SNOWFLAKES AND SABOTAGE

WOLF SHIFTER KINGS

BOOK THREE

BELLA MOONDRAGON

To Alanis. I wish nothing but the best for you both.

CONTENTS

ANOTHER IMPOSSIBILITY

Hollis

By the Goddess, I feel like shit. My head aches, my skin burns, and I am far too hot. I told Father sleeping in the carriage away from Escuro wouldn't work out for any of us—if I feel like this, I can only imagine how he's doing this morning. We could've left this morning without losing any face after whatever fight he had with King Kieran. I'd be shocked if those Dun's Crossing types got up before ten in the morning, even with their ridiculous ritual slated for today.

I groan and stretch. My skin pulls at itself, and the burning intensifies. Like the damned carriage actually cut me up.

At that thought, a memory bursts through my mind. Splintering wood, blood running down my pelt. Did I fucking shift last night? Did I break the carriage? I search my mind for any other clues.

All that comes to me is the grayish blur of the Haze.

I suck in a deep breath, and I know something is impossibly wrong. Father had his fight before sunset, and we left a few minutes after. Eva and I shouldn't have even been close enough for the Haze to reach us. We talked about it and were even a little disappointed. It's been weeks since both of us turned twenty-one, her the day after me, and we're ready to start our lives together, just like we've always planned. Eva's had her wedding dress ready since we were sixteen. But if that's all I can remember, it did reach us. Which means I should be smelling cinnamon and jasmine right now. Not this foreign blend of blackberries and something I can only describe as sunshine.

What the fuck?

Slowly, I open my eyes. Someone's head lays on my chest. Their pale, blonde head, where Eva's scarlet hair should be. Something throbs painfully on my shoulders, but I ignore it. Blonde means Dun's Crossing, more likely than not, but I can't recognize whoever it might be from the top of her head.

Dun's Crossing. This has to be some kind of ploy by King Kieran. Relief washes through my body. He realized Eva and I got caught in the Haze, separated us after we fell asleep, and gave each of us to different members of his own court. It sounds like something King Gavin would do if Father displeased him. Which means all I need to do is extricate myself before anyone sees, find Eva, and we can leave just like Father wanted to.

Unfortunately, stealth has never been my strong suit. I'd much rather toss the stranger off me and bolt out of the clearing for my real mate—maybe with a pitstop to show King Kieran exactly who the fuck he's messing with. I keep telling Father we're wasting our time, trying to find the right moment to break off the alliance with Dun's Crossing. King Kieran doesn't have the power his father had for reprisal. We should end it now—before we get dragged back in.

I lift the strange woman's head—her hair is like silk through my fingers; King Kieran has decent taste—and begin to slide my body out from under her. The half-dead grass tears and crumples. My clothes are somewhere with the remains of the carriage, probably to the north. Maybe I can find Eva on the way and—

"Mmn?" the strange woman mumbles.

I jump up, drop her head. It bounces off the ground, and her eyes shoot open.

Pale blue eyes in an oval-shaped, angular face. A face I know well because I barely saw Eva without her in our last couple of weeks at Solberg Castle.

The woman who sits up and stares at me in confusion is Princess Candace.

King Kieran's cockier than I thought.

"What are you doing?" she asks.

"Getting out before your brother's plan works." I cross my arms. My shoulder throbs again. What the fuck did I do to it?

"His… plan?" Candace blinks tiredly. I never realized what a perfect mouth she has, so much fuller than the rest of her siblings.

That's why this is a fucking trick, Hollis. Keep your head on straight.

"He and my father fought," I say. "We were leaving before our name got muddied by this ridiculous castle-in-the-air scheme of yours."

Hurt flashes across her face. "You don't think the rejuvenation's going to work?"

"Well, how could it?" I take a step back. She's obviously just trying to keep me here long enough for someone to catch us. I'm almost sorry to hurt her—I think Eva really considers her a friend—but I won't let her brother make me a pawn in his game because I think she's got a nice laugh. "The effects of wolfsbane are permanent. Everyone knows that."

The scars on Luna Estrella are enough to prove it.

"I—" She shakes her head. "What does this have to do with the Haze? Why are you running away?"

"Because you're not my mate." This time, my shoulder sears like my arm is about to fall off. More memories of last night leak in. Someone's teeth in my arm—but they had to have been Eva's. I don't need to check the bite to know its shape. "King Kieran had you sneak in after I fell asleep. To humiliate us after their fight."

Her soft mouth falls slightly open. Her pale eyes shine with what look like tears. My shoulder might not be where the bite is; it might be infected or something. I stare at the ground. As long as I don't look at her, I can get out of here. I can find Eva and let her make it up to her friend.

"You really think I would do that?" Candace asks quietly.

I glance up. She's curled her knees half up to her chest, blocking a lot of her body. Her narrow hips give way to an ass that would fit perfectly into my hands. Her pale skin shines in the morning light. And there, above the plush swell of breast I remember from last night, sits a still red, barely snowflake-shaped mating mark.

The kind you can only get from someone born in Snowcrest Canyon.

My skin goes cold. My stomach drops. There's… there's no way. I'm promised to Eva. She's promised to me. Three hundred years of various members of the Kar and Skadis families born within a week of each other have mated when the Haze arrives. Our families are intertwined through history, though not so closely as to have ramifications on our genes. I can't be the one to break the tradition.

Father's face appears in my mind, glowering with that sickening hint of resigned disappointment in his eyes. Like he always expected something like this.

"Of course, I believe it," I spit. "What the fuck other explanation do you suggest?"

"That the Goddess brought us together?" She stares at the dead, broken grass where we lay mere minutes ago. "Kieran, Anwen… even when it seems like the Goddess or the Haze has made a mistake, it's always right."

"Well, not this time." I keep backing up. A tactical retreat. "This place is fucked up. The Haze probably can't work right since *your father* destroyed the land here."

She flinches. "I wasn't even born yet when that happened."

"Whatever you say. He's still your family." Fuck, Eva's going to be mad. Candace looks like a bird with a broken wing. But she'll understand when I explain what kind of insanity King Kieran put us through. "But you know I'm right. Look at this."

I gesture at the ruined land around us. Even with the first warmth of spring in the air, there's no sign of life in the leafless, black-gray trees surrounding the clearing we slept in. I break off a piece of bark, and it crumbles like sand in my hand. My shoulder is going to kill me if I don't reach Eva soon.

Candace takes it in with wide, wet eyes. I've never even really liked women with the sharp, fragile look she has. I've never liked women other than Eva. Hell, I've never looked. I was always just going to fall in love with her someday.

"I'm telling you," she murmurs. "There's no way around the Haze."

"I'm not in the business of rolling over whenever some foreign princess tells me there's no way." I shake my head. There's just... no way.

I turn on my heel and throw myself into a shift. My fur, a red so deep it looks black in most lights, bursts from my skin, and I hit the ground running. Sore muscles groan and stretch. I put my nose to the air.

There. Cinnamon and jasmine. King Kieran didn't even have the decency to drag Eva far enough away that I couldn't smell her.

This will be over soon. No matter how much my shoulder hurts.

SUPPORT

Candace

AT THE TREE LINE WHERE THE HALF-DESTROYED WOODS GIVE WAY TO the large, open area full of all the various delegations' colorful tents, someone laid out piles of clothes for anyone drawn into the Haze. I hover nearby, waiting for a moment when no one is looking.

I can't let them see the burning mark on my collarbone. If someone asks me anything, I'm going to lose the shreds of composure I gained sitting alone after Hollis left and break down, which I absolutely can't right now. The rejuvenation ritual starts in—I glance at the sky—less than an hour, when the sun fully crests the horizon. Raven and Estrella need me. I can worry about the fact that my mate thinks I'm a cruel joke after that.

Mother's voice echoes in my head. *"A daughter is an alliance. Your only job, when your Haze comes, is to convince the Goddess to make you a good one."*

If my mate doesn't want me, what am I then? Nothing at all?

My lower lip wobbles, and I sink my teeth into it. Bad train of thought. That doesn't matter right now.

A cluster of girls, two of which sport mating marks on their backs and chests, pull three dresses from the pile and finally leave. I take the split-second opening to dart in, grab one for myself, and dress alone in the tree line.

Hollis was right about one thing. Escuro looks so much worse than I even feared. The trees and grass are all the same gray as Estrella's scars. I was always impressed by Luna Delaney, keeping her pack alive under such difficult circumstances, but now I think she must have even more magic than I realize.

With my thoughts on the real adversity people here have overcome, I set off through the sprawling camp to the tents we set up upon our arrival yesterday. On the way, I pass Mother's prison wagon. Nearly a full platoon of soldiers stand around it. Finn thinks it's overkill, but I understand. Until a few days ago, Nessa sat in the dungeon at Solberg Castle next to Mother. Taner led a mission to apprehend her on the border of Snowcrest a few months back. Then, while we were in the process of transferring Mother to the prison cart for this trip, Nessa somehow escaped. Just the idea of her out there somewhere makes me sick. She doesn't seem to have her father's violence—despite her involvement in the plot against Anwen and Estrella, she never held a weapon—but I know her–better than almost anyone else. I don't think this will be the last we hear of her.

Our trio of silver-and-blue striped tents is a busy warren of activity. Servants dart back and forth between the three. Reddish smoke puffs out of the Sundrop Gem tent nearby, where I expect Raven and Estrella are finishing the final batch of their concoction. I duck into the tent Ingrid and I are going to share for the length of our stay here.

"Thank the Goddess!" she says as I walk in. "I was about to send out search parties. Did you and your mate decide you could squeeze in another round?"

"Ingrid!" I squeal.

She laughs, fidgeting with her hair in the mirror. Long, blonde strands dangle messily out the back. She never can do it on her own.

I step closer, release the combs attempting to hold her hair in place, and start over. "I didn't actually meet my mate."

She looks at me in the mirror. "Truly?"

I nod as pain streaks through my body and turns my vision slightly gray at the edges. "No one called to me."

"I'm sorry." She pats my hand. "Or congratulations? It seemed like you didn't want to go."

"Just tired from the trip." I need to distract her. "Where did you get this dress? I don't think I've seen it yet, and it really suits you."

Ingrid smiles and plucks at the sea foam-colored fabric. "I got the idea from Estrella and made the gown myself. Well, with a little of Bright's help. She complained the whole time. Our whole court's more colorful, now that Anwen is over there. Have you noticed?"

"I did." I push a bejeweled comb into place in her hair, then the second. "You're so lucky your hair is thick enough to hold these. You and Mother both."

She laughs. "We could hold them in your hair if you even let me use a little glue."

"Never!" I put a hand to my nearly waist-length hair. It's too fine for anything but a few pins and the braided styles Tess is so talented at, but I still love it.

"Fine, fine." Ingrid shakes her head. "Let me help you pick something out."

I smile. "Of—"

If I let her pick out the dress, she'll choose something I need help getting into. Ingrid's taste has always been elaborate. And then she'll see the mark. She'll know I lied.

"Of course not," I say.

Ingrid blinks. "Why not?"

"Because…." I glance at the flap of our tent. "Because when I was walking in, I overheard one of the servants saying they needed music for the ritual, and I happen to know you brought your lute."

Ingrid blushes prettily. Mother always said she had a perfect strawberries-and-cream complexion.

"I did, but I wasn't thinking—"

"Go see!" I put the final comb in her hair and squeeze her shoulders. "You're so talented. There's no way you won't improve the ritual."

"Okay!" She bounces up, glowing with excitement. "I'll go talk to Raven and Estrella. They'll know what they need."

She scurries out of the tent, and I slump onto my bed. I didn't hear anything about music, but I know those two won't be able to refuse an excited Ingrid. And she really is talented on that lute of hers. A few days of hearing about how wonderful my sisters—by blood or otherwise—are sounds like a much nicer time than a few days fending off Ingrid's questions.

A trumpet blares three blasts to indicate the ritual will start in half an hour. I really do have to get dressed. I strip out of the clothes I found at the edge of the trees and sort through my dresses. A soft brown one with a high neckline catches my attention. Just the sort of thing to let me fade into the background while the rest of them take the spotlight. Normally, I'd pick one of the gray-greens that brings out the hints of color in my eyes. Mother said they made me look pretty as a picture. But today, disappearing sounds better than anything else I can imagine. I put on undergarments and slip the dress on over my head. With everything fastened and tightened, it hides my unimpressive behind and draws polite attention to my chest —but never so much that my future mate could get jealous.

Not future mate anymore. Just mate. Who doesn't want me.

Tears well up in my eyes, and I swipe them away. Not now. After the ritual. Or maybe when we get home. Then, I'll confess to everyone. Kieran and Raven won't mind me staying in the castle for the rest of my life. Kieran doesn't care nearly as much about marriage alliances as Father did.

Right?

My stomach starts twisting itself into knots, and I know I need to go. I smooth down my dress one last time, leave my hair loose, and rejoin the world outside the scant privacy of the tent.

Estrella and Raven stand in the middle of the chaos. Estrella clutches what looks like a wine decanter, but judging by the ribbons of gold threading through the liquid within, that's the concoction she and Raven have been working on almost nonstop since Raven used an early version of it to save Estrella's life from her own wolfsbane encounter. Raven presses a hand to her own back, her swollen belly jutting out ahead of her like another participant in their conversation. I step up to them.

"When we introduce the serum, I think," Estrella is saying.

Raven nods slowly. "That would be a nice time for some music. It would make the whole thing a little more atmospheric." She smiles at me. "Good morning."

Estrella smirks. "How was—"

I put a hand up. "No mate. Keep talking about the ritual."

The wave of pain that sweeps through me is so severe I almost lose my footing. Estrella studies me, but Raven has too much on her mind to do anything but plunge forward.

"Shouldn't the holy woman be here by now?" she asks.

"Yana will meet us at the site," Estrella replies.

Another trumpet. Two, this time.

"Which we should be moving toward." She hefts the decanter carefully. "Are we ready?"

"I think so." Raven's smile is a little worried.

I put my hands on both of their shoulders. "The two of you are some of the smartest women I've ever met. I'm sure you're ready. This is going to be incredible."

"Thank you." Raven kisses my cheek awkwardly around her belly.

Estrella chuckles. "With you on our side, how could we fail?"

Ingrid sprints up to us, lute in hand. "What are you still doing here? We have to go!"

"All right, all right." I begin escorting everyone toward the ritual site Estrella and Raven picked out. We join a flow of well-dressed nobility, all heading to the spot. If they're right—and I really do think they are, no matter what certain Snowcrest princes might say—we are all about to see the closest thing to a miracle anyone other than the Goddess Herself can produce.

That is almost enough to make me forget the burning in my collarbone and the sinking feeling that I've failed the one job I was ever given.

REJUVENATION

Hollis

Eva shakes her head. "I just don't know how we didn't find each other."

"It's strange," I agree, my mark burning.

When I found her, asleep in the nook of a tree, I looked her over for a mating mark before I even woke her up. All the way over. Not a single sign of the snowflake shape. Not even a red spot that might turn into a snowflake when the swelling goes down.

"But it's a good sign neither of us found anyone else," I add.

She grins as she scrapes her red hair up into a bun. We are standing amidst the flow of people, all headed to the spot on the edge of the camp we were told upon arrival to avoid.

"Definitely better."

That fucking bite sears. I cling to the pain.

I stayed in my wolf form all the way back to camp, pretending I was still under the effects of the Haze. Sniffing Eva, running circles around her, just acting like an idiot. She laughed so hard she had to catch herself on my back a couple of times. Her fingers in my fur felt so normal, so familiar, that I almost forgot what I was hiding. Then, she'd say something about how it was weird we didn't mate, and it would start hurting all over again. As long as it hurts, I can't forget. The ruined land did something to the Haze. This is a mistake.

"Maybe it didn't work because we were at the edge," I say. "The Haze only affected us enough to make us shift, not to make us mate."

She scratches one of the matching scrapes on her arm—she burst out of the carriage as well. "Do you really think that's possible?"

"What else could it be?" If anyone could hear the real question in my voice, the hope for any other explanation for what the hell happened last night, it would be her.

"I don't know." She shakes her head. "I suppose you must be right. Why else would we destroy your father's carriages and not find anyone?"

"Exactly."

Eva adjusts the neck of her gown, framing her breasts perfectly. There's a small freckle on the top of the left one, a freckle I've spent half my life looking forward to tasting. I stare at it now, trying to remember why I wanted it so badly.

"Hey." She bumps her hip into mine. "Watch the eyes, or rumor is going to spread that we really did mate."

I jerk my gaze away. We stop at the edge of the crowd, almost too far away to see. There must be a hundred or more people here, even more than the gathering for Luna Estrella and King Anwen's wedding that wasn't.

"Do you actually think this is going to work?" I ask.

"Candace does," she says.

Another lance of pain.

"Yeah? Did you talk about it?"

"Not much." Eva's face glows with a smile. "We had too much else to talk about. Did you know they have ruddy-chested flycatchers in Dun's Crossing?"

I laugh. "I don't even know what that is."

She rolls her eyes. "I *told* you. They're descendants of—"

"Thank you all for coming to this miracle, this new beginning for my kingdom." King Cole's voice echoes over the crowd. "Our beautiful daughter has been working for months with the Luna of Sundrop Gem on what we all thought was impossible: a cure for wolfsbane poisoning."

Murmurs ripple through the crowd. I guess not everyone knew why we were all dragged out here. Eva takes my hand and tugs me forward.

"I want to see," she hisses.

I let her lead me and rub my thumb over the pen callus on her finger I know so well. My mark is going to kill me if Father doesn't.

"Thank you, Father," Luna Raven says. "I had a whole speech prepared, but then our little heir kept me up all night."

Laughter surrounds us. Eva pulls me up onto the wooden support around a tentpole, just high enough off the ground that we can see over the crowd's heads.

Luna Delaney and King Cole have stepped to the side, leaving Luna Raven, Luna Estrella, a woman in holy robes, and—I squint—a blonde with a lute in the middle of a clear space encircled by rocks, next to a massive dead tree. Luna Estrella squeezes Luna Raven's hand and steps forward holding a massive jug.

"Yana," she says, "will you perform the blessing?"

There she is. Right behind Luna Raven, next to the prison cart that holds Rowena Solberg. She's wearing a brown dress that almost reaches her chin. My stomach drops. My skin goes cold.

My mate doesn't look at me.

"By the light of the Goddess," the holy woman prays, "and by Her darkness, we find our way. For too long, we have been haunted by one impossible specter. One threat from which there is no recovery. By Her grace and wisdom, may we finally overcome it."

Father steps up next to the wooden structure Eva and I stand on. I raise my eyebrows.

'I thought you left,' I say to him through the mind-link. *'King Kieran delivered an insult too great to be expected to bear?'*

'Hush,' Father replies without looking at me. *'We cannot look distracted.'*

I exchange a look with Eva, who shrugs. She's right. There's no reason to reopen the events of last night any more than necessary right now. I just need to focus on the stupid ritual. If it works, there'll be a party. If it doesn't, there'll be some kind of celebration anyway. Then, we get to leave, and I get to spend the rest of my life figuring out how to destroy the false mate bond this place gave me.

The holy woman puts her hand on the trunk of the tree. "This is where the original injury was dealt. The heart of Escuro, its oldest oak, which extends roots into the waters from which the people here drew their life. Here, it will be repaired."

Luna Estrella hefts the jug. "In this, I hold redemption. Rejuvenation. The work of a woman harmed almost as directly by Gavin Solberg as her people's land—"

"And of one who ended a centuries-long feud between Dun's Crossing and Sundrop Gem," Luna Raven adds.

The other queen smiles. "Redemption. Rejuvenation. Forgiveness. With the Goddess' blessing, we give this to Escuro. To the world."

She upends the jug, and the whole crowd falls silent. Only the musician keeps playing.

A stream of burgundy liquid threaded with gold pours out, thicker than wine but thinner than blood. The smell is strange—half a dozen plants, something like dirt or grit, a warmth I can't quite explain. But the liquid puddles between the roots of the tree and just…sits there.

Shit. It's actually not going to work.

Eva leans up on her tiptoes. "Something's happening."

"What?" I grab her wrist to keep her from toppling over. I don't see anything.

Something gurgles before she can answer, and I do see it. The liquid is draining into the ground very slowly. Just like any liquid would. I open my mouth to tell Eva she's missing the clouds for the silver linings again.

Bright, golden light flashes like a single burst of fire. I wince and shut my eyes. Gasps echo through the crowd.

'Hollis, look!' Eva says in my head.

I open my eyes again, and for a split second, wonder if what the

Lunas actually made was some sort of mass teleportation potion. The cracked, dead grass under their feet is replaced by a lush blanket of green. As I watch, a pale wildflower sprouts out of the ground and blossoms. But the biggest transformation is the tree itself. The blighted, leafless trunk behind them now spreads the first shoots of green overhead. Its bark is golden and lustrous, except in a few places where gray veins match the scar on Luna Estrella's neck. Actually, all the new growth has those, but just a little. A handful of blades of gray grass wave in the breeze with their neighbors, vital but forever marked by what happened here.

A fucking miracle. That's what happened here today.

Luna Delaney bursts into tears. Luna Raven races for her mother, and the two of them clutch each other.

King Cole steps forward and clears his throat. "A celebration is in order!"

Cheers ripple through the crowd. They did it. They fucking did it.

"Tonight, at sunset, on this very spot." His voice is thick with emotion, and I roll my eyes. I know he's out of practice, but a king should be able to hold himself together a little better. "We shall honor the restoration of Escuro!"

More cheers. I jump down off the platform and hold a hand out for Eva to do the same. "Can we talk about your departure now, Father?"

He stares down at me, eyes nearly hidden under his heavy brows. "I do not know what you mean."

Without another word, he turns and walks away. Eva hops down, and something crunches under her feet. I look down. The grass under our feet is still dry and dead. As delegates begin to filter away, the effect becomes clearer—a perfect circle of restored land, surrounded by the same destruction as before. Judging by the cluster of important people around the oak tree, they've noticed too. Candace looks worried.

"What?" Eva asks.

I shake my head, look at the ground. "Just thinking about how good this is actually going to be."

EXHAUSTION

Candace

"Look at this!" Estrella holds a single piece of green grass up in front of my eyes. "It's alive."

"I'm so happy for you." I force a smile. Despite the realization that this first application only affected the area right around where they put what they've started calling the elixir, Raven and Estrella are walking on air. Raven's barely left her parents' side, both because I know she doesn't see them as often as she'd like and because they're the only ones here who know what Escuro used to look like.

"Perhaps we could use the elixir to create more oases in Sundrop." She grabs my hands. "The applications are endless. There is no wound we cannot heal."

"It really is amazing." My mark aches. I didn't see Hollis at the ritual, but even just smelling him in the crowd made me sick. With the celebration tonight, I just want to lie down.

"Are you all right?" Ingrid asks as she walks up. "You look pale."

"Just tired." I offer another wan smile. "I didn't exactly get much sleep last night. I could use a nap before the celebration."

"By the Goddess, I'm so sorry." Estrella releases me. "Go, rest. We can speak later."

'I'll keep them distracted,' Ingrid says through the mind-link. *'The tent isn't exactly soundproof.'*

'Thank you,' I reply. *'And give Raven my congratulations.'*

'Of course.'

I leave the ritual site, my steps dragging over new grass and old. I dodge chattering groups—most excited, some jealous—and wend my way through back alleys. At least Kieran and Anwen had some privacy when they were fighting the mate bond. They didn't have to do it in the middle of a campground with a hundred of their closest potential political allies. I would give almost anything for a real door I could shut between me and the world.

"I didn't expect to see you here." The voice is oily smooth, perfectly even. "Finally come to visit your mother?"

I twist and discover my back route has led me past where her prison cart is parked. Guards at attention surround it, and Mother's pale, long-fingered hand drapes out from between the bars. Dirt makes small crescents under her nails.

Before everything that's happened this past year, Mother was my closest confidant after Ingrid. I know what she's done, who she's hurt. But I can't tell anyone what happened between Hollis and I—except the one woman no one would talk to or trust.

"Open the door." I lift my chin, try to look like I have the authority to do what I'm doing. "I wish to speak to her inside."

The guards exchange looks. One of their gazes goes hazy with a mind-link. "King Kieran says she may," he reports a second later.

I try to keep my posture as they let me into the cramped wagon. Only a few shafts of morning light creep through the bars, just enough to illuminate the wide bench Mother obviously has to use as a bed and the chamber pot off to the side. A tray with a few food scraps and a pail of water promise Kieran is actually improving the dungeon conditions as he said he would, but seeing her like this is still jarring.

"How long has it been?" Mother fixes a lock of lank blonde hair.

I swallow. "Sev-seven months."

She purses her lips. "I thought I raised you better than that."

I flinch. I know I should have been visiting her. I did, a few times. In the beginning. Before the grime truly settled onto her—she refuses to bathe when offered water—and I could no longer look at her without acknowledging the truth.

The woman who raised me is a prisoner, and I am letting her stay one.

"I'm sorry," I mumble.

"I can't hear you," she says.

"My apologies, Mother." I force volume into my voice. "I have been—" Saying busy will only irritate her further. "Barred" is a lie, and I've been trying to stop lying since I realized just how like them it made me. "Frightened."

A small smile crosses her face. "Of what, darling?"

You. What your imprisonment means. How much I'm your daughter.

"I don't know." I shake my head. "I didn't know."

"But you do now?" She takes my hand, silver manacles around her wrists rattling.

Why does Kieran have her chained in silver? Mother is originally from Lightning Cape, a kingdom to the south Father conquered a few months after they mated, so she has some extremely minor wind magic, but nothing she's ever used for more than whisking a quill she didn't want to stand to retrieve into her hand.

Or pushing things off a table to make a servant she was displeased with keep cleaning.

I blink. "Something happened last night."

"Your first Haze." Mother's smile is sickly sweet, like she doesn't quite know how to do it anymore. "Did you—?"

I nod.

"And he frightens you."

'*No.*' My face burns as I mind-link Mother for the first time in almost a year. '*He...he doesn't want me.*'

"Oh, darling." She cups my cheek. The silver stings my chin. "Who would?"

"What?" I flinch back like she hit me.

"Imprisonment gives someone a lot of time to think." Her smile sharpens into something dangerous. "And I've been thinking you're a disloyal bitch I wasted my energy trying to raise into a lady."

My pulse roars in my ears. "You don't mean that."

"Oh, but I do." She stares out of the bars. "You were my favorite, and you left me here to rot. You don't even visit. What is a mother supposed to think?"

I open and close my mouth. Nothing comes out. Mother was always cruel to Raven, but not to me. This is a woman I've never seen before.

"Yes, I've had a lot of time. Before the chains, I used that time to train my magic, but since then, I can only think." She stares at me, her eyes burning into mine. "You never truly took my lessons to heart. If you were meant to be the sort of woman I wanted, you wouldn't have had to work so hard. I certainly didn't. So I don't blame the unfortunate man the Goddess placed in your path. I'd help him run away." Her mouth flattens into a line. "If I could."

"I'm leaving." My voice wavers. I knock on the door for the guards to let me out.

"Of course, you are." Mother grins viciously. "That's the only skill you ever learned. Burying your head in the sand and letting other people get their hands dirty."

The door to the cart creaks open, and I explode out into the sunshine. I don't know when I started crying, but tears streak down my cheeks. The guards regard me awkwardly, not quite sure whether they should offer to help or leave me alone.

"Don't tell anyone about this." Before they can reply, I stumble away from the prison cart.

Luckily, when I reach our tent, there are still only a few people there. Most of the staff and family seem to still be at the ritual site. I plunge into the relative darkness of the tent and throw myself down on the bed, all thoughts of a nap gone. My shoulders shake with sobs. Mother's right. It shouldn't be this hard to make people like me. There must be something wrong with me. I just wish I knew what it was.

Eventually, my sobs peter out. I am exhausted. I said I was going to na—

THE ACRID STINK OF HOT METAL AND BLOOD CONSUMES ME. MORE blood than I've ever seen before, ever smelled before. Slowly, other details filter in. The air stings my skin—grit, flying in every direction. Pained screams echo from everywhere, those of the tortured and dying. Howls mix and meld and split apart in an aching cacophony. Finally, I manage to open my eyes.

I stand in the center of a blasted battlefield with a war raging around me. Dark mountains loom over the destroyed earth. A wolf lands at my feet, screaming in a half-human voice as another wolf tears it to bloody shreds. I try to recoil, but I can't control my body.

Instead, I lift up, up, up. With every foot I climb, I expect to see the edge of the fighting. It must end somewhere. But it stretches ever onward, horizon to horizon. My stomach churns. I would be sick, if I had enough control of my mouth.

I stare down over a war worse than anything Father ever created. The tiny sliver of peace Kieran clawed back is destroyed, forgotten in a disaster the likes of which the world has never seen. And everyone is dying.

I SHOOT UP IN BED, DRENCHED IN COLD SWEAT. THE LIGHT OUTSIDE THE tent flap is darker, approaching sunset. My head pounds. That dream felt so impossibly real that I know it's going to come true someday. Maybe soon. I have to tell—

Hollis's words ring in my ears. Mother's, too. Who would I tell? Who would believe me? No one even thinks my dreams are premonitions.

Ingrid lifts the tent flap. "Hey. I kept them away for as long as I could, but we have to start getting ready now. Are you okay?"

I wipe my face and force a smile. "Just woke up."

NOTHING TO CELEBRATE

Hollis

"So I said, 'Who are you kidding? Your wolf doesn't even have two ears.'" Lord Gunnar, one of the Snowcrest nobles Father begrudgingly agreed to bring on the trip, bursts into laughter at his own joke.

Father nods once, crisply, and takes another drink from his cup. Zain, my Beta whenever I take the throne, just sips his drink. Eva laughs politely. I put on my fakest laugh—Gunnar likes the sound of his own voice too much to ever notice me.

Around us, the celebration is in full swing. The early spring air here is warm enough that I didn't have to wear my cloak over my tunic and pants, but Eva is wrapped in fur over a fine, sky-blue dress that cups every inch of her body and still didn't make me look twice at her. Couples spin around the oak tree, which someone strung lanterns in the branches of, and music plays from a dozen different performers scattered around the space. For being put together in the afternoon, it's decent, but I miss the celebrations at home. Their alcohol is bullshit.

Father looks at me. "Have you made inroads with the other delegates?"

He's searching for other allies. He says he wants to know we have someone backing us before breaking ties with Dun's Crossing. I still think he's being too cautious, but he's the one who left his Beta, Eva's father, at home to run the kingdom in his absence because he doesn't trust anyone else. Caution has been his middle name for a long time now.

"I'm friends with Candace Solberg," Eva says.

Father's face shutters. "Not them."

I squeeze her hand. *'We're trying to get away from Dun's Crossing.'*

'Why?' Eva demands. *'I like Candace.'*

My mark burns. I need to do something about it. Between the ritual and now, I finally looked at the damned thing. When I saw the rays of a sun shining back at me, I almost puked. Somehow. Candace bit me. I just need to figure out what about this fucked up place made that happen.

'Because the Solbergs can't be trusted,' I reply.

"I've met a couple of guys," Zain offers. "They were talking about doing a friendly spar tomorrow. Hollis, you want to join?"

"Sure," I say, barely hearing him. "I'll be there."

Father grunts, pleased. My chest warms. Military and combat prowess is the one thing we share these days.

"Ah! King Andri, Prince Hollis," someone says.

Father and I turn in unison. King Kieran and Luna Raven approach. Even in the dim light of the night, her stomach is impossible to miss. I'm shocked her healer allows her out of bed.

"King Kieran." Father clasps his hand. "Luna Raven. Impressive work."

"Thank you." She curtsies awkwardly. King Kieran has to help her regain her feet. "It seems I specialize in bringing new life to the world these days."

"When are you due?" Eva asks.

"Soon," Luna Raven groans.

I sip my weak wine to cover my eye roll. She seems nice enough, but she's way too casual. No poise, no grace. In the few memories of Mother I still have, she carried herself like she was always walking on a cloud.

"Snowcrest is honored by our small role in this miracle," Father says. "Enjoy your success."

King Kieran and Luna Raven say their goodbyes and move off. As Lord Gunnar launches into a tirade about how they didn't even acknowledge him, I scan the party again.

I haven't seen Candace yet. Which is good. I don't want to, not after this morning. But at this point, I'm starting to suspect she actually might not be coming. So I can start my plan.

If I was at home, I'd go to the library. Since Mother's death, our collection's become more and more military texts, but I'm sure there's still some history in there. Something that would tell me about the Haze and the times it backfired. Instead, I'm stuck in a fucking field, and that means my only resources are the people around me.

I kiss Eva on the cheek. "I'm going to go see if they have anything stronger."

"Bring some back if they do," she replies.

I laugh and escape the group.

'Need a hand?' Zain asks.

I tell him no. He is my Beta, and I trust him with my life, but I don't trust anyone with this kind of secret.

After a brief, failed search for harder liquor, I ask a woman to dance, and the plan begins.

"You're from Escuro, aren't you?" I ask as we spin around the tree.

She giggles. "How did you know?"

The dark hair and eyes, the dress that looks like nobody's seen it in the light in twenty years, the vague aura of social ineptitude.

"Lucky guess," I reply. "Are you mated?"

She giggles again. I tighten my hold on her and hope she finds that romantic. This kind of information-gathering is not where my strengths lie.

"No." Her eyelashes flutter so much I actually wonder if she has something stuck in her eyes. "But I could be."

"Oh yeah?" I dip her to hide my expression. "Do you know anyone who is?"

"Loads of people." She leans closer, her licorice smell clouding the air. "I was out in the Haze last night. Were you?"

"Missed it." That's the story I'm giving Eva, so it's good enough for this stranger. "So the Haze has been working in Escuro? People are happy with their mates?"

"Um… yeah?" She looks at me strangely. "Why?"

Fuck. "I'm writing a book."

"Ooh, tell me more!"

The rest of the night goes a lot like that. Finding someone who could have answers, asking questions that are supposed to be subtle, and either hitting a wall or ending up in another ridiculous lie. By the time I wander off the dance floor, half the gathering must believe I'm writing a book or a paper or a poem when I haven't written anything but a tactical map in years. And every time, I get the same answers: the Haze is dangerous in Escuro. Some of the plants here have been so ruined by wolfsbane that they're unsafe to touch. But when people risk it, everything proceeds normally. The bites are normal, the couples are normal, everyone is happy. This holds true both before and after King Gavin's death, a line of questioning I thought would be useful and mostly got me weird looks.

Two more days. Then, I can go home and see if there's a way to break a mating bond, even if it's a legitimate one. Or I can just never see Candace again and learn to shoot my bow through the agony in my shoulder.

I stomp over to the table set up for the delegates from Snowcrest Canyon and stop cold. Eva and Candace sit there, laughing like one of them just told the funniest joke in the world. Candace's head is thrown back, her blonde hair cascading away from her face like a dying ray of light, and she clutches her stomach over her grayish-blue gown like she might burst a rib from laughing too hard. Eva looks perfectly at peace, like she's laughing with an old friend instead of a woman she visited in person for a week and has been writing letters to sometimes since.

A feeling I don't know how to name crunches through my chest.

I'm in the middle of a Goddess-damned party. I crush the feeling down and saunter over to them like there's nothing in the world wrong with the woman I'm supposed to be mated to and the one who tricked the Goddess Herself to mate with me sitting together.

"What's so funny?" I drop into the seat next to Eva and sling my arm around her shoulders.

Eva swipes a tear from her eye. "Candace was telling me a story about the ruddy-breasted flycatchers, and—"

I snort.

Out of the corner of my eye, I watch Candace's face fall. Her gaze lands squarely on my arm.

"What?" Eva says.

"Oh, come on, you expect me to believe a fucking bird story is that funny?" I chuckle. "You were talking about something actually interesting. Tell me."

"It really was a bird story," Candace says quietly.

My mark screams. That's my mate, sitting across from me, looking like a kicked puppy. Every instinct in my body howls for me to shut up and apologize. But I didn't get this far in life by listening to my instincts.

"By the Goddess, really?" I shake my head. "Can we talk about something interesting now, then? I'm here, and unlike Eva, I've got standards."

Eva shakes her head. "Did you find the drinks, then?"

"I couldn't find shit. It's like people in Dun's Crossing have no idea how to have fun." I turn to Eva and direct the next comment only to her, over the torturous agony in my shoulder. "Maybe that's why the funniest thing you could find over here was a story about a bird."

My mark doesn't matter. Just two more days, and then I'll figure out how to get rid of it.

It's that, or I have no idea what my future looks like anymore.

NOT LIKE THEM

Candace

I SHRINK LOWER IN MY SEAT. MY MARK BRANDS MY SKIN LIKE A HOT iron, and I just swallow the pain. Eva found me hiding out at the edge of the party, trying to convince myself to join in and risk seeing either of them. I tried to warn her that I wasn't very good company, but she's too good of a friend to take no for an answer.

That only makes me feel worse.

"He's right," I say numbly. "It wasn't very funny."

"See?" Hollis grins at Eva. "Even she admits it. Nobody likes bird stories."

I nod. I've heard that enough, though usually without the edge of venom in Hollis's voice right now.

"*Please* can we talk about something interesting?" he says.

Eva's gaze flickers between the two of us. I can't read anything in her green eyes, which are so like Hollis's.

"What in the world are you doing?" She shrugs out from under his arm.

I suck in a breath. I've never heard her sound so offended before.

Hollis puts up his hands. "I'm just trying to make this party fun—"

"No, you're being a dick." She glares at him. "Look, I'm really sorry you didn't get to have sex last night. Mating would've made everything a lot easier. But that doesn't mean you get to take your bad mood out on our friend."

My stomach twists itself into sick, acidic knots. What would Eva say if she knew Hollis was behaving like this because he did mate last night? Because the mark of my teeth is searing itself into his shoulder? Memories flash through my mind—his strong, competent hands, his hot mouth, his smell so potent in the night.

"It was a joke," Hollis says. "I'm sorry you didn't have sex last night, but you used to have a sense of humor."

I wince. He's lashing out at everyone. I can't let him hurt Eva. But I can't find my tongue to stand up for her like she deserves either.

"Don't waste your time lying to me." She crosses her arms. "I know when you're joking, and I want you to apologize."

I could tell Eva. I could pull her aside, whisper it quietly. I could stand on the table and declare it, explain why Hollis is being so cruel right here and now. I could do anything but sit here in complete and total silence, like I did when I watched Mother beat Raven.

"Fuck no," Hollis scoffs. "Candace knows it was a joke. Don't you?"

Finally, he looks at me. There's a hard mask over the depths I saw in his green eyes last night, something cold and harsh. He's hiding from what happened.

"You don't have to answer that." Worry and frustration wrinkle Eva's brow. She has no idea what's going on with Hollis. "You don't have to do anything he tells you to."

There's my opening, if I want it. But what good would telling Eva really do? Hollis is obviously never going to accept me as his mate. If I stay quiet, I'm the only one who has to hurt. Clearly, Hollis isn't.

"Thank you." I put my hand on Eva's. "I don't think he was joking, but I have other rounds to make, so I'd rather just go."

She frowns at me like she's trying to read my thoughts through my skull. I pray she can't. Between memories of Hollis and my latest dream, there's nothing in there I want her to see.

Finally, she nods. "All right. But just say the word, and I'll kick him out myself."

"Understood." I stand and walk away from the table with no idea where I'm going. I've made all my rounds, and I have no real interest in talking to any of these people again. All the smiles, the music—it's too much. I just want to lie down and forget I ever met anyone from Snowcrest Canyon.

If this is the last time I'm going to see him, I deserve one last glance. I look back over my shoulder.

Eva is talking to Hollis seriously, visibly still upset with him. But he's watching me, his eyes unguarded but holding an expression I can't understand. As soon as we make eye contact, he looks away.

I turn around and keep walking. My feet lead me to the edge of the celebration where the lights are dimmer, and the music is quieter. The remains of a headache from my dream pulses in my temples in time with my aching mark. I watch the party spin on without me.

On a normal night, I'd be on the dance floor, matching Anwen partner-for-partner. Or, I suppose Baz now. Anwen hasn't been more than six feet from Estrella since the two of them arrived. Dance lessons were one of my favorites growing up and the easiest skill we were forced to learn. If I can impress a man with my grace, I don't have to know all the right words like Anwen always seemed to or have the royal bearing Kieran was born with.

The two of them twirl by with their wives, Kieran and Raven slower than the music calls for. I smile and wave when they do, but something in my chest aches. Growing up, Kieran was properly scary. He had a temper, and he tormented Raven almost as much as Mother and Father. Anwen didn't scare me, exactly, but he had a way of always popping up where I least expected him with the piece of information I least wanted him to have. They were both dangerous. And so was I, though in my own small ways. I ran the variety of noble daughters with an iron fist, passing down edicts about who could and could not be invited here or there. We were our parents' children. But now, they have Estrella and Raven. Their mates softened them, showed them a way to be better. I've been trying to find my way ever since that dream, the one that showed me how wrong I was about Raven, but I was looking forward to my other half—wondering how he would balance me out. Now, I'm destined to remain off-balance forever, fighting the cruelty in my blood.

Ingrid's smell catches my nose. Of course, she's out here. And I think my own head might not be the best place for me right now. I follow the trail around the circle of the party until I find her fidgeting with the draping sleeves of her gown.

"I let Kieran introduce me to everyone he wanted," she says defensively before I even open my mouth.

I smile. Ingrid hates balls and other big celebrations. She can't stand people talking about nothing over the music she'd rather be listening to—and she seems to have escaped the cruelty that infected her three oldest siblings. I wonder what that's like.

"I wasn't going to accuse you of anything."

"Thank the Goddess." She deflates. "Because I didn't, he still has a few 'suitors' picked out."

"Really?" A chill runs down my spine. Mother used to introduce us around like she could convince the Goddess to mate us to certain men just by putting us in their proximity. I assumed Kieran would've stopped that practice.

She waves a hand flippantly. "Suitors, allies–they're all boring people with no opinions they're willing to share."

I exhale in a gust. He has stopped.

"You look wound up." A small smile creeps over Ingrid's lips. "Don't tell me you're not even enjoying this."

Usually, I'm on the dance floor, keeping up with Anwen partner for partner. I shrug.

"It's been a long couple of days."

She grabs my hand. "Sneak out with me."

"What? No. Kieran will notice and—" And what? Get upset? The worst he can do is yell. After Mother, and Hollis, and the mark that won't let me relax, a little yelling might be downright peaceful.

Ingrid's smile grows. "See? You're considering it. That's how I know you need this. If you're tired enough to consider breaking the rules, you have to."

I look at the party behind us. Eva and Hollis are dancing now, seemingly over whatever happened at the table already. My mark hurts, but so does my chest.

"Okay," I say.

Ingrid claps her hands together. "Here's what we're going to do—"

I STAND IN THE MIDDLE OF THE ASHEN BATTLEFIELD, TAKING IN THE suffering around me. I open my mouth and—

Something shakes my shoulder. I blink awake and rub my eyes. Ingrid's plan worked like a charm, but she wanted to stay up and talk, so I can't have been asleep for more than an hour yet.

The thing shakes me again. I turn and see a hand reaching through a split in the tent. My heart hammers. I take a deep breath.

Pine. Amber. Snow.

Hollis is standing outside my tent, waking me up in the middle of the night.

"Don't scream," he whispers. "This is important."

My stomach twists. His scent is intoxicating, but after the way he treated me, I feel like I'm already hungover.

"What?" I ask.

"Can we talk?"

COMMON GROUND

Hollis

Through the darkness, Candace's pale brow wrinkles. I clench my fists.

"Why?" she asks.

Hell of a question. One I have no idea how to answer.

"Eva gave you a chance to tell her everything. To make me look like the asshole." I study her through the gap I sliced in the side of her tent. "Why didn't you?"

She bites her lower lip and looks at the ground. Silvery moonlight casts her face in stark colors, but I can just barely make out some redness around her eyes. Was she… crying?

My mark screams.

"I didn't want to hurt her," Candace mumbles. "This way, I'm the only one hurt."

The pain redoubles. That thing in my chest jumps like a guard dog who heard a strange noise. She really believes she's the only one this is hurting.

Focus, Hollis. You came here for a reason.

And that reason is the look on her face when she glanced back as she left. It wasn't hurt or humiliation or even the want I spotted for just a second when she woke up this morning. It was concern.

When Eva and I returned to our tent after the celebration, everything was back to normal between us. She was teasing me about my two left feet, and I was complaining the music was impossible to dance to. Habit took over, and I started pulling off my tunic.

I came this close to showing her my mark. This close to ruining everything. Because I was having fun with her, the woman who *should* be my mate. Drastic times call for drastic measures, so I need the help of the woman who shouldn't help me with the one thing we agree about.

"I don't want to hurt her either," I say. "It's the last fucking thing I want."

Candace swallows visibly. "So?"

"So the mark isn't just hurting you."

She looks up at me, hope shining in her soft blue eyes.

"Physically, I mean." I rub my aching shoulder. "And we can't exactly talk to other people about this."

"You want my help figuring out how to break the bond," she says slowly.

Fuck. Every time I think the mark can't hurt any worse, it finds a new way, digging burning spoons in behind my eyes.

"Yes." I smile as confidently as I can. "So it stops hurting all three of us."

"Okay," she says.

"Okay?" My eyebrows shoot up. "Okay. Thank you."

She slides off her bed and away from me without a word. When she returns, she's wrapped a heavy robe over the white nightgown I was trying very hard not to notice. I help her climb out through the gap in the side of the tent then offer her my arm.

Candace stares at it for a long second.

"Eva talks about you a lot." She begins walking away.

"Good things?" I hurry to catch up.

She glances at me out of the corner of her eye. "Mostly."

I grimace. "Did she tell you the blueberry story?"

A smile pulls at Candace's lips that answers the question for her.

"She tells it wrong every time." I shake my head.

"Then tell me the right version."

I look around the silent campground. The moon is already dipping toward the horizon, the small hours of the morning creeping up on us. Almost no one is awake, and the few who are don't pay any attention to a couple more shapes in the night.

"Fine," I grumble. "You have to understand, this was a few weeks after my mother died."

Candace puts a hand on my arm. "I am sorry about that."

The strange feeling in my chest reacts, and I pull away from her touch. She tucks her hand into a pocket of her robe wordlessly.

"When I was even younger, she showed Eva and I this patch of winter blueberries. They grow on the mountain Kar Castle sits atop, but only in a few places. So, the two of us were sitting in this dead boring history lesson, and I looked out the window, and I could've sworn I saw the patch. The very one she showed us."

Candace covers her mouth to hide a small laugh.

I bump my hip into hers. "Don't laugh! I told you, Eva has it all wrong, so you don't know the end yet."

She nods seriously.

"Our history tutor was easy to distract—just tell him Kaiya, one of the maids, was nearby, and he disappeared. We got rid of them and snuck out onto the grounds." I glance at Candace. The moonlight turns her cornsilk hair to liquid silver. My heart skips a beat, and I plunge onward. "At this point, I could shift with some reliability, but Eva couldn't."

"So you shifted and let her ride you," Candace supplies.

I allow myself a small smile. "We did that a lot back then. Anyway, I put my nose to the ground, and we start running. In addition to winter blueberries, ice ivy also grows around the castle. And the berries look almost exactly the same."

"Except icy ivy is poisonous." She is clearly fighting to hold back laughter again.

I roll my eyes. "By the time I tracked down a patch of anything, Eva was freezing, and I was starving. Because I'm a gentleman, I made us a fire while *she* picked the berries."

"She picked them?" Candace's mouth opens in shock.

"Skipped that part, huh?" I grin triumphantly. "She always does. The rest is true—we ate about a dozen each before starting the trek home then made a pie with the rest when we got back. Both of us got violently ill, but not before the cook convinced Father to have a slice of the pie." I expected him to be furious, but he never actually said a word about it. He would've been furious before Mother died.

"Eva described the illness in a little more detail." Candace giggles. "But you're correct, she doesn't tell it right."

"See? You can trust me." An impulse to take her arm again sweeps through me, but I squash it. People might not be listening, but anyone could see us.

"You grew up together, didn't you?" she asks.

I nod. "I never had any siblings, and there weren't many other children in the castle. We spent all of our time together."

"She's your best friend," Candace says.

I've never put it like that, but she's not wrong.

"Do you love her?" she asks quietly.

I open my mouth, and nothing comes out. Eva is my promised. I care about her more than almost anyone in the world. She's the person I go to with good news and bad, the one who makes me laugh. And I'm going to fall in love with her when the Haze—

Well. I should have fallen in love with her. Not that I know what falling in love feels like.

That strangeness in my chest twinges again. I've never gotten that with Eva. I've never looked at her and thought about what the moonlight did to her hair or how kissable her mouth looked. Fuck.

"I didn't ask you out here to be put on trial." I pull away from Candace—when did we get so close?—and a dark shape catches my eye. The prison wagon. "I might as well ask you how you're out here celebrating when your mother is imprisoned right over there."

"That's the least of my concerns," Candace mumbles.

For the first time in a long time with anyone other than Eva or Father, I want to know more. "What do you mean?"

She jerks her head up like she forgot I was here. "Oh. Um, just with the bond, and the ritual not working fully…." She toes some dead grass.

I peer at her. "You're lying."

Her mouth tightens. "Those are significant concerns of mine."

"But there's something more." Somehow, I can already tell in the pinch of her brow and the way she won't look at me.

"It doesn't matter." She shakes her head. "If you asked my siblings, they'd tell you it's just something I made up in my head."

We pass the wagon and approach the newly vital tree. Lights still hang from its branches, burning low, but the rest of the celebration is abandoned. There's just us. I remember all my failed attempts at getting information out of people here. Subtlety isn't my art.

I lean against the tree and cross my arms. "I'm not like your siblings. Give me a shot."

She stares at me for a long moment. "You're not going to use this to make fun of me the next time you feel uncomfortable?"

I stiffen. "No."

She keeps staring at me, like she's taking me apart, climbing inside my head. How does she already know me so well?

"I won't," I say less defensively. "I promise."

"All right." She takes a deep breath. "Since I was a kid, I've been getting these… dreams. The royal family of Dun's Crossing doesn't have any magic, but somehow, I do. My dreams—some of them—come true. I can tell when I'm having them. They feel different. More real." She shakes her head. "I dreamt of you. Down to the blood."

"Holy shit," I murmur.

"I knew you wouldn't believe me." She starts to turn away.

I grab her wrist. Her skin is warm and smooth under my hand. "I do. Magic is strange, and no one understands it as well as they say they do. But why is that a problem now?"

She studies me like she's searching for signs I'm making fun of her.

"I'm not a good liar," I say.

A small smile softens her face. "That, I believe." She turns back, but I don't release her wrist. The pain in my mark finally fades.

"I've been having a new dream. One that prophesies war worse than anything my father started." She swallows. "And once the dreams start, whatever they're predicting usually happens soon."

I reel back a step. War. It would be a chance to prove myself to my father—and a guarantee of thousands of deaths.

"You believe me," she says incredulously.

"Of course." I exhale slowly. "We need to—"

"No one believes me." She takes a step closer. Gold and silver play over her skin like a dance.

Candace kisses me.

FIGHTING THE INSTINCT

Candace

MY HEART HAMMERS AS MY LIPS SLIDE OVER HOLLIS'S. HE TASTES EVEN stronger than he smells, like a winter day I'm watching through a window. My heart flutters. My stomach clenches.

Hollis pulls back. His eyes are wide, pupils nearly swallowing green iris. "We can't."

Right. My mark sears, and I drop my gaze. We were just talking about all the reasons why we can't do this. Who it will hurt.

"Not here." He takes my hand.

Bright, burning hope lights in my chest. I scamper after him, out of the soft lights strung in the branches. Can he feel my heart pounding against the thin skin of my wrist? When he glances back at me, is he worried or just checking to see if I'm still following?

Hollis leads us to a small cluster of half-living trees, outside the ring of light and away from any other tents. I take a step forward, ready to kiss him again. He really believes me.

He frowns, and a muscle in his jaw tenses.

"What?" I ask softly.

"I—we—" He shakes his head.

I study the restrained movement in his legs, the tautness of his hand in mine. He wants to run. My stomach churns, but I want to run too. We shouldn't do this. I open my mouth to say just that.

He drops my wrist, grabs my waist, and crushes me to his body. I yelp, but his lips swallow the sound. His tongue dances into my open mouth, and I twine mine with his. His taste is potent, almost intoxicating. The first snow of the season in a pine forest, the promise of a hot drink when I get wherever I'm going. Ice and warmth in a complicated blend, neither as intense without the other. I slide my hands into his dark hair and hold on tight.

My heavy robe dulls the sensation of his hands sliding over my hips, my chest. The spring air tempts me despite the chill. I force my hands between us and yank the tie holding my robe closed. It falls open, and Hollis pushes it off my shoulders. I moan as his touch intensifies, nothing between us but thin, white cotton.

He cups one of my thighs and hooks my leg around his waist. Hardness presses into my warm center. I grind against him with another moan.

"Shush," he murmurs. "No one is nearby, but…."

He doesn't have to finish the sentence. I know the stakes. And through my vague memories of the Haze, I know I won't be able to keep quiet while he's touching me. With shaking fingers, I untie the cravat around his neck. Hollis stares at me blankly.

"I saw this once, in a book one of my brothers left out," I whisper. It sounds better than admitting I know it from watching Father bring prisoners of war back to the castle. Then, I stuff the cravat into my mouth, silken fabric brushing over my tongue.

Hollis's gaze goes dark. He strokes my cheek and opens his mouth as if to say something then closes it again. Before I can ask, he lifts me off my feet and lays me down on my fallen robe, his body covering every inch of mine.

I moan, and it comes out no louder than the beat of a bird's wings. My skin hums with want, and Hollis is quick to provide.

He presses his mouth to my neck, my collarbone, devouring in bites rough enough to feel but gentle enough not to mark. I squirm underneath him. He unties the neck of my nightgown easily, and I drag his mouth lower, onto the top slopes of my breasts. It's all he can reach. My body pulses, craving his touch where I need it most.

I have a robe to wear back to the tent.

My nails sharpen to claws, and I shred the front of my nightgown. It falls to the sides, and Hollis growls as he takes one of my nipples in his mouth. Lightning arcs through me. I clutch his hair once again, holding him so he can never get away. He palms my other breast in the same rhythm, nearly as hungry as we were the first night. My legs smear past each other when I tense them. I'm already soaked.

The embroidery on his vest and tunic scrape over my chest. I groan, release his hair, and begin pulling at his clothes. I'm barely wearing the sleeves of my nightgown anymore. I want to see him.

Hollis ignores my growing frenzy, focusing all his attention on my breasts. Here, he leaves behind a trail of kisses, covering nearly every inch of pale flesh. Right now, there's only us. There's only the sparks in my veins and the all-consuming want between my thighs. I thrust up into him and brush against the stiffness in his pants.

He's going to know I've never done this before.

I can't wait another second, and this is the only weapon I have.

I reach between us and grasp his cock.

Hollis grunts. "Softer."

I loosen my grasp with a small grimace. He's been inside me, but I've never touched him like this. Blindly, I undo his trousers and reach inside. Beads of wetness collect at the head, and it twitches when I run my thumb over them. He makes a soft, abortive sound that seems to be his own muffled moan. I wrap my fingers around him, and he thrusts into my hand as he switches his mouth to my other breast.

My nipple pebbles in the night air, cold for the second before he covers it with his hand. Slowly, I stroke him inside the prison of his pants. The angle is awkward, but touching him is exhilarating.

Hollis releases my breast, finally, and begins kissing down my chest. Soft nips of warmth chase his mouth, spurring the want between my legs higher than the want in my chest. I lose my grasp on his cock as he moves and grab his hair once more. His teeth scrape over my inner thigh, and then he pauses.

I lean up on one elbow to look at him. Hollis lays, frozen, staring at the apex of my legs. All his muscles have gone tense again. The spell is breaking. We are not two people in the night. We're not even two mates, really. A world expands in my mind's eye. One where I am learning how to touch him at the beginning of a lifetime of pleasure. Where one day I'll hear him fully. Where one day he'll mark my neck if he wants, grab me where anyone could see. An impossible world that he's realizing will never come.

Tears prick my eyes.

Hollis runs his fingers between my legs, a series of tiny explosions of pleasure, and his whole body melts. He moves sinuously as he returns to kissing my thighs and spreads the wetness everywhere he can reach. My breath whooshes out of my chest in a single gust, and I lie back. His mind must be telling him to leave, just like mine is. But our instincts are stronger. We can't fight them.

He fucks one finger into me, then a second. I arch, taut with want. His name comes out muffled through my makeshift gag. My first peak is already approaching, hot and fast. Every time he sinks his mouth onto my thighs, it gets a little closer. My tears spill, but something as complex as sadness or yearning is gone from my mind. I am all pleasure.

Hollis curls his fingers, and I shake apart around him. He strokes me through the tiny earthquakes that follow. My breath comes back to me slowly through the gag, and I fight the encroaching reality of the situation.

Clothing rustles. I squeeze my eyes tighter and hope. When he lies back down on top of me, it's skin on skin. I know I was right. There's nothing here but us and the trees now. He lines himself up with my entrance. My walls flutter in yet another echo of the peak, and he slides in.

The gag barely muffles my near-scream. A few birds fly off at the sudden noise. I lurch up into him, wrap my arms around his neck and my legs around his waist like that'll keep him from ever going away again. It only drives him deeper, at a new angle. I tremble as he thrusts. His grunts start to grow in volume, and part of me wants to shush him. The rest wants to soak up every sound, every breath, every second before this ends.

With his hands hungry on my breasts, his mouth on my neck and dancing over my mark, Hollis reaches the apex first. He stiffens over me with a raspy noise that could, if I really want to hear it, sound like my name. I cling to him tighter. Even as he softens inside me, he keeps thrusting. Our sweat mingles. Our skin sticks together. My second orgasm crashes through me like a tree falling in a storm, leaving only devastation in its wake.

Hollis rolls off me, onto the forest floor. His chest rises and falls, the coating of dark hair drawing dramatic swirls on his pale skin. My stomach twists as the only two thoughts I can think take center stage in my mind.

How can I stay away from Hollis now?

How can I not without destroying Eva?

I pull his cravat out of my mouth, push to my feet, and grab my robe.

"Where are you going?" Hollis asks.

"We—" Can't do this. Should never have done this. "—can't get caught."

I tie my robe back on and leave, the fact that I didn't tell him we couldn't do it again pulsating in my mind.

A WAY FORWARD

Hollis

I watch Candace disappear through the still mostly leafless trees, and that thing in my chest crunches. Fuck that. I crunch it back. That was… fuck, I don't know, a mistake. A lapse in judgment. But sleeping with her makes sense. It's all animal. Wishing she would stay? That's unacceptable.

Slowly, I dress. Most of my clothes are in one pile, but I tuck the cravat soaked with her saliva in my pocket. Nobody's going to notice I'm not wearing it anymore. I'll just drop it in the laundry, and no one will be any wiser.

Our tent is on the north side of camp, so I turn and march toward it. And Eva. Who's supposed to be my mate. I tracked down Candace to protect Eva, not hurt her even worse. It was a stupid fucking plan, all emotion and no logic.

The lights on the old oak fade back into view, along with the memory of Candace's face when I said I believed her. Was it such a stupid plan? Candace has the kind of heart I honestly didn't believe people had outside of storybooks, and I can tell she cares about Eva. She doesn't want to hurt her either.

Shit. Instincts were supposed to be these animal things, all physical. But there's no instinct to explain the crunch in my chest when she leaves, the softness when I look at her. Maybe, between the two of us, we could come up with some kind of plan? A way to tell Eva that hurts her the least? If anyone can do it, it's Candace.

Which leaves the problem of the war to me.

AFTER THE NEXT DAY'S REVITALIZATION—JUST AS MUCH POMP AND circumstance, a lot more spreading green—I sit with Zain in the shade of my tent. The exponential growth has the whole gathering excited. Group after group wanders by, chattering about it.

Candace stood at the front with her family, like last time, but she wore a gray dress this time. We haven't spoken since last night. It's harder to find time than I would've guessed with how disorganized the whole campground seems to be.

"A war?" Disbelief threads through Zain's voice as he lounges in the low chair across the matching table from mine. "Why the fuck are you asking about war?"

The leafy branches of the old oak loom over a line of tents. I can't explain without telling him why Candace and I were alone together, and I'm not telling anyone about the mark until I talk to her again. We need to come up with a plan—and as much as I trust Zain in a fight, he's a shit secret-keeper.

"Call it a feeling." I shrug. "There's something in the air."

"I think that's excitement, but fine. I'm still finding my in with the other delegates." He shakes his head. "None of them seem like they're about to start a war."

"I haven't exactly started making friends either." I frown. Candace and Eva have been consuming my thoughts. Worse, half the kingdoms seem like they're run by a pack of toddlers, and the other half are so uptight I'd be surprised if they didn't have an ancestral stick for jamming up their asses. Father's right, Snowcrest really is the only place with the right balance.

"Really?" Zain smirks. "I heard a rumor you're writing a book on Escuro, which is funny because I'm only half sure you remember how to write."

I force myself to laugh and mentally curse yet another bullshit plan. Of course, that rumor would spread.

"Trying to figure out if they're starting the war?" he asks.

Thank fuck. An excuse I didn't have to come up with. I nod. "As you could probably tell, I didn't make a lot of progress."

Zain snorts and pushes his auburn hair out of his face. "You, trying to talk to people? I'm shocked it didn't work."

"Dickhead." I elbow him in the ribs, hard. Diplomacy isn't my strong suit, but it's not like I walked up to people and started cursing them out. I deserve a little more credit, and my second-oldest friend knows it.

Because he's my second-oldest friend, Zain ducks my second swing with a laugh. "All right, I'm focused. The Solbergs have had six or eight chances to start a war on unsuspecting kingdoms since Gavin died, and they haven't, so I don't think it's them."

"Or they're spectacular manipulators hoping you'll think exactly that." The idea seems a lot less palatable than it did when I woke up the morning after the Haze. "Maybe they need Escuro strong first."

"Why?" Zain shakes his head. "No, I think your best bet's one of the other kingdoms. Things are in flux right now—it's the perfect chance for a lesser kingdom to strike, especially if they've been building strength quietly."

Father strides into sight, pauses slightly, then joins us in the shade.

"Boys," he says.

"King Andri." Zain bows.

"Father." I don't. Zain's being ridiculous.

"This ritual works." Father stares at the mottled green and gray ground.

"Did you hear anything else about it?" I ask. "Like, are the wolves of Escuro being affected?"

Father shakes his head. "Unless delirium is an effect."

I laugh. "Zain and I were talking about who might take advantage of a gathering like this."

Father raises an eyebrow. "The Solbergs. The Sollabellas—Sundrop Gem barely speaks politics yet. Escuro cannot be discounted. I have never trusted Oakspring Dunes."

"Is there anyone you do trust?" Zain asks with half a smile.

"Our people." Father nods. "A few others, here and there. The wolves of Starfall Mountain were once honorable."

I haven't heard the name Starfall since King Gavin destroyed them, a few weeks before he showed up on our doorstep, and Father allied with him.

"Thornwinter Swamp," he adds.

Mother's pack, before she moved to Snowcrest. An idea strikes me. *'Go start making friends,'* I tell Zain. *'I'll catch up.'*

'You sure?' he asks.

I nod.

He stands with a groan. "Well, I've got plans with a few other delegates. Lilywind set up something like a bar on the east side of camp, and—"

Father waves his hand dismissively. Zain's talking more than he has to—Father's already waiting for him to leave. He does without another word.

"There was no Skadi daughter your age, right?" I ask. "That's why you and Mother…."

Father frowns. "If there were, we would be mated."

"Of course," I say quickly. "I've just been thinking about it since I reached maturity."

He grunts.

"Uncle Misael, his wife isn't a Skadi either, right?" I scowl at my hands in my lap. This is why half the camp thinks I'm writing a book. This whole subtle manipulation thing comes as easily to me as sewing does to swords.

"No." Father folds his hands behind his back and starts to turn. "I ought—"

"Hang on," I blurt.

He looks at me. Shit. Now, I need something good.

"Other delegates have been asking," I say. "They don't understand our traditions, and honestly, I haven't done as good a job learning them as I should've."

Father sighs, and that fucking look, the "I've been waiting for this" look flashes through his eyes like a knife through my gut. But he takes Zain's empty chair.

"Whenever a daughter of Skadi and a son of Kar are born within a week of each other, they are mates," he says. "May skip whole generations. Soren believes magic equally targets far-flung branches of family trees. I believe him a romantic fool." He shakes his head almost indulgently at his absent Beta.

I smile tightly. "Has there ever been a son and daughter born at the right time that don't mate?"

"No." He stares at me. "Once, our families ruled Snowcrest Canyon back and forth every generation. Even then, it happened. My mother believed it an old spell."

I've never heard of an ancient spell being broken. One old enough to span centuries of history, back when the magic beneath Snowcrest made sense to the people who lived there? It's impossible.

Until now.

"Why do you ask these things?" Father says. "Eva said you were too far from the Haze. You were not taken."

"We weren't!" I hop up. "Just close enough for the transformation. And I am sorry about the carriage, I will fix that as soon as we get home."

Father stares at me, his eyes fathomless. I wish like hell I could read him, but the older he gets, the more lines collect on his face, and the more impossible it gets. Disappointed is a safe bet. Distrustful is another one.

"Eva just called." I tap the side of my head, indicating a mind-link I didn't receive. "She needs help with one of her bird things."

Father nods. That's as close to a dismissal as I'm going to get, so I turn tail and rush off in any direction before he can say another word.

I need to talk to Candace. Not the least because it seems like talking to anybody else backfires on me.

A MONSTER

Candace

RAVEN LOWERS HERSELF INTO HER CHAIR WITH A GRUNT THAT DOESN'T dampen the glowing smile on her face. "The calculations are in. Almost twice the area we revitalized yesterday returned today."

Estrella blinks quickly, like she's warding off tears. "I never dreamt—"

"None of us did." Raven takes her hand then turns to me. "And thank you for being here. Between my pregnancy fog and Estrella's power exhaustion, we need someone with a clear head."

I smile. "I'm just happy I can help."

That is true. Since I left Hollis, I've been sick with anxiety. Every time I close my eyes, I picture the battlefield—the battlefield only he and I believe in. And then, I picture Eva. We've already lied to her for two days. Staying quiet any longer will only make it worse, but telling her is going to destroy her.

"…All right?" Estrella says, looking at me.

I blink. I didn't hear a word. "Um—"

Raven chuckles. "Still tired? I was exhausted for almost a week after the Haze."

Relief washes over me. "Yes. That's it. What were you saying?"

"According to the calculations Raven brought us, it should take perhaps a week to revitalize all the destroyed land," Estrella says. "Possibly more."

"And the spring equinox is in ten days." Raven smiles tiredly. "Which will officially put me a full two weeks after Fleming said I would give birth."

I rub her shoulder. She must be so uncomfortable, both physically and with having Fleming so far away. I get itchy if I think about it for too long. He makes the medication I have to take every afternoon for the heart condition I was born with, and even though I have enough, losing access to the source is nerve-wracking.

"I was saying it might be nice to formally extend our stay through the equinox." Estrella rubs her tired eyes. Concocting the revitalization potion several days in a row is draining her reserves like a sleepless night would. "We can formally unite all the kingdoms under the banner of celebration, even if we cannot do anything more at this time."

I nod even as my stomach twists. This is my chance to tell them about my dream, the threat to peace on the horizon.

"I'll send out some messengers, ask who will stay," I say instead.

"Thank you." Raven smiles. "I'll speak to Mother and Father first. They are technically hosting the event."

"Let me know." My smile feels tight. "Anything else?"

AFTER SPLITTING UP FROM THE MEETING WITH OUR OWN ASSIGNMENTS —mine being to wait, as usual—I dodge Ingrid and dart out of our circle of tents. I know it's silly, but something in my gut tells me she'll know what happened last night just by looking at me, and I can't face that right now. I need to talk to Hollis. I don't even know what he's thinking—

"Candace!" Eva calls.

My skin prickles as I turn with another tight smile. She darts through the flow of people toward me. They turn and stare as she passes, the few loose tendrils of her red hair flying in the wind and her skirt rustling. She really is beautiful.

"Hello," I say as she skids to a stop next to me.

"I was coming to find you," she says breathlessly. "There's a Tapia's pheasant on the west side of camp."

My jaw drops. "No one has seen a Tapia's pheasant—"

"Since King Gavin poisoned Escuro!" She grabs my hand and takes off through camp once more. I mumble apologies as I stumble in her wake. The last thing I need is for Mother to ask me about this later.

But when we emerge to the west, near a small cluster of barely leafed trees, and I catch sight of the green-and-purple reflective tail dragging along the ground, every other thought leaves my mind. I squat to get a better view of the impossible bird. Is the ritual bringing back wildlife, not just because there's food here again, but magically? Everyone agrees the Tapia's pheasant was practically extinct. Yet, this one squeaks a mating call as it struts from one tree to the next, its feathers catching the light.

"Isn't it beautiful?" Eva sits on the ground next to me. "I'm so glad I'm here."

"Me too." I glance at her. She looks perfectly relaxed. If Hollis believed me—

No. She's going to receive enough bad news, if we can ever figure out a way to tell her. She doesn't need to worry about this.

"Even if the Haze didn't work." She smiles ruefully. "It's so weird. I've never heard of anything like it."

"And if it worked, you and Hollis…."

"Would've mated." Her smile turns dreamy.

"How does that all work?" I ask, my gaze trained on the pheasant. "Being promised to one another. I thought the Goddess took the reins during the Haze."

She laughs. "I take it your mother didn't talk to you about it much?"

I shake my head furiously. "Once, she handed me a book on the matter and left. Raven and I didn't exactly have a sibling relationship growing up either."

"Then you've come to the right place." Eva plucks a piece of grass from the ground and begins shredding it. "I may not remember Mother, but Eyana, my oldest sister, mated during her very first Haze, almost four years ago. And the castle tutors made sure I knew *everything* about my role as a promised."

"Yuck." I wrinkle my nose. My main tutor was a graying older man called Mathis, and I don't want to imagine him telling me anything about mating. "I don't need the, um, physical details."

"Yuck is right. I'm happy to skip them." She grins. "So I can tell you that, while the Goddess does take over, we know what She's going to do. My family and Hollis's used to trade the throne back and forth every generation or so. And do you know a great way to end a generation?"

"Kill the current Alpha and Luna." I wince. That's the sort of plan my parents would've come up with.

She nods. "After a couple of blood-soaked centuries, people realized a Skadi and a Kar born right near each other ended up mated nearly every generation. And one of our holy women revealed that was a gift from the Goddess, a chance to stop fighting. So one of my ancestors and one of Hollis's struck the compromise. The Kars would keep the throne, but whichever one of their sons mated to one of us would become Alpha, regardless of succession." She shrugs. "We know what's going to happen because we trust the Goddess doesn't want the killing to start again."

I put every iota of willpower I have into watching the pheasant instead of blurting out the dream that's been haunting my sleep. Maybe the Goddess isn't the benevolent deity we've all been led to believe in. Maybe She wants there to be death in the world, and when Kieran stopped Father, She had to come up with a new way to make it happen.

Maybe I'm the new way.

"Did you mind?" My voice rasps out of my throat, jagged and uneven.

Out of the corner of my eye, I watch Eva glance at me. "Mind what?"

"Being the sacrificial lamb." I try to smile. "Having your whole life laid out for you, just because of when you were born."

She sighs and leans back on her hands. "I think I might've if I didn't like the plan so much."

I raise an eyebrow.

"Well, it's not like spending my life with Hollis will be so terrible." She giggles. "Even if he does poison me sometimes."

The blueberry story. I open my mouth to tell her I heard the full version from him, then shut it again. How could I possibly explain why we were together? Or when?

"You can tell me," she says, like I was going to share a secret.

"Oh." I fidget with the hem of my dress. "I was just going to say that you watched him grow up, go through all his awkward phases. You still want to marry him?"

"He saw me through mine." Her smile is soft, nostalgic. "I think there's something special about having known someone your whole life. I don't know how people mate with strangers or even just acquaintances. I like knowing the man behind the animal."

The pheasant's rusty call echoes a little louder, and we both turn. Bobbing out of the brush is another bird, smaller, grayer. A female! This isn't a once-in-a-lifetime miracle. We're witnessing the rebirth of the species.

That still isn't enough to keep my skin from crawling. I am just as cruel as Mother and Father. Worse, because Hollis avoided the question when I asked if he loved Eva, but I can see the difference in the way the two of them speak about each other anyway. They're undeniably close, but Hollis talks about her the way I talk about Finn.

And she talks about him the same way I do.

Eva clasps her hands under her chin as the two birds circle each other, no idea about the monster sitting next to her.

PROTECTION

Hollis

"No, anchor your fingers at your ear." I yank Ty's elbow back until his fingers are at least near his ear. The young noble from Tansy Beach trembles.

'It's like he's never lifted a fucking weapon.' I growl at Zain.

'He probably hasn't,' Zain replies. *'Tansy Beach is weird about human fighting.'*

"Breathe and release," I say to the kid anyway.

His breath shudders out from between pursed lips, and his fingers slip off the string, knocking the arrow loose. It falls in the grass at his feet as the bowstring *twangs*.

"Ow!" he yelps.

"I told you to watch your grip." If I stick with him a second longer, I'm going to take his fucking head off, so I turn to the next delegate in the line of archers Zain and I are ostensibly training with.

Training? Certainly. With, not so much.

The noble from Oakspring Dunes releases a little more steadily.

His arrow thuds into the ground, point buried in the dirt, almost a dozen feet away.

"Good work," I say through gritted teeth.

"Makai," he supplies like I was looking for his name.

Then, like there aren't arrows flying wildly in the loose direction of the targets Zain and I set up after the revitalization this morning, he bounces forward to go pick up his arrow. I grab him by the collar and jerk him back.

"These people might not be trained marksmen, but until you get the all-clear, you stay behind the fucking line," I snarl.

Makai flinches. "Sorry."

I force myself to release him. This archery practice is the plan Zain and I came up with to actually get to know some of the other delegates, maybe figure out who the hell is looking to start a war, but it's quickly spiraling out of control. After two more days of revitalization, small swirls of gray darken the grass like poorly mixed dye, but almost everything else is alive. Now, they're trying to spread the magic to the furthest reaches of the kingdom, and with nothing *right here* to look at anymore, all the other delegates are restless. What was a small group of nobles we invited is now a wandering line of almost twenty shifters, some of which haven't even reached the age to enter the Haze yet, struggling against the lightest bows our guards packed for the trip.

Worse, I've only been able to see Candace for a couple of moments every day. Not nearly long enough for us to actually fucking talk about anything. Just enough to taste her and know she wasn't actually running away after our night together.

Zain walks up and claps me on the shoulder. *'Break soon? Or would you rather start this famed war by killing someone's crown prince?'*

I take in a deep breath. I crave her so badly I smell her blackberry-and-sunshine scent on the wind when she isn't even around. *'Break. Let's—'*

The smell grows stronger. Too strong to be my imagination. I glance around and spot a head of pale blonde hair disappearing between two tents. She's here—and it looks like she's headed to our spot.

'Let's split up so I can cool off. Take them to the Lilywind camp.'

Zain looks at me disbelievingly. I stare back at him.

'Whatever.' He claps his hands. "Hey! Water break at the bar."

Nobles shuffle after him, immediately lured by the temptation of alcohol. They're all going to be even shittier shots by the time I get back.

Candace is worth it. I take off after her, trying to be subtle.

Really, I should just stop trying. Two envoys from Whaleberry Harbor stop me for a "quick chat" that I definitely piss them off getting myself out of, and when I try to flatten myself against a tent like the scout trainer at home is always telling people to, I catch my foot in the ropes holding it up and tumble ass-over-teakettle into the dirt. A few ladies walk by, snickering.

At this point, I'll look more normal just walking through camp like myself and letting the rumor mill do what it wants.

Luckily, I could pick Candace's scent out of a perfumery. I track her through the warren of tents striped with different family colors to the edge of the campground then pause before stepping into view. She might want privacy.

"You're right," she says.

"I always am," a woman replies in a voice I don't recognize.

She's talking to someone. All the way out here. Who—

A soldier in Dun's Crossing silver and blue marches past the two tents I'm tucked between. I duck back. Of course. Rowena Solberg's prison wagon is out here. Which means I really should leave. Eavesdropping is the coward's path, as Father says.

"But what do I do?" Emotion cracks Candace's voice. "He's my mate."

If I can hear them, so can the guards. Does everyone in Dun's Crossing know? I have to stay, to find out what I'm dealing with. Ice flows through my veins, and I exhale slowly, painting the air in front of me with my breath. I might not be used to sneaking around, but Eva and I specialized in making sure tutors didn't know we'd ever left the room. A thin sheet of ice, thickened in the right places, creates the illusion of nothing but shadows in a place. It only works if you've got a tutor dumb enough not to realize he shouldn't let the crown prince sit in the back row, but it's perfect for something like this. It hardens into place, and I relax.

"...Doesn't matter," Rowena is saying. "There is nothing to do. For you. That's why you're here, after all."

Candace blows out a sharp breath. "I'm here because I convinced Kieran to allow me to assign your guards."

Thank the Goddess. But I don't leave my spot. Listening a little longer can't hurt, now that I'm here.

"And because...." She pauses. "Because you're the only one who will understand."

"I do," Rowena coos, sickeningly sweet. "Though I'd understand better if you told me who, exactly, your mate was."

"When you mated with Father, did you know?" Candace's voice breaks on the last word.

My chest aches.

"I knew he was the prince." Rowena lingers over the title like it's candy. "I knew I was blessed to have him."

"Did you know what he'd become?" Her voice is almost a whisper.

There's a long, tense pause. Something hot simmers in my veins. Is she asking if I'm going to become like Gavin Solberg?

"I hoped," Rowena says crisply.

Why King Kieran and Queen Raven haven't just killed her yet, I'll never know. I clench my fists.

"So he might not know about me." Candace's relief is palpable.

I feel like I'm going to puke. There's no one in the world less likely to become her father than her.

"For that, you'd have to ask your father if he knew about me. Oh, wait, you can't. Because your brothers murdered him and locked me up." Rowena laughs, high and cold. "But I wouldn't worry too much— you didn't learn nearly enough from me that there's any chance he doesn't already know what you are."

The simmering something bursts into burning rage. My ice

dissolves in an instant as my emotions slip out of my control and my mark screams.

"I'm going to destroy everything," Candace says. "The Goddess declared it."

"I could've—"

Their words fall on deaf ears as I stride out of my hiding spot. Soldiers shout and run toward me, but I ignore them, my gaze locked on the dark prison wagon alone in the middle of the clearing. Smartly, Rowena falls silent. Only the memory of Father's voice in my head, warning me not to start an international fucking incident, keeps me from spearing the wagon with enough ice to slaughter Rowena where she sits.

"Who—" Candace's face appears at the barred window on the door. "Oh."

"Good afternoon." I wave like I was just walking by, but I doubt my face is hiding anything. "I thought I heard you, so I came looking. Sorry to barge in."

"Well, hello." Rowena's voice purrs from deeper in the wagon, but I still can't see her. "I don't believe I've had the pleasure—"

"He's not a threat," Candace says quickly.

The soldiers leveling weapons and shifting around me take a couple of steps back. I didn't even notice how close they'd gotten.

"Let me out," she demands.

"Now, darling, don't you want to introduce me to your... friend?" Rowena asks, sickly sweet again.

Candace ignores her. I clench my fists as one of the soldiers runs over to the door with a jangling ring of keys and unlocks it.

Something moves. A shape I can barely make out in the gloom. Then, it resolves into a woman. I met Queen Rowena at Mother's funeral, I believe, and a few other times over the years, but the dirt-encrusted woman in the darkness of the wagon looks more like a monster out of a fairytale than the icy queen I half-remember.

Candace steps out with her arms wrapped around herself like she's cold, and I jerk my attention to her. I have to get her out of here.

Before I actually decide to kill Rowena just to stop her from saying shit like that to my mate ever again.

"Goodbye, Mother," Candace says without looking back. "We have somewhere else to be."

"I thought he was just wandering by." She approaches the window as the guard slams the door shut again. "Come visit again soon, darling. And bring… him."

The last thing I see before Candace pulls me away is her expression, far too sharp to be called a smile.

STRONG

Candace

I TUG HOLLIS AWAY BY THE WRIST—THE LEAST ROMANTIC PLACE I could grab him, because even though I assigned all my favorite guards to Mother, I don't trust anyone enough to actually admit who my mate is—and pray under my breath that he actually was just walking by. If he overheard a single word of that, he'll never look at me again. After the past few days of stealing moments with him, a pattern is becoming obvious. The times he stays with me come after I've been strong. During the Haze, I was too out of my mind to worry. Since then, he likes me when I walk away rather than take his teasing, when I admit a dream that makes me sound insane to believe, when I sneak away with him rather than attending to my responsibilities.

And if those are the times I feel most like Eva, that's just not something I'm going to think about.

But if he heard me with Mother... I'm never weaker or smaller than I am when I'm with her. Going to her at all is a weakness. I just need to talk to someone, and I know what Ingrid would say. She'd tell me I'm being ridiculous, to stand up for myself and declare my mate to the world. If he doesn't want me, everyone should know that he's disobeying the Goddess.

The times Hollis seems to like me best are the ones I feel most like Ingrid, too.

We arrive in the small circle of now fully living trees that has become our spot over the past few days—far enough away from everything that no one can overhear us if we're reasonably quiet, close enough that no one asks questions about how long we're taking to get places when summoned. Small, dark purple wildflowers dot the tall grass. A squirrel chitters in the branches. A bit away, a thrush sings.

"So," Hollis says, "your mother."

Panic fills my limbs, only to be chased away by the ice of Mother's voice: *Your greatest weapon is your body. If you won't use it in the mate bond, where will you?*

I throw my arms around Hollis's neck and crush my mouth to his. Fear dampens the usual thrill of his taste. His hands find my hips, and he falls into rhythm. Since the night after the first ritual, we haven't stolen enough time to have sex yet, but this is quickly becoming familiar. When I realized that yesterday, it filled me with warmth. Today, it makes me taste bile.

Hollis pulls back. "I don't know how long I have. I'm supposed to be cooling off so I don't kick the asses of the morons I'm trying to teach how to shoot."

Mother again. *Men like to talk about two things: themselves and your body. Keep the conversation to those, and you'll break hearts.*

"I bet you're a great teacher." I force a giggle and run one of my hands down to his bicep. "You're certainly strong enough."

He laughs. "I'm a crap teacher. Strength only makes me a better archer."

"You could teach me." I smile coyly. "It can't be that hard."

Just like she promised, I watch his pride ruffle.

"I don't have a bow here, but I promise it's not as easy as it looks." His grip on my waist tightens. "It's all about control."

I lean into him, appreciating the hint of a rasp in his voice. "Controlling what?"

"Everything." He bends down until I can feel his breath on my face. "Do you think you could do that?"

"I could try." I purse my lips slightly, trying to tempt him into kissing me.

Instead, he spins me around, pressing his front to my back. With one hand, he points my face at nothing in the brush and pulls my arms up as though I am holding a bow. I start to forget why I was distracting him in the first place, if I even was. It's so easy to lose myself with him.

"Inhale," he murmurs in my ear. His hand glides down my chest, lingering on my clothed breasts before settling on my stomach. "Can you feel it?"

His hardness against me? I grind against him. "Yes."

His laughter is more air than sound. "The tension in your abdomen, carrying up into your arms when you inhale."

"Then no." I laugh fully. "I just feel like an idiot."

"Well, you're not holding a bow," he grumbles. "It's different."

I twist in his grasp to face him once more. His hands drag on my dress, pulling my skirt higher. "I believe you completely. But I think I'll stick to fighting as a wolf."

"You fight?" He smirks down at me.

"I know… some self-defense."

His smile only grows. "Then stop this."

Before I can blink, Hollis hooks his arms under both my thighs and lifts me off the ground. Instead of fighting him, I wrap my legs around his waist and hold on. Want courses through me.

"Some self-defense." He chuckles.

"You're not going to hurt me." The words taste bitter in my mouth, but I cover them with another kiss.

Hollis melts into me. There's no shake in his arms, no hint that holding me is any strain. He could throw me all around this clearing without breaking a sweat. I clutch him tighter as desire begins to burn between my legs. He only has a few minutes, but maybe we could—

A branch snaps. Hollis rips back from the kiss and drops me in a flutter of skirts. I grab another tree so I don't fall over. When I look at him to demand what he's thinking, I find him trained like a scout wolf in the direction of the sound.

My heart pangs. Over the past few days, he seemed less and less like he was fighting the instinct to bolt when we were together. I thought he was actually getting used to the idea. Getting used to me.

A thin, brown rabbit hops out of the bushes in the direction of the noise, sees us, and bolts back the way it came.

"Why so jumpy?" I push to my feet and brush myself off. "It's just a rabbit."

"Because—" He turns back to me, and the words seem to catch in his throat. "Well, there's a reason we're here and not in my tent."

My mark aches. "Right. We should probably go. There shouldn't be anywhere that *we* are, not like this."

He stares at me for a long moment. "I have enjoyed these past couple of days."

Me too. And that's the worst part.

"But you don't think we're in a place to start telling people, do you?" He stuffs his hands in his pockets. "We haven't talked about anything yet."

He's right. Of course, he's right. And there's no way to tell anyone —other than Mother—without telling everyone. That's why even Ingrid doesn't know yet.

"No, I don't." I stare at the bushes the rabbit hopped off through, wishing I could follow. "We need a plan."

"Right." He takes a step closer. "But we don't have time to come up with one now. I need to leave before people start wondering."

I look up into his green eyes, trying to read whatever truth exists in them. "It would be really, really bad if people found out."

"Exactly."

He leans in to kiss me again, not hearing the difference between the two things we said. Telling Eva, especially without a plan, would be catastrophic. But her finding out any other way would be much, much worse.

I tilt my head up, and our mouths meet. It's what I'm supposed to do. Be the mate he wants. And he's not exactly signaling subtly, his hands roaming over me again. But suddenly, the kiss feels hollow. What did Eva say? She wants to know the man beneath the animal. Hollis and I made perfect sense during the Haze, when we're having sex, and we make no sense outside of it. I'm still just the animal to him.

Something sharper than desire burns through me. Hollis likes me when I'm strong. When I make the dangerous choice instead of the safe one. I break the kiss.

"What am I to you?" I ask. "A body–or a person?"

He takes a step back like I tried to hit him. His already pale skin goes paler. "A body? What do you mean?"

That thing keeps burning. "I mean, is what we have just physical? Do I exist to you when you're not touching me?"

"Of course you exist." He cups my hip gently, like I'm a hot stove he's afraid of burning himself on. "And we will talk. But right now, we don't have time."

"We're never going to have time." I pull out of his grasp. "We had ten days. Five, now. And then we disappear to different kingdoms. So should we talk when we can or waste that time touching each other?"

Something in him hardens. He scoffs. "You call that a waste? It seemed like—"

"I do," I say over his words. "When the other option is figuring out our future, I do."

"Our future?" His eyebrows shoot up to his hairline. "Look, I just came here to make out for a couple of minutes. You can talk about the future with someone else because I don't see one for myself with"—he looks me up and down—"*this* person, okay?"

My mark sears like it covers every inch of my skin as Hollis shakes his head and leaves without another word.

Good work, Candace. Really strong.

DRINKING BUDDIES

Hollis

I STORM OUT OF THE COPSE OF TREES, CLENCHING AND UNCLENCHING
my hands. I have to hit something. There has to be something in this
Goddess-forsaken place for me to hit. I march back to the mock-
training ground Zain and I slapped together, still empty, but we've
only finished the fucking archery part.

It's better than nothing. I shoulder one of the heavy bows, nock an
arrow, and let it fly. Bullseye.

Inhale, aim, fire, exhale. The next arrow lands directly next to it.

Tension knots my muscles, over tightens my grip. The third
quivers in the ring just outside the bullseye, its bright-red fletching
taunting me. I throw the bow down in the grass and storm down the
shooting range. *All fucking clear*. And I have to get that last arrow out
before anybody else sees it. I haven't missed the bullseye from this
close since I was sixteen.

I'm not an idiot. I know I went a little overboard. The look in her
eyes is going to haunt me in my dreams tonight; she was like a baby
bird looking at a foot coming down on top of it, her soft blue irises

shimmering with tears. And I knew she just had this awful talk with her mother, though she made it fucking hard to remember. But what the hell was she expecting, cornering me like that after we agreed that wasn't a good time to talk?

At the target, I rip the arrows free one after the next, not nearly as careful as I should be. One of the heads chips. I snap the arrow over my knee and throw it on the ground. The blacksmith fucking hates reforging chipped arrows, and I know our coffers are full enough for one replacement.

She clearly wasn't going to let it drop. She left me with no choice. I scrape my hands through my hair. I need to talk to—

Eva. Dammit.

'Still at the bar?' I ask Zain through mind-link.

'Fuck training. These guys are way better at drinking like they wanna die,' he slurs back.

Good enough for me. I abandon the weapons, knowing Father's going to be pissed about that later, and storm off.

Music and laughter leak out of the bar Lilywind set up at the center of their circle of tents. It's audible almost a hundred feet away. I crack my knuckles as I approach. Hopefully, they don't mind bar fights.

Zain, the other delegates, and a couple of dozen clay steins fill the middle table. They're laughing louder and more drunkenly than anyone else. They've even collected a couple of other patrons, including Candace's younger brother, Finn.

"Hollis!" Zain yells as I walk in. "Another round!"

A woman in an apron walks over with another tray of steins and starts handing them out. A very small part of me is impressed. How the hell did Lilywind know to bring all this crap? Then, the woman pushes a beer into my hands, and I stop being anything but very thirsty. I tip the mug to my lips, chasing away the taste of her.

"Chug! Chug! Chug!" Someone starts chanting, and what seems like the rest of the bar joins in.

Breathless, I tilt my head back and finish off the last foamy dregs then slam the stein on the table. The group roars, and I grin.

Forget Eva. *This* is what I need. Applause is even better than punching something.

"What the fuck happened to you?" Zain hands me another stein, this one half-finished, as I sit on the low-slung bench.

Every head turns in my direction. Father would want me to give some civilized, political answer.

"I've got a girl," I say. "Needed some time with her."

Laughter and hoots fill the air. Someone claps me on the shoulder, sloshing more beer on the already sticky table.

"I thought you didn't mate." Zain shakes his head. He doesn't believe me.

"Who said I fucking did?" I raise my beer and cover the pain in my mark by chugging it, too.

"I thought you were some kind of monk." Finn raises his stein to me with a smirk. "Aren't you *promised?*"

"Fuck that!" Ty hollers. "You should get what you can."

"See, that's what I think." I gesture to him with my beer. "She's not exactly on the same page."

Zain shakes his head and groans. "That is the worst."

I nod, bolstered by the agreement.

"Today, we were having a nice time when she fucking corners me, demands to know what kind of future I see for us." I laugh. Saying it out loud, here, it sounds so ridiculous.

"What'd you say?" Finn asks.

"I told her I didn't have a future with anyone who asked those kinds of questions."

More laughter. My smile grows. I can barely feel the mark's sting. I'm not the problem, Candace is. She demanded answers after we agreed that it wasn't the time to talk. What did she expect? I chug my beer, and before I can even put the stein down, someone is shoving another one in my hand. Zain is right. Training was useless. Drinking is obviously where these delegates shine.

King Anwen shoulders one of the lower-level nobles out of the way and sits down next to his brother. Immediately, Finn stops laughing and straightens up. So do most of the lower-level nobles, and I realize there's music playing from somewhere that I haven't been able to hear this whole time.

"What's so funny?" King Anwen asks.

Finn shakes his head at me. I roll my eyes. Sure, his brother's a king, but he's been king for less than a year, and I'm a crown prince. And neither of them even know I'm talking about their sister.

"I was just telling these guys how I handle women who don't listen." I lean back in my seat and wave my beer. It's heavier than I remember. Some spills over the side. "I've been having a great time with this girl, but she interrupted that to ask about our future after we already said we weren't going to talk about that, so I put her back in her place."

King Anwen closes his eyes and takes a long, deep breath. Brave man. I wouldn't want to smell this place any more than I have to.

"Finn," he says. "Thump Prince Hollis on the back of the head for me so I don't have to start an international incident."

"Hey—"

Finn stands up and obeys before I can get a full sentence out. He doesn't thump me hard—he's too scared, I bet—but the blow jars my brain enough to speed the arrival of my hangover.

"What the fuck do you think you're doing?" I demand. "I'll start an international incident all over your ass, no matter whether the king or some barely crown prince hits me."

"You like this girl?" Anwen asks calmly.

I splutter. "Stand up and fucking face me. Man to man."

"You like her enough to keep spending time with her, at least." Anwen clenches his jaw. "And she likes you enough that she does, too."

"Who cares?" My blood boils in my veins. I lurch to my feet, ready to fight. Where's the squirrelly bastard I remember from his wedding? I should've pissed him right off by now.

"If you wanted to treat her like a man, you could've reminded her you weren't going to talk about big stuff right then." He looks up at me, completely unperturbed. "Or you could've told her the truth, which is that you're too damn scared of what a future with her might mean to face it."

I lunge across the table with a punch, but Zain catches me before I can make contact. Everyone starts muttering, taking sides. I grit my teeth and glare at Anwen. Last time I saw him, he needed my fucking help. Where the hell does he get off talking to me like this now?

"Being scared is normal." Anwen stands. "Reacting like a child and blowing up instead of facing your fear isn't. If you actually like her, or you just want to stop being a chickenshit, go to her and tell her that." He pulls Finn up. "But we're leaving."

The two of them walk away. Dead, flat silence fills the bar in their wake. I clench and unclench my fists around nothing. I don't even remember putting down my stein. A hangover pulses in my temples. Zain's arm around my chest is the only thing keeping me from taking off after that so-called king and teaching him a lesson he won't forget.

Somewhere deep down in my chest, a voice that sounds uncomfortably like Eva's reminds me no one has ever talked to me like that before. But that stupid fucking voice doesn't mean that he was being disrespectful. It means he was acting like an older brother.

Or a father.

I crush the voice to pieces, shove every thought it put in my head away, and order another round. The best way out of a hangover is to go deeper.

BLESSING OR CURSE

Candace

TWO DAYS LATER, INGRID CHATTERS ABOUT A MUSIC DISCUSSION SHE had with some Lilywind noble as she, Finn, and I head to the rejuvenation ritual. I want to listen. I really do. But my eyelids droop, my muscles burn, and it's taking all my concentration to keep my skirt from dragging in the mud after last night's rain. Every night, I have the dream. Sometimes more than once. Every night, it's the same, and it always wakes me up. Between that and my burning mark, I'm surprised I'm getting any sleep at all. At least the cool, slightly misty air makes it unpleasant enough out here that I'm at no real risk of falling asleep.

We take our usual places behind Raven, Estrella, and now Kieran at the center of the crowd. Kieran holds the jug. Magic exhaustion slows Estrella's limbs, and Raven looks like she's about to pop. Yet another companion to my late, lonely nights are her soft groans from the tent nearby as she struggles to get comfortable around the swelling balloon of her stomach. I don't think I've seen her without a frown in days, though she always tries to speak nicely. I can't resent her slips. My patience is quickly wearing out too, and I don't have a little person dancing a jig on my insides.

Slowly, the rest of the crowd gathers. Every day, it's a little smaller, but I haven't yet seen a ritual without at least one representative of each kingdom. At this point, it's mostly a blessing and promise, a few hours later, that some far away part of Escuro has sprung back to life. There's a feeling in the air like the end of a ball, when everyone is waiting for the clock to strike midnight so they can go home. And midnight—in this case, the equinox—is fast approaching. That's what drags my gaze across the crowd to where the group from Snowcrest Canyon always stands.

As always, I see King Andri first. With his height, his hair, and his scowl, he's impossible to miss. Next to him, I spot the bright red of Eva's curls. We've spent much of the last two days together, and my stomach still twists every time I look at her. Mother's words ring in my head, and visions of war dance behind my eyes. But even that has nothing on the heart-pounding panic of looking for Hollis next to them.

There he is. Half-hidden behind his father, looking drowsy but present. After his comment about the future, I didn't think we would ever speak again. I certainly didn't intend to speak to him. But then he found me, and we went on a walk. He didn't say a word about our future until the end. He didn't say a word about our relationship. I just saw glimpses of the person in all of Eva's stories, the one I watched walk through the halls of Solberg Castle laughing with her. And as he was leaving me back at my tent, he peeked up through his soot-colored eyelashes and said he didn't want to talk about the future then. No promises, not even an apology, but my heart melted. I didn't grow up around my brothers not to recognize the closest a man like Hollis can come to an apology. So I decided to enjoy our time and wait. Clearly, he's willing to change. He just needs time.

Like every other morning, the soldiers roll out Rowena's prison wagon. Goosebumps cover my skin, and I slide past Ingrid and Finn to put as much space between us as possible. Ever since Hollis caught us, it just feels too dangerous to go back. I'll handle the dreams and my worries about Hollis on my own. Apparently, he's been looking into who might start a war, and the idea of telling him it's me makes me want to go lie down until the equinox.

"Good morning," Raven manages, leaning heavily on Kieran's arm.

"Good morning," Estrella says through a yawn.

"As our work stretches on," Kieran says, "my lady wife has decided to open the floor for who might give a blessing. After all, we're all here because the revitalization of our world is important to all of us, and the Goddess bestows her blessings equally."

A spring bird sings a mating call. No one raises their hand.

"Anyone?" Kieran's voice goes a little tight. "There are no wrong words."

'If I have to ask again, one of you is volunteering,' he says through the mind-link. Judging by Finn's and Ingrid's reactions, they received it too.

Still, no one answers. He starts to open his mouth. I scrape together a few shreds of confidence to give the blessing I seriously doubt my younger siblings will volunteer for.

"I will." Mother's voice, louder than I've heard it in a long time, echoes from within the walls of her prison wagon.

"No—" Kieran starts to lurch forward, but Raven grabs onto his arm as she tips without his support.

A wind whips up, blotting out the sound of his voice. Mother said something about her powers, didn't she? But this is impossible. She's never been able to move more than a few sheets of paper with her wind.

"I would like to thank the Goddess," she says with a laugh in her voice, "for my backstabbing children. The eldest, who overthrew me. The second, who turned his back on his kingdom. The two youngest, who hide behind the shield of their older siblings to excuse their actions. And most of all, my bastard daughter, Candace."

My stomach plummets. Whispers ripple through the assembled crowd. Someone shrieks, "What?" and I'm worried it's me.

The wind grows. "Not a drop of Solberg blood runs through her veins. Not even a drop from Dun's Crossing. My dearly departed

Gavin was off on some campaign of violence when a charming rogue whose name I don't even remember sauntered into the castle."

My world narrows to the patch of grass directly at my feet. If I don't look away, I won't collapse. There are footsteps. More conversation. People are shouting, but I can't hear anyone other than Mother.

"Oh, Gavin was furious at first." She sounds delighted at the prospect. "Until Fleming declared I was going to give birth to a little bitch, and I reminded Gavin of the blessing and curse of his line—all sons." She laughs. "A girl would secure alliances without all the blood he so loved to splash around in. Of course, the bastard couldn't even do that correctly. She—"

Mother's words cut off abruptly with a rattle of wood on metal. Dimly, I become aware someone is holding my arm. Ingrid.

"It's okay," she whispers. "You're okay." Over and over again, like a mantra. Like four simple words will be enough to change the fact that my whole life is a lie.

I am not a princess. I'm not my father's daughter. I am all my mother and some stranger. Some rogue. I'm an embarrassment to Kieran's reign, to the whole family. What will this mean for Ingrid's prospects?

Where will I go?

"Shut the fuck up," someone growls.

My head feels like it weighs a thousand pounds, but I raise it anyway. My beloved patch of grass disappears from view, and I look at the wagon. All my favorite guards crowd tightly around it, but there are others. Kieran—one glance at the center of the clearing shows Raven clinging to a wobbling Estrella—Anwen, Finn. And the owner of the voice that made me look up, the only spot of green in the silver-and-blue fray. Hollis, hammering on the door to my mother's wagon, attempting to silence her.

Why? He never really liked me in the first place, and now I'm less than nothing to him. A stranger at a royal celebration.

Ingrid squeezes my arm. "I don't care what she says. You're my sister, and I know everyone else feels the same. That's why they're over there, why Eva sent Prince Hollis."

My stomach churns. I can't listen to her now. Quiet falls, but not really. Every other delegation murmurs amongst themselves, amongst each other. I can't make out words, but I don't need to. They're all looking at me. Pity, embarrassment, and disgust blur in their gazes.

Rogues vary wildly, but I've never heard about them being particularly cruel, just selfish. Which means all the cruelty I spent years honing to a fine point and wielding over the castle doesn't come from some inescapable biology. I may have gotten some from Mother, but I chose it.

I sink to my knees in the mud. I'm the same monster I thought they were. An intentional one. No excuses to hide behind.

The murmuring grows. Ingrid tugs on my arm, saying something about getting out of here.

A scream rends the air. Pure, animal pain. My thousand-pound head twists toward the new sound.

Raven crumples out of Estrella's grasp, cradling her stomach. "I'm going into labor."

FOR THE BEST

Hollis

"Fuck," King Kieran hisses under his breath.

I stare into the depths of the prison wagon, rage pounding like a heartbeat through my veins. "Go. I'll keep an eye on her."

He looks at me for a second, and I fucking know he's about to ask why. I don't have an answer. I think I might've exchanged a look with Eva before taking off, and that might be enough, but I don't give a shit right now. All I know is the monster in this rolling cell needs to be dropped into the deepest, darkest pit I can find as quickly as I can fucking find it. For the first time, I'm grateful we're in Escuro. Deep, dark pits seem like their specialty.

Before he can say a word, Luna Raven screams again, and his decision is made. He takes off, along with his two brothers. I cling to the bars at the front of the wagon for another second, glaring into the darkness. This close, even in the thin, cold rain, I can make out more of Rowena than I could the other day. She looks like one big mat of fur, except for the jingling silver manacles around her wrists and her glittering eyes.

"Move out." I jump off the wagon. "Now."

The Solberg guards respond with almost the same crispness and speed I'd expect at home. Someone must've told them to listen. I take the left flank position, between Rowena and the crowd. Candace's shattered face floats in my mind's eye as we march. Each drum-beat step sends another pulse of anger through me. It was like watching someone kick a puppy in slow motion. When the ex-queen offered to speak, Candace's whole body curled in on itself defensively. When she said the word *bastard*, Candace's eyebrows knitted, her mouth turned down, and her eyes went vacant. But what made me move was when Rowena laughed, and Candace rocked like she was hit. My mark shrieked, and I just started running.

Her wagon wheels into its usual place, marked by deep dents in the lush, green grass like Rowena's presence keeps the land dead. The rest of the guards fan out to their usual positions. They've got a soldier's disinterest in the royal drama, which is probably why Candace assigned them here in the first place. It's an impressive thought. Yet another reason I didn't doubt for a fucking second that she was royalty.

Didn't. Past tense.

There's no denying Candace didn't know about this. That, or she's the best fucking actor in the world, and I don't think she is. But everybody's just taking the word of a snake they chained up because she was too dangerous to leave loose. I've got the distance from the problem to remember that.

I swing up onto the front of the wagon again and peer through the bars.

"Very gallant," Rowena says. "I see why she wants you to love her so badly."

I crack my knuckles around the bars. "Prove it."

"You don't believe me?" Her smirk catches a sliver of light. "How novel."

I snort. "Right, you've been a paragon of truth in your life."

"I think you'll find I've lied much less than any of you believe from your high horses." She prowls closer to the door. "I'll answer your question on one condition."

It's doubtful that I'll fulfill it. "What?"

"Believe me when I tell you I'm giving you the answer to save you from that traitorous little bitch," she snarls. "I hand-raised her in my image, and she chose the whore daughter of Escuro over me. She'll do the same to you. Just wait."

"Sure." I poured my anger over the word. "Now, your proof?"

"Go to wherever she's sleeping. By her bed, you'll find a vial labeled *heart*. Take one of the tablets, and I promise, your eyes will turn as blue as mine. The little bitch was born with her father's brown eyes." She sneers. "If that's not enough proof, find someone with magic. I can only do so much."

I leap off the wagon without another word. She's a waste of breath —but she's also given me a chance to prove her wrong. I stride through camp thinking about nothing but the vial. I'll just find it, prove her wrong, and then… go back to having no clue what comes next.

That's a problem for later.

The Solberg tent circle is in chaos. People dart in and out of the main royal tent where Raven screams through the birth. I wince. It sounds painful, but at least I don't have to worry about my total inability to sneak. I dart into Candace's tent and head for the low cot she's been sleeping on. There's nothing on the floor, but a leather satchel hangs off one of the posts. I open it carefully to find a few beauty supplies and a carved, wooden box. That, I slip out and set on the bed. A few minutes of fidgeting, and I find the hidden clasp that opens it.

Inside sits a glass vial with, in the jagged hand of a healer, a label reading "heart." I swallow. That doesn't mean anything. I pluck it from the velvet cushion and shake one of the tablets out into my palm. It's powdery and white, and I raise it to my lips.

My mark pulses.

What the fuck am I thinking? If I take this, I'm going to have to explain to everyone why my eyes are suddenly Solberg blue. I pocket the tablet, put everything back, and slip out of the chaos just as easily as I slipped in. From their spot, it's not far to the Lilywind bar. Unlike the last time I was here, conversation is all muted murmurs, and no one is laughing. Like the last time, Ty sits at one of the tables, nursing a drink. I slip into the seat across from him.

"Were you there?" he asks.

I nod. "That queen's a real bitch."

"Huh?" Ty frowns at me. "Oh, yeah, I guess. But she finally told the truth. The rest of the family is all liars."

I didn't feel bad about my plan when I sat down. Now, I really don't.

"Hey, one of the serving girl's boobs fell out of her dress." I point behind him.

Ty turns immediately. I crumble the tablet into his drink.

"Damn," I say. "She's really fast, sorry."

"Helluva day," Ty mutters as he turns back. "I miss the most interesting ritual of this whole damn trip and seeing some boob."

"Some people are just unlucky, I guess." I watch intently as he picks up his beer and sips it.

His eyes remain dully olive green. My heart leaps. Rowena's the fucking liar.

"You can say that again." He shakes his head. "Fuck it, I'm going to go find somewhere worth being. No offense."

"None taken," I murmur as he chugs the rest of his beer.

"I'll see you for archery tomorrow?" He sets his mug down and looks at me.

Through ice-blue eyes, like any Solberg.

"Show up at archery, and I'll knock your teeth in," I snarl. He can't do fucking anything right, and nobody can make me put up with him. I storm out of the bar, back toward the Solberg tents with no goal in mind. Rowena could've known she was going to do this and switched the tablets. Or had someone switch them. Or maybe a side effect of Candace's heart medication is turning non-blue eyes blue. There has to be something I'm missing.

'Where are you?' I ask Eva through the mind-link.

'With Candace,' she replies.

My heart skips about fourteen beats. Should I go see them together?

'In Raven's tent,' she adds.

No. Facing the two of them together would be hard enough without all the screaming. I'm better off nowhere near there. Maybe I'll shift, try to work off some of whatever is rumbling through my chest like a thunderstorm.

"Son." Father's bass cuts through the endless whispering covering the camp.

I jerk my head up and find him sitting on one of the benches lining the main path, close enough to the Solberg tents that I can still hear the screaming. To be fair, I don't know if there's anywhere in this camp you can't.

"Father." I sit next to him. "Why are you here?"

He grunts. "Where else is there?"

The circle of Snowcrest tents he barely leaves for anything other than the rituals he dutifully attends every morning and the occasional diplomatic meal, I think.

"Of course," I say.

Camp noises fill the silence between us. My pulse leaps and jumps like a professional dancer. He's thinking something, and I have no clue what.

"Those Solberg guards aren't trained as shitty as I feared," I venture.

He snorts. "You should've stayed put."

There it is. "Why?"

"Confirmed our alliance." Father shakes his head. "Put us in a mess we don't need."

"But Eva—"

"Is too involved. Now, I know why I never liked that bastard."

I close my eyes and draw in a long, slow breath. "King Kieran?"

Father laughs bitterly. "Both. The cuckoo and the heir who didn't notice it."

He means Candace. He thinks she stole her place in that family. Something in my chest cracks, but from it comes cold reason.

Even if we could explain ourselves to Eva, there was no way our relationship would ever work. One time, I convinced Father to have venison for dinner when he wanted veal, and that's the biggest concession I ever got out of him. The idea of me mated to, much less marrying, anyone but Eva would've been a nearly impossible sell. And now that everyone knows Candace is… whatever she is, it actually is impossible. We were a mistake. Mating makes things simple, so when it was this hard, I should've known. Candace and I have to stop pretending.

Maybe this is for the best.

A NEW HEIR

Candace

"Here we go." Raven's Aunt Nola holds out a squalling, still bloody, bundle of baby.

Kieran accepts it like he barely notices the blood. Raven just slumps back against her pillows, sweat-soaked and panting.

"We have a son." Kieran's grin could light up a whole castle.

"Lemme see'm," Raven mumbles.

I twist the towel I was blotting her forehead with between my fingers and try to stay in this moment. In here, nothing matters other than the exhausted, beatific smile that parts Raven's lips when Kieran lays her son on her chest. Out there—

I'm not thinking about that. Right now, I am nothing more than a new aunt.

"He is wonderful," Estrella breathes, reaching for Anwen's hand. Before long, I get the feeling the two of them will have an heir of their own.

"Really beautiful," I manage. It's true, with a smear of dark hair already covering his forehead and what look like Solberg-blue eyes. "What are you going to call him?"

Kieran and Raven exchange a look.

"Altair," she says.

Eva steps back into the tent with a bucket of water. "I brought—damn, did I miss it?"

I nod. She hurries over to join the circle of cooing family members, and it feels right. She talks about his tiny feet with Ingrid and nudges me when it's my turn to talk. But when she opened the tent, she let in a breath of fresh air, and now I can't stop thinking about how everything reeks like blood.

"I'll be back," I mumble to whoever's listening. I don't even know if anyone responds. It's so easy to forget about me already.

Outside of the tent, I suck down mouthfuls of air that taste like anything but the sour iron of all my worst memories. Watching Raven get beaten time after time, never saying a word. Walking past the dungeon and pretending I didn't smell what was going on down there from the top of the stairs. Greeting Fath—

King Gavin. Ex-King Gavin. He's not my father, and he knew all along that he never was. Are any of those memories actually mine? Why did I get lessons and dresses and exotic sweets brought home from his "diplomatic trips" abroad when Raven got nothing but pain and torture? I should've been on the floor next to her. I'm less than she is. Not someone else's royalty, not royal at all. A half-noble from nowhere.

By the time the first sob breaks my lips, my eyes are so foggy with tears I can barely see. I have to get inside. No one can see me like this.

Or can they? What difference does my appearance make if I'm no one?

"Candace?" Hollis says.

His voice washes over me like walking inside after a day out in the snow. Warmth and safety and the promise of a comfortable night's sleep. I twist toward the sound and throw my arms around his neck, feeling like the one time I had too much wine with dinner and the room went fuzzy. I am no one. Nothing matters. And I want my mate.

"Hey! Okay, can you walk with me a little?" He untangles my arms and takes me by the hand.

Of course, I want to say. Anything you want. But I don't know how to move my mouth without vomiting.

Hollis pulls me into my own tent, and my nose twitches. I want him so badly it's almost like his scent beat us in here. As soon as the flap falls shut behind us, I lean up on my tiptoes and try to kiss him.

My lips brush the palm of his hand. Which he put between my mouth and his. My mark screams, but that has nothing on the feeling like I've just been punched in the center of my chest. I sit down on my bed hard.

"You too?" I whisper.

He winces and pulls his hand back. "No. Yes. It's… complicated."

"Do you think I'm—" I can't wrap my lips around the word. "Or not?"

Hollis sighs and crouches next to my bed. "I talked to your mother."

"Never do that," I hiss. "She'll hurt you."

"I know." He rubs my knee through my mud- and blood-stained dress. That must be a good sign. "But everyone was just believing her, so I had to ask if she had any proof."

A small break opens in the clouds of my thoughts. "Did she?"

After a long, painful silence, he nods. "I think. It seemed like proof. Maybe stop taking your heart medication for a couple days, look in the mirror, and then we'll know."

My skin grows cold. "How do you know about that? My parents made me promise never to tell anyone."

"She told me." He shakes his head. "But we're getting off topic. I don't want to talk about your parents. I want to talk about mine."

"Okay?" I say slowly.

"My father," he corrects. "I was talking to him earlier."

I close my eyes. I don't really want to hear what the grumpy old Alpha thinks of me now.

"We've been so focused on Eva that we forgot about the rest of the world," Hollis says.

Icy fear takes root behind the aching impact of his rejection. "What do you mean?"

"I mean getting him to accept anyone other than Eva was always going to be an uphill battle, and he could easily disinherit me for Eva–or someone else."

"Your throne?" I say dully. "That's what you're worried about right now?"

"Not my throne." He runs a hand through his hair. "My future. I was raised to be an Alpha King. There's no one else able to take on that role in Snowcrest. And I'm not ready to do anything else."

"Your throne," I repeat like it'll make more sense the more I say it.

"It probably wasn't going to work anyway!" Hollis says slightly louder. "This isn't exactly a surprise."

"And what is this?" I ask.

"I'm—" He stares at a point over my shoulder.

I meet his green gaze and hold it. "You're what? Say it to my face."

"I'm telling you this is over," he says through gritted teeth. "I think you're only going to get more hurt if we keep pretending this can turn into something more, so I'm ending it."

A gaping pit opens in my chest, swallowing the ache, the ice, everything into a bottomless nothingness. Tears pour down my cheeks. I wrap my arms around myself, the only thing holding me together.

"You were the one thing I thought I could count on," I whisper through my sobs.

"That's not true," he says comfortingly. "You can count on your sisters. On Eva."

My stomach wrenches like it's trying to break its own neck. I can count on Eva because I've spent days lying to her face on behalf of the coward in front of me, telling me this was probably never going to work out anyway. Bile sinks searing fingers into my throat, and I lose all ability to tell what hurts where anymore. I am a writhing ball of pain and utter humiliation.

Who was I kidding, trying not to be like my parents these past few months? Have I even changed at all? I've been kinder to people who are useful to me or who can't leave because of blood or marriage. But I lie, I cheat, I do whatever I must to get the things I want. I was raised in my mother's image, and that makes me a monster. Just yesterday, Hollis and I were lying in our spot, half-dressed and giggling over our secret. Laughing that we were hurting people.

There's a reason I've been dreaming of war. I thought I would start it with my stupid, useless heart. But that was yet another fanciful lie. I'm starting this war that's going to destroy the world because I am exactly the daughter the Solbergs wanted–because I let them make me into it.

"Shit." Hollis looks at me with something like concern in his eyes. "I know this is the worst time to do this. We could maybe keep something? Meet in the trees after dark, maybe we each make a couple visits to each other's kingdoms a year after this?"

"In secret." I'm not asking.

"Well… yeah." He rubs the back of his neck. "It's like I said—"

I don't want to hear what he has to say again. Something hot bubbles up inside me. Standing, I put my hands on his chest and shove him back. He barely moves. Too stupidly strong.

"Go," I sob.

"I—"

"I don't care!" Something in my throat scratches raw. Nobody cares. I'm just a body to him, just a piece of meat. My future is to be alone. By the Goddess, I should've seen that coming a mile away. Who would want me? "I never want to see you again."

"Never?" he asks quietly.

I'm done. I drop back to my bed and bury my face in my pillows and sob. Hollis lingers for a long moment, drifting a little closer, then a little farther away. Finally, his scent leaves the tent altogether.

My tears only come harder. Now, I'm alone.

STIFF UPPER LIP

Hollis

Outside the tent, Candace's sobs sound as loud as Raven's screams did not too long ago, but nothing changes in the flow of frantic traffic between the other tents. Almost everyone heads for the largest one, half of them clutching gifts, to pay fealty to the new baby prince.

Something in my chest crumples.

If I was a good person—the man she seems to think I am, if she made the mistake of counting on me—I would walk back into that tent and hold her. Fuck Father, fuck whatever other consequences might follow. The mark on my shoulder certainly agrees, screaming almost louder than her in waves of pulsating pain. But what she and the mark don't understand is that being a good person comes second to being a good prince, and I was only raised to do one of them well. The heart whining in my chest is almost a waste of an organ at this point. I've let it shrink and wither for so long that sometimes I'm surprised it still beats. So Candace's sobs don't inspire anything in me that my mother's didn't one of the last times I talked to her.

My memories of Mother are few and far between. More of them have faded in the almost twelve years since her death. When I picture her now, she looks more like the portrait hanging in the gallery hall than a living, breathing woman. But there's one memory that always stays crystal clear. Sharp enough to cut, if I remember it too often.

A couple days before she died, she called me into her room. Just me. I pushed open the door, my then nine-year-old hand barely large enough to wrap around the handle of the royal bedchamber Father had abandoned to be Mother's sickroom. I don't think I'll ever forget the smell of that room. Mother had been sick for a while, not that Father was telling anybody, and the astringent stink of the royal healer's poultices hung heavy in the air. None of them had helped.

She laid in the massive bed, smaller than I'd ever seen her. Her dark hair hung limply against her cheeks where it didn't stick to patches of sweat. The only blotches of color on her pale face were raised red spots on her cheeks one of my tutors had explained meant her fever was high again.

"Open the curtains." Her voice rasped weakly. "Then come sit next to me."

I obeyed as quickly as I could. Father and I had a talk the day before. He didn't think she had long left, and I didn't want to waste a second. Perched on the mattress next to her, I waited while she coughed. As always, she tried to hide the splatter of blood on the sleeve of her nightgown. As usual, it didn't work.

Mother wrapped her twig-like fingers around mine and looked at me, tears shining in her warm eyes. "I love you. You know that, don't you, my little holly berry?"

The old nickname just stung. I squeezed her hand and didn't say anything.

"And I always will." She looked away from me, at the night sky shining through the curtains I'd opened. "When… when I'm gone, you can look up at the stars and know I'm watching over you. Wherever you are, that's where I'll be." A tear streaked down her cheek.

A sadness too deep to understand roared in my chest.

Father had made sure to mention another thing during my talk with him the day before. Snowcrest Canyon would mourn the loss of their queen, so they needed to know their king and crown prince remained strong. They could only grieve Mother fully, as they needed to, if they knew they could rely on us. It was my responsibility as their prince to keep a stiff upper lip.

So when I looked at the silvery tear track on Mother's sunken cheek, when everything in me screamed to throw myself on her and sob and beg the Goddess to change Her mind, I held onto Father's words. Our people needed us. I sniffed once and trained my gaze on the window. Just like the smell of that room, her broken little inhale when I looked away is unforgettable, still ringing in my ears. Echoing in Candace's barely hidden sobs in the tent in front of me.

I swallow, sniffle once, and walk away. It's better that she learns now. I can't be relied on.

The next two days pass in a blur. Luna Estrella alone carries out the revitalization rituals, and since Rowena isn't allowed back, she keeps opening up the blessing for any who will give it. Something about the first one being a total disaster seems to have broken the ice. At least no one can give the worst blessing of the event. Rumors about Candace swirl, spurred on by the fact that nobody sees her. She's not at the rituals, not getting food at communal mealtimes, nothing.

Not that I'm keeping track. I, in fact, am doing the exact opposite. I've been so caught up in her that I've been neglecting my responsibilities. Even if she's not the person I'm going to spend my life with, I still believe in her dream. There's just no reason for her to lie, or to seem so scared if she is. So I throw myself into making alliances. Since training in archery was pissing me off more than helping, Zain and I set up some hand-to-hand sparring. Sometimes in wolf form, sometimes with weapons. It lets me keep an eye on Ty, who does show up with those same blue eyes the very next morning, though they're gone by lunch. His eye color is yet another topic of the endless conversation that seems to be the lifeblood of this fucking place. Popular theories include the Lilywind delegation testing drugs in the drinks at their bar, which doesn't make anyone stop going, and fringe side effects of the revitalization. No one connects it with what happened to Candace. No one seems like they're going to start a war to end all wars.

Between the twice-daily sparring sessions and the drinking that follows, I spend time with Eva. More time. Intentional time. If whatever Candace and I had is doomed, there's only one option. I need to figure out how to convince Eva either that we're mated—virtually impossible, with the sun-shaped mark on my shoulder—or to tell everyone that we're mated and hope whoever her true mate is never appears. I'm not stupid enough to think it's going to be an easy sell. But we've been raised our whole lives as each other's mates. Spending forever together, even if it's under slightly false pretenses, can't be that hard to wrap her mind around. Someday. Once we're back where we were before we arrived here.

In the late afternoon on the second day after Rowena made her announcement, Eva and I lie in the grass near the edge of camp, blowing bubbles out of a soap liquid someone named Nikos from Thunderpeak traded her. They dance through the sky overhead, tiny pockets of rainbow light.

"No." Eva shakes her head, smiling just a little. "You're making that up."

"I'm not!" I lean up on one elbow to look at her. "I really heard someone in the bar claim rainbows are evil because they're the opposite of the moon."

"I just refuse to believe anyone can be so stupid." She exhales a gentle half-laugh, the most I've gotten out of her in two days. I don't have to ask to know the Candace situation is bothering her. Not least because I saw her outside the circle of Solberg tents yesterday, fighting with Princess Ingrid about whether or not she could visit.

Silence falls. I focus on blowing the biggest bubble I can through the contraption of sticks and string Nikos gave Eva with the liquid. Slowly but surely, the curve expands. Bigger, bigger—

"Have you seen her?" Eva asks.

The bubble pops. Bitter soap rains down on my face.

"No." I scrub a hand over my skin to remove the worst of it. "Why would they let me in?"

"I don't know." She shakes her head. "Maybe because you helped get rid of her monster of a mother?"

I shrug. This is a dangerous path to walk down. My brain starts wondering—is Eva banned because of me? Does Ingrid or any of them know about us? Am I so much of an ass that I've damaged our alliance with Dun's Crossing?

"If only I knew what was going on." Eva sounds wistful. "If I could just tell her this doesn't change anything for me."

"She'd probably really appreciate that." Candace's words about relying on Eva echo through my mind, and my mouth burns.

"If only." Eva sighs. "I'm sorry. I don't mean to bring the mood down. You've been so strong about this for me."

That's what I'm good at. Swallowing whatever I have to for my people.

Eva shifts slightly, twisting her hand to lay palm-up in the grass. Perfect to hold. My mark screams as I take it. We've held hands a million times, but it didn't mean anything before we came of age. Now, every touch feels important. Judging by the flutter of a smile on her lips, she feels the same.

I suck in a deep breath then brush a gentle kiss over her lips. We've kissed before, secret experiments in hidden corners of the castle. I still remember the clench in my gut, the craving for more. Now, I feel sick.

Eva lights up when I pull back, and I crush the sick feeling into nothingness. This is my promised, my wife, and I'm going to love her as well as I can. It's what a prince should do.

UNPRETTY FACE

Candace

FOR THE THIRD MORNING IN A ROW, I PULL MY COVERS OVER MY HEAD as lunch approaches and rub eyes gritty from crying.

Well, not exactly the third morning in a row. The very next day, I tried. I got up, made myself beautiful even as Ingrid fluttered around me, saying I didn't have to go out if I didn't want to. But I knew Estrella was exhausted, and there was no way Raven would be well enough to handle the ritual yet. I wouldn't leave my sister-in-law by herself. Then, I stepped out of the tent—not even out of our cluster of tents, just my very own—and the whispers started.

Is it true?

Look at her brave face.

How sad.

Bastard.

Bastard.

Bastard.

And I decided that, if I'm not a princess, I don't owe the world a brave face. I didn't have to make the worst day of my life into something pretty for them to coo over. I turned on my heel, marched back into the tent, and haven't come out since. For three days, I've been lying here, alternating between crying and staring at the striped-fabric ceiling, working up the energy to cry again. I've only seen Ingrid because I can't reasonably shut her out. Even I'm not mean enough to damn her to sharing a tent with Finn and his Beta. I can smell them from here.

If I lived in a perfect world, I'd let Eva visit too. I really miss her. I know she'd bring all the news I'm actually interested in and gloss over everything I'm not. But she's too sweet not to try to bring Hollis—

A dry sob breaks through my lips. I can't even think his name without his last words stabbing through my chest. The tent doesn't smell like him anymore, thankfully. The first day was torture, inhaling that homey scent all day. Ingrid kept asking what was making me break down so often, and I couldn't tell her. If thinking about him destroys me, I can't imagine what attempting to say his name would do.

The flap at the front of the tent rises, and Ingrid steps in. "Hi."

I burrow deeper in my blankets. Because I'm a glutton for punishment, I took *his* advice. I stopped taking my heart medication. Part of me figured if he was wrong, and Mother was right, if skipping a few doses killed me, then at least I'd never have to endure the shame of leaving the tent again. The first day, I felt a little strange. Today, my eyes won't stop itching. He wasn't very specific, just something about looking in the mirror, but I haven't been able to check. I don't want to find out through Ingrid's eyes, no matter how kind she's been.

"So, not much better." The world beyond my blankets darkens again as she likely lets the tent flap swing shut. "I brought you breakfast." A wooden tray thuds on the dressing table we set up across from her bed. "They had those rolls you liked so much yesterday again."

I'd managed not to cry for the length of eating the roll, which Ingrid took as a great sign. I figured it was probably luck.

"Do you want me to stay or go?" she asks. "I'll do whatever you like. Because, you know, you're my sister. Just as much as you always have been."

I swallow the sting. She keeps saying things like that. I know Ingrid barely bothers to lie, but believing her is like getting out of bed or thinking *his* name. Impossible.

"Okay." She doesn't even sound hurt. I don't deserve her. "Well, I've got a couple visitors for you, if you're willing. And they're really excited to see you."

"I said no visitors." My voice creaks, rusty after days of silence.

"You might want to reconsider." I can hear her smile. "Raven's up and about, finally, and Altair misses his aunt."

Tears prick at the corners of my eyes. That squirming bundle of new life was the only good thing about that day. I've always loved babies, the smaller the better.

"Bring me the hand mirror." I have to know. No one can see me until I do.

Moments later, the metal handle of the mirror prods my shoulder. I take it without looking at her then hold it up in the hidden hollow of my blankets.

A stranger's eyes stare back at me. Numbness chases a sharp spike of pain that he was right. The icy blue I've had and loved my whole life, the color that marked me as a Solberg, is gone. In its place is a warm hazel, all brown and gold with the barest hint of green. A color I might even call pretty on someone else. In my face, it looks monstrous.

Outside the tent, someone makes the tiniest whimper I've ever heard. My heart squeezes.

"They can come in, but no lights." I sit up. "And don't ask, please."

Ingrid nods and starts to turn away, but her gaze locks on mine. She's noticed. Of course. Every muscle in my body tenses.

She turns back for the flap without a word. I thank the Goddess I have even a half-sister like her. A shaft of light pierces the darkness of the tent, and Raven steps inside, holding a bundle in her arms.

"This is your Aunt Candace," Raven says softly but with a tiny edge, like she's daring me to object. "You met her the day you were born."

Altair whimpers again, and Raven strokes his head.

"He's just confused. He usually passes out right after feeding, but he's still awake." She looks at me. "I figured this was as good an opportunity as any to bring him to you."

"Can I hold him?" I hold out my arms.

"Be careful with his head." Raven hands him over gently. "We don't know if he inherited his father's thick skull yet."

"A Solberg baby?" Ingrid smirks. "Of course he did."

I wrap my arms around the plush bundle of blanket and baby. Barely poking out of the thick quilt, Altair screws up his face like he's about to wail and lets out another tiny whimper. I smile down at him. He's so precious, so light and so heavy at once.

"Don't let him fool you." Raven lowers herself into the chair at the dressing table tiredly. "He can scream with the best of them when he gets going."

"I've heard him," I murmur, not wanting to speak any louder than his tiny ears can handle.

Ingrid and Raven start talking about something, but I'm not listening. Altair works a tiny fist out of the swaddle of blankets and swings it at nothing. His blue eyes flutter open for a second, then shut again, dark eyelashes stark against his round, red cheeks. A whole new life. A future for Dun's Crossing after Mother and Father, just sitting in my arms.

"Your eyes," Raven says suddenly.

A future that I'm not a part of, I remind myself as reality crashes back in. My smile dies on my lips.

"I thought I said not to ask."

"I'm not." Raven lifts her hands defensively. "I just didn't know what to not ask about."

I squeeze my eyes shut, like I can hide them now that she's seen. "Don't tell anyone."

"I'll shut up anyone I hear talking about it." Ingrid cracks her knuckles.

I shake my head and clutch Altair closer. No one else should be hurt on my behalf. Last year, I'd be out in the crowd, gossiping with the rest of them.

"I wanted to ask how you're doing," Raven says carefully.

"Don't." The one moment of peace I've had since then slides through my fingers like sand in an hourglass. Even looking at Altair isn't distracting anymore.

"Rowena—"

"I said don't." My voice whips out, sharper than I've ever heard it.

'I think you need to hear this,' Raven says through the mind-link.

I curl in on myself, wishing there was some way to block my mental ears.

'Rowena is a horrible, small woman who finds all her happiness in making others miserable,' Raven says. *'For a long time, I was her main target. She hit me when I "broke the rules," sure, but more often when she and Gavin were fighting, or something didn't go her way, or she was* bored. *The things she says and does tell people about her, not about the people she does them to.'*

My stomach twists in nauseating knots. I never realized how bad it was. How many of those boredom beatings did I stand idly by through, content with whatever lie Mother fed us about her reasons? How many did she even bother to justify like that? Raven deserves the Solberg name. She always has, and she's living proof that I don't.

"Take him back." I thrust Altair out.

"I don't think you're hearing what I'm saying." Raven accepts her son with a frown. "I mean you shouldn't let her define you. She doesn't deserve that honor."

I duck back under the blankets. "Thank you for visiting. Please go away now."

In silence, Raven and Altair leave. I can only tell by the flicker of light at the door.

"Candace," Ingrid says.

"Please." My voice breaks.

She leaves, too, and I return to my self-imposed exile.

WRONG

Hollis

My plan to act like I actually believe Eva is going to be my wife is going great—except for the fact that I basically haven't slept since I started it because my mark hurts so Goddess-damned bad. That'll fade. I know it will. Because I do believe Eva's going to be my wife. It's what everyone expects, what they need. Even Mother would be proud.

The next afternoon, Father clears his throat as I'm headed out to meet Eva.

"Yes?" I pause at the mouth of our tent.

"You think I don't notice." He grunts. "I notice. The whole camp buzzes. You and Eva, going around not just like friends. Like sweethearts."

I told Zain to make sure people knew about it. I figured it might overtake some of the talk about Candace. It absolutely hasn't, but at least it's doing something. A sparkle of what I might call pride shines in Father's eyes.

"Next Haze, all your waiting will end," he says. "Until then, give her this."

He slides a narrow, dark, wooden box across the table he's sitting at to me. I pick it up and open it. The hinges still glide like the last time someone reached for the necklace inside was only yesterday. But I recognize the gold chain studded with tiny, green stones immediately. Mother wore it when she sat for her portrait. If I really dredge back into my memories, I think she wore it more often than not. I finger the cast-gold pendant in the middle and try to understand its shape, but it's no clearer here than it was hanging in the gallery.

"Your mother brought little from her home," Father says. "It pained her. On our wedding day, I made this with my own hands. The symbol is the crest of Thornwinter Swamp." He peers at it. "Or it's meant to be."

I blink several times. My father is actually talking to me? Mentioning Mother directly? Telling a personal story? I must still be asleep.

He clears his throat. "Give to Eva. It will suit her. Someday, make your own."

My gut drops. This is a piece of jewelry he handmade for the woman he loved, and he's giving it to me so I can give it to the woman I love. But he has no idea who that is. And I have no idea if there is one.

"Thank you," I manage, snapping the box shut. "I'll make sure to find the right moment."

"Do not wait." He waves me off, clearly having filled his emotional-moment quota for the day.

I stumble out into the spring sunshine, my head spinning. I'll walk up to Eva and give her the necklace. Mother loved her. And I love her, in my own way. Just not the way Father loved Mother.

A vision pops into my mind, Candace wearing the necklace. It warms her cold complexion—and clashes with her eyes. I shove the vision away. That's the Haze talking, not my mind. I square my shoulders and march off to meet Eva.

"Hi!" She waves as she bounces out of a sewing circle with a few other ladies, trailing several threads behind her.

I pluck one out of the air. "I think you might still be attached."

She groans. "I knew I forgot something."

One of the other women in the circle snips the trailing threads before Eva can even reach for a pair of scissors then exchanges looks with the others. I search my chest for the protective rage that always seems to manifest when something like that happens to Candace. I'm pissed—they're being judgmental and ridiculous—but it's very easy to resist the desire to knock their heads together. Violence obviously isn't the answer.

Dammit.

Eva tucks her sewing into a bag and takes my hand. We walk everywhere hand-in-hand now. I never noticed how thin her fingers are before, almost skin and bone.

"So, what would you like to do?" she asks. "I know some people are starting to set up for the spring equinox party in a couple of days. We could go help."

I wrinkle my nose. "No, thanks. We show up, someone decides what the event really needs is an ice sculpture, and then that's our next three days."

She laughs. "All right, all right. What's your bright idea?"

We pass the flourishing old oak, and I catch sight of the copse of trees Candace and I used to meet in behind it. I could take her there and give her the necklace.

"I... don't know," I say instead. "Ty and a few of his friends are hosting a game tournament in their tent."

"Yuck."

"We could go for a run." I eye the rest of the woods, green and beautiful once more. "I haven't, really, since everything came back to life." *Deep breath.* "And I'd love to see it with you."

She grins, exposing her one chipped tooth from a painted-rock prank back when we couldn't have been more than twelve, and steps behind a tree without another word. A moment later, she darts off.

'Catch me if you can!' she calls through the mind-link.

In wolf form, I can't give her the necklace if I want to. I stuff her clothes and mine in her sewing bag, then shift and give chase.

Escuro flies by. I barely notice it. My attention remains locked on Eva's bright-red tail disappearing between the trees. She hasn't outrun me since we both hit puberty, but I haven't given her this much of a head start in ages. The rhythm of my paws on the dirt almost makes me forget the disaster I'm running away from. Almost.

I catch her tail between my teeth, gently, and Eva explodes back into human form with a laugh, hiding her naked body in a patch of tall grass..

"Dammit!" She pulls leaves out of her hair. "I thought I had you."

I pull her clothes out of the bag silently before ducking behind a tree to shift and get dressed myself. This place really is beautiful, even with the marks the wolfsbane left on it. The faint veins and splatters of gray look like they belong. Which means this is the perfect moment to give her the necklace.

"You haven't got me yet." I run my finger over the necklace box. "But, you know, we're supposed to be running together."

"That's the words of a man scared I'll beat him one day." She smooths her dress down.

I shake my head. "More like one who really cares about you. So, um"—I rub my fingers over the box. My stomach revolts. My shoulder screams—"thanks for the run."

What's wrong with me?

Eva studies me. "Something's wrong. What is it?"

She knows me so well that something truth-shaped stumbles out of my mouth. "I'm worried about Candace."

"Me too." She sits on the ground. "I still haven't been allowed to see her."

I pocket the box. "I wish there was something we could do."

Like my chance to help didn't pass me by with all the grace and subtlety of a ballista bolt.

Eva smiles. "Maybe there is."

❄

As the sun sets behind us, I take a step back to behold our handiwork. A behemoth of scavenged supplies, held together with rope and a prayer.

Eva grins, the orange sunset coloring her face. "It's perfect."

"I think it's better than your surprise party, at least." I nudge her.

She rolls her eyes at me. "We have no idea whether her isolation is her idea or someone else's. I think, if we could've snuck a party's worth of fun for just the three of us under the back wall of her tent, you might've been very surprised by the response."

I think she would've been, but I keep that to myself. I'm not reopening the trap of actually seeing Candace that I so narrowly avoided at the beginning of this.

"All I'm saying is, this way she feels like we're there for her whether she wants company or not."

"You already won." Eva swats me. "Stop bragging and help me turn the damned thing on."

I grab the bucket of water from the well someone from Tansy Beach summoned in the middle of camp. "Are you sure it's going to work?"

"I'd be more sure if we went with the pheasant call, like I suggested." Eva stares at the device like she can tell how effective it is just by looking.

"Her favorite bird is the ash warbler, and they're not usually around here." I shrug. "Won't she notice that more than the pheasant she saw here?"

Eva shakes her head. "Someday, I'll find out how you remembered that and I didn't. You're just lucky she attached a flute that played the call to one of her letters."

Lucky was right. I just assumed Eva would know Candace's favorite. Only after the words left my lips did I realize she'd told me that while we were taking a break to catch our breaths in our spot, cornsilk hair hanging tousled over her face and lips swollen. Just remembering that makes my mark ache.

"You're stalling." Eva grabs the bucket, climbs the tiny step stool we borrowed, and pours the water into the top of what should hopefully be a reusable bird-caller.

My heart jumps into my throat. Water tumbles down the couple of ramps Eva insisted it needed to get fast enough, then hits the damaged carriage wheel Makai was happy to hand over when we came asking. The carriage wheel pulls a rope, which raises and lowers a narrow fan attached to that flute Candace sent.

Soft, lilting birdsong fills the air.

"Yes!" Eva runs back and throws her arms around my neck.

Building a completely new machine with no supplies and fewer skills was easier than wrapping my arms around Eva's waist. The necklace burns in my pocket. Someday, soon, everything will stop feeling so wrong. I just know it.

ENOUGH

Candace

I'M SITTING AT THE DRESSING TABLE, FIXING MY HAIR FOR THE FIRST time in days, when a bird starts singing right outside my tent. An ash warbler. For the third time since sunset yesterday. I almost smile.

When it first happened, I made Ingrid go check. We were way outside of where the warbler should be, and if it was lost, I'd consider leaving my tent to make sure it got home. The last thing I expected was for her to report some kind of insane contraption making the noise. If it weren't for the flute attached at the bottom, I'd have no idea what was happening. But now, every time the singing starts again, I know Eva is out there, trying to reach me however she can.

Another couple of visits from Altair haven't hurt, either. Raven has stopped trying to talk about Mother, which I appreciate. I'd much rather talk about the newest Solberg, all the tiny changes he goes through every day. Today, he opened his eyes for longer than yesterday. Tomorrow, who knows?

I take a deep breath and look at myself in the mirror. Same face, same hair, different eyes. The tablets I've been taking every day for as long as I can remember did nothing but turn my eyes the right color to blend in. Looking at them makes my skin itch, but I force myself to hold my own gaze for another breath. This is me. Princess Candace Solberg is dead. Kieran says—through Raven—that he has no intention of formally removing me from the line of succession, which I know he means well, but she is dead. She died the moment Mother made her announcement. No matter what title I hold, there will soon be no noble in the world that doesn't know the truth. This is the person Ingrid, Raven, Altair, and Eva care enough about to chase down even when I'm trying to chase them all away.

The warbler's song slows then peters out, leaving me with just the hazel eyes in the mirror and the question of what's left after Princess Candace.

Ingrid steps into our tent, and her face lights up. "Look who's out of bed!"

A nearly overwhelming instinct begs me to dive back underneath the covers, like she's going to drag me out to the next ritual just because I combed my hair. I take another deep breath and stay seated. It's not like I want to go back to bed anyway. Something like energy flickers through my veins, antsy and aimless.

"How did you start playing the lute?" I blurt.

She blinks. "I just picked it up one day, when that traveling music tutor was visiting. I was awful." She laughs. "Do you remember?"

I shake my head. "Mother said music was a waste of my time. I took extra lessons with Corinne, the housekeeper, whenever that tutor visited."

"Right." Ingrid worries her thumbnail.

"Stop that," I say in the exact same tone Mother always did.

Both of us freeze. Slowly, Ingrid lowers her thumb.

"I didn't mean that." I rub my hands over my face like I can scrub mother from my mind. "I meant… I meant to ask how you didn't put it down. Your lute."

She sits on the edge of her bed and blows out a breath. "I didn't know I was awful. All I knew was that I liked the way the neck fit in my hands, and I liked the poofy pants the troubadours in town wore."

"That's it?" That sounds impossible. "What about your drawing?"

She glances at the cup of charcoal next to her bed. "I plucked one out of a dead fireplace and started drawing on the walls. Corinne was furious, but Father said I had promise. I kept going half to prove him wrong."

Every interest she's ever had comes with a similar story when I ask. It struck her fancy one day, so she pursued it. If she liked it, she continued. If not, she abandoned it without a second thought.

"Do you think you're done?" I ask quietly. "Picking up new hobbies?"

She laughs then stops when she realizes I'm not joking. "Um, no. I think I'll be done once I take my place in the night sky, and only then if the Goddess doesn't have stellar sculpture or something."

I lean back in my chair, struggling to wrap my mind around the sheer breadth of the world as Ingrid sees it. There is no limit to her life, to what she can try—not just try–*be*. If Princess Candace Solberg is dead, could Candace of no particular last name live a life like that?

"Why do you ask?" Ingrid cocks her head to the side, her hair falling over her shoulder in a rain of golden curls.

"I need help." The words burst from my mouth on a single breath, and I wince. "There has to be something after hermithood in this tent, and I'm trying to figure out what that looks like."

"Now that's something I can help with." Her smile is sharp with confidence. "Are you looking for hobbies specifically?"

I'm looking for the woman that belongs to these hazel eyes. "Hobbies seem like a good place to start."

She nods. "And the bird thing…?"

I purse my lips. I love birdwatching. There's a magic in watching them move back and forth like clockwork every season, in new life springing from nothing based on instinct alone. But that fidgety energy burns in my veins, and I know it's not enough. Birdwatching is a waiting game. Something I do alone in high towers when no one gives me something else to do. I can't build a life around that. Not anymore.

"I want something more active," I say. "Like you. I want to... I don't know... make something?"

"Easy." Ingrid claps her hands together. "Have you ever done any fine arts? Drawing, painting, sculpting?"

I shake my head. Yet another class Mother thought was filling my head up with nonsense.

"Okay. I know you don't read a lot, but what about writing?"

My one adventure into journaling ended when Mother said she found it under my pillow and was disappointed to hear I didn't like my fourteenth-birthday gown. If I hated it so much, I could appear before the kingdom in my birthday suit. That night, I'd burned the journal and never looked back.

I shake my head.

"Hmm." Ingrid taps her chin. "You've got an eye for color."

"That's true." I need it to bring out what little I could with the simple gowns in Dun's Crossing. "What can I do with that?"

"Painting, again. Design." She grins. "Flower-arranging."

"Oh, of course." I stand and mock-curtsy with my nightgown. "Hello, nice to meet you. My name is Candace, and my one true passion in life is flower-arranging."

Ingrid giggles. "All right, all right! What else do you like?"

Lying in bed. Making Mother smile. Impressing people.

"Dancing?" I say.

"Dancing," Ingrid repeats with a lot more confidence. "Now, that's something."

"Maybe." I sit back down and twist my hair around one of my fingers. "I only know how to dance at balls. I spend more time flattering my partners than anything else."

"But you like it?" She hops up off her bed and crosses the room to sit at my feet. "Because you can learn how to dance by yourself, for yourself."

"I do," I find myself saying. "I just don't know if it's enough—"

She grabs both of my hands. "It doesn't have to be."

"What?"

"That's the secret. Nothing has to be the thing that changes your life, makes you who you are, or whatever." She smiles up at me, her blue eyes dancing with excitement. "If you never stop learning, you never run out of chances to find your favorite thing."

My heart squeezes. She really, truly believes that. She might believe it hard enough that I can, too.

"Okay." I squeeze her hands. "I'm a dancer."

She shakes her head. "You're Candace, and you dance."

I take in a breath. "I dance."

"Good!" She kisses both my cheeks. "Now, I have to go because I promised Estrella I was just going to grab my lute and come back, but I will return with dinner and anything I can find out about people here who know how to dance."

"You can find out?" I raise an eyebrow.

She rolls her eyes. "Fine, Estrella and Anwen can find out. You think you'd be nicer after I helped you like that."

Ingrid whisks out of the tent into her wide-open world with no idea how much her parting comment stings. I twist and look in the mirror again. My features become those of Nessa Winters, still missing after her escape from the dungeon. She was raised to be cruel, and it caught up with her. Then, they become Ingrid's. She, somehow, isn't our parents' daughter. I don't know what makes the difference. I don't know who gave me these hazel eyes. Maybe that's another interest to power the person I will be—finding out whether you really can become someone other than who you were raised to be, even without the healing influence of your mate.

My mark burns, and Altair starts his pre-dinner wail. The Goddess knows everything. She guides us to our other halves, the people who can make us into the best versions of ourselves. But I've heard Anwen talk about how he and Estrella got together. She and their love made huge differences, started changing him almost immediately. Still, when he was a little tipsy one night, he swore to me that he'd still be alone if not for a talk he had with Kieran. I don't need my mate to grow.

'Someone come save me,' Kieran calls across mind-link. *'I'm talking to*

an ancient Snowcrester who won't take my signals, and I can hear my son crying.'

'Be there in two,' Finn replies.

I don't need my mate to have children either. And I do want those. My very own little squalling messes, keeping me up and driving me crazy and filling my life with so much love. I'll love them more than I ever could have loved Hollis. The hazel eyes in the mirror grow shiny with tears, but they don't look sad. Disappointed, a little bittersweet, but not sad. Once this is done, I'll return to the castle just long enough to find a husband in town. It's not like any noble will have me now. Someone I can care about, if not love, and who will love our children. And I'll watch birds, and dance, and do whatever comes after that.

And that will have to be enough.

THE DEFINITION OF INSANITY

Hollis

I'M A MORON. WORSE THAN THAT, I'M INSANE. THAT'S WHAT MOTHER
said when she found out I'd stuck my tongue to the frozen pole
outside of the kitchen three times in a week and basically skinned the
damn thing every time. But every time, I thought it would be like in a
story Eva and I read, where it tasted exactly like peppermint.
Creeping through the maze of tents in the dead of night, holding the
jewelry box inside my pocket, feels like walking out to that pole the
fourth time. Like knowing it's going to hurt bad enough that I can't
possibly justify it–and doing it anyway.

Paper crinkles in my pocket. I know I'm going to have to explain
this, somehow, but I couldn't sit in the tent with a sleeping Eva and
write a note to Candace. So I guess I'm going to do that crouched
outside of her tent like a monster in the night.

I am a moron.

At least my tossing and turning kept me awake long enough that
everyone else is asleep. I don't have to worry about my ability to

sneak in addition to my sanity. Before long, I find myself crouching outside her tent with my heart in my fucking mouth.

Like licking the pole a fourth time.

I slip the paper, quill, and ink out of my pocket, then scrawl her name at the top of the page. No greeting, no honorific. We're past all of that now. Then, I stare at the blank page.

Letter-writing's never been a strong suit of mine. Eva's the one who communicates for the both of us, more often than not. I'm not afraid of giving my opinion by any stretch of the imagination—but anywhere outside of training our soldiers, I apparently have a tendency to come off *harsh*. Eva knows all the niceties, the ways to make people respond how I want them to without just ordering them. I don't know that there are any niceties for this.

This was my mother's, I write. The words look heavy on the page, but they won't mean as much to her.

I loved my mother, I add.

Ridiculous. I scratch it out.

My father made this because she didn't have any jewelry, and I thought —what? That Candace didn't have any? How did Father tell it so the little chain was so important, so dense with love and a want to make someone happy?

Can I make any of that matter when we have no life to spend together?

I pull in a deep breath. I'm a fucking prince. I know how to express myself. I attack the paper again.

The next time I look up, three sheets of paper lay crumpled around my feet, and the moon is on its way back toward the horizon. That one was too much, that one too little, and that one barely anything at all. I have one fucking page left. One chance to keep her from assuming it's a mistake and asking if anyone is looking for it, ruining any chance we have of keeping the events of the Haze a secret.

I write her name at the top of the page again. I've been trying to use Father's words, but maybe that's not the right way.

Before Mother's death—before she even got sick—she used to

read to me at night sometimes. Her favorite was a story about a princess locked in a tower and a prince that visited her every single day even though neither of them could find each other during the Haze to confirm they were each other's true mates. Every day, they talked for hours. How to get her out, and what they would do when they could. They tried a thousand methods, but the tower was protected in old magic, too strong for either of them to break through on their own.

Everyone in the prince's life told him he was being ridiculous, especially when he started locking himself away during Hazes. He needed to give up on this girl and make a real life for himself. But he brought his loved ones to meet her, and they saw how true the love between the princess and him was. One day, when he was old and gray and so was she, he convinced enough of them to come help him. The old magic was too powerful for two, but for a hundred? The stones of the tower fell away, and the two lovers were finally united.

When I was younger, I thought it was a tragedy. They missed all that time together. I asked her to stop reading it because it was such a sad story. But I remember Mother just shaking her head and saying they didn't miss anything. They loved each other the whole time, and that's all two people really need.

My quill flows across the page, writing down every word of the story. Mother's voice rings in my ears, soft over familiar phrases. When I'm done, I don't read it over. I'll just crumple it up if I do. But I scribble one last thing at the end.

Even if the tower never falls....

Seconds tick away as I stare at the unfinished sentence. What the hell do I say? That I love her? I don't even think that's true. I know my feelings about her are different than I've ever felt for Eva, but love? No fucking way. Instead, I put a period at the end of the sentence, scratch an H into the bottom of the page, wrap it around the box, and slide it under the wall of her tent.

Nothing happens.

Part of me really thought she was awake on the other side, listening to me scribble and pace and mutter under my breath. But this is better. This way, I don't have to hear her read my note and laugh. Because she's going to. What the fuck was I thinking, writing a fairytale? I peer at the bottom of the tent. I could just wedge my hand under there, grab the box back—

No. I've never second-guessed myself like this before, and I'm not about to start now. I straighten up, hold my head high. Crown Prince Hollis Kar. This was my last misstep, the words at the end of the page of the shitty fairytale somebody could write about Candace and I. When I wake up in the morning, I'm not even going to pretend there's another option for me anymore. I'm going to marry Eva, be happy with her, and that's going to be enough.

I gather up my evidence, turn on my heel, and start marching back to our tent. Morning is starting to threaten, but I have more than enough time to walk back. My steps feel lighter, without the necklace weighing me down. The decision is made. No regrets, no looking back. The future I've spent my whole life planning for seems possible again. The searing ache in my mating mark already feels halfway normal, something I could learn to live with. Father will be proud. Eva will be thrilled.

Something rustles, not far away. I duck my head and hunch. If they can't identify me, there's less to worry about.

There! Darting between two tents. Too big to be anything but a shifter, moving quickly on all fours. I keep walking like I didn't even notice and sniff the air as subtly as I can.

My sense of smell has never been the strongest, especially in human form, but I can still pick up enough to confirm it's a shifter. Something fruity, something floral, and… cold. My stomach drops.

The shifter running through the night alongside me is from Snowcrest Canyon.

All stealth goes out the window. I tip my nose to the sky and inhale deeper. I need more information. Father wouldn't skulk like this, but Eva might think she's setting up for the greatest prank of all time.

Whoever they are, they're already moving away. Dammit. Fruit, floral... that's almost nothing to go on. Eva's scent of cinnamon and jasmine—

Goddess above, I'm so fucking stupid. There are three scents in this world I can recognize without a second thought. Father's, Eva's, and my own. If Eva really was following me, I wouldn't be standing here wondering. It'd hit me like a punch to the gut. That's probably just Zain sneaking back after some ill-considered tryst or one of the other nobles Father insisted on bringing. The wolf seemed smaller than a lot of the ones we brought, but that could well be a trick of the light. I roll out my shoulders and continue walking back to the tent.

Only when my hand hits the entrance flap do I realize the other shifter wasn't headed in this direction, toward the circle of Snowcrest tents. And they weren't actually headed away, either. It looked like they were coming from outside the gathering altogether, headed to something inside.

Which means they're probably a late-arriving delegate or someone craving a hunt. I'm overthinking things. I slide through the tent flap, inhale a lungful of Eva's thick scent, and slide into bed.

BRAND NEW

Candace

I wake early the next morning, and the world feels a little less like a yawning maw of disaster than it has recently. It's not that hard to sit up in bed, and when I see the faint line of sunlight poking through the tent flap, I basically smile. Today, I don't care what people think about Princess Candace. I'm starting a brand new life as just Candace, someone who dances. Nobody even has opinions about her yet.

Just Candace is going to the revitalization ritual to support her loved ones, I decide. I slide out of bed and start pawing through my trunk for something to wear. All the dresses are plain, simple, not meant to draw attention so much as hold it once it's caught. Dresses that let me fade into the background unless I want to be seen. On this brand-new day, I don't like any of them. I wish I had some options like Estrella does, or like Ingrid kept in the back of her closet while Mother and Father still held the throne. For months, I've been eyeing a dusty rose fabric Bright, the royal seamstress, keeps as hidden as she can. When we leave, I'll see about getting something made from that.

For now, I pull out my once-favorite dress, a greenish gray, and push the trunk back beneath my bed.

It hits something with a quiet *thud*. I frown. There shouldn't be anything else under there. I shove one arm beneath my bed and grope wildly until my hand lands on something hard. And...papery? I pull it out.

After unfolding the letter wrapped around the wooden box and opening it to reveal a necklace inside, I burst into tears. What does he mean, if the tower never falls? He's the one who said—to use his metaphor—it never could. He said we had to stop. He abandoned me when I needed him most, like I never even mattered. And now he does this? Is he ever going to let me get over him?

"Candace?" Ingrid says sleepily.

Princess Candace couldn't breathe a word about this to anyone because of the political implications. Just Candace is tired and so lonely. I launch myself off the floor and throw my arms around my sister. My whole body shakes with sobs as she hugs me back.

"Tough morning?" She pats my back. "And, uh, what do you have there?"

"A rejection present from Hollis Kar," I blurt.

Ingrid grabs me by the shoulders and pulls me back so she can look in my eyes. "You're... not kidding."

I shake my head, still crying. "The Haze—I lied. I did mate with someone. Him. And for a couple of days, I really thought it was going to work out, but he says it can't, and I want to move on, but he gave me this." I shove the note and box at her.

She reads quickly, one hand still on me, her eyebrows ticking higher and higher with every line.

"Sorry, and why can't this work out?" she asks when she's done.

"Because of Eva," I sob. "I can't—I'll be a monster—"

She hugs me again. "You won't. The Goddess did this to you. If there's one thing the disasters of the last few Hazes have taught us, it's that fighting the Haze is a waste of time. If Eva is really as great as you say she is, she'll understand.

"His father will never accept me," I mumble into her shoulder. "Because I'm a bastard."

"I don't care about his father, and neither should he." Ingrid's voice burns. "That's no reason to turn down the smartest, nicest, most beautiful woman I know."

I laugh wetly. "The order of an Alpha?"

"Yes." She clutches me tighter, immediately furious on my behalf. "Do you want me to fight King Andri for you? Because I will do it."

My dream burns itself into the backs of my eyelids. Is this how I start it? By unleashing Ingrid's protective instincts on the world?

"No," I say sharply. "I don't want anyone to know."

"You shouldn't have to—"

"Everyone is talking about me enough." My voice breaks.

"The offer remains." She kisses the side of my head, and I remember the first day she got taller than me and realized she could do that. "Just—the Moon Goddess knows the two of you can be happy if you're both willing to put in the work. Clearly, he was dropped on his head often enough that he's not, but that doesn't mean you can't put the work into yourself. And I'll help wherever I can."

"I know." I squeeze her. "I love you. Now, let's get dressed."

"I love you too." The same furious determination shines in her eyes and her voice as she lets me go.

It's not new, but maybe not everything needs to be.

RIGHT ON TIME, INGRID AND I STEP OUT OF THE TENT, ARM-IN-ARM. Real sunlight hits my face for the first time since Mother denounced me. It's warmer, more springlike than it was a few days ago. It promises a fresh start for me and Escuro.

"Estrella has been going over to set up early," Ingrid says. "So we should just meet her over there."

I nod. Just... leave the circle of our tents.

"You can do this," she whispers.

"Isn't the big sister's job to set the good example?" I reply with a smile.

"Maybe you set a good enough one to convince me of all this." She wiggles her eyebrows.

As I laugh, we step out into the campground proper. Perfect timing. Ingrid really is good. But the change is still immediate. Every group we pass turns to watch us. One person walks backward for several paces, just to stare at me for longer. I hear a few snippets of whispers—my name, the word *bastard*, worse things that Ingrid starts talking over as soon as she starts to hear them. Apparently, she got a lot of great information about people who could teach me how to dance better. The topic makes it a little easier to focus on my future, my imaginary husband and kids, beyond the castle I grew up in.

"Candace!" someone yells.

I wince. Then, I smell the air—cinnamon and jasmine.

Eva collides with my back and throws her arms around me. "I was on my way to fill up the bird caller again when I heard you were out. Oh, I'm so glad to see you."

My stomach churns. The necklace hidden between my mattress and bed frame in the tent should probably be hers. But if Hollis is telling the truth, at least I'm not keeping her from her happy ending anymore. I twist and hug her back.

"I missed you," I admit.

"I missed you, too." Her smile glows in the morning sun. "I have so much to tell you. Hollis has been fascinating company—oh, you have to see him!"

"And I will," I say quickly, my heart in my throat. "But right now, I have to go help set up the ritual."

"Can I come help if I promise not to say anything?" She stares at me, begging with her eyes.

'I think you could tell her,' Ingrid says through the mind-link. *'She's weird like you. She'd get it.'*

'If it's not happening, there's no point,' I reply. *'I'll just hurt her.'*

Ingrid purses her lips.

"Of course," I say. I really did miss Eva.

Eva loops her arm through my free one, and the three of us take off down the path. I struggle to keep up just a little. The sun and the noise is already starting to get overwhelming after so long in the dark and quiet. My head aches.

"Did you hear that?" Ingrid asks suddenly.

"What?" I glance around and realize fewer people are looking at me.

"They said—"

'Rogue captured on the outside of camp,' Kieran tells us both. *'He was behaving suspiciously, trying to get in. Escuro soldiers picked him up and are bringing him to Alpha Cole and Luna Delaney.'*

"Prisoner for Escuro," Ingrid says, an interested smile pulling at her lips. "They'll be at the ritual."

"Let's hurry!" Eva declares.

Like she's reading the mind of the crowd, more and more people start to join us on our path to the ritual site. More than I saw at the last ritual I attended, days ago. They press close as space becomes scarce, suddenly no longer afraid to touch the bastard when there's fresher gossip on offer. When did I become so cynical?

We arrive at the site, so beautiful after so many days of magic here. Estrella stands below the oak, jug between her feet. As expected, Alpha Cole and Luna Delaney lean on each other next to her, frowning. Unexpectedly, Raven is with them, though she sits in a chair cradling Altair in her arms. Ingrid leads me through the crowd to our spot behind the tree and a little to the left. Anwen's already there, holding space open at the very front. Thankfully, away from Mother's prison wagon which towers at the edge of the crowd, too far for most people to hear her. Finn scowls on the other side as we slip into place.

"Coming back?" Anwen murmurs as I take my spot next to him.

"More like rejoining the living." Finn smirks.

"Don't be a dick," Ingrid snaps.

I start to wince then swallow the instinct. Maybe just Candace doesn't mind a crude word every now and then. Princess Ingrid seems not to.

The crowd parts as one, like a wave drawing back from the shore, and a few Escuro soldiers march a man in patchwork leather to the middle of the ritual space. He stares at the ground, his dirty blond hair covering his face. The soldiers throw him down on his knees, and his scent fills the air. Underneath the reek of unwashed body, he smells like untamed nature. Like a summer day and charcoal. It's not unpleasant.

Alpha Cole steps forward. "This is no trial, just a friendly interview. What brings you here…?"

"Kash," the rogue spits.

"That's him." Mother's voice carries over the crowd, impossibly loud for how far away she is. "That man is my bitch daughter's father."

He looks up, and I meet his hazel eyes. My skin turns to ice, and I sway.

TIRED OF WONDERING

Hollis

"Oh, shit," Zain whispers.

A gasp ripples back through the crowd, and I grit my teeth. I knew I shouldn't have fucking come. I haven't been in days. After Rowena's last "blessing," I came once or twice to just see if Candace was here, but when she wasn't, it obviously wasn't worth my time. The blessings are all the same, and any change is happening miles away. But I woke up to find Eva gone and Zain out of his mind about some rumor he'd heard but couldn't focus long enough to give me details about, so I let him drag me here.

Okay, I was terrified she got the necklace and decided to make a public announcement about everything that happened between us. But somehow, this is still worse. I crane my neck to try to get a glimpse over the thick crowd at this Kash.

He looks like any other rogue—leather armor he clearly stole or made himself in the woods, scars all over what little exposed skin there is, leaves and twigs sticking out of every crevice like he's never had a bath. I suppose his hair is a little like the color of Candace's, but from this distance, I can't see anything else. It's all bullshit.

"She expects us to believe this just happened on the first day she shows her face in public again?" someone nearby asks. "Does the bastard think we're fucking stupid?"

"I'll bet you twenty gold pieces that the next words out of his mouth reveal him to be the king of some kingdom no one's ever heard of, so she's not *really* a bastard."

The first person snorts, and my blood boils.

"Shut the fuck up," I snap. "Can't you see she's going through something?"

They laugh and step a little away. Zain nudges me.

'Are you okay?' he asks.

I ignore him and freeze a plinth of ice under my feet, growing it taller and taller until I can actually see over the crowd. I need to know if she's here.

She is. Of course she is. Bracketed by Eva and Ingrid, who seem to be holding her up. There isn't the same numbness in her face as last time, but clearly, she didn't plan a single second of this. Anyone who thinks she did is a moron.

Masochistically, my gaze drops to her throat. No necklace. Mine or another. My mark aches, but I push the thought away. Maybe she didn't find it. Or even Mother's story wasn't enough.

"What? You don't believe me?" Rowena asks.

Wind whips through the crowd. Alpha Cole and Luna Delaney look at Queen Raven. Queen Raven looks at Candace. Ingrid tries to step in front of her... I guess sister is still the right term, but Candace puts a hand on her shoulder. She's regained her feet, and her hair shines in the light, unbound. She takes a step forward, and I see her eyes.

They're brown now. If Ty's blue eyes weren't enough proof, this certainly is.

And she'll suit the necklace much better.

I crush that thought immediately.

"I am just as tired of wondering as any of you," she says, her voice strong and clear. It makes me want to stand up straighter, be the man she thought I was.

"If either of you have any proof of your claims, provide it now." She lifts her chin.

She looks like a painting, the sun dappled through the leaves of the tree highlighting her hair and confidence shining through every inch of her body. I've never seen her like this before. The closest I ever came was when she demanded to know what we were to each other, and then, she was mussed and seemed barely sure she was actually saying the words. This is a different woman entirely.

My heart skips a beat.

"Permission to stand?" The rogue, Kash, has a leathery voice that sounds nothing like hers. Just more proof this is another cruel trick by Rowena.

Alpha Cole nods. Kash climbs to his feet.

"Assuming I recognize that voice correctly as Queen Rowena Solberg, I'm happy to volunteer that I did fuck her, some twenty-odd years ago." He chuckles. "And enough I definitely could've left something of myself behind."

Cocky son of a bitch. I'll knock his teeth down his throat before I let him brag about that again.

"Former queen," Candace corrects smoothly. "She's been deposed for crimes against the citizens of Dun's Crossing and the world."

"She's a liar!" Rowena yells. "They were *jealous*, all of them!"

I cup my hands around my mouth. "Sounding a little crazy, Rowena."

Scattered laughter ripples through the crowd. I smirk. Candace doesn't even look in my direction, which can only mean she already knows it's me. My smirk dies.

"Anything else?" Candace asks. "Any real proof?"

A woman steps forward. "I'm an envoy from Cirrus Summit. We have powers related to family, and mine can tell the true parentage of a child, if all potential parents are present. I... I can tell you, one way or the other."

"Thank you," Candace says. "Do you need my mother?"

The woman nods. A handful of Dun's Crossing soldiers begin wheeling her prison wagon to the front. I abandon my plinth of ice rather than being crushed under its wheels and build up a new one in the spot I'm pushed to immediately.

Zain stares at me. "What the hell has gotten into you?"

"She's Eva's friend," I reply. "And mine, to an extent."

He shakes his head. "Your father's going to kick your ass if you end up embroiled in something."

I can't take a breath without remembering that.

The wagon rolls to a stop next to Kash, the woman from Cirrus Summit, and Candace. She closes her eyes as the woman takes her hand. Rowena's thin wrist still barely fits through the bars, but it's enough for the queen to grab the woman who takes hold of Kash with her other hand. All four of them go silent and still.

In a crowd of a couple hundred standing on grass, we could've heard a pin drop. I wonder how many of these people realized that, with Gavin dead, there was no way to ever fully confirm that Candace wasn't a bastard. Rowena didn't seem to be lying, but she'd still set herself up to never be proven wrong.

The woman's head jerks back hard enough that I wince, and when she opens her eyes, silvery light pours out.

"What the fuck does that mean?" I mutter.

A moment later, the light fades, and she shakes herself out.

"These two," she says, "*are* the parents of Candace Solberg."

A million conversations break out around me.

"Can you believe—"

"—just some rogue?"

"What did Gavin—"

"How did Kash—"

I tune them all out. I don't give a fuck about the opinions of a couple of bored nobles who don't know a damned thing about the woman they're all so obsessed with. All I care about is her.

Her dark eyes shine, and she blinks several times as she looks at Kash. Her father. He starts to reach a hand out toward her, but before he gets close enough to touch, what feels like an army of her family surrounds her. The people she was raised to call her siblings—even Finn, the smirking one Zain still drinks with. All their mates, and their mates' families. Eva. So many people she disappears at the center of them, completely surrounded by love.

Something in my chest aches. I let the plinth melt until I'm below the level of the crowd once more. Zain elbows me. I elbow him back, harder, and don't look at him. I am not one of the people who love Candace, and I never will be.

The prison wagon trundles back to the outskirts of the crowd. I don't know where Kash is. Conversation about Candace keeps getting louder as people decide on theories and argue about them.

"Attention," Alpha Cole barks.

Slowly, everyone falls silent.

"My kingdom is being reborn after decades of suffering," he says. "And I am not so small minded as to think rebirth is only for the land. In that spirit, I'd like to request Princess Candace gives today's blessing."

"Just Candace," she says. "Please."

Her voice rolls through me like thick, sweet honey. I want to see her again, but I repress the instinct. Instead. I just close my eyes and listen.

"Alpha Cole is right about rebirth," she says. "But it's not limited to me either. Every day we wake up, the Goddess gives us another chance to be the people She knows we can be. To be brave, kind, true. Sometimes, it's easy to forget that those are qualities to work for rather than being born with. So I bless this land with the Goddess' belief in us and with our endless ability to try again."

Magic shudders along the ground, a sure sign they've poured that jug, but I barely notice it. Because I'm selfish enough to think Candace might just be talking about me.

FATHER DEAREST

Candace

I PACE OUTSIDE THE GRAY AND BLACK TENT ALPHA COLE AND LUNA Delaney have been staying in, where they took Kash after the ritual. Going anywhere else seemed wrong. My stomach twists and jounces like it did when I let Ingrid convince me to sled down one of the castle roofs during a particularly bad snowstorm.

Inside this tent sits my father. My real father. Not King Gavin, a rogue named Kash who I can smell from out here.

How is any of this happening? The ritual certainly isn't secret, but he had twenty years to seek me out before now. I've been outside the castle many times over the years. I've even been out without Mother and Fath—King Gavin–if only to the village near the castle. There's just no reason he only found me after Mother told everyone he existed.

Unless she made it happen.

The tent opens, and Kieran steps out, followed quickly by Alpha Cole and Luna Delaney. She hugs me tightly. Even though she has Raven back, children separated from their parents are a particular sore spot of hers. Alpha Cole just pats me on the shoulder, his eyes so like Raven's twinkling kindly. Then, the two of them stride away.

"What's going on?" I ask.

Kieran leads me a couple of steps away. "They've agreed to release him into our custody. Our soldiers will pick him up just as soon as we have a place to keep him."

My stomach twists a few more times. "Did… did you talk to him?"

"He's not very talkative." Kieran eyes me. "He just keeps asking for you."

"Oh." My chest aches like someone punched me.

He hesitates then wraps his arms awkwardly around me.

Growing up, Kieran was the crown prince who liked to curse where I could hear him so I'd react. Now, he's someone completely new. But I'll take a hug from anyone right now.

"Raven says promising not to remove you from the line of succession wasn't the right move," he mumbles. "Too political."

"I understood."

He shakes his head. "You deserve to hear it. I don't care what that man is—whether he's the missing piece you've been looking for or a threat we have to take out before heading home. You're my sister, and nothing he or anyone else says can change that."

I melt into his arms, and he holds me a little more naturally.

"Thank you," I whisper.

"Should've said it earlier," he replies. "Who he is doesn't change who you are."

Tears prick the corners of my eyes, and I know what I have to do. I squeeze Kieran tight, then let go and step back.

"I'm going in." I take a deep breath. "I want to talk to him."

Kieran's eyebrows shoot up. "Are you certain?"

"If you're right, then I have to." I offer him a weak smile.

He nods like he understands—maybe he does, after killing his father—then pulls the tent flap aside and barks that all the Escuro soldiers need to wait outside. Princess Candace requires privacy.

"Just Candace. Please."

He frowns. "Okay, Candace."

I step into the tent with my father.

The inside is gloomy, like most aboveground buildings in Escuro are. Their eyes still aren't adjusted to the sunlight. But I can make out a shape in front of a small fire below a hole in the ceiling, hunched over what smells like a leg of some cooked bird and eating like it's his last meal.

"Kash?" I say tentatively.

"Candace!" He lurches to his feet, sending the plate on his lap clattering.

I skitter back a step. His ankles are manacled so he can't run, but the chain between the cuffs on his wrists is so long he can almost spread them wide enough for a hug. Grease drips down his arms.

But he has those eyes.

"Sorry." He scoops the plate off the floor and sets it on the low bench he was sitting on. "Not used to all this finery. Would've worked great if we were in my old shanty." His smile is crooked, and the firelight casts the handful of thick scars slicing through his face in stark shadow.

"I—" My voice breaks. Oh, Goddess, I'm going to be sick.

"Wine?" He grabs a goblet on the bench and thrusts it at me. Red liquid sloshes over the side.

I shake my head then clear my throat. "You wanted to speak to me?"

"That's why I'm here, after all. Mind if I sit?"

I shake my head. He plops back down on the bench, takes another bite of the meat in his hand, and washes it down with wine.

"To talk to me?" I ask.

He nods. "News of Gavin's death just reached my corner of the world. The old bastard was the only thing keeping me away, so I figured I'd come see you."

Questions swirl in my mind, each screaming over the next to be asked. His hair catches the light. It isn't the same color as mine, a little warmer and more honeyed, but it falls out of his ponytail into his eyes in a way I'm intimately familiar with.

"Is your hair too fine to stay back?" I ask.

He raises his eyebrows. "Sure is. Why?"

"Add a comb to the ties you use to hold it. Or a clip that looks a bit like a crab claw." I snap my fingers together a few times, like he hasn't seen far more of the world than I have.

"I'll see what I can do." He grins. "I take it you got that from yours truly."

"I certainly didn't get it from Mother." I run my fingers through my own hair. My thoughts start to fall into order. He's a real person, a part of my blood. The tiny similarity makes it all seem so much more real. "How did you know to come here?"

"You ever spent much time with a rogue?" His tilted grin shines with mischief and grease.

"No."

"Well then I s'pose you'll just have to trust me when I say our tracking skills tend to be better than any you raise in your kingdoms. All I needed was a breath of your scent."

"My scent?" I frown. "How did you get that?"

His eyes widen slightly. "Figured it out on my own and what I remembered of Rowena."

My heart skips a few beats. Saying her name summons her into the room, reminds me of what I was so scared of outside. He could just be another part of her plan. I've heard of Cirrus Summit having powers related to blood, so there's no reason to disbelieve that, but that doesn't mean he's telling me the truth.

"Okay," I say slowly. "And… you said you had been staying away because of King Gavin?"

Something sharp flashes in Kash's eyes. "Yes ma'am. Much as I hate to admit it, I've known about you since your mother did. Gavin raged up and down the castle, demanding she destroy you by whatever means necessary. He wasn't going to lower himself to raise another man's child." He clenches his fist around his wine glass. "Many's the nights I thought about killing him for the things he said about my flesh and blood."

My doubt burns away. This, Kash means with all his heart—I think.

"Then, some healer or wizard told him you were gonna be a girl, and his tune changed. I've always thought Rowena did something there." He shakes his head. "Suddenly, I could have all the gold I could carry if I never set foot in Dun's Crossing again."

A sick, icy ache spreads over my skin. "And you took it?"

"I didn't have another choice." He lunges toward me again, and a chain linking his manacles to something deep in the ground rattles taut. "I left for the same reason I didn't kill him—if I had, you and me would've been in deep shit. Never safe again."

"That makes sense." From a selfish perspective. I take a few steps back, making sure I'm out of range of his reach.

"I knew you'd understand." Relief crashes over his face. "I don't give a rat's ass about Rowena or whyever the hell she's locked up. I just want to get to know my daughter."

I don't know the last time somebody smiled like he is while calling me that. I let out a long breath.

"It… might be nice to get to know you, too." Kieran's words ring in my ears, but I can't accept that they're true without knowing who Kash is. "Can we start with you? Why are you a rogue?"

He huffs a laugh. "Curious. That's a familiar trait, and half the answer you're looking for. I grew up part of a pack, like anybody else, but it all seemed too Goddess-damned small. Why hole up in one little spot when there's so much to see?"

"You ran away?" My heart hammers. I can't imagine doing that.

"Depends what counts as running." His smile grows bittersweet. "No one's disappointed I haven't come home. There's no home to come to."

That, too, feels true. Kash is alone—or an incredible liar.

"So there was no reason not to chase the wind wherever it led." His grin brightens again. "I pick my paths by heart, chase any smell that catches my fancy, don't answer to no one I don't agree with. Tell me that doesn't sound like a better deal."

Last year, I would've disagreed in a heartbeat. After everything that's happened, I can't. I'd miss my family, but I wouldn't have to worry about Mother or Hollis again.

"See?" He tosses the now-bare bone of the bird leg onto the plate. "I knew you were mine even before you stepped out. There's something in our bones."

"Where are your bones from?" I blurt.

"Don't matter much anymore." He wipes his hands on his pants. "Tell me, did you get any of my powers? I know Solbergs don't have shit."

"The dreams are from you?" The second I say it, it sounds so obvious. No one has powers they don't inherit.

"Ha! Another prophet in the family."

His grin is so bright, it burns in my chest. If I told him about the war I've been dreaming about, he'd believe me. He might even be able to help me make sense of it. I open my mouth to confess.

"I know they can be rough, so I'm happy to talk about the dreams," he says. "I'm here for you, kiddo."

He also might run directly to Mother. I snap my mouth shut again and glance at the tent flap. This was a ridiculous idea. I should just leave. Kash stares at me for a long second then runs his hand through his hair.

"I get it." His matching gaze meets mine. "I probably seem like a shithead showing up at just the wrong time. But I'm meeting someone I've loved for twenty years now." He jingles the chains around his wrists. "I want to tell you everything, hear everything about you, but it's gonna be tough when I'm locked up for doing nothing more than walking up to the edge of a party. Is there any chance your old man could get a little benefit of the doubt?"

He's asking to be freed. Kash wants to wander freely, able to access me whenever. My stomach flips over and over. Worse than the sledding by far. I don't know anything about him, and I don't have any reason to trust him—

A few strands of honey-blond hair fall from his ponytail into his face, and I make my decision.

OVERKILL

Hollis

FATHER AND I STRIDE THROUGH THE CAMPGROUND, ON THE WAY TO lunch with a few representatives of Lightning Cape. He might be the only person in a mile radius who can think or talk about anything other than Kash's sudden appearance at the ritual this morning. I'm certainly not. I haven't seen a glimpse of her since she left the ritual following that fucking rogue. Nobody seems to know anything new—well, I bet Eva does, but I haven't seen her either. The information blackout sets my teeth on edge. One of them should've told me something by now. A huge event is happening in my mate's life, and—

"You are distracted," Father grunts.

"No," I lie immediately.

"What did I say?" He raises one bushy eyebrow.

I scrub through my memory for what he was talking about. Fuck, for anything he's ever said about Lightning Cape.

"That the wind powers of their royal family are a strong military match for our snow powers, so we'd fight well together," I guess.

He scowls. I guessed wrong, and now he's even more pissed than he would've been. This is why I don't fucking lie.

"Go back to camp," he says.

"What? No, you need me."

"I need someone smart and young." He harrumphs. "Doesn't have to be you."

No, no, no. "I swear to the Goddess, I'll pay attention from now on. What were you saying?"

"The king and queen have a young son, same age as Soren's youngest girl. If we could arrange a trip when a Haze was incoming —"

"Maybe they'd mate, and the alliance would be a lock." I nod. "It'll be a few years, though. Emiliana is only eighteen."

Father waves my concern aside. "We build until then. It will only help."

"Okay. In the meantime—"

The smell of blackberries and sunshine catches my nose, and I jerk my head up just as the rest of the crowd around us goes almost silent. There, stepping out of the circle of Solberg tents, is Candace.

And Kash.

I sneer automatically. From a distance, I thought he looked like any other rogue. Up close, it's much worse. Even if I ignore the fact that he's filthy—which he makes very fucking hard—I can't miss the way his eyes dart around, scanning the crowd, or the arm around her shoulders he's clearly trying to use to look relaxed. If he tried to catch my attention on the streets of the town around the palace, I'd have him arrested before he finished his sentence. Even if he wasn't doing anything illicit right then, he would be soon. *Untrustworthy* rolls off him in waves.

Yet, Candace seems to be letting him drape his arm around her. I really thought she was smarter than that.

"Do not tell me you've fallen for their petty gossip," Father says. "We have real business."

"Right." I shake my head to clear her out of it—doesn't work, with her scent in the air—and try to remember what I was saying. "Uh, in the meantime, we need something else to offer them. Military might is always a strong offer."

"Too far." Father frowns. "Our troops would require months to cross the world to their aid."

Whispers swirl through the air, difficult to ignore. A lot of them comment on Kash's reek. Couldn't she have at least convinced him to bathe first? Others talk about the coincidental timing, and as much as I don't believe Candace had any idea Kash was still alive before this morning, I understand them a little better now. The two do look surprisingly cozy. Others still discuss what this means for Rowena, if anything. I remain solidly on the side of nothing, with a side of executing her so she can't try anything like this again.

Father clears his throat. Right, I'm paying attention.

"What if we gave them strategic advice? Letters travel faster than soldiers," I say.

He grunts thoughtfully. He doesn't think it's a terrible idea.

As Kash and Candace are about to pass us, he leans in and kisses her on the forehead. Her face crumples in discomfort, and with her nose, it can't be a new reaction to the smell. She doesn't want him touching her like that. But she doesn't shove him off and knock his teeth in for good measure. She doesn't say a Goddess-damned word, and she smiles at him when he pulls back.

My blood bursts into a hot boil. If she won't do it, I—

"She humiliates the whole family, cavorting with that rogue." Father shakes his head. "If she continues, they will be destroyed within a month. Mark my words."

His words are like a bucket of freezing water to the face. I can't do anything. Not in public, and if the fact she's still not wearing the necklace is anything to go by, she'd probably stop me in private too. For the sake of Father, Eva, and Snowcrest, I gave up that right. I conjure a piece of ice into one of my clenched fists and squeeze it until it starts to melt.

"We will see," I say. "Now, about Lightning Cape—"

❄

THE LUNCH LASTS FOREVER. EVERY TIME I START TO GET DISTRACTED BY the whispering farther down the long table we're eating at, I freeze another piece of ice and let it melt. It keeps me focused. Enough. By the end of the meal, Father is shaking hands with Alpha Iraj and promising to speak again soon, and I'm about to vibrate out of my skin. We leave the tent, and words burst from my mouth before I can catch them.

"Would you like to discuss how that went, or am I dismissed?"

He eyes me, then sighs. "Dismissed."

The sigh stings, but I take off so fast that I almost leave it behind me. Eva has to be somewhere in this Goddess-forsaken camp, and I'm going to find her. I know she knows something.

Tracking by scent in human form is virtually impossible, which is likely why I end up outside the ring of Solberg tents. And once I'm there, it only makes sense to slip my hand under the outer wall of Candace's. Just to see if she didn't find the necklace. If she didn't, I'll… fuck, I don't know. Push it farther? Take it back?

I'm saved from making the decision by finding only grass where I know the necklace box was. My mark sears as I straighten. She found it and isn't wearing it. That's fine. I'm fine.

I turn on my heel and return to tracking Eva, which is miraculously easier with that question answered. I find her with a cluster of women from a variety of kingdoms, for once sitting back and not talking.

'Hey,' I say through the mind-link. '*I've been looking for you.*'

'*Don't tell me you want to know what I saw of Kash, too,*' she answers wryly.

'*No.*' It's only half a lie. '*I want to know about Candace.*'

'*That, I'll talk about.*' She says her goodbyes, extricates herself from the circle, then joins me. As soon as we're out of sight, she shakes off her whole body like a wolf caught in the rain.

"I can't stand how everyone is talking about this," she declares. "It's monstrous."

"So she's taking it hard?" I ask.

"I don't think she knows how she's taking it yet, but there's so much pressure to have an answer because people won't stop talking." Eva scowls at the nearest passing group, like they personally have been whispering in Candace's ear.

I crush down my instincts and sling an arm around her waist. She doesn't fit quite as well as Candace, but we fall into step immediately.

"Kicking the ass of everybody here won't help," I whisper in her ear.

She giggles, then frowns at me. "I'm not ready to be distracted yet."

I hold up my free hand innocently, and something releases in my chest. Permission not to flirt with the woman who's going to be my wife shouldn't feel so good.

"Have you seen her with him? He's out because he said it would make it easier for them to get to know one another." She rolls her eyes aggressively.

"That sounds like a lie." My grip on her tightens as my anger kicks back up.

"Right?" She shakes her head. "And he's really grabby with her. She doesn't know how to stop him yet, but it's way too much even if she could. Like he wants to jump into the role of father imme-diately."

"Overkill," I snarl.

"Exactly." She grabs at the empty air in front of her. "Ooh, if I could get my hands on him in a way that wouldn't bother her—"

"Should we return to the ass-kicking dilemma?"

She bumps my hip with hers. "I think Kash wants more than he's letting on. I can't just sit back and do nothing."

An idea strikes me like lightning.

"Maybe you could," I say, "if I don't."

Eva frowns. "Say more."

"You don't want to hurt your friendship with Candace. She and I are… less close." Pain stabs through my mark. "What if I stuck close until we figure out what Kash is thinking? Just so there's someone there to intervene if things take a turn."

She stares at me. My heart pounds. Was that a step too far? Does she suspect something?

Eva throws her arms around my neck. "That's perfect! I'll cover for you with King Andri if you need to miss something important."

"Anything for you." I hug her back, smelling blackberries instead of jasmine.

FAMILY DINNER

Candace

"Thank you." I smile up at Kash—he suggested I call him Father, but that still seems too strange—as he hands me a bowl of noodle soup in one of the long food tents that's sprung up in my handful of days in isolation.

"Just let me know if you want seconds." He tosses his hair over his shoulder and sits on the long bench between Kieran and me.

Judging by the scent wafting off the soup, which I can just make out despite his closeness, this is going to be too rich for me to finish the bowl I already have. Long, thick noodles and chunks of some meat float in a rich broth flavored with a cacophony of herbs. Still, I nod.

"So, Kash," Raven says, "I'd love to know a little more about you."

"Me?" He seems surprised.

I drag my spoon through my soup. This polite, awkward conversation is the conceit of this little dinner—introducing the new family to the old. Or the real family to the fake, if I can really count Mother as family. My siblings line the benches. Ingrid sits directly across from me, looking between Kash and I like she's trying to find similarities. Only a private conversation with Raven convinced her to come at all. Finn takes up far too much bench on the other side of me from Kash, all his attention on his own food. Kieran rocks a sleeping Altair beside an exhausted-looking Raven, and Estrella and Anwen sit opposite Kash.

Laughter breaks out at the other end of the tent, reminding me I'm not just surrounded by people with some claim to the title "family" but also several dozen complete strangers who've been talking about me behind my back. My temples throb.

"I like to think of myself as a puffball seed." Kash grins easily. "I go where the wind pushes me. Simple as that."

I spoon up a bite of the soup, blowing on it gently. Once again, the description echoes in my chest. There's something about it—

"Hmm." Raven nods encouragingly, but I can see the tightness of confusion between her brows. There's something about the way he describes being a rogue that's so unfamiliar it's intoxicating. I eat my soup.

"What about you all?" Kash asks. "I wasn't up on much royal gossip, but last I was around the palace, weren't you two twins?"

I inhale a noodle and start hacking. Kash thumps on my back.

"There you go, baby girl. Clear it out however you gotta."

Something fever-hot crawls up my spine as I finally manage to swallow. He keeps just barely overstepping the lines like that.

He's probably just nervous, I remind myself. *He basically told you as much.*

He rubs my back in small circles, and I wish there was a way to make him stop that didn't make me look like a monster.

'Okay?' Ingrid asks me.

I nod. If I say anything about how Kash makes me feel, they're all going to overreact. There's one thing I want out of this dinner—no new rumors about me.

"Well," Kieran begins, "to answer your question, that was a lie my father told. Luna Raven is the daughter of the king and queen of Escuro. King Gavin kidnapped her as a baby."

Kash snorts. "That sounds like Gavin to me."

Anwen's hold on his fork tightens. Finn raises his glass as if to cheers Kash's words. I shove food into my mouth as quickly as I can. Perhaps if I finish eating, I can go, and the rest of them can figure out what claim they have over me amongst themselves.

Is that a rogue instinct? My father's blood, making itself known after years of repressing it? Maybe he's why I had to work so hard during Mother's lessons, why I was always happier dancing than chit chatting during balls. Maybe I'm not meant to sit still on a throne or otherwise.

"He was a complex man," Raven says, her voice conciliatory.

"You can say that again." Kash swigs his drink, droplets of red wine spilling into his beard.

"So, you knew him?" Anwen asks tightly.

"Ah, let's not dredge up old pains." Kash slings his arm around my shoulders and pulls me slightly closer to him on the bench. "We're all here for Candace, right? Let's talk about her."

"I've already told you so much about myself." I smile and extricate myself as carefully as I can.

He lets me go easily. He always does. That feverish feeling still surges every time.

"So much? Ha! I don't know a damned thing." He smiles around at the rest of the table. "Y'all grew up with my girl. I want to hear about everything I missed."

My face warms. "There's not—"

"One time, Candace barged into a tense political meeting completely nude," Finn offers.

Kash sputters a laugh. "Now, I know you're my daughter. How old?"

My stomach churns around the soup I've guzzled down. "I was *three*. Which means Finn doesn't even properly remember the story, he just remembers Fath—"

Kash's eyebrows raise. Everyone turns to me.

"Mother told that story," Ingrid blurts.

"Not anyone else," Kieran agrees.

'*Thank you,*' I tell both of them.

"It's all right," Kash says. "It's not like I don't know someone else raised my girl. Ain't gotta lie on my account."

"I'm going to stop calling him that." I nod to myself. "Not just to make you comfortable."

"You don't gotta do anything to make me comfortable." He grins. "Unless King Kieran here is offering up some kind of recompense for the twenty years his father stole from me."

The already half-dead mood at the table collapses completely. While the rest of the tent remains loud, the silence around us is almost deafening. There it is. The real reason he's here. He wants another payoff, just like King Gavin gave him so many years ago.

Kash bursts out laughing. Hand on his belly, head thrown back, full-throated laughter. The rest of us just watch him. My heart sits heavy in my chest, making it even harder to keep the soup down.

"Shit." He wipes a tear from his eye. "Rowena had a sense of humor, back in the day, but I see she didn't much bother to pass that down."

"That was… a joke?" Kieran asks.

"Hell yeah." Kash finishes the wine in his goblet and slams it back down on the table. "You think I'd just drop that into the middle of a conversation? They teach a couple manners even to the farmers and rogues you lot don't think about."

Estrella laughs first, but I can tell it's more out of magic exhaustion than humor. Raven joins in for similar reasons a moment later. I crack a smile as soft, stilted chuckles attempt to alleviate the tension surrounding us.

'*You believe me, don't you, baby girl?*' Kash asks me through the mind-link.

I jump so much my knees crash into the underside of the table.

"Candace?" Ingrid's gaze darts to Kash accusingly.

"Shiver." I smile. '*I'm sorry. I forgot you could probably do that.*'

'*No worries,*' he replies. '*But you do, don't you? You know that's not why I'm out here, right?*'

He's out here because… because I couldn't have both of my

parents imprisoned. Because if there is part of me that's good, it's him. Because we have the same hair.

'Right.'

Kash nods like he believes me. "Seriously, this time, tough stuff aside. Don't even say the bas—motherfucker's name. Just tell me about Candace and the rest of you only."

"Candace learned the alphabet before me," Raven says slowly.

"The brains didn't come from me." Kash pats my knee, and the dinner starts to take on something like a rhythm.

A strained, painful rhythm, but a rhythm all the same. My half-siblings dredge the depths of their memories for any anecdotes that don't even hint at the way we grew up. Most of the time, they fail. There are constant pauses, spaces where Mother or Father or the way Raven was treated would fit in. But in between them are some genuinely sweet moments. Ones I'd forgotten. Ingrid brags about sledding down the roof. Finn replies with the fact that he tried it right after us and broke his leg. Kieran chuckles through the story of my earliest attempt at declamation, where I said two words and ran off the stage sobbing that I didn't know how to talk.

Anwen doesn't really speak. At first, I think it's because he doesn't have any good stories about me. Then, I realize—laughter a split-second too late, ramrod straight posture, slightly hazed eyes never leaving Kash. He's watching, wielding his skill at reading people and reporting every single detail to Kieran.

Or is it Estrella now? She glances at him every now and again, often with a minute nod. Their entwined hands sit on the table, her moonstone ring shining in the candlelight. Maybe her magic exhaustion is more of a posture, at least for tonight. A chance for both of them to watch.

On the other side of Kash, Altair hiccups in his sleep. Oh, Raven mentioned this. That's a sign of—

Before I can finish the thought, Kieran transfers his young son off his shoulder and into Raven's arm. She begins singing softly to him and adjusts the neck of her gown so he can breastfeed before he even properly wakes. Kieran rubs her shoulders briefly, then pours Anwen another glass of wine from the decanter in the middle of the table without being asked.

The ache in my chest grows. The two of them move like two limbs of the same creature, taking care of all of us. I want these stories, the people surrounding me, to be enough. But I also want that.

I shake my head. I don't need a mate. Maybe Kash could fill the hole. I've never had a father I could be close with. I ignore the brief shoulder pat he gives me in response to another story and decide to tell him about the dream that's been haunting me. Whether his powers tell him anymore or not, his response will tell me what I need to know about him.

Maybe. The last person I trusted like this was Hollis.

There's no way to know without trying. I reach for Kash in my mind, ensure only the two of us are linked, and start to ask if I can pull him away for a moment.

The smell of pine, amber, and snow overwhelms me as Hollis slides onto the bench between us.

PARTY-CRASHER

Hollis

I squeeze between Candace and her so-called father with a comfortable smile on my face. *I'm just sitting down for dinner with friends*, I tell myself. *They invited me. There's every reason for me to be here.*

Hell, it's not like I'm going to come up with a reasonable excuse for why I'm doing this.

"It's been an interesting day, huh?" I say.

"Certainly." King Kieran frowns at me. "If you don't mind—"

"I will take more wine, thank you." I hold my hand out for the decanter in front of the king.

His jaw works, but he hands it to me. I was right. They have too much at stake, with everything going on, to make a scene about me being here.

"What did you think of the ritual?" I ask King Anwen and Luna Estrella.

"Very unique." Luna Estrella smiles tightly.

"What about you, Princess Candace?" Saying her name feels a little like swallowing a sword, but I fight to keep my smile fixed. I must look like an insane jester.

She just nods. Doesn't look away from her plate, doesn't open her mouth.

Right. That makes sense.

"Sorry." Kash offers me a small smile. "Who are you?"

I bow. "Prince Hollis Kar of Snowcrest Canyon."

The part of my sentence where I explain what the hell I'm doing here disappears in silence. After a long moment, Kash nods.

"Well, good to meet you. We're trading stories about my girl, if you've got any."

I glance around the table. "Most of mine are second hand from my promised, Lady Eva, but I'd love to hear yours."

"Hey, I'll take second hand as well as anything else." Kash claps me on the shoulder a little too hard. "Go ahead!"

The Solbergs fracture into different conversations, clearly uninterested in anything I have to say. Except one. Across the table, Princess Ingrid is staring at me. No, not staring—glaring.

What the fuck is that about?

"Boyo?" Kash says.

"Right." I plaster that fake smile back on. "Lady Eva and Candace are close friends. Did you know Candace is an avid birdwatcher?"

"Well, who'd have thunk?" Kash grins. "Truly, I'll take anything."

I launch into a story I half remember about some... pheasants, or something, while watching Kash intently. I'm already achieving everything I hoped. If he's smacking me on the shoulder, he's not grabbing her. But this is the closest I've gotten to him, and reading people might not exactly be my strong suit, but I'm no slouch.

His hazel eyes—fuck, they really look exactly like hers—wander while I talk. Every time I gesture, he follows the movement. When other people move, he whips to them. I recognize the look from our scouts—he's used to watching his own back in dangerous situations. What I can't tell is whether he's still watching out of habit or because he thinks he's in danger here.

His smell is like a wall, damn near impossible to puncture. As he slaps his knee, laughing over some story I think I told wrong, I consider whether that might be on purpose. The other person up late last night—I assumed it was Zain, but when I asked him about last night's conquest, he said he'd failed. Could the body odor be covering something I'd already smelled?

"When did you get in?" I ask.

"This morning." He frowns at me. "Damned guards picked me up the second I got within sight. Why?"

If Eva were here, she'd know whether he was lying. Whoever was skulking around in the darkness smelled like Snowcrest or another mountain pack. Maybe I can use that.

"Just wondering how the trip was." Goddess, that sounds like bullshit to me. "Where were you coming from? Somewhere near home?"

He snorts. "Home isn't a concept most rogues hold to."

"Well, you must've come from a pack originally."

His smile tightens slightly. "I s'pose. I came from a little farm to the east, stuck between a couple different packs. Mama swore allegiance one way, Papa the other."

Nowhere near Snowcrest, if he's telling the truth. I nod and sip my wine. It's tart, sharp—just like the smell of blackberries behind me that is taking up way too much of the brain I need to be able to lie to this man.

"So you went off on your own?" I ask. "Why?"

"That really is the most interesting why to you royal types." He shakes his head. "May as well ask why you're staying."

"My people need me," I say automatically.

He smirks. "Can't say I haven't heard that before. Mostly from my not-so-good friend Gavin."

Kash might be the only person in this whole damned campground who says King Gavin's name that confidently.

Candace laughs behind me. Both Kash and I twitch toward her.

"Just how do you know my girl, after all?" he asks.

"Friend of a friend." My mark burns. Talking to him has been a fucking waste of time. I still don't trust him as far as I can throw him, and he's asking questions I don't want to answer. "I actually have to pass on a message for that friend, if you don't mind." I twist and tap Candace on the shoulder.

She stiffens like I struck her with lightning then turns very slowly. "What?"

"Eva wanted me to let me know that if there's anything you need, she's there for you." Smiling at Candace is easy. My face stops feeling like a painful rictus of forced cheer.

Her now-dark gaze roams my face, searching for something. "Is that why you're here?"

Just like the rest of her family, she won't buck social convention to refuse me. Especially when no one knows what happened between us.

"That, and a few other reasons." I spin my cup between two fingers. "I wanted to pick your brain about something."

"What?" Prince Finn smirks.

"Father is thinking about doing something like this around Snow-crest," I lie quickly. "Show off the castle, maybe some of our local highlights. I wanted to get any tips you had about setting this up, anything you'd do differently."

"Don't invite your mother," Candace mutters.

Finn laughs. Candace claps a hand over her mouth.

"It's okay." I… actually mean that. I want to tell her more about Mother, not hear less. "I won't invite any outside agitators."

She nods gratefully. I remind myself I'm just here on protection detail.

"Convincing people to stay for the party tomorrow has been a real bitch," Finn says.

"The spring equinox ball." Fuck, I almost forgot about that. "Why?"

"It wasn't originally planned." Candace shrugs. "Convincing people to make plans is easier than changing them."

"Is that true of you too?" I ask.

She bites her lip and stares at her food. "I like to think I'm pretty flexible."

"That so?" My cock hardens, remembering all the positions I've had her in.

Her cheeks turn a pretty pink. "That's not what I meant."

"What did you mean?"

"I mean I'm not so stubborn I'm impossible to talk to." Her voice whips out, sharp and jagged.

"See, I'd think that would make you so obliging you couldn't find your own opinions."

"No, but it does make me so obliging that when I do, people react like I've grown two heads." She narrows her eyes at me.

My mark burns slightly, but I find myself smiling. Going back and forth with her like this is as easy as breathing, like it's never been with anyone.

Anyone but Eva.

I shove that thought away. "Are you certain you didn't grow two heads? Things have been so busy, I'm not sure you'd notice."

"I'm pretty sure." She gets so close to me I can barely see her mouth anymore, but that doesn't make me want to kiss her any less.

"Ah, Pri—Candace?" a new voice says.

We both twist to see a middle-aged woman standing behind us.

"I heard from Princess Ingrid you were looking for a dance teacher." She pulls a handkerchief through her fingers over and over again. "Lady Edwina, at your service."

"Dance teacher?" I raise my eyebrows.

"Thank you, Lady Edwina," Candace says tightly. "We'll speak *later.*"

"Practicing for the ball tomorrow night?" I ask. "You know, in Snowcrest, the spring equinox is a fertility ritual."

"Does that mean you'll be going with Lady Eva?" King Anwen asks suddenly, his eyes hard. "Or someone else?"

Candace stiffens, and I wish like hell I could tell her she's got nothing to worry about. Her brother's thinking about the time he treated me like a fucking child in a bar a few days ago. Judging by the daggers flashing in his mate's eyes, both of them think I'm sleeping around on Eva, nothing more.

Well, I am. Or was.

My mark screams.

"I'm going," I say as politely as I can. "And, of course, so is Lady Eva, so we will go together."

"Hm." Anwen eyes me but doesn't say another word.

"And the rest of you?" I gesture to the table.

Everyone mumbles their assent, including Kash.

"Well, then it will be a beautiful equinox." I grin. "I hope to dance with you, Luna Raven." I reach for her hand, and maybe more from exhaustion than anything else, she accepts a kiss on the back. "Luna Estrella." She looks more irritated, but she doesn't stop me either. "Princess Candace." I hold my hand out.

She looks like someone is jabbing her with hot pokers, but she puts her palm in mine. I brush a kiss over her soft skin, inhaling her scent. Then, I release. Protection detail only.

"And Princess Ingrid!" I reach for her hand.

She yanks it back. "I don't like strangers very much."

I bow. "Still."

"I wouldn't hold your breath." Ingrid glares at me steadily.

Lovely girl.

SPRING EQUINOX

Candace

"What do you think?" Ingrid asks. "The green or the gold?"

I study the dresses hanging from each of her arms. The green is a soft sea foam, a frothy thing that makes her look like she's just stepped off the top of a wave, especially when she lets me style her hair. But the gold, embroidered with deep blue, makes her shine even at the edge of the ball, where I know she's going to be spending most of the night.

"You can't go wrong." I smile.

She rolls her eyes. "You're just saying that because you're excited you don't have any admirers hanging around."

"Can you blame me?" I drop onto my cot and scowl at the new squeak of the wooden box hidden between the mattress and the frame. "They are relentless."

Ingrid laughs.

Ever since dinner last nice, I cannot take two steps outside of this tent without Kash, Hollis, or Kash *and* Hollis appearing out of nowhere to escort me wherever I'm going. Days of not even hearing

from Hollis, much less seeing him, have disappeared. Kash remains…
overenthusiastic. Between the two of them, I sometimes feel more
like a venison shank caught between two wolves than a person. Even
worse, with Hollis always around, I haven't found a spare second to
talk to Kash about my dream. At least both of them were scared off
when I said Ingrid and I were going to start getting ready for
tonight's ball three hours before it started.

Of course, we didn't actually begin getting ready until a few
minutes ago, after an hour of blessed peace and quiet.

"I just wish I knew why," I say. "Why now? Why both of them?"

"Maybe Hollis is doing this because he knows it's going to irritate
you." Ingrid holds the gowns up against her body, one by one.

My mark throbs. "He wouldn't. Not out of nowhere."

"Maybe he's jealous." She turns back to me, frustration blazing in
her eyes. "Now that somebody else wants you, he wants you back."

"Ew!" I wrinkle my nose. "Kash is—"

"Not like that." Ingrid shakes her head. "Just in any way. Whatever
else Kash is, he isn't exactly subtle about how much his connection to
you matters."

I shrug, and she turns back to the mirror. What she's saying makes
some sense… or it would, if I could believe that Hollis cared at all.

"Not quite sure how to knock on these," Kash calls from outside.

Ingrid groans. "Seems like your freedom was short-lived."

I hop up, shaking my head. "I told him to come. I need to talk to
him for a second."

"Mind-link me if I should have an emergency to get you out." She
grabs my hand for a second as I brush past her and outside.

Kash grins. "He—I thought you were getting ready?"

I swallow a wince and don't look at the robe I'm wearing or my
loose hair. "Ingrid is going first. I'm helping her."

"Guess I got a lot to learn." He nudges a rock across the ground.
"So, there ain't much time left until sunset, and I don't expect we'll
have a lot of privacy. What did you want to ask me?"

My stomach swoops. He thinks I invited him here to ask him to
escort me to the ball. Where Hollis couldn't intervene.

"Not ask." I smile to cover my worry. "Tell."

He laughs. "Well, I'm glad you got a bit of my confidence."

"I've been having this dream."

Kash's face falls. He really isn't a very good liar—so is he telling the truth about everything else?

I'll know when I finish this.

"What sort of dream?" he asks.

Details spool off my tongue. The war, the blood, the devastation. The way it all feels so much realer than a normal dream. How I've had it nearly every time I close my eyes for almost two weeks now.

He blows out a long breath and rubs a hand over his face. "Well, repeated dreams about the same shit tend to be some kind of turning point. Major life events and all."

I nod. "But what about *this* dream? Is there a chance it's more like a metaphor than anything real?"

"A chance? Sure." The smile he offers me looks strained. "I haven't been having anything like it, which means either I'm not likely to get caught up in a world-spanning war, or, I guess, that your mind's reimagining another conflict as a war."

"Okay." If he's not having similar dreams, then him being here probably isn't what's going to start it, at least. Or it really is a metaphor. Maybe I've been waking up every night because everything with Hollis feels like the end of the world, and I scared him and Kash for no reason.

Kash grabs me by the shoulders and meets my gaze. "Hey. I know the pressure you're under, trying to figure out what to do with this information. Ain't nothing scarier in this life. But you're my girl, and I trust you'll make the right call."

I study his eyes. No flicker of a lie in there. Some part of him does trust me. Maybe that's the answer I was looking for, more than anything specific he had to say about this dream.

"Now." He grins. "Who has the honor of taking my girl to this shindig?"

No one, unless Ingrid counts. Mother's voice rings in my ears— telling him I'm going alone is an invitation for him to ask me. I could say Finn, but that means relying on Finn to be willing. Kieran and Anwen will be too busy with their wives.

Hollis is taking Eva. Obviously.

"Well," I say slowly, "I was hoping you would."

Kash's face lights up, and he hugs me tight. "Why, I'd love to."

"Thank you." I struggle to suck in a full breath within his arms. "But I really have to finish getting ready."

"Course." He releases me. "So do I!"

I turn and step back into the tent. Ingrid looks at me with wide eyes.

"Maybe he'll bathe?" she says.

JUST AFTER SUNSET, I STAND JUST OUTSIDE THE LIGHT CAST BY THE OAK tree at the center of the ball, fidgeting with the sleeves of my dress. Ingrid chose the gold, in the end, then insisted I wear the green. I tried to refuse. She's always been thinner than me, so a dress that on her skims a suggestion of curves has me threatening to burst out every time I move. But she wouldn't take no for an answer, and as mixed scents cloud the air, twining with wild music humming over the crowd, I wonder if she wasn't right. The spring equinox is a time of fertility everywhere, no matter what Hollis says, and wearing a bit less makes sense here.

"How'd I do?" Kash asks from behind me.

I spin around and realize how he snuck up on me. He actually did bathe. His sandy hair is back in a ponytail—with the clip I suggested to keep it in place. His wrinkles and scars are a bit less dramatic without dirt outlining every crevice, and he's traded his leathers for something approaching court attire.

"Very impressive," I say honestly.

"That's what I was hoping for." He puts out his arm. "You look lovely, but I'm going to have to be fending boys off all night."

My face warms. Normally, that's Kieran's threat to make.

"Let's go inside."

The page standing at the outside of the gathering takes one look at us then holds his trumpet to his lips. "Candace and her father, Kash."

No titles, no fanfare. I step into the ring of lights on Kash's arm. Everyone nearby turns and stares. The whispers begin a second later.

With the heavy thump of drums and birdlike trill of some flute, they're a little easier to ignore. That–or practice.

"Dancing first?" Kash asks. "Or would you prefer a drink?"

I glance at him. "You're more comfortable here than I would've expected."

His hold on me tightens, but he smiles. "You really think we didn't have the occasional holiday out in the sticks? A party's a party, baby."

That makes sense. Mostly. The spring equinox ball is probably more like something a farmer would have than anything else.

"Candace!" Eva floats over, resplendent in a pure-white gown that highlights her every curve.

I release him to hug her. "You're gorgeous."

"By the Goddess, so are you!" she replies.

"Evening." Kash nods at her "Helluva party."

"Isn't it?" Eva barely glances at him, all of her attention on me. "I heard you're dancing more now."

"You did?" I frown then realize Hollis must have told her.

Some of my worry about his behavior the last two days eases. If he's telling her, then he's not sneaking around.

"Care to show me?" She bows elaborately and holds out her hand.

Kash stiffens slightly. "I was hoping for the first dance."

"Later." I pat his arm and pray that's enough to tide him over. "I doubt I'll see Lady Eva much tonight."

Then, I put my hand in hers, and we spin off into the crowd.

"I haven't started my lessons yet," I admit. "No time."

"Oh, I assumed." She grins. "But I bet I'm a better dance partner than a rogue."

I giggle, and guilt burns in my gut. "He's really not so bad. I can tell he's family."

She waves my words away. "I believe you, but I'm not here to talk about your father."

"Oh?" I raise an eyebrow. Eva usually gossips for business, not for pleasure.

"I need advice about Hollis," she whispers.

The guilt intensifies. Nausea claws at my throat. "Okay."

"He's been... different lately." She smiles. "More romantic. Like we're really going somewhere."

My mark screams. I shouldn't be surprised, but that doesn't make it hurt any less.

"Tonight, he's been all over me. Paying me a million compliments, holding me, everything." She leans closer with a surreptitious smile. "I think we might sleep together tonight, even though we're not mated yet. I've never done that before. Do you have any advice?"

"I haven't either." The lie stumbles off my tongue, and I miss the next step of the dance. "Wh...why do you think that?"

She shrugs. "You just seem really confident lately, and I was wondering."

"Well, I haven't." *Moon Goddess, hear my prayer, strike me dead where I stand.* "So just—"

The music switches, and I recognize the cue to change partners.

"Just hold that thought until I see you again!" I smile as I transfer into the arms of a stranger.

And another stranger. And another. I laugh, I flirt, I feel like a porcelain statue of myself. Exactly what Mother always wanted. But I don't look for Hollis in the crowd. I can't. Because if I see him with her, it's all over.

At the end of the song, I consider leaving the dance floor. My legs ache, and I'm getting tired.

'Seems like you're without a partner,' Kash says. *'And I've got my dancing shoes on.'*

If he grabs me and starts pushing me around now, I'm going to lose it. So I spin around and throw myself into the arms of the nearest person on the floor.

Pine. Amber. Snow.

Oh no.

ANYONE BUT HER

Hollis

Fuck.

As soon as I saw Candace walk in, I knew I was in trouble. She's dressed like I've never seen her before. Tight green fabric cups her breasts and ass like I want to, trailing from the hem up to a loop hooked over her finger to keep her mobile enough to dance. Her hair spills loosely out of some complicated bun, shining in the low light like spun gold. She's a Goddess-damned nymph of the equinox, a walking dream. But before we arrived, Eva said she had a plan for keeping Kash and Candace apart tonight. She officially released me from protection detail. So I've been doing the only fucking smart thing—avoiding Candace like the plague. Every time I look at her, I picture the necklace dangling in the empty space of her shockingly low neckline.

Well, the times when I'm behaving, I picture that. The times when I'm not, I picture her spread out before me like a meal I have all the time in the world to enjoy.

But now, she's in my arms, blinking up at me like a deer that just saw a wolf bounding at it. She fits fucking perfectly. The music is loud, intoxicating, and so is her smell.

"Dance with me," she whispers. "Or Kash will."

That's all the invitation I need.

Automatically, my feet find the steps of the one courtly dance I ever really managed to learn. Candace stumbles slightly, and I realize the problem—I'm used to Eva's longer stride.

Growing up, I mostly danced with Eva, but a handful of older court ladies wanted to be indulged by the young prince. At Father's insistence, I became... passable. I don't step on toes. I don't lead aimlessly. But I've never really liked dancing. It's sort of like the first stages of archery practice, when my trainer made me imitate the motions of drawing and firing without an arrow or a bow. It was a show of physical prowess with no meaning and the most human thing I can imagine, far more human that the human-form hunting other kingdoms think we're so strange for.

Not with Candace. She dances like liquid. Every step contains the shadow of the next, the echo of the one before it, weaving together into a tapestry of movement like nothing I've seen before. Like she doesn't even have to think about the moves. They exist, deep in her bones, and something in the music just pulls them out.

I correct my stride to hers, and I can almost feel them. The steps map out more easily in my mind. The rhythm of the music pounds behind my breastbone like a second heartbeat. I could almost close my eyes without losing my place—and somehow, she's not fighting me for the lead. She's pulling a dance out of me I didn't even know I had.

Like magic.

"You look—"

"Don't," she says. "Not tonight."

"Why not tonight?" I frown. "Tonight seems like a hell of a time."

"Because I already talked to Eva," she snaps.

I blink. Eva looks... well, she looks like Eva in a nice dress. The white highlights her red hair. That's pretty much all I noticed.

"Don't act like you don't know what I'm talking about," she hisses.

"I don't." I glance around the outside of the crowded dance floor, looking for Eva. She left me a few seconds ago because she needed a drink, but she didn't say anything about having a particularly tense conversation with Candace.

"She mentioned tonight." Candace's cheeks pink. "And… something related to the, you know, fertility element you were talking about."

My mark urges me forward, begs me to run my thumb over the heated points of her cheeks, to taste her lips. Only years of restraint are enough to crush the urge and actually hear what she's saying.

"Eva said she was going to fuck me tonight?" I blurt.

Candace quickly goes from pink to red, and she ducks her face. "The reverse, more accurately."

"That I was going to fuck her," I mumble.

Candace stiffens in my arms. Together, we miss the next step, and the one after. A music cue tells us it's time to switch partners, and she starts to pull away, but I hold her tight. She can't leave like this. I don't know if I can let her leave at all.

She doesn't fight me for long. The relief of her relaxing into my arms almost takes me out at the knees.

"Is it true?" she asks.

"Kind of," I find myself saying.

Blonde eyebrows lift, and her plush lips part.

"I… meant to," I admit. "I thought it would be enough. Make everyone stop asking about the failed Haze. Give her something to hold onto."

Candace's face crumples. "Right. Because you've made your decision, and she's going to be your wife. Hollis, let me go."

My chest aches as my mark begins to burn.

"I can't."

She looks up at me, surprise painting her face again.

"I want to," I say through gritted teeth. "I'm supposed to. But every time I get my hands on you, I just fucking can't."

She stares up at me in silence for a long, painful moment. One song transforms into the next. I stare down at her soft face, the hazel eyes that suit her so much more than the blue. They're soft, kind, but far more complex than anyone thinks at a single glance. Beautiful.

How could I possibly leave this ball with anyone but her?

"Tell me about the necklace," she says.

Not a question. An order. She already barely reminds me of the woman I woke up next to that first morning.

"It was my mother's," I say. "I don't know if that actually made it into the final draft of the letter."

She shakes her head. "Draft?"

I've already made a complete fool of myself. "There were four. One of them actually explained the necklace. Father made it for her when he realized how little she had to remind her of home. That symbol in the middle—it's the symbol of her kingdom, hammered out by the clumsy fingers of a king."

Tears fill her eyes, shining even brighter under the lights. "Hollis, why did you give it to me?"

I open my mouth, and nothing comes out. How the hell am I supposed to explain that giving her that answer is impossible? That it breaks the promise of the necklace, the promise I made to myself that night? It was supposed to be my last indulgence. My last step outside the lines before settling down to life with Eva who's waiting for me somewhere here to grab her and kiss her and start that life even though the thought of it makes me sick. The thought of releasing Candace, that is.

A storm of emotions swirls around me, a potent reminder why I don't fucking indulge all the stupid little whims and pains of whatever remains of my heart. If I'd cried with Mother that day, I never would've stopped. If I hold onto Candace now, kiss her now, I'll never stop.

And Father needs me.

"I want to be happy," Candace says quietly.

"You deserve to be." My voice comes out husky and low.

"Waiting for you is…." She shakes her head. "I can't keep doing it."

"I'm not asking you to." I try to smile, but it feels more like a grimace. "Neither of us can."

She exhales slowly. "But I'm not good at giving up, and right now, you're making that impossible."

Her words hit like a punch to the chest. Everything I've done has just been giving her hope. Making her think there's a chance when I know there isn't one.

"So I'm asking you to decide." She nods to herself. "I've asked before, but this is the last night, Hollis. It's our last chance. After this, we return to kingdoms separated by two weeks of travel, and I will move on with my life if you tell me to."

Fucking words. I'm so much better at action. There's no way to explain the impulses pulling me in a thousand directions, the fact that I'm doubting myself for the first time in my Goddess-damned life because of her.

The song ends. I stand there in total silence, holding her, waiting for the next to start. If it ever will.

"I'm going to our spot," she says. "There's nothing else here for me anyway."

Then, she pulls away, and even I'm not selfish enough to try to hold onto her. My arms remain wrapped around empty air. The next song hums into being, and I drop them to my sides before someone else can take them as an invitation.

Candace didn't say she'll hold onto hope if I meet her there. She didn't say she'll give up if I don't. She didn't fucking need to because I already know her almost as well as I know Eva or myself.

'She's leaving!' Eva calls over mind-link. *'Should I go after her?'*

It's a hell of a question.

OUT OF MY SYSTEM

Candace

I PACE BACK AND FORTH UNDER THE MOONLIGHT, THE HEM OF MY GOWN swishing over the grass. Alone.

Of course, I'm alone. Hollis has been more than clear—there is no future for us. Throwing myself at him one last time was obviously nothing more than another chance to humiliate myself. Mother always said I had a soft heart, that disappointment would be what killed me in the end because I couldn't ever stop trying. I clutch my skirts in both hands and stare up at the moon.

Please, I pray to the Goddess with no real idea what I'm praying for. To let him go? To hear him pushing through the brush toward me? Just over a week ago, I knew exactly what my future looked like, and now I have no idea.

Standing there, under the lights, in his arms, it seemed so obvious. I needed a chance to close the book on Hollis. On the life I imagined we could have together. If I could simply have him one last time, I could forget about him. I could stop waiting for the tower to fall.

Perhaps this is a better way to understand that. I just wish it didn't hurt so much.

Something rustles behind me, and I whip around, an excuse already on my lips. I needed to catch my breath before returning to the party, isn't the light so beautiful here, I'm only—

"Candace," Hollis breathes.

My heart leaps into my throat. He's here.

There's nothing else to say.

We collide in the center of the tiny clearing that holds most of our memories. My mouth on his, his hands in my hair. His teeth sink into my lower lip, and I gasp open underneath him. He licks into my mouth. Pine, amber, and snow dance on my tongue for the last time.

I shove my hands up under his tunic, grab at the cool skin there. Coarse hair scrapes over my hands. It covers his chest, leads in a tempting trail down to the waistband of his pants. I salivate. There's so much we still haven't done.

Tonight, I won't leave regretting anything.

He grabs my dress as I sink to my knees in front of him, pulling the fabric. It strains over my curves, and something rips, but then spring air whispers over my skin. Only a corset and underskirt cover me. But I can't think about that now, when I'm stripping his pants down to his ankles and taking in the cock I've only really felt. The swollen length of it juts proudly out of the nest of dark hair at the bottom of that trail. A bead of something milky shimmers on the tip.

I take him in my mouth.

Kissing him makes his smell overwhelming. With him heavy on my tongue, I'm surrounded by pine, amber, and snow. I am shedding my winter clothes in the warmth of a fire someone I love set to warm me. I am cupping my hands around a hot beverage and shivering in the best way as tense muscles relax. He is a symphony of tastes and smells, and I imprint them into my mind one by one.

He threads his hand through my hair, destroying the careful updo I spent so long on, and squeezes tight. I moan around him, and he bucks forward.

Fuck.

The last time I touched him, he told me to be careful, to be gentle. Want throbs like a second heartbeat between my legs, and I can't. I swallow him down to the same frantic beat. The hair on his legs scrapes my cheeks, more scrapes my nose. I savor every scratch. The tip of him nudges the back of my throat, and my gag reflex flutters, but I choke it down. I'm not pulling back now. Not when he's growling, deep in his throat, and holding onto me like I'm the only thing keeping him anchored to the ground. I can just barely hear the music from the party still raging on, not far away, but he sounds so much sweeter.

He grunts. "Don't… want to…."

Hollis doesn't need to finish his sentence for me to know I'm going to ignore him. I want to taste him like he's tasted me. I want to watch his face as he reaches the heights of pleasure. I want all of him, for the very last time.

I grab the backs of his legs and hold him in place. He groans, but his thrusts don't slow. I hollow my cheeks and move with him. He's close. I can feel it in the tightening of his muscles, the stumbling of his rhythm. So close.

He rams himself forward and goes taut. Salty, musky liquid pours down my throat, hot and still tasting of him. I moan around his length and swallow as much as I can.

Mere moments later, he pulls back, grabs me, and lifts me into a kiss. His taste blurs between us. I shove my tongue between his lips, dancing along the jagged line of his incisors and tasting every inch of him. More. I need more.

His fingers fumble at the tie of my underskirt. I help him, and it puddles around my feet. Neither of us bother with my corset, though he pulls one breast free of the boned top. Then, his hand is dancing between my legs, spreading the wetness there across the insides of my thighs as he finds the bud that drives me wild. My knees weaken, and I cling to him.

"Hollis," I whisper.

"Someday, you'll scream my name," he replies.

His words disappear in the haze of pleasure rippling up from the apex of my thighs. I can only pull at his tunic, freeing enough of his skin to sink my teeth into. The scar of my sun-shaped mark winks back at me. I bite down there, an echo of the force used that first night, because he's got to be hiding it. Here, I can mark him as much as I want and never worry. I've already done everything I can.

He groans, and his fingers jerk. One slides to my entrance, and I roll my hips against him. I need the sweet pressure of him inside me.

Hollis understands without a word. Two fingers thrust home, and only my mouth on his shoulder keeps me from crying out loudly enough that the whole party would hear us. I roll one of my own nipples, plucking and teasing like he usually does.

I can teach this to my eventual husband, a small part of me notes. He won't understand me as innately as Hollis does, as perfectly, but this is not the end of pleasure, even if it's the pinnacle.

My whole body hums, careening toward the apex. I shudder around his fingers. Hollis hooks his arm under one of my legs, knocking me off balance, forcing me to lean my whole weight against him. He fucks another finger inside, and the three of them hit a new place. Something that makes me see stars.

"Just like that," he murmurs. "So beautiful for me. My mate."

Once upon a time, I thought those words would mean something. Now, they mean this one beautiful man, who throws me around and wrings pleasure out of me like I've never felt before. I moan wordlessly. There's nothing more to say.

"Not like this." He pulls his fingers back with a lasciviously wet sound.

I whine at the loss.

"Tonight, I'm finishing inside you." He drops my leg, then spins me around and bends me over with a firm hand on my back.

I twist pliantly at his silent orders. This way, I can only see the lush green of Escuro, restored. The trees that shield us from the crowd that can never know. I brace my hands on the ground and thank them for growing, for healing. Without them, I would be alone at the spring equinox.

Hollis palms my ass, then nudges my entrance. He's only half-hard, still recovering from my mouth, but he threads himself inside. There's no waiting tonight. I rock back, feeling him grow and harden inside me. In this position, I have nothing but my willpower to hold back my moans.

A challenge I am going to rise to.

"Fuck," he mumbles.

With his hands on my hips, he starts. I meet every thrust, roll back in rhythm. My hair hangs in my face. My breasts sway, brushing the dew-tipped grass. Suddenly, the dew grows much colder and clings to me, sweet and sharp.

Ice. Hollis froze the dew without losing rhythm, and he's caressing my breasts with it. I bite down on my own lip as hard as I can to hold back the feeling of being surrounded by him, of the pleasure I barely lost during the change in position. I am a spark about to burst into flame, and he is the ice drawing out the moment of explosion, second by painful, beautiful second.

Someone screams. High, pained, almost animal. It tears through me, and I jerk my head up, pleasure slipping through my fingers.

A pale face stares out from the circle of trees. A pale face above a paler dress, topped with fire-red hair.

Eva.

No.

WORST CASE

Hollis

I LOCK EYES WITH EVA. TEARS SHINE IN HER GREEN GAZE. THAT, I CAN handle. But the pained pinch of her eyebrows when Candace picks her head up is too damn much.

"This isn't what it looks like." I yank back from Candace without a second fucking thought.

Eva's gaze drops to my cock, standing at attention, glistening with both of our juices.

Shit.

"I can explain." Candace straightens, fumbling to stuff her ice-covered breasts back into her corset.

Finally, Eva's gaze trails to the snowflake-shaped bite on Candace's collarbone. She makes a small, soft, punched-out noise.

This can't be fucking happening.

"Plea—"

Eva shifts and sprints away before I can even finish the word.

I feel like someone scooped out my guts and dumped them on the grass in front of me. I feel like a prisoner marching to the gallows. I feel like the stupidest, sickest fuck in a hundred-mile radius, and even worse, I know I'm right.

"We have to—"

"—find her," Candace finishes.

Where my guts once were, a firework of warmth explodes. With her hair hanging in her face, naked from the waist down, on the worst night of my life, Candace somehow still knows exactly what to say.

Now, I just need some of that to talk to Eva,

Candace puts her nose to the air. "She went north, but she's already wheeling back around. It doesn't seem like she's running away."

"We'll cover more ground separately," I say.

Candace nods, and part of me wonders if she's also thinking about the other reason to split up—I doubt Eva wants to hear from both of us.

I don't get to ask before she shifts into a sleek, gray wolf and bolts off into the trees.

I follow suit, my own wolf wrapping me in a world of physical sensation that still can't blot out the guts-on-the-ground feeling.

My best friend. My best fucking friend. Forget tradition, forget being promised to each other, Eva is and always has been my best friend. She's been at my side through all my best and worst moments, just like I've been at her side through hers. That's why it was so easy to imagine walking away from Candace and spending my life with her. I've been practicing for twenty years. And a life with one's best friend is most people's dream come true.

I've never seen Eva look like that before.

At her mother's funeral, an event I remember stories of more than any actual memories, Father let me sit with her family. The whole time in the temple, I held her hand. She stared blankly ahead, shaking with tears she almost didn't seem to notice she was shedding. Afterward, we went outside with all her sisters. Every single one of the four of them just wanted to sit in a sleigh, silently. Even little baby Emi, only a few days old. But I knew better—or at least, I did for Eva. So I started making ice sculptures. A whole little ice play, retelling a story that had made Eva laugh in class a few days ago. I did silly voices for all the characters, made them move like I never had before, threw everything into the play. Her sisters barely looked up, but at the very end, Eva smiled. And I felt like I was already king of Snowcrest in that second.

Now, I've ruined everything. Because I was too much of a selfish fucking prick to talk to Eva before following Candace away. Because I was too Goddess-damned scared that talking to her would take up tonight, and I couldn't wait to spend the rest of my life with Candace.

At my mother's funeral, she held my hand, just like I had hers, so long ago. I didn't cry. I just stood next to Father and said the words he'd taught me to the endless line of approaching dignitaries. There was no time to hide away, and Eva was never as good at constructs of ice as I was. But that night, she crept into my room. We were just barely old enough that she wasn't allowed anymore, a new rule Father and Lord Soren agreed on, but she scaled the outside of the castle to reach my window. I remember letting her in with numb hands, and the smile on her face when she showed me the book of stories our tutor had been reading from so long ago. Just seeing it startled half a laugh out of me, and that was enough. We stayed up all night, huddled around a candle, reading the stories aloud to each other and putting in curse words wherever we thought the fairytale characters really ought to be cursing. It was the first time I imagined a world without Mother that didn't just feel… empty.

My nose isn't nearly as Goddess-damned good as Candace's. I lose the trail she pointed me on quickly. My brain whirls. Would Eva have turned back north, run all the way home? No. She faces her problems head-on, always has. When one of our tutors tried to focus all his attention on me, neglecting Eva and the other students, she'd stuck to my side and taught the other kids after class while I spoke to Father. When a few noblewomen from the east tried to start a rumor that one of her friends was secretly a foundling, Eva and I fought them in a courtyard, even though they were adults.

But this is nothing like anything I've seen her face before. She stayed, stood her ground, stared at us until she saw the mark. Until she realized, for the first time, that we might not be on the same side.

Goddess above, I am so fucking stupid.

By the time the sun starts to rise, I realize I've made the biggest mistake of my life. I've covered every path I think she might've taken, and there's nothing. Just… nothing. My tail droops as I turn and trudge back to camp. I could run all the way back to Snowcrest and not find a thing. Eva knows me too well. She can avoid me for the rest of her days, if she wants to.

As I approach the copse of trees to grab my clothes, a new smell reaches my nose. Blackberries and sunshine. Candace, her gray ears low and her steps equally plodding. She didn't find Eva either.

In silence, we shift into human form and redress with our backs to each other. I sling my vest over my bare chest, the remains of my shredded tunic laughing from the grass. At least my pants are only destroyed at the ankles, making them a little easier to wriggle up over my sweat-soaked body. When I turn around, Candace is using a hairpin to hold the split side of her dress closed over her bare chest. My feet move without thought, and suddenly, I'm helping her. Our fingers brush. That firework of warmth echoes hollowly in my chest.

"We should have told her," Candace murmurs.

There's nothing I can say to that.

Together, we join the flow of half-dressed, slightly swaying nobility headed toward the old oak for the final revitalization ritual. At least we don't stand out. A few times, Candace starts to drift away from me, but I grab her and pull her back. I've lost Eva, destroyed the most important person in my life, but I won't have nothing to show for it. As soon as this is done, I'm talking to Father. I don't care what he says. Candace is my mate, and we're going to have to find a way to make that work.

The crowd stops. I can just barely make out the branches of the oak overhead. We're here, far enough away that we can't see a thing.

"My family—"

"Can wait," I say. "They have a ritual to run."

Candace looks down at herself and winces. "They can help us find Eva after."

I nod. Father certainly won't.

"By the light of the Goddess," Luna Estrella declares, "and by Her darkness, we find our way. On this last day, as we give her last blessing, I ask who would speak the final words of this miracle."

"I will," Eva says.

Candace and I jerk our heads up at the same time. She's here!

'Please don't run away!' I yell over mind-link. *'We have to talk.'*

For the first time in my whole fucking life, my words slam against a wall in Eva's mind. She won't let me in.

"She's not listening." I grab Candace's hand, and we start fighting our way through the crowd together.

Eva's so close I can smell her, even through the press of bodies. Her and—someone else. Someone from Snowcrest. Someone familiar that I can't place.

"This truly has been a miracle," Eva says. "My eyes are open to possibilities I've never considered."

Her voice sounds like glass. So hard and brittle I almost don't recognize it. I shoulder people out of the way without a glance. I have to get to her.

"Like seeing my promised mated with another," she declares.

Candace and I burst out of the front edge of the crowd. Eva looks at us, an echo of that sound she made in her eyes.

"The bastard Candace stole Prince Hollis during the Haze!" Eva dumps the jug of potion onto the ground with a flourish and a bitter grin.

The ground rumbles as the magic spreads. Conversation breaks out like a storm. People flood at us from all directions. Like someone grabbed either side of my ribcage and started pulling, I'm torn in two directions. Eva is leaving—and someone is tugging Candace out of my grasp.

I hesitate, and both of them disappear in the chaos.

CHAOS

Candace

"No!" I shout as I'm ripped away from Hollis. Like anyone will hear me over the chaos the crowd has broken out into.

It's worse than any other ritual—or maybe this is the only one I've been in the crowd during. Scents buffet me from every direction—flowers, trees, body odor, stale alcohol. Someone shoves me to one side, and another person pushes me right back. I try to fight, but I don't even know what I'm fighting for. To reach Hollis? Last night was supposed to be our last time together, a goodbye to what we could've been. His attachment to me today is… I'm not sure. Guilt, maybe?

Or, a small part of me suggests, *he actually came because he wants to be with you.*

That part keeps getting me in trouble. Last night was supposed to be about killing it as well, and yet here it is again.

"I can't imagine," someone says to the person next to them. "Do you think she found them together?"

Eva. The look she gave me last night stabs through me, all hurt and accusation. She was right. I finally find her after a whole night of looking, and I'm thinking about myself. Wondering what last night meant to Hollis. It doesn't matter—not us, not my parents, nothing but the fact that I took the heart of someone I really care about and crushed it like a bug. I need to find Eva. She's what matters most. I gather myself and start pushing through the crowd.

A smell catches my nose. Caramel and sweetcress. I look up and find Estrella standing in front of me.

"Candace." She hugs me quickly, tightly. "Come with me. We have to get you out of here."

I shake my head. "Did you see which way Eva went?"

Estrella's eyebrows knit, making her look even more exhausted. "You're going after her?"

"I have to." It's the only thing I can hold onto in this chaos, burning like a beacon in my mind.

"May the Goddess guide your steps." Estrella kisses each of my cheeks lightly. "She knows what we need better than we often do."

I nod and barrel into the crowd once more. My nose is almost useless in the crush from any distance, but I have to try. Eva is here somewhere. She should be right ahead, but simple ideas like "right" and "ahead" are impossible to make sense of. My gown strains where I pinned it, threatening to burst and expose me in front of all these people. I don't have another way to fix it, so I just keep running.

Conversation swirls around me. I lose track of how many times someone shouts, "There's the bastard!" I don't lose track of how many times people sneer and hurry away from my touch before I can shove them, like something about me is dirty now.

"Hey!" Ingrid yells. "Over here!"

On instinct, I wheel toward her voice.

"By the Goddess, I've been looking for you." She grabs both of my wrists. "Move. Now."

"Eva needs me," I repeat.

Ingrid stares at me for a second. She looks fresh, like the surrounding cacophony can't reach her somehow. She squeezes me, lets me go, and drapes a cloak she was wearing around my shoulders to hide my bursting dress.

"I'm sorry it happened like this, but I'm glad he can't hide anymore."

I can't reply to that now. What happens after I leave this crush of people is another Candace's problem. More Candaces seem to keep splintering off.

There! Jasmine. I whip around and start burrowing in a new direction.

My legs ache. I ran all night, tracing a wisp of a scent trail deeper and deeper into the woods. It feels ridiculous now. Eva couldn't have gone that way and appeared at the ritual when she did. I must have confused her with someone else, or picked up an old trail, or—

I never really wanted to find her in the first place?

I shake that thought away. Of course, I wanted to find her. I *want* to find her. There has to be something I can say, some explanation I can give, that makes this all make sense to her. It was the last night, Hollis is hers—the throb in my mark almost makes me scream—I only did what I did to protect her.

All lined up like that in my mind, those excuses sound a lot like something Mother would say. She only ever wanted to protect us.

Someone grabs me by the shoulders, but instead of shoving, they hold on. My heart leaps into my throat as I twist to see who has me.

Kieran's pale face looms out of the crowd. His ice-blue eyes are wide, and the silver-and-blue sash he wears at rituals to declare him Alpha King of Dun's Crossing dangles off one shoulder.

'Diplomatic tensions are dissolving,' he tells me through the mind-link. *'Snowcrest is furious. Other kingdoms are saying that we're traitors. We have to go.'*

'Snowcrest is furious?' I ask. *'Or King Andri?'*

'They're the same right now,' he snaps. *'Anwen's working with Alpha Cole to dissolve the crowd, so you and I just need to get out of here.'*

Responses tumble through my mind. Kieran looks five years older than he was when he took the throne. Altair is back in the tent with a nanny, but I can almost read Kieran's worries about him in his eyes. Adding to his diplomatic chaos would be cruel.

"Candace!" someone shouts.

Not someone. Hollis. In all the noise and furor, he's looking for me. My heart skips a beat, and that little part of me screams to go to him. Maybe splitting up was a ridiculous waste of time. Maybe we can only find and face Eva together. Maybe he already has her.

'No.' I free myself from Kieran's grasp. '*I have another plan.*'

Kieran snarls, but the sound is so thick with exhaustion and worry I can't be scared. '*I am Alpha. My plan—*'

I shove a yelling noblewoman in between the two of us and duck low in the crowd. Kieran's shouts ring in my mind, demanding that I come back, but I ignore him. He didn't come back when he was "chasing" an escaped Raven. I can't do it now.

All I can do is try to remember where Hollis's shout came from and find his scent. I take bruise after bruise—elbows in the ribs, kicks to the knees, headbutts. My whole body aches. But I can smell him. I must be getting close.

I explode out of the crowd, into the relative quiet surrounding it. Mother's prison wagon looms dark against the bright sky, surrounded by soldiers at attention. I turn to leave.

"Oh, my darling," she says. "Wonderful work."

My stomach swoops. I pause. Why is she complimenting me?

"Lying was never your strongest weapon, but you must've been practicing." She laughs wildly. "You must've lied well enough to convince the Goddess Herself. There's no other way a bastard like you wins a prince!"

Wind whips through my hair as I throw myself back into the crowd, eyes burning with tears. I didn't want this, never asked for it, but who's going to believe that? Mother's right. Convincing people— through lies or otherwise—was always a stumbling block for me.

"No!" a heavy, bass voice thunders. "There is no proof. I do not accept."

Something toward that voice smells like snow. I'm so lost, so upside-down, that I charge after it without a second thought.

"Lady Eva is wrong," the voice continues. "She only wanted to make a scene."

Eva would never. Maybe my nose is ruined. Anyone from Snowcrest should know her well enough to know that Eva doesn't have an attention-seeking bone in her body.

"Pah!" The man attached to the voice sounds disgusted. "That's no proof. You could have done that with paints."

I keep pushing. More bruises collect on my skin. I stumble, and someone knees me right below my eye. The burst of pain almost makes me throw up, but I force myself back to my feet.

"The Haze cannot work here!" the man declares. "The land is too sick, too destroyed."

Suddenly, I place the voice. King Andri, using almost the exact same words Hollis did when I first woke up next to him. I burst through the final layer of crowd and find him standing in a small pocket of peace, surrounded by several other Snowcrest nobles I've seen around—and Hollis.

"The Solbergs destroy all they touch." King Andri's face is red and tight with rage. "They knew the Haze could not work here, and they set all this up. To humiliate us."

Hollis stares at the ground. He doesn't fight back, doesn't disagree. Eva is nowhere to be seen.

"Not *they*," another noble in the circle says. "*She*."

King Andri backhands the noble without a breath of hesitation. "Get out of my sight. That bastard did not do this. Kieran is the danger. She is a mere pawn."

Hollis's shoulders tighten as the noble scrambles away, but he still doesn't say a thing. My body starts to go fuzzy, then numb.

"Something is wrong." King Andri nods resolutely to himself. "We do not rest until we find it and restore our name."

I can't fight him. Not if Hollis won't so much as shake his Goddess-damned head in disagreement. I step back into the crowd before he can see me.

I'm sorry, I say to Kieran. *I'll go now.*

TRADITION

Hollis

"WE WILL NOT DISCUSS THIS IN PUBLIC." FATHER SCOWLS AT THE CHAOS of the crowd then turns and storms out.

Like a dog on a fucking leash, I chase after him with the rest of the Snowcrest delegates. My ears are ringing, my heart's damn near pounded itself to mush against my ribcage, and my eyes burn from a night spent awake. I can barely think about any of that.

Where is Eva? Where is Candace?

The second we break the edge of the crowd, he picks up his rant again.

"We never should have indulged this Solberg scum." Father is almost purple with rage, angrier than I've ever seen him before. "This is what comes of mixing with other kingdoms. At home, the Haze would have worked properly. Tradition would have asserted itself."

At home, we would've known immediately that Eva and I weren't mates. There would've been weeks and months of experimentation to figure out why. We both would've been miserable.

Fuck, maybe that's better than this.

Twice, Eva has run away now. It's like I barely know her anymore. Like this betrayal turned her into someone new.

"Do you understand what they've done?" Father grabs me by the shoulders and shakes me. "Centuries of peace and tradition, shattered."

"They?" I manage.

"Solberg scum." He releases me harshly, halfway to a shove. "Twisted the magic, tricked all our minds. They did this. Using the bastard is just more insulting."

My mark sears into my anger. He can't talk about Candace like that. She's more than a bastard, more than a pawn. I open my mouth to yell at my father for the first time in my life—

And remember the soft parting of Eva's lips last night.

Father's never going to listen. If I don't stand up for Candace, my mark keeps hurting. For hurting both of them, that's what I deserve.

"Send a messenger to Lord Soren," Father barks. "He will not learn this news from anyone but me."

One of the other nobles hurries off to do that. I keep pace with Father through a nearly empty camp. Almost everyone remains at the ritual site behind us.

"What do you think he'll say?" The words burn almost as much as my mark. I should be looking for Candace—for Eva—for both of them.

"What I am saying," Father snaps. "This is a mistake that must be set to rights. He knows us too well to assume deliberate insult. At home, we will find answers."

My gut sinks like a rock. The only answers I want are about apologizing to Eva. After last night, I know there's no happiness for me without Candace. The mate bond is worth fighting for.

"Once you're away from the influence of the bastard vixen, their sick magic should revert." Father strides toward our tents.

I stumble as a wave of pain nearly knocks me off my feet. My mate. He's talking about my mate like that.

"You can't—"

He holds open the flap of his tent and gestures for me to go inside.

"I will, and so will you. For our people's sake."

I hesitate. Snowcrest needs me to be the leader they were expecting, the prince who obeys tradition and leads them like they need to be led. Father is wrong about Candace, about today, but it would've been so much fucking easier if I just mated with Eva. If I could just walk into the Goddess-damned tent without leaving parts of me outside.

"Zain," Father growls.

My would-be Beta snaps to attention in the small cloud of Snowcrest delegates surrounding us.

"Stay with the prince. Keep him here. Temper the magic in him." Father looks at me with that old, resigned disappointment in his eyes. "I'll make arrangements. We leave the second they are complete."

Zain nods sharply and nudges me into Father's tent. A babysitter. He assigned me my own fucking Beta as a babysitter. I'm a failure the likes of which he never could've imagined, and now, I can't even be trusted to sit fucking still.

The tent flap swings closed behind us, and I can't even think that he's wrong. If Zain wasn't here, I'd be pulling up the stakes at the back and heading out to find Eva and Candace the second I couldn't hear Father anymore.

"Dammit!" I kick a table sitting off to the side, and pain radiates up my leg.

"Hell of a day," Zain replies evenly.

"Shut the fuck up." I scrub my hands through my hair. "You don't know."

He pulls a flask out of an inner pocket of his vest, takes a swig, and holds it out to me. "I wonder why the fuck that is?"

I snatch the flask and pour burning liquor down my throat. The slick taste of black licorice coats my mouth, Zain's favorite, but I don't even grimace today. It'll keep the alcohol from dulling my senses too much.

"I couldn't fucking tell you." I wipe my mouth on my bare arm.

"Give me one good Goddess-damned reason why not." His voice is sharper than I expect, and I glance at him.

Zain and I have always been close. Having an actual guy friend was useful growing up, but every time something actually important happened, I went to Eva. But I'm starting to wonder if I know any of the people I spent my whole life with because I barely recognize him either. Instead of the casual, laid-back posture and easy smile I'm used to, Zain is a knotted ball of tension. Every muscle in his body is locked. Unlike me and half the crowd at the ritual, he's fully dressed, and a sword gleams on his hip.

"You're pissed," I say.

He barks a laugh. "More like furious. I'm supposed to be your right fucking hand, and now I'm the asshole with my jaw in the dirt, trying to figure out how we're going to fight Dun's Crossing because you've been too Goddess-damned distracted to think about it."

"You are." I cross my arms. "You're just a shit secret-keeper, and I couldn't let this get out."

"Who did you tell?" Zain glares at me.

"No one." Fuck, that feels stupid now. "Candace and I were the only ones who knew. That's why Eva—" My voice rolls over and dies before I can say another word.

"That shit about the war was a distraction, wasn't it?"

"I wouldn't do that," I say.

He studies me then shakes his head. "Goddess above, you're fucking stupid."

My eyebrows shoot up. "What?"

"You spent ten days sitting on a powder keg with the ability to destroy the whole fucking kingdom, and you didn't tell your right hand or your best friend?" Zain shakes his head again. "King Andri leads the kingdom alone, but most Alphas don't."

Alone is the way I work best. I like people for the occasional celebration, to bounce ideas off sometimes as a blank canvas, but I've built our army alone, earned the scraps of Father's praise alone, become the man I am today... because of Eva. And Candace. And Zain. And a thousand other people who bothered to teach me something.

I sink down onto Father's bed. "I might be fucking stupid."

"Give the man a prize." Zain claps me on the shoulder, takes his flask back, and swigs it again. "Look, this isn't the end of the fucking world."

I stare at him blankly. So, Zain having advice worth listening to is a fluke at the end of the world. Good to know.

"You and Eva have fought before," he says. "You remember the great fork catastrophe?"

I snort. Back when we were barely eight, Eva declared she had one favorite fork. She ate with it every meal, nearly refused to touch another one. But I was going through a rebellious phase, so I gave her fork to another girl in the castle. She yelled at me as soon as she found out, and I didn't stop discovering forks in my bed for weeks.

If Eva started yelling last night, I'd know what the fuck to do. The face she made is new, branded into the center of my chest.

"This is different," I mutter.

Zain knocks his shoulder into mine. "That was different. It was the first time you ever fought. Maybe this is your first big fight. All I know is, you guys always find a way to make up. It's practically tradition." He chuckles. "Course, I assumed that was because you were fated to be together."

I grimace.

"Not funny yet. Got it." Zain tucks his flask away. "Just talk to me next time. And trust whatever it is the two of you have."

Trust. Not exactly my strong suit. But as he leans back in a chair next to the table and shuts his eyes, I wonder if his advice doesn't apply to both of the women my instincts are screaming at me to go after. I have no way to reach Eva. Father had Lord Gunnar looking for her the second after the announcement, and even he couldn't find her. But I can trust in what I have with Candace. I just need to make sure she knows I trust it.

While Zain is distracted, I grab one of the scraps of paper Father always keeps by the head of his bed for late-night messages and scribble a few words. Then, I freeze an icicle in my palm, breathe life into it, and tie the scrap around its neck. It slithers out a tiny gap in the tent and disappears.

ANOTHER BAD IDEA

Candace

I sit at a makeshift table in the center of Kieran and Raven's tent, surrounded by people with various claims to being my family, all talking over each other about the mess I've made. Even Kash, my father, is here, for reasons I might never understand.

"She didn't do anything wrong!" Ingrid smacks the flat of her hand on the table. "You didn't tell Father who you were really mated to, did you?"

Kieran exhales painfully slow through his nose, looking like he's about to start pulling his hair out. "I was being blackmailed. And I had reason to believe my mate was my twin sister, not the crown prince of our strongest ally."

"Some prince he is." Ingrid snorts loudly.

"Shush," Raven says automatically, bouncing a dozing Altair. "I just got him to fall asleep. Please."

Ingrid puts her hands up defensively. "I'm just saying that, if you let Candace tell her side of the story, you'll realize Hollis is the real problem."

"*Prince* Hollis," Kieran corrects with narrowed eyes.

Ingrid rolls her eyes and slumps back in her chair, a near-perfect mirror of Finn, who's barely glanced up from the table since we finished dragging all the smaller ones together.

"I am not sure that's fair," Estrella says. "The mate bond is often an intensely stressful process. People behave in ways they otherwise might not."

Anwen takes her hand and smiles ruefully. "She means to say some people freak out and act like assholes."

"No, he's just an asshole," Ingrid replies.

"Ingrid," Kieran hisses.

She shrugs.

'*Seems to me he is,*' Kash says through the mind-link.

"We are here to discuss solutions because this affects all of us," Kieran says. "But we should have started with the person at the heart of this. Candace, do you have anything you'd like to say?"

Do I? My stomach churns, gnawing at nothing but the nightmare that started last night and seems well on its way to continuing for days. My head spins. I look at Kash, across the table from me. His hazel eyes shine with tempting promise, and everything he's ever said about being a rogue echoes in my mind. My muscles ache to throw me into a shift, to sprint out of this tent without a plan. Freedom seems impossible any other way.

"We need to find Eva," I say.

Kieran sighs. "Why? She has no direct connection to the throne."

Because she's my friend. Because, if I can make things right with her, maybe I'm not the monster I fear I am. Because all of this is my fault, and she's the one who's most hurt.

I open my mouth, but the exhaustion lining Kieran's face makes me close it again. He doesn't care about any of that. I just shrug.

"I like any plan that doesn't involve pandering to Hollis," Ingrid offers.

"Nobody's suggesting that," Anwen says. "Just that, while there will be diplomatic repercussions, a mate bond is a mate bond. The Goddess brought the two of you together."

"And you deserve the opportunity to discover what that could mean for you," Estrella finishes with a smile at Anwen.

They don't understand. Them being together was hard for them, not the rest of us.

"Okay!" Kieran almost shouts, patience visibly frayed.

Altair stirs. Raven glares at her husband and returns to rocking their baby with all her focus.

Kieran runs a hand through his hair and takes a deep breath. "Okay, I'd like to focus this meeting on diplomatic outcomes. Candace can make whatever decisions she likes about her romantic life once we figure out how to reclaim our alliances."

"Reclaim?" I ask.

He glances at me, blue eyes stormy, then away again. "Are you able to endure a conversation focused on politics?"

I feel like I'm at the center of a storm pulling me in a thousand directions. I nod.

"I have soldiers in plain clothes out amidst the crowd, joining conversations and sharing what they learn with me through the mind-link." He stands like the news is too big to say while sitting down. "We are in the initial blush of reactions, which means some of these will cool, but public opinion of Dun's Crossing and the Solberg family is rapidly shifting to the negative."

I suck in a sharp breath.

"So swiftly?" Estrella asks. "After everything with Sundrop Gem, after these days of revitalizing Escuro?"

Kieran nods solemnly.

"How?" I whisper. "Why?"

"It's been building." He's not looking at me again. "Mother's outbursts haven't been popular. People have begun to believe that she is not imprisoned for her crimes but in fact a way for us to reclaim the spotlight from Escuro and the powerful magic being worked here."

My stomach sinks lower and lower. Because of me. All because of me.

"What?" Ingrid scowls. "You'd think assassinating your own father would be enough to prove that you didn't agree with him. Throw Mother in the dungeon with Hollis, when we get around to that stage."

Anwen winces.

"We're not throwing Hollis in the dungeon," Kieran says tightly. "Not least because, in addition to losing almost all of the goodwill we've built up with other kingdoms, this… incident severely damaged our relationship to our strongest ally."

Estrella and Raven speak simultaneously.

"Sundrop Gem?"

"Escuro?"

Kieran clenches his jaw. "Our strongest non-familial ally. Father worked with King Andri for most of his reign."

The two Lunas seem satisfied. I can only think about the phrase *severely damaged*. It plays through my mind over and over again. I need to find Eva. I need to talk to Hollis. And I need to make certain that my brother doesn't have to start from scratch because the Goddess decided I needed the ability to make a complete fool of myself and everyone I love.

"Early reports from the Snowcrest camp are negative," Kieran continues. "King Andri is already making plans to leave immediately. He'll be gone within the hour."

"Stall him," Ingrid suggests. "Kidnap Hollis, and toss him in with Mother."

Kieran tenses like he's about to snap at Ingrid again then glances at Altair and stops. I grab her wrist.

'You don't need to do that,' I tell her.

'Someone needs to!' she replies.

I swallow another wave of nausea. I'm pulling actual siblings apart. There has to be something I can do.

"There has to be something we can do," Anwen says. "At the very least, we could stall them long enough to get a plan together."

Kieran shakes his head. "No, I think—"

I tune him out. There has to be something I can do, and this might be it. I know King Andri better than almost anyone else in the room, though only secondhand through Hollis's stories. But if someone ever needed to stop Mother from doing something and had only my stories to go on, I'm sure they could.

My mind scrolls back through everything I've learned. He made that necklace for his wife, which shows that he loved her. He gave it to Hollis for Eva, which shows that he believes in tradition. That, of course, I already knew and is at least half of the problem. And I don't even know any traditional forms of apology in Snowcrest.

Focus, Candace! Or you're going to lose everything.

I don't need base facts about King Andri, I need to know how he likes his problems to be handled. He appeared in stories about Hollis getting up to mischief only at the end to yell. He put Hollis in charge of their country's army just before King Gavin died, and Hollis was intensely proud of that fact. So he values physical might and trusts Hollis immensely.

Any solutions involving Hollis are impossible. I can't reach him, and I wouldn't know what to say if I could.

I'm wrong about the stories, I suddenly remember. There was exactly one where, after Eva and Hollis got up to some mess, he didn't get in trouble. It was the one with the mattress sledding down the stairs, but the part that matters is that Hollis went to his father and told him everything before anyone else could. He didn't get found out, didn't even have any good reason to suspect he would, he just confessed and apologized. King Andri values clear, direct communication without having to demand it of people.

We've got half an hour to convince him to sit down with Kieran if we want any chance of smoothing this over.

"I have an idea," I say, interrupting Anwen.

Kieran smiles tiredly. "Is this about Eva again? I know she's your friend, but we really don't have the time."

"It's not—"

Anwen pats my shoulder. "Hollis, then? I get wanting to see your mate, but I don't know if reuniting you is the best idea right now."

"No—"

Kash leans forward. "You know, when rogues get into territory disputes, we settle 'em all one way. Mano a mano."

"A duel?" Kieran raises one eyebrow. "It's quick, at least."

Even Kash gets listened to over me. But can I blame them? I'm the genius who had the bright idea to sleep with my mate on the exact same night I knew my dear friend wanted to. Who didn't warn anyone in time to get out ahead of this problem. Every problem we're —they're—now facing comes as a direct result of my bad ideas.

I wouldn't want to hear from me either.

THE REST OF MY LIFE

Candace

I FOLD DRESSES INTO MY TRUNK AND LISTEN TO THE COMMOTION OF the rest of the encampment breaking down outside. Kieran decided that letting King Andri cool off would yield the best results, so we're leaving just as quickly as everybody else. This weird pocket of time with so many people in one place is dissolving as fast as it came together.

An icicle slithers under the wall of the tent with a piece of paper wrapped around it. My heart jumps into my throat. Hollis? Eva? I glance over my shoulder at Ingrid, but she's off in her own world, humming to herself as she packs up our vanity.

I pretend to drop something, crouch, and unwind the paper. The icicle melts into water the second I do. My hands shake as I unfold the paper and smooth its crumpled edges, but there's no reason. Only five words greet me.

The tower is still falling.

Hollis. Disappointment and relief twist in my gut. He really meant last night. He came because he wanted to try to be something, and no matter what I heard his father say, he's not giving up.

Am I?

Something crashes outside, and two people begin shouting. That's been happening a lot. Tempers are high.

"All good?" Ingrid asks.

I shoot to my feet and crumple the sliver of paper into the bodice of my dress. "Yeah. I just dropped a button.

Ingrid nods and turns back to her task. The paper crinkles against my skin. My heart pounds in time with its movement.

Over the course of this trip, I've lost so much. My name, my family, my friends. I've destroyed even more. If Hollis truly believes… I can't lose him too. I can't lose everything. Even if I have no idea what his hope or mine will mean for us.

Less than an hour later, a few of Kieran's men load trunks onto carriages to take us back to Dun's Crossing. I can't look anywhere out here without seeing proof of the damage. More people are fighting. Half a dozen kingdoms are already gone. No one looks at us as we get ready to leave.

"Didn't think you'd leave without me, did you?" Kash saunters up to the carriages with a small leather bag over one shoulder.

Kieran raises his eyebrows. "Are you coming to Dun's Crossing with us?"

"Course I am." He slings an arm around my shoulders. "I still have a lifetime to make up with my girl. I'll get it in time, since I can't get it any other way."

Tension ripples through the group. Kash has been mentioning what Kieran owes him more and more often. I still think it's a joke, but every time it comes up, I believe that a little less.

"Mind if I ride with you?" he asks me.

I wish intensely that Mother and King Gavin had had another child, but Finn, Ingrid, and I have a four-seat carriage to ourselves. So I just nod.

We could throw him in the dungeon, too, Ingrid offers.

With a small smile, I climb into the carriage. Finn is already inside, staring out the window with that flat expression of his I've never figured out how to read. I look out the window with him, and my chest aches. The green and gray striped Snowcrest tents are already gone. Hollis is headed home, a two-week journey from where I'm headed.

I stuff my hand into the small purse tied at my waist and cup the note I stashed there earlier. There's no chance for us. I'm not stupid. Kieran's plan isn't going to work, and our diplomatic relations with Snowcrest are probably damaged forever. But as Kash slides into the carriage next to me and asks for yet another round of stories, I run my thumb over the words inscribed on the tiny page. He believes. And if he believes, I can find a way to believe, too.

THE TRIP HOME IS UNEVENTFUL, AND SO IS THE WEEK THAT FOLLOWS. A somber cloud hangs over the whole castle, like even the staff and the nobles who didn't come can feel the ripples of what happened in Escuro. Kieran writes letter after letter, trying to patch back together a relationship with any of the kingdoms that had been present. He won't tell anyone exactly how it's going, but judging by the increasingly dark bags under his eyes at dinner every night, not well. Altair is grumpy for the first few days back as well, his screams echoing through the halls. He didn't take to the journey back, and the having to settle into his new home isn't helping. I barely see Raven.

Honestly, I barely see anyone other than Ingrid and Kash. Finn is up to whatever he's usually doing in the village around the castle, only appearing when his presence is demanded. The rest of the nobles avoid me. Kieran keeps saying he's going to make a formal proclamation that I'm not being removed from the line of succession—he doesn't have to report a non-change; he just believes it will change people's opinions—but he hasn't had the time. Ingrid spends as much time as she can with me, trying to distract me with new games she's come up with and threats to jail King Andri, but she's got so much going on. She offers to give up some of the seemingly thousand skills she's learning to be with me more. I refuse. She's got the life I dreamt for myself back in that tent where everything changed, and I won't take it from her.

That leaves me with Kash as company. He likes to walk through the castle with me while I point out places where different things happened. And to eat every meal together. And to spend almost every second that I'm not asleep by my side—making up for lost time, always. By the second day, I'm making up excuses to sit in my room alone instead.

In my room, I pen letter after letter to Eva. Long, flowery apologies. Descriptions of the birds here. Short, simple apologies. Rambling screeds about nothing. Every single time I sign my name at the bottom, I look back over the letter before immediately tossing it into the fire. Where would I send it? What little court gossip Ingrid is willing to dredge up for me has no indication of whether Eva's returned or remains missing. And there's nothing I can say to fix this, not with Hollis's note tucked into my nightstand.

I don't write Hollis. Opening that door is too painful.

Days drip past. I try to learn more dances, to pick up other hobbies, but none of them hold my attention. I spend hours huddled in a cloak in the pubs in town, watching the crowd for any potential husbands and nursing a drink. Every man I see falls short of Hollis. This one has dark hair, but it doesn't have his thickness or luster. That one his confident way of walking into a room without any of the brains or prowess to back it up. One after the next, viable suitors fail. I want my mate. Not a pale replacement.

I have the blood-soaked dream every single night. Every time, I expect it to horrify me less. Every time, I wake up soaked in sweat and panting.

The one thing I don't do is visit Mother, who's been returned to the dungeon once more. I don't want to hear what else she thinks about this disaster. I don't think I could survive it.

But as time oozes from one minute, one hour, one day into the next, I start to wonder if I can survive this. If I can live the rest of my life trying to fill a hole I know the person who made it wants filled as much as I do. Two weeks away, the other half of my heart beats. Everything sours without it.

One day, as I'm writing my hundredth letter to Eva, Kieran reaches out to me through the mind-link. *I need to talk to you about something." Meet me in my office as soon as you can.'*

There's no panic or urgency in his voice. Nothing has happened. But "as soon as you can" still sounds like the first new thing in my world since arriving home. I toss the half-finished draft into the fire and hurry to his office.

Inside, Kieran sits at a desk covered in papers. There's no sign Raven's been using the workspace next to him. He smiles tiredly as I walk in and gestures to a second chair.

"I'm telling you this because I think you deserve to know," he says.

"All right." I sit. "Is everyone okay?"

He glances at the piles of papers then shakes his head. "As much as they were. A week has passed, and it's time to begin making moves to rectify our political position."

I nod, hope starting to fill my chest. He wants me to do something, go somewhere—maybe even Snowcrest!

"A diplomatic mission to Kar Castle leaves tomorrow morning," Kieran says.

I grin. "I can be packed. I can't—"

"You can't go," he says.

My stomach drops. "You're joking, right?"

He shakes his head. I study his face, and there's not a flicker of humor. Just more and more lines. It's hard to believe he's only a few years older than me anymore.

"You can't do this," I say. "He's—I'm—"

"You're the people at the heart of this conflict. Reintroducing you two is more likely to fan the flames than cool them."

My mark aches. "I need him. You wouldn't let anyone force you away from Raven."

A pained expression flickers across his face. "This is the smartest choice for the kingdom. As royalty, we're responsible for more than just our own wants."

Does he think I don't know that? Mother drilled everyone else's needs—wants—*whims* into my head above my own. But I can't live like this. Not when I know there's a chance.

"Kieran, please," I whisper.

He clenches his jaw and remains silent. His decision is already made.

Fine. I bolt up from my chair and storm out. Kieran's decision is made, and so is mine.

RESOLUTE

Candace

WHEN THE SUN RISES THE NEXT MORNING, IT FINDS ME CROUCHING IN
the stables, sandwiched between one of Finn's favorite stallions and
Ingrid. It lights the wild grin that's barely left her face since I barged
into her drawing practice yesterday and declared Kieran didn't
control me. She immediately bounced out of her seat, hugged me, and
said she'd been waiting her whole life for me to start breaking rules. I
don't know if I believe her, but she's thrown herself into this scheme
with a gusto I didn't know even she held for scheming.

"Okay," she whispers like we're not in the stall with the mare
because it's least likely to spook. "Time for the final stage. Are you
ready?"

I nod sharply. The time for wondering, for questioning my decisions, is over. We've got one very narrow window, or this all falls
apart.

"Spectacular." Ingrid's grin widens. "Let's move."

I grab the small bag of clothes and supplies I wasn't able to sneak
into Ingrid's full trunk and creep out of the stall with her on my heels.

Up in the castle right now, Kieran is probably checking on the pile of pillows "sleeping" in my bed to ensure I'm not trying pretty much this.

No, I'm kidding myself. Ingrid insisted on setting up the pillows, but no one is going to think for a second that I would disobey Kieran's direct order. But I'm tired of hunting for myself while everyone else keeps dictating who that is, what it means, what I can and can't do. If I ever want to find a life for myself, one that makes me happy, I need to stop listening.

So Ingrid and I pause against the wall of the last horse stall and wait for the creak of the carriage house door. Emerie is on duty this morning, and apparently, he never latches doors behind him. Ingrid knows more about the inner workings of our castle than I think I ever have, and I'm happy to rely on her expertise now.

Creeeeak.

I grin. A few soft footsteps on hay, and he's gone. We dart into the carriage house attached to the stable.

Ingrid groans. "How are we supposed to know which one he's going to take?"

I look at the dozen carriages lined up, sniff the air, then point. "That one."

She turns to me with wide eyes. "What?"

I scurry over to it, conscious of how little time we have. "You, Kieran, Taner, and Finn, right?"

"And Kash." She rolls her eyes. "Apparently, he's not letting Kieran out of his sight until they come to an agreement."

My stomach starts to drop, but I remind myself that's a problem for later. Someone starts whistling faintly. The grooms could come back any second.

"This carriage sits six comfortably so it's perfect for a long trip for four or five. Padded walls to keep out Snowcrest's weather. And"—I sniff the air again—"you smell that?"

Ingrid shakes her head.

"Neatsfoot oil." I smile. "Someone's already started setting up for horses."

She shakes her head in disbelief. "I trust you. Let's finish this."

Together, we squeeze me into the drop compartment in the floor for valuables, which Ingrid offered to fill herself. It's a tight fit, but the ride should be fairly comfortable, and Ingrid swears she'll be able to sneak me food until I can reveal myself. I take a deep breath before she closes the lid over me.

I'm making the right choice for me. Everything else will follow.

FOUR DAYS INTO THE JOURNEY, WHEN TURNING AROUND TO SEND ME back would add a whole week to Kieran's timeline, I crawl out and reveal myself. Part of me expects Kieran to start yelling like Father used to. Instead, he just takes a deep breath, closes his eyes for a minute, and then chuckles tiredly.

"I'd have done the same thing," he says. "But I still wish you hadn't."

"I'm glad you understand why I had to." I squish myself onto the bench next to him.

The rest of the trip passes uneventfully. Two full weeks of trundling over countryside, through forests, and up into the imposing mountain range I've seen on the horizon my whole life. The higher we climb, the fewer signs we can see of spring. Snow still clings to dark peaks, and everyone has to huddle close or pull extra layers out of their bags. Ingrid and I share a large blanket. Finn tries to refuse any additional layers at all, but when Kieran catches him shivering and starting to turn blue, he's forced into a few extra tunics. Kash offers to help keep me warm, and I almost refuse, but he radiates more heat than a fireplace. His arm around my shoulder is an uncomplicated boon for the first time since meeting him. My breath sparkles in the air in front of me, which makes Ingrid laugh and create bigger clouds, but I can only think about the note in my purse and the fact that I still haven't heard anything about Eva. The higher we climb, the closer I get to the reason I've thrown caution to the wind for the first time in my life. A few environmental changes barely catch my notice.

"Coming up!" the driver on the front of the carriage calls.

Ingrid presses her face to the window. I try to look and almost end up tumbling into Taner's lap. But finally, the carriage pulls to a stop, and someone opens the door for us to exit.

According to protocol, Kieran exits first, with Taner right on his heels. Then, Finn and Ingrid, since they're the only actual heirs. Last of all, Kash and I step out, and I pull my hood over my head to hide myself as much as I can.

Only years of good breeding keep my jaw from dropping as I look up into the sky at Kar Castle. Nestled between two mountains and made of the same stone, it looks more like another peak than something people actually built. Pointed, near-black towers jab up at perfect angles, dusted with their own powdery coating of snow. Unless there's much more of the castle behind the front, it's much narrower than our castle, but it's easily the tallest building I've ever seen, scraping the very sky.

Ingrid grabs my hand. *'Good luck.'*

'I think I'm going to need it,' I reply.

She squeezes my hand, a wordless promise that she's on my side no matter what happens. The deep green double doors swing open. My heart skips a beat. I'm about to see Hollis for the first time in weeks.

One person steps out. I squint, trying to make out details through the glare off the snow. Was he allowed to greet us by himself? That's very nontraditional.

The approaching figure picks their head up, and I see red hair atop far too slim a body to be King Andri. A tiny frown creases Kieran's brow. Something is wrong.

"Ah!" The figure bows. "Allow me to introduce myself—I am Lord Gunnar Ahlm—and deliver Alpha King Andri's apologies. He would have loved to greet you in person, but he simply didn't have the time."

'Don't,' Kieran warns all of us. *'King Andri is angry, and he has a right to be. We'll survive a little insult.'*

I don't know which of us he's warning. But I know sending someone in his stead, and not even his Beta or son, is one of the simplest, most cutting slights King Andri could've delivered before we even walk through his front door.

"It is a pleasure to meet you, Lord Gunnar." Kieran bows deeply, and we all follow suit. "I understand the pressures on an Alpha's time better than anyone, so no apologies are needed. Does our host know when he might be able to fit a conversation into his schedule?"

Lord Gunnar smiles tightly. "Not that I am aware of."

The flat refusal hangs dead in the icy air. There's no open, nothing to try to talk around or through. King Andri isn't just angry, he's furious. Something burns in my gut. I should've stood my ground, back in Escuro. He wouldn't be this upset if I had.

I think.

No. I'm listening to myself now.

"One moment." Lord Gunnar starts pointing to us one by one. "It appears you made an error in your letter. You said five guests, but I count six."

"There was a slight change of plans," Kieran says. "Allow me to introduce—"

I straighten, and my hood falls back. "Candace. I believe we've met."

Lord Gunnar looks like he just bit into a lemon. "Hm. Yes. The first five of you can follow me. Candace"—he says my name like it hurts him to do so—"please speak with Helga, our housekeeper, and she'll see what we can arrange for you quickly."

I curtsy. "Thank you, Lord Gunnar."

My manners seem to irritate him more. That's one thing all of Mother's lessons were good for.

'Sorry,' Ingrid says.

'Don't be.' I smile. '*Without you, I wouldn't have even gotten this far.*'

She leaves with everyone else, and I step into the soaring entryway of the castle. A broad, sour-looking woman looks me up and down.

"Follow me." She turns and marches to the left, away from the sweeping staircase everyone else ascended.

Up a much smaller, switch-backed stair, the woman I assume is Helga deposits me in front of a simple wooden door, grunts something about my bag being up shortly, and leaves before I can thank her. I push open the door and take in my room.

A single room, with a comfortable enough looking bed. No fire flickers in the grate, and I rub my arms for warmth. It's a far cry from anything I have at home, but it outdoes anything Raven ever had. And I'm not here for the room. I'm here to make things right.

Someone knocks on my door.

BREATH OF FRESH AIR

Hollis

"Come in?" Candace calls hesitantly through the door of one of the lesser guest rooms.

I breathe in a sharp breath. I can smell her even through the door, blackberries and sunshine. Knocking—rather than just tearing down the door like I wanted to the second Lord Gunnar told Father about the additional guest in the Dun's Crossing party—was almost impossible. Now that I'm here, opening the door almost seems harder. Three weeks apart. The longest three weeks of my fucking life. And now she's just on the other side of a heavy wooden door, close enough that I can hear her moving on the other side. It's too good to be true. Especially after weeks of rotating between training our troops and searching high and low for Eva. I've barely been sleeping or eating.

My hand shakes with anticipation as I open the door.

Candace turns. Mid-morning sunset illuminates in her long, corn-silk hair, highlighting the curve of her neck as she swallows heavily.

She's wearing a simple traveling dress, plain brown fabric with little ornamentation, but it looks like royal robes to me. The high waist pushes up her breasts just enough to make my mouth water. Exhaustion leaves dark smudges under her eyes. Maybe she missed me as much as I missed her, like someone cut my fucking arm off and expected me to keep going like normal.

Fuck it. I've waited long enough.

I cross the room in three steps, wrap my arms around her, and pull her into a kiss. Her taste explodes through my mouth, delicate and sweet. I run my tongue over her full lower lip, fist my hands in the wool of her dress. She bends against me like a branch in the wind. A low groan rumbles in my throat, and I clutch her closer.

'Too long,' I think through the mind-link we don't yet share. 'Too long, and never again.'

She braces her hands against the thick velvet on my chest. I gasp in a breath between her lips rather than get any farther away from her. For the first time in Goddess only knows how long, my mark doesn't hurt. If I only think about her, I can pretend nothing does.

Candace shoves me back. I could hold on if I wanted to, keep her crushed against me, but I take a step back. Agony rips through my mark, but I step back.

She looks at me, her lips swollen, her chest rising and falling faster than before. I swallow hard and fold my hands behind my back so I don't grab her again.

"The door is open," she says.

I conjure another living icicle and creak it shut, then smile. "Better?"

She chews on her lower lip. "I got your note. But—"

"Don't say but." I step closer, still not grabbing, but just to feel her warmth in front of me.

She doesn't back up, and her gaze drops to the slightly undone neck of my tunic. "But I haven't heard anything about Eva, and I'm here for her."

My gut sinks. "Just her."

Candace's hazel eyes shine when she pulls them back to my face. Then, she reaches into the bodice of her dress and pulls out Mother's necklace, pinned where no one can see it. "Maybe not just her."

A slow grin spreads across my face.

"But that night…." She takes a deep breath. "It was supposed to be our last time together. Closure, so I could live a life without you."

I remember the look in her eyes when she told me where she'd be and shake my head. "I don't believe that."

Her eyebrows shoot up. "It was. That was my deal with myself."

"I keep making those same deals." I cup her face. "I kept following you and Kash around the camp because I told Eva I would be your bodyguard until we figured out that your father could be trusted. Nothing more. And the first fucking night, I almost asked you to the equinox ball in front of your whole family." I smile ruefully. "There's no resisting what we have when we're together."

Candace crosses her arms. "I need to see Eva. Fix things with her. Then… then we can talk."

After the weeks I've had, that feels like a confession of love on bended knee.

I sit in the one chair in front of her fireplace. It wheezes under my weight, and I make a mental note to talk to Helga about fixing up the furniture in the lesser guest wing one of these days. Candace perches on the edge of her bed.

"I'm not sure where Eva is," I admit. "We've been searching, but we've only heard rumors. And she was the best one for figuring out what to make of those."

Candace's face falls.

I nod and rub my hands on my pants. "We've got teams searching everywhere, but our biggest clue actually came from her father."

"Lord Soren," Candace says numbly. "Where is he?"

I grimace at the memory of our return home. Soren greeted the caravan at the gate, redder than Father with rage. His bellowing was hard to follow, threading together fights from their childhood between him and Father with ancient slights between our families and this latest issue, but one thing was very clear: someone had warned him. And given that Father hadn't allowed a single person in our group to rest long enough to pen a letter, much less send one, there was only one way that could've happened. Eva had returned home and told him everything.

Of course, when I told Father I was pretty sure Eva had beaten us home enough to tell Soren everything, he rejected the idea immediately. Eva had, at maximum, an hour's head start on us, and we'd left with one fewer carriage than we'd arrived in—the one I had destroyed the night of the Haze. The one she'd used kicked out of had been patched up. She couldn't have run all the way back to Snowcrest faster than the carriages. She would've tired out too quickly. But Father hasn't been in the mood to listen to anyone lately, so I'm ignoring him. The fact that she couldn't have beaten us back on foot doesn't mean I'm wrong, it just means she had help.

And I have no fucking idea who from.

"He's back on Skadi Peak," I say. "He left the day we got home, after he screamed at Father and me on the front steps."

"Can we visit?" Candace stands. "I want to talk to him, see if he knows where Eva is."

"I tried that last week." I sigh. "Skadi lands are now completely protected by their personal guard. No one is allowed without direct invitation from Soren himself."

"So Eva is there." Relief washes over her face. "Thank the Goddess."

"It's better than living off the land." I study Candace, trying to figure out why this is such good news to her. "But we still can't reach her."

"Yet." Candace nods resolutely. "But I'll find a way."

"We'll find a way." I stand with her.

She looks at me then asks quietly, "Why do you want to talk to Eva?"

"To explain," I answer immediately. "I can make her understand." In the weeks of loneliness, I've gotten more and more sure of that.

Eva is reasonable. She was just… shocked. And now, Soren's keeping her trapped so she can't actually start to recover. I know Eva. She doesn't sulk like this.

Candace shakes her head. "I hope so. I want to fix things with her. But I also just want to apologize. She deserves that, whether she accepts it or not."

"Sure." I smile. "Apologies, explanations, all of it. Together, we can find a way."

She looks at me a little strangely. "And you're not just doing this because I mentioned her?"

The fragile scaffolding keeping me from completely falling apart shudders. If I think about Eva for too long, it starts to crumble. I'm not used to this… eating away at me. Emotions are supposed to appear and then die when I push them away. They're not supposed to take up residence in my gut and gnaw every time I crack open the door. If I stay focused on the next step, and the next, I can keep going. If not—

"No," I find myself admitting. "I miss her."

Candace finally closes the distance between us and embraces me. She just lays her head on my chest and stays there. Like opening the door when I knew she was on the other side, I struggle to lift my arms and hug her back. It's too much all at once.

"Being away from you was awful," she admits to my shirt. "But I don't know how to have both. You and her. And I don't think either of us are willing to lose her."

Choosing Candace over Eva never even crossed my mind. I need them both. But maybe, just maybe, that's the answer. Maybe Eva needs us both too. The scaffolding stops shaking. I hold Candace, bury my nose in her hair, and take my first breath of fresh air in weeks.

"I'm not. But I can figure this out." I smile against her head. "If you'll let me, I'll find a way for you to get everything you want. You just have to agree."

Candace remains silent in my arms. Painful seconds tick away.

Can she hear my thundering heartbeat? I know I can do this, but offering it feels a little like peeling my skin off so she can see the vulnerable parts of me underneath. I'll turn the world upside down for her—and myself inside-out if she refuses.

"Okay," she says. "I'll let you try, at least. But we do this together."

"Together," I agree.

RISK-TAKING

Candace

"This is a bad idea." Ingrid crosses her arms and glares at her door, like Hollis is just outside of it.

He's not. He's in my room, waiting for me to come back after I told him his idea was a bad one and that I needed to get someone else's opinion first.

"Is it a bad idea because it's Hollis's or because it's a bad idea?" I ask.

"What difference does it make?" She rolls her eyes. "All of his ideas are bad. I can't believe I smuggled you all the way here, and you're reconciling with him."

"What did you think I was coming here for?"

"Eva," Ingrid says defensively. "Yourself? I don't know, I just got excited."

"Well, this is for me." I sigh. "Kash is my father, biologically. Getting him on our side might not be the worst idea."

Ingrid blows out a long breath that sends the hair in her face flying. "It sounds like you've already made your decision. But I don't trust either of them. I think you're better off working on Raven—"

"Who's at home with Altair." I shrug helplessly. "There's no one easy here. At least Kash wants to get on my good side."

Not that that had stopped him from continuing to make comments about some kind of deal with Kieran. At this point, he makes everyone uncomfortable. Kieran still believes he's earnest, just a little mercenary. Finn made a few comments on the journey here that make it very clear he thinks Kash is just part of Mother's latest scheme. I'm not sure.

So I guess I'm going to go talk to him and find out.

"Thank you," I say before Ingrid can keep arguing.

"Maybe someday you'll listen to me." She kisses me on the cheek to show she's not really upset, and I leave.

Back in my room, Hollis is thrilled, and he insists we immediately head out to find Kash. I have nothing else to do in this castle, so we leave. Hollis seems different here. Surer of himself, and he was already cocky in Escuro. He stands perfectly straight, snaps crisp salutes to the soldiers we pass in the halls, never misses a step as he leads me through his towering home. Maybe it's just that we're not hiding. We haven't really talked about what we are right now, but the whole castle knows we're mates. He doesn't grab my hand, kiss me, even stand particularly close, but he's not watching for every noise or movement anymore. It's easier. Like it was the few times Eva made the two of us talk, back at home before Anwen's wedding. I could get used to this.

If we can find Eva. If we can apologize. If we can have both. But it's easier to believe Hollis can make that true when he's so unflinching.

"There." I twist my head to the left, sniffing. Hot dirt and charcoal. Kash.

Hollis snorts. "That makes sense."

"Why?" I frown as he leads me through a narrow door.

Immediately, the air becomes hazy and humid. The carefully

bricked walls quickly dissolve into craggy, natural stone. I pick out other scents—birch, minerals—as we descend.

"This is one of the most popular parts of Kar Castle." Hollis pushes open a final half-door to reveal pools of steam water, sunk into the stone. "The sauna."

Kash waves a bouquet of branches at us from where he sits on one of the low benches along the wall, intensifying the birch smell. "My girl! And the boy that brought us all here. Hell of a place you've got."

"Glad you're enjoying it," Hollis says.

I pluck at the neck of my gown and silently thank the Goddess when a cloud of steam moves, revealing the towel wrapped securely around Kash's waist. It also reveals the plate of food next to him, which he happily takes a bite from as we approach.

"What brings you here?" Kash pats the bench on his other side, only offering space to me.

I take a deep breath and accept it. Hollis sheds his vest and remains standing. I wish I could take off a layer. The heat is already getting overwhelming.

"We wanted to talk to you," I say. "About… us."

"The three of us?" He raises an eyebrow.

"Us." Hollis gestures at me and then himself. "There were a lot of opinions the day the news broke, and we don't feel like we got yours."

"And I want it." The words feel less like a lie than I thought they would. Maybe it would just be nice to know one person doesn't think my feelings for Hollis are a mistake or a catastrophe.

"Looking for your old man's approval, huh?" Kash grins. "Well, I gotta admit, I don't have too many feelings. I don't think I understand the situation well enough."

Hollis nods. "For centuries, my family and Eva's—"

"The girl who revealed to everyone that we are mates," I interject.

"Right. We've been mated to each other when we're born close enough together, which Eva and I were." Hollis runs a hand through his hair. "So I grew up my whole life knowing who I'd wake up to after the Haze, but I didn't."

"And so did Eva," I add. "She's a close friend of mine, and I knew this would hurt her, so we decided… not to pursue the relationship."

Kash frowns. "Then how'd she find out? See a mark?"

"In effect." Hollis stares at the rocky floor.

"He's softening it." I bite my lip. "We didn't not pursue as much as we intended to, and she caught us. We made a terrible, selfish mistake that's caused a lot of problems, and we just want to fix them."

"I understand that." Kash nods slowly. "And now, you're…?"

I look at Hollis. Hollis looks at me. It's my answer to give.

"Trying to figure out if a relationship is possible."

Kash chuckles. "Always is. Just take my path."

A vision of Hollis and I, sprinting through the trees together, happy and free, expands in my mind. My chest aches with want. But that's just another selfish choice. And even if this works out, if the tower falls without crushing anyone beneath it, Hollis can't be all I am.

"I've got responsibilities I can't just abandon," Hollis says. "But you've got to admit, the consequences are a little steep for a stupid mistake."

"Oh, sure." Kash nods easily. "Royalty tends to do that, 'specially when there's tradition involved."

"So you think we should be together?" I ask. Hope blossoms, fragile but bright.

"The Goddess certainly does, and no one survives long after disagreeing with Her." He takes another bite of his food.

I frown. That's not a commitment. "If somebody else asked you about this, what would you say?"

"That I want whatever gives me the most time with you."

Hollis's frown matches mine. "And what do you think does that?"

"Frankly, kid, I doubt you do at all." Kash leans back against the wall. "Sorry."

"But you want a relationship with me." My mind refuses to accept his blank denial of the very idea of the conversation. "Doesn't that mean you want me to be happy?"

"Course I do." He slings a heavy, sweaty arm around my shoulders. The birch branches he's holding dampen my gown. "But is he really what's gonna make you happy? I've gone my whole life without a mate, and the only thing missing from my life was you."

Hollis clenches his jaw and wipes his forehead. He's getting frustrated. So am I.

"There are already too many people in my life with their own ideas about what's best for me." I twist to meet Kash's gaze. "I'm asking you to be different. To stand up for me like King Gavin never would've."

"Don't bring that piece of shit up to me like that." The potent, burning rage that flashes through his eyes is as readable as words on a page from this distance.

Old instincts snap on like magic. I need to defuse his anger before it rages out of control.

"I'm sorry," I say. "I know you're nothing like him. He's just the only comparison I have for fathers."

"Mine isn't exactly lining up to attend our wedding either," Hollis offers.

I shake my head at him minutely. He's only going to complicate this situation, and I feel like I'm finally about to discover why Kash is here, the answer I've been looking for all along.

Kash sighs. "I know you'd never try to hurt me, baby. Don't think I'm mad at you."

"I don't." I lean against him despite the heat. "You're mad for me, right? Because he separated us?"

Kash's laugh is more air than sound. "I'm mad for a lot of reasons, and you're certainly one of them."

Not just me. "Did you really love my mother?"

"Rowena? I'd sooner love a snake that just bit me," he replies.

I chew on my lip to hide a frown. "You know so much about me, but I feel like I still don't know anything about you, and I want to. I don't even know why else you'd be angry at King Gavin."

Kash kisses me on the top of the head, lingering even longer than he usually does. For once, it feels more like buying time than trying to force me into something.

"Let's just say Gavin took a lot from me. A lot I can't ever get back."

Hollis and I exchange a look. There are pieces missing still, but for the first time, I really believe Kash. At the very least, he's not *just* here because Mother asked him to be.

"Then this is your chance to get back at him from beyond the grave." Hollis takes a step forward. "Build accepting our relationship into your deal with King Kieran, and Gavin will roll in his grave."

Kash snorts and releases me. "You've got balls. But I've already done all I can on that front. This is what you want?"

I nod. It's the first step to having enough options that I can figure it out, at least.

"All right. Then when it's just the three of us, I'm your biggest fan. But I can't risk my position here for a relationship that by your own telling's already been on and off a dozen times." He whacks the birch branches against his bare chest and closes his eyes.

Conversation over.

Just like our chances.

SNOWBALL FIGHT

Hollis

MY FIRST PLAN DIDN'T WORK OUT. HELL, I HAVEN'T SEEN PAW NOR TAIL of Kash since that disastrous conversation with him. I have no idea why it went to shit. It really seemed like we were onto something, like Candace was about to unearth some big secret... and then he just shut down.

I roll out my shoulders. I'm not dwelling on old plans today. Not when I've got a new one to try.

Thank the Goddess I do. Candace hasn't come to see me since Kash turned us down, and it's making me a little itchy.

I crack my knuckles then rap on her plain, wooden door. She opens it, raises one golden eyebrow.

My breath catches. Fuck, I'm so glad she's here. Even if she says she's mostly here for Eva, even if we can't figure this out and she leaves again, just having her here is like taking a physical weight off my chest. Being able to knock on her door means both of us stand a shot of getting out of this.

"I have a new plan," I say.

Candace smiles tiredly. "Is it that you're going to get Kieran a meeting with your father?"

I grimace. "He asked if I still considered myself prince of Snow-crest when I mentioned it, or if I'd given my loyalty fully over to you."

"That sounds like King Andri." Candace glances behind her, worry in her hazel eyes. "I feel like I'm making everything worse."

"No." I grab her hand with both of mine. "Not for me, at least."

She studies me for a long, quiet moment. Her lips flicker between a smile and a frown.

"What's your idea?"

I grin. "We go for a run."

MY BREATH PUFFS IN ICY CLOUDS, AND SNOW CRUNCHES UNDER MY paws as I wait in the courtyard for Candace. The spring thaw we experienced in Escuro won't reach up into our mountains until June or July, but my thick, dark red fur keeps me more than warm enough. No, I'm just antsy because she wanted to change by herself. She didn't want me to see her.

But she's coming. And we're going to find something

The Skadi manor is highly protected, and so much has changed, but I still think I know Eva. She won't be able to stay locked up in there. Not after life in the palace and the surrounding town. She needs her freedom. So Candace and I are going to search the town and the palace grounds. If she needed air, a chance to breathe, Eva would come here. She's never really lived anywhere else.

Candace woofs beyond me, and I twist around. She circles the corner of the stable with a satchel, likely carrying clothes, over one shoulder. Her gray fur looks like a smudge of shadow against the bright, white snow.

Eva used to say I look like a drop of blood.

I pad over to her, wish we had the mind-link, and nudge her shoulder. She gestures with her head toward the gate. I shake mine.

No. We start on the palace grounds, by the back of the castle where there aren't walls so much as cliffs so craggy that it's worthless for any enemy to try to advance from that side. With a deep breath, I take off.

Snow flies. Candace lopes alongside me, her muscles shifting and lengthening under her thinner coat. The brilliant, midday sun highlights additional colors in her fur—hints of brown, white, even silver. Like her new eyes, there's so much to see below the surface. She puts her nose to the air, wet black skin twitching. Every breath that fills my lungs only smells like her. Like summer in the middle of late winter. Like the fresh air and warmth I've been waiting for.

I lead her around the castle, heading for the crags Eva and I have climbed so often. Escaping, sneaking back in. The towers loom over us. Is Father watching? What about her family? The hairs on the back of my neck prickle.

Candace is still sniffing, but she hasn't taken off in a new direction. She doesn't smell anything. Eva's not here now, or she covered her tracks well enough that even Candace can't find them.

Fuck it. I offer one short, sharp bark of warning, then wheel in a new direction. The grounds stretch the farthest to the east, and there's a less patrolled gate there. It's just as reasonable a place to start —and as soon as we round the first peak, we'll be out of sight of the castle.

Candace turns with me easily. My mouth falls open, and my tongue lolls out of my mouth. We don't even need the mind-link to communicate.

This path leads us beside the icy training yard we only use during the short summer months, and the one target I cleared off to be able to shoot to clear my mind before she arrived. I watch her glance at it then at me. Yet another thing I don't have to explain. My heart thuds out of time, too fast and too slow at once.

Open the east gate, I call through the mind-link to the soldiers that should be on guard there at this time.

They do as they're told, and metal whines in the distance. Candace pricks an ear then picks up speed. Fuck. I can't explain to her that's just my orders being followed. She doesn't even know there's a gate over here.

Before I can think twice, I launch myself at her. She's faster than I expected, but the snow slows her a little, so I catch her in the ribs. We roll, tumble over each other, and land in a heap. I shift back into human and meet her massive, wolfish gaze.

"The gate out," I say. "I asked for it to be opened."

She blinks slowly. Her gaze trails from my face down to my bare chest, and I shiver. Not from the cold.

Then, she flashes into human form, scoops up a handful of snow, and smashes it against my face. The feeling of her bare skin against mine makes me too slow to react. She shifts back into a wolf before I've even wiped the snow from my cheek and bolts toward the noise.

Oh, she's going to pay for that.

Fur explodes from my skin, and I hit the ground running. She should've known better than to start a snowball fight with someone who grew up here. As I run, I let ice sparkle over my tongue, then scoop a mouthful of snow up off the ground. The eastern gate comes into view, already open. Candace barrels through it without a glance back, but I close my lips around my weapon anyway.

Outside the castle walls, she slows slightly, glances back at me. Mistake. I whip my head back, then forward, spitting the now-icy snowball at her. She yelps as it shatters against her coat, then snarls and lowers her chest to the ground.

She wants to play.

I mimic the gesture, my chest bright and warm despite the cold. And I scoop up another mouthful of snow.

She sprints away, her high whine informing me she thinks it's unfair that I can throw snowballs as a wolf, too. I just hurl it at her and huff a canine laugh. I could have the snowballs throw themselves if I really wanted to win. But in the spirit of fairness, I chase her toward a small cluster of conifers I know lays not far outside the walls, pelting her with snow the whole time. She dodges, weaves, tries to circle behind me and trip me up. I dance over her efforts with a wide grin. She's not used to a wolf as big as I am or the uneven terrain beneath the ice.

I leap into the trees and begin sprinting side-to-side through them, an old trick Father taught me for agility.

Candace takes the cover for the opportunity it is. Her high, clear laugh echoes off the frozen trees, and a snowball crashes into my side, knocking me off rhythm. I slam into the next tree. She only laughs harder.

I shift. "Oh, that's how you want to play it?"

With a wave of my hands, I conjure a snowball the size of a small boulder and heft it. Where is she? I scan the trees for any movement.

There! A bare heel disappearing behind a trunk, part way to becoming a paw again. Which means she'll come out—

Candace barks as my snowball catches her in the head and shoulders. I shift back and bolt toward her. I'm used to fighting like this with Eva, who has her own powers to counter me with. Did I hit Candace too hard? Is she okay?

I stop next to her prone body. Her back leg twitches, slams into the trunk of a nearby tree.

A branch full of snow lands on top of me, and her eyes pop open, sparkling with amusement. I shake off, then shift, hoping she'll get this message as much as she did the others.

Candace hesitates, then becomes human underneath me. I press a kiss to her lips before she can change her mind. She's freezing, obviously not suited for the weather, so I cover her with my body. Or maybe that's just to feel her skin all over mine. She arches up into me all the same.

Finally, I pull back to suck in a breath.

"We should keep searching for Eva." She smiles ruefully.

I stare down into her eyes, at her pink cheeks and swollen lips. We should keep searching for Eva. We will.

But for the first time since Eva ran away from us, and maybe longer than that, I think I can see a future I want to live through.

PAYING ATTENTION

Candace

"King Andri has refused my latest meeting request," Kieran says.

Taner groans. Finn rolls his eyes. Ingrid cracks her knuckles and glares at the portrait of the king that hangs over the small sitting room they've been granted to use for their meetings.

I scratch a line through the bottom entry on our list of potential options, *Run into him on the way somewhere else and try to get a commitment while he's not paying much attention.*

"Did he refuse it, or did you not actually run into him?" Finn asks.

Kieran grits his teeth. "I didn't run into him long enough to have a conversation."

"That weasel." Ingrid shakes her head. "I bet he ran away from you on purpose."

"He had the grace not to actually run, at least."

Taner runs a hand through his hair. "All right, we need a new plan. Candace, anything?"

I perk up slightly. Kieran's Beta is asking for my opinion?

"Well—"

"Left on the list, I mean," he says.

Right. Of course. I search the sheet of paper I offered to take notes on when we started having these meetings a week ago. Suggestions meander this way and that, nowhere near a neat column. Even though I'm taking notes, other people keep adding things as they see fit. Kieran's scrawl crowds in around the top, Taner's at odd angles on the sides, even Ingrid's flowing script dots the page here and there. Finding anything takes several seconds of concentrated effort—and filtering out a few suggestions I've struck off without attempting because I know they're going to fail. Whoever put *Lock him in a room and just start having a meeting* needs to have their quill removed.

"Um…no," I say. "That's everything we've come up with so far."

Kieran blows out a long breath. "New plans, anybody? Go."

"Have we tried sending a formal letter requesting a meeting?" Taner asks.

"Before we arrived and after," Kieran says. "What about requesting through an intermediary?"

I scan the list. "We've tried using that lord who greeted us and a few other nobles to no avail."

Taner rubs his hands over the velvet of his armchair. "You know, I've actually started making a couple friends."

Kieran's eyebrows fly up. "You have?"

He nods. "If you let them talk about their human-form hunting thing, they're a lot friendlier. This one guy, Zain, has been most open to talking."

Zain is Hollis's Beta—and King Andri hates that fact. Apparently, Betas are sworn to their potential Alphas young in Snowcrest, and Zain comes from a family King Andri wanted an alliance with, but he thinks Zain grew up into someone who's going to be useless to Hollis, once he takes the throne.

"Someone who's actually open to our cause is a miracle from the Goddess Herself." Kieran rubs his face tiredly. "All the other intermediaries claimed they asked, but I wouldn't be surprised if King Andri didn't hear from a single one of them."

"Can we give him a message to pass? Something really specific?" Ingrid frowns. "Based on what I've seen of Zain, he's not the most responsible wolf in the castle."

"Clever." Kieran pulls out another piece of paper and starts writing. "Taner, do you think he'll go for that?"

I open my mouth to warn them, and King Andri's painted gaze lands heavily on my shoulders. He might not like Zain, but he hates me.

"He definitely will." Taner grins. "I think this stands a real chance."

I close my mouth again. Taner, Kieran, even Ingrid… they have heads for politics. There's a reason I'm mostly here to take notes. And that reason is that I was never supposed to be here in the first place.

Kieran looks up. "Is there anything we can offer him to secure the meeting?"

"You've tried apologizing in advance and offering a new alliance with Dun's Crossing, terms to be negotiated in the meeting," I rattle off.

"What about some kind of gift?" Taner suggests.

"No way." Ingrid crosses her arms. "We're already offering too much."

"Not the way he sees it."

King Andri's portrait glares down at me, a reminder of the one thing he'd truly love—my removal from his castle. And his future. If the endless stream of magicians and academics into the palace is anything to go by, he hasn't given up the hope that he can break the mate bond between Hollis and me. Just thinking about it makes my mark ache. Hollis has shown up at my room every other day with some new plan to try to convince everyone we can be together without destroying the world, and none of them have worked yet, but just knowing he's going to be there… it's sort of like a new hobby. An interim one, to bridge the gap between Princess Candace and who I might turn into. I don't want to lose that.

Maybe I don't have to. Hollis and I made it into town the other day, and it's really not far from the castle. If Kieran paid for my accommodation in an inn there, that might go some way toward easing the tension. Maybe mine and Kash's. He's still enjoying the palace far more than he has any right to.

"Perfect." Kieran scribbles a few more words. "The land north of the Sapphire River has been contested for too long."

Ceding land before they even talk is kind—King Gavin overran it before he made the initial alliance with Snowcrest—but King Andri will see that as weakness. He'll know he can ask for almost anything and get it.

I frown. "Maybe—"

Kieran dots an emphatic period onto his note. "Write down whatever you're thinking, and we'll try it if we need to come up with another idea."

I duck my head and write, *I leave,* on one of the few remaining spaces of bare paper. It's not like they can make King Andri any angrier. Maybe next time.

Kieran and Taner leave to give the note and instructions to Zain. Ingrid kisses me on the forehead and says she's off to hide from the palace tutor. I pack up my writing implements quietly.

"You know," Finn flicks ash off the table indolently, "I'm about ready to go home."

"You were ready to go home once the carriage left the stable." Finn has been sulking since we arrived. I've heard more than one comment about him not being the crown prince anymore.

He rolls his eyes. "Whatever. All I'm saying is, if you know how to end this faster, fucking saying it might help."

I blink. "What?"

"I don't care what you do or who you are. Live your life. Make your choices. But"—he shoves out of his chair—"nobody's ever going to know your ideas are worth trying if you never say them."

He leaves without another word. I sit, frozen, for several long seconds. That's the longest speech I've ever heard him give. Finn was… paying attention? To me? And enough to notice all the times I almost spoke up. Maybe he's seen me with Hollis and suspects I have additional insight. I stare at the door he left open. Or maybe he just wants to hear my opinion.

That feels impossible. But I believe everything he said about not caring what I do, and the rest didn't sound like, say, Ingrid trying to reach me via Finn. When I finally unfreeze, I write down a few more ideas I've had. There will be another one of these meetings, and I might like to be prepared.

THAT AFTERNOON, INSPIRED BY THE BEAUTIFUL-IF-TERRIFYING PAINTING of King Andri, I sit in front of an easel in the portrait gallery. The light slants through the high windows, casting exciting shadows on the ancient art that I want to capture. Some Alpha whose name I don't know stares down at me as I swirl my brush through what I'm hoping is the color of his eyes.

I lift the brush and compare the two. Mine is too blue… and I'm not really sure I should start with the eyes on a blank canvas, now that I think about it.

Footsteps echo behind me. I twist. Hollis's dark hair appears at the top of the stairs, followed by the rest of him.

"Helga said I'd find you here." He smiles. "Taking up painting?"

"Trying to." I push hair out of my face and look at the ancient patriarch again. Hollis has his nose. "I don't think it's going very well."

"I'm sure it's—" He circles around so he can see my completely blank canvas. "Well, it can't actually be bad yet. You haven't started."

I laugh and watch his face transform. This new, soft expression he seems to keep hidden just for when he makes me smile warms me like his scent. And it doesn't appear in any of the severe portraits lining this hall.

"Just be grateful I didn't decide to paint that one." I point at a particularly awkward painting of what looks like eight- or nine-year-old Hollis.

"I am." He rubs my shoulders gently. "I have a much better one in my quarters, if you'd like to see it."

My gaze drifts from his scrunched face to the next portrait over. King Andri and a beautiful woman, holding hands. She wears the necklace I keep pinned inside my bodice and smiles at King Andri. Luna Queen Lara.

Nobody is ever going to know...

"Your mother is beautiful," I say. "Do you miss her?"

BEFORE

Hollis

I TAKE A FULL STEP BACK FROM CANDACE BEFORE MY BRAIN CATCHES UP with my body. We were supposed to go try to get some of the staff on our side today—and if the idea appealed, maybe have a private lunch in the kitchen, without all the pressure of a formal meal. Talking about Mother is… not exactly the opposite but far from what I was hoping for.

I don't talk about Mother to anyone. A few days after the funeral, Eva asked me if I was sad, and I told her never to ask me that again. She hasn't broken that rule since. I have no map for conversations like this.

My mouth opens without a specific instruction. My chest puffs, and my brows furrow. I don't know what I'm going to say, but I know I'm going to regret it.

Candace holds up a hand, silencing me. "I understand. That was a bad idea."

She starts to turn back to her painting, but not before I watch disappointment flicker over her face. Pain aches through me—but not from my mark. Something deeper inside me hurts at the thought of disappointing her. I want—need–to prove I'm worth all the risks she took to be here.

Worth what we did to Eva.

I grab her wrist. She freezes.

"I—" can't finish my sentence. A thousand of Father's lectures echo through my head, one after the next. A bottle catches my eye, some alcohol she was probably using to thin paint. Can't be good for me. I snag the bottle and take a few swigs anyway. It sears down my throat like poison.

Candace watches me with worried eyes. The world dulls slightly, and I take a deep breath. Her scent enfolds me.

"I remember the day that was painted." I turn to the portrait, one of my favorites of Mother.

It's not an answer to her question, but it's something. She relaxes slightly in my grasp. I slide my fingers down to hold her hand without looking at her.

Mother and Father stare back at me from the canvas. She is still healthy, without even the shadows under her eyes that appeared in later paintings—all of which Father hid away in some attic. She's wearing my favorite dress of hers at the time, a deep plum frock that I liked because it was soft to bury my face in, and her hair curls tightly around her cheeks. Father is smaller than he is now, but not by much. I honestly think it's a trick of the painter because I remember him being huge when I was younger. But the artist did something in the brushstrokes around his shoulders, his eyes, to make him look like he matches Mother perfectly. Both proud royals, chins high, looking out over their people, but not dominating them. Just waiting for the next request they can fulfill to keep their kingdom happy. Father's heavy cloak blends slightly into the dark background, and the ghost of a smile turns up the corners of his lips. Mother bends outward from the canvas like she's waiting for me to start talking.

"Her royal portrait hangs in the throne room, but she never liked it." I smile at the memory. "Grandmother made her sit the day after her wedding, and she was already pregnant with me. She always claimed you could see the morning sickness on her face."

Candace joins me at the railing overlooking the far side of the gallery but doesn't say a word.

"This portrait was a present from Father, for the anniversary of their five years on the throne, and it was supposed to be just her." I glance at the bottle of alcohol again. The pit of my stomach burns, but maybe another swig wouldn't hurt.

Candace plucks it from my fingers and sets it back down on her easel, not out of reach of either of us. It's just a quiet concern. Fuck, that might actually make it easier to keep talking than the alcohol would've.

"She sat in the east tower library, her favorite one." I trail my fingers over the railing. "But after a few scheduling issues, the painter could only come on a day she'd promised to spend with me. So she sat me down before he arrived to explain the situation."

She smiles. "I'm sure you took that well."

"At five?" I snort. "Believe it or not, I liked being told *no* even less back then."

"Hard to imagine." She leans against my shoulder, warm and grounding.

"Long story short, I pitched a fit." I shake my head. "She finally told the painter she'd sit with me in the room, or not at all."

Candace giggles. "Don't tell me that's when you gained your taste for paint thinner."

"No, but I did eat a fistful of blue paint I've never seen come back out." I stare at the portrait. "You see how she's looking just a little to the left?"

She nods.

"She's watching me. I think." My eyes burn. "I spent the whole session trying to distract her, make her break, and that's all that made it into the final painting."

That, and her smile. It doesn't appear in any of her other paintings because that was the one she kept reserved for Father and me.

"But if it was just the two of you...how is King Andri in the portrait?"

"He dropped in for a visit just after her session started," I say, "and discovered me running around, trying to make a mess of everything."

Candace tenses up again. I know what she's thinking. There's a reason I was avoiding this part of the story, after all.

"He tried to bribe me away—horseback riding, going for a run, finally letting me hold a sword. But nothing worked because I'd been promised a day with Mother." I grip the banister tightly, glance at Candace out of the corner of my eye. "So he sat down next to her, offered the painter some ridiculous sum to add him to the canvas, and told me he wanted to see which of them I could distract more."

Her eyebrows raise. "Oh."

"What?" I don't know why I'm asking. She's surprised because the Father I knew before Mother died and after are two completely different men. Now, she's going to pity me for what I lost. Or think I should've been enough to keep him the way he was before.

Or, worst of all, assume he hasn't changed behind closed doors. The King Andri the public knew always was more severe.

"I guess I just never really considered that your father could've changed," she says quietly.

"That happens when you lose the love of your life," I snap.

She nods. "This might sound strange, but... do you miss him?"

"How could I? He's right upstairs." I cross my arms and stare at the floor instead of the portrait. This was a stupid idea, and now I feel like I'm going to puke.

"I just mean—" She sighs. "I don't know. For my parents, there is no before. I don't really have any kind memories of my fath—King Gavin or my mother."

Her soft, sad smile tears at something in my chest. Father and I aren't as close as we used to be, but I have these little pieces of proof that he loves me. That he can love me.

"I can't imagine what it's like to have that and lose it." She puts her hand over mine on the banister.

My eyes sting. Fuck, I'm actually tearing up. I haven't cried since...

maybe since before Mother died. When I told Eva not to ask me, suddenly everybody else stopped as well. And I didn't really want them to ask—she obviously did me a favor by spreading the word that they shouldn't—but it meant I haven't heard anything more than empty condolences from strangers for years. I try not to think about Mother or even Father when he had her.

"I miss them both," I admit.

Candace's smile in the corner of my eye aches. "I'm so sorry you lost them."

I scrub at my face. What am I doing? We're in public. I'm still the crown fucking prince. I can't go around breaking down in the middle of the castle, especially when the kingdom is in such a tense spot.

"You know, I have to go." I pull back from her touch, even though it hurts like hell.

She stares at me for a long moment, afternoon light making magic in her hazel eyes. It pulls out the hints of gold, of green. She looks like a kaleidoscope, shifting colors I could fall into and never stop watching.

Then, she dusts herself off and starts packing up the paints on her easel.

"What are you doing?" I ask.

She doesn't look up from her work. "If you're going, so am I."

I scrub at my eyes even harder.

UNAFRAID

Candace

heart pounding. If Finn didn't talk to me after the meeting, I would've let Hollis whisk me on whatever adventure he had planned for today. I never would've heard the story about his mother—and he wouldn't have told it. Judging by his occasional sniffle, just talking about her uncorked something inside him. Something I think needed to be uncorked a long time ago. My heart aches for the wistful smile he gave the portrait. I've got three parents, and there isn't a painting of any of them I'd look at like that. Maybe having a before is worse, in some ways. He knows exactly what he lost—who his parents could've been, if he were a little luckier.

Hollis opens a door and lets me into a small sitting room. I take one of the couches in front of the dead fireplace. He stirs it to life, hesitates, then takes the seat next to me instead of one of the others.

"Do you want to keep talking about her?" I take his hand.

"No. Yes." He shakes his head. "I'm… not sure."

I stroke the back of his hand with my thumb. "I'm here regardless."

He leans back against the couch. "Feels a little uneven now."

"Why?"

"I just unloaded all that shit onto you, and I don't think I've asked you how you even feel about Kash yet."

I blow out a long breath. "Honestly, I have no idea how I feel about Kash. It's still too new."

He laughs. "Then you sort of know how I'm doing."

"I have no idea how I feel about most things right now."

"Including me?" Hollis asks softly.

I glance at him out of the corner of my eye. His dark hair falls into his face, and his eyes are rimmed with red from the tears he refuses to cry. Vulnerable, not dangerous. My heart skips a beat.

"I know how I feel about you," I say slowly. "I'm just not sure what to do about it."

"I think I do." He almost sounds surprised at himself. "But we have to agree, and I don't think you will yet."

"Yet?" A smile tugs at my lips.

"Yet." He nods confidently. "But I'm happy to start trying to convince you."

I squeeze his hand. "Good luck."

Hollis captures my lips in a hungry kiss. His taste is even homier after a week within these walls, like it's something ingrained in him simply by growing up here. But no one else I've ever met from Snowcrest seems like they would taste quite as delicious. Quite as safe.

After a moment, I pull back. I have no idea where we are in the palace, but Hollis didn't lock the door, so we could be caught at any moment. He threads a hand through my hair and rolls us so I'm pinned to the couch.

With a chuckle, he kisses down the side of my face and along my jaw. I watch his eyes flicker closed. He drops a last, soft kiss on my lips, then drags his teeth down my neck to my pulse point. I hiss, and he bites down, sucking a mark into the skin.

"Hollis!" I gasp.

"What?" He looks up at me, green eyes half-lidded. "We have nothing to hide."

We have… nothing to hide. For the very first time since the Haze, it doesn't matter if anyone finds us. They already know.

Want courses through me like a rushing river on the heels of realization, and I start pulling at Hollis's clothes with a growl. He snaps to attention, shedding off his complicated layers. When our fingers tangle on his buttons, I start unfastening mine instead. The faster I can touch him, feel him fully, the better.

Once everything is gone, he crushes me back onto the couch, skin against skin. He pins my arms over my head and devours my neck. His cock presses against my thigh. His dark hair grazes over my skin in the wake of his mouth, soothing the bites and scrapes he leaves behind. I moan at a particularly sharp sting and arch up into him.

"Louder," he murmurs.

His hands leave mine and start roaming across my body. Tracing the curve of my hip, the bottom curve of my breasts. He continues down from my neck onto the tender skin there and sucks a nipple into his mouth.

Louder, it turns out, is an easy command to follow when you're not afraid of being caught. His name swirls in my mouth, stumbles out on another groan, and I feel his smile against my chest.

When he brings a hand up to tease my other nipple, I remember I can actually move my arms. One hand, I thread instantly into his hair and tug. The vibrations of his grumble ripple through me. The other, I slip down his back, nails out, scratching red lines I can't see. I need to mark him as much as he's marking me, however I have to. Each line of scratches pulls a sharp bite from him. Pain, pleasure, and the comfort of knowing we don't have to hide or alchemize into something far more potent. Moans pour from my lips heedlessly. Hollis squeezes my hip and slots one of his legs between mine.

I roll against the sweet pressure on instinct. Wetness smears over his skin—I'm dripping already. He moves with me, our bodies undulating like the rise and fall of a wave. My mouth finds his shoulder, and I bite down.

Another moan escapes me as I arch into his mouth, feeling an increase in friction. I squeeze his hips desperately, nails biting into skin. Hollis hisses and bites down nearly as hard.

His name passes my lips on a terse groan.

Hollis ducks his head lower, freeing his shoulder from my mouth, and sucks a mark into the thin skin over my hip bone. I thread a second hand into his hair and hold on tightly. Animal instinct consumes me. I am want, need, and nothing more.

He reaches between my legs, spreads them, and rubs his thumb over me lightly. The contrast between his earlier roughness makes me gasp. He barely strokes me, just enough to send shocks up my spine.

"Please," I whimper. "At least come here."

Hollis releases my hip and brings his face back up to mine. His breath splashes over my lips. I claim his mouth. *Want, need, take.*

Without warning, he thrusts two fingers into me. Euphoria careens through my limbs. I fight his hold on my leg to wrap it around him for more pressure, but he holds tight. I am his to do with as he pleases, and I'm going to know it as much as the rest of the world.

It's a welcome reminder. We've been apart for too long.

A third finger joins his first two, but he doesn't speed up or release my leg. I groan against his lips, begging wordlessly.

"You want me?" he asks against my lips.

I nod.

"Are you ready?"

My forehead knocks against his as I nod even harder. The pain barely registers. I was ready as soon as I realized we're free.

He releases my leg, and I fold it around him. His soft chuckle doesn't loosen my grip, but even knowing what comes next, I falter when he removes his fingers. I was so close.

His tip brushes over my skin briefly, hard and hot, and then he plunges into me.

"Hollis!" I yelp.

"Candace," he replies.

I lock my legs around his waist, holding him as close as I can for as long as I can. He stays for a long moment, his hips against my hips, just luxuriating in the fullness. The completeness.

Hollis pulls back, breaking my hold with very little effort. Later, I'll consider if I should train my legs more to be able to stop him next time. Now, every iota of my thoughts hangs on the long, slow slide of his cock. Is he going to turn the pace to molasses, torture me again?

I should've known better. Hollis missed me as much as I missed him. He slams into me with just as much force as before, then sets a bruising pace. I scrape my nails along his back with every thrust. A sheen of sweat glimmers on his body, sticking our skin together, but he doesn't slow. I lower my mouth to his neck and suck a deeper, more purple bruise than he left anywhere on me. Pleasure swirls, so intense my eyes start to water. Nothing to hide. Nothing to be afraid of. Just problems to face and conquer together.

"Candace," he gasps into my hair.

"Hollis," I groan.

His rhythm goes erratic. His fingers slip between us, teasing my sensitive bud. My breath scrapes out of my throat. Hollis pounds into me one last time, then stiffens. His climax sends me over the edge, shaking and moaning with reckless abandon.

Instead of pulling out, he lays his head on my chest, still sheathed inside me. I release my grasp on his hair and stroke it gently. I can't wait to parade around the castle with my new necklace of bruises— but I might want to hold him like this more.

SEE YOU NOW

Hollis

A few days later, I sit in Father's tapestry-covered office for
one of our weekly meetings, warming my hands over his fire.

"What are you smiling about?" he snaps. "Our southwestern
border has been attacked."

"By rogues." I try to swallow my grin, but it's impossible. It's been
impossible since my talk with Candace in the gallery and the evening
that followed. Since then, I've seen her almost every day, and at least
half the time, I don't even have to seek her out. She's actually coming
to find me, taking my hand, pulling me into hidden rooms for a
repeat performance. It finally feels like what I always expected
finding my mate would be.

"Is the bastard's father not a rogue?" Father huffs. "He could be
ordering them. Arranging the attacks."

I pull the map he was looking at closer to me and point at the
three pins. "There's a couple dozen miles between each of these, but
the attacks were only a day apart. Either he's got three separate
groups he's ordering around—"

"Not impossible."

"*Or* they're unconnected. There was a group of similar attacks last spring in the east."

"Testing our borders." Father crosses his arms. "You cannot know how long they've been planning for."

A quick glance tells me I'm not convincing him. Again. Since Candace and her family arrived—maybe since we came home—he's been even more unreachable than usual. There's only one way to deal with him when he gets like this, and it's to excel.

"I'll pick out a squadron of scouts," I say. "They'll be able to tell us whether the rogues are operating tactically, or more like rogues usually do."

Father huffs and stares at the fire. I study his face. I've been going to the portrait gallery more often now, and I never realized how different he looks from that painting with Mother. It's more than the intervening years. The lines on his face, the threads of gray in his hair —those all make sense. What I see in the gallery and don't see in the man in front of me is a spark in his eyes. The Father in the portrait, the one I hazily remember, looks like he wants to get up in the morning.

Is this what I looked like before Candace arrived?

"What's next?" I ask.

"Grain deliveries." He turns away from the fire. "Winter stretches on, north of Kar Castle."

"Is there something wrong?" We always deliver grain this time of year.

"Troops that would escort it have been recalled to the castle." He paces to his desk. "We have no escort."

"Then we just use those troops." I shake my head. "We don't need three squadrons here. Even if Dun's Crossing is planning something —which I seriously doubt—there are six of them."

"Inside our walls," Father says stubbornly. "Refusing protection from an enemy inside is sheer recklessness."

I pull a map of Kar Castle across the table to me and study the plans like I don't already know them by heart. Thick walls, small floors that stack one on top of the next like the sedimentary rock of the mountain beneath us. Looking at it now, I realize how tightly contained and controlled it is. Nearly every tower can see a handful of others. The tiny levels mean anyone else on the floor can often hear you. Gaining the element of surprise within our walls would be nearly impossible.

"An additional squadron is just going to make defending ourselves harder." I drag my fingers over the narrow staircases that thread up each tower. "They'll get in each other's way."

"They are your men. Did you not train them how to walk in orderly lines?"

"I did." I tap the stairs harder. "But it doesn't matter how orderly the lines are when there's barely enough space to fit two adults side-by-side. More of them just means more congestion."

"We will station them on relevant floors," Father says.

"And when we guess wrong?"

"They will have orders to remain in place." He glowers down at me. "They do follow orders, do they not?"

I clamp down on the frustration bubbling through me. My men are the most impeccably trained soldiers I've ever seen, and Father knows it. Especially after the gathering in Escuro—the other kingdoms had some men in uniform I'd hardly believe understood how to follow directions, much less orders. Father is under a lot of strain, some of which I've caused. I just need to prove to him my plan is the right one.

"Of course they do," I say "But if we're just keeping bodies around to hold position throughout the castle, the additional squadron is barely helping."

"Their presence shows we are strong." Father shakes his head. "I will not send them away."

"They're for show?" My eyebrows shoot up, and I start to lose a little control over that frustration. "You're the one who taught me pretending to be what you're not is the refuge of weak men."

"Snowcrest is strong." He slams his fist down on the table. "I pretend at nothing!"

"You *pretend* to be larger than we are." I gesture at the maps and papers showing the extent of our lands, our forces. "We are strong, we are powerful, and we are *small*. You're puffing yourself up like a frightened cat to try to intimidate the largest kingdom in the world."

"Frightened?" Father scoffs. "I do not fear Alpha King Kieran. He lacks his father's mettle."

"His father's cruelty," I reply. "And I don't think idolizing King Gavin is going to help us with shit here."

"King Gavin was a monster," Father says. "A brutally effective monster. And while I do not believe his son has the necessary monstrosity to destroy us, he does have the reckless confidence to attempt it."

"Fuck, if you're trying to scare him out of making a move, send the squadron with the grain and hire civilians to stand around looking impressive." I throw my hands up. "I haven't heard a word from you about alternate ways to get the grain north, and I don't believe we should starve our people because a diplomat *might* try something."

Father looks at me slowly. I hold his gaze. He's been difficult to reason with lately, but that's happened sporadically for my whole life. It's not exactly a surprise that King Andri is difficult to bargain with. So I know how these disagreements go. We've each made our points, and it's time for one of us to agree with the other. Sometimes, Father is right. Other times, he isn't, but I don't see much danger in following his path. And most rarely, I argue my side well enough that he comes around. This beat of quiet, sizing each other up, is the turning point. One of us must concede—and since a whole portion of the kingdom potentially going hungry is at stake, I'm not backing down.

"You think yourself so clever," Father says.

"I—what?"

He stands, lumbering like his wolf. "You know *nothing*."

"They're my men. I know their capabilities. And Kar Castle—"

"Has been my home for far longer than it's been yours." His voice cracks through the air, sharp and hard. "You are the reason we have enemies within our walls. The reason they remain here instead of leaving after nearly two weeks of silence. If you had not marked the bastard, Alpha Kieran would turn tail like any reasonable diplomat."

"Don't call her that." I jump to my feet, protective rage burning away any scraps of frustration. "Her name is Candace, and if her brother is staying here for her sake, then I think that says a hell of a lot about his character."

Father laughs. "This is no time for jokes. Alpha Kieran has no more character than a twig or stone."

"He's standing by Candace in a difficult time. When he doesn't have to." I stare Father down, trying to sear my point into his head. "I think that's brave."

"It's ridiculous, and that is how I know your plan will fail. You are still a child, Hollis, and I've let you forget that for too long."

"Then how are you going to feed the north?"

"I will find a way." Father glares steadily at me. "We prepare to send grain early, to avoid any potential lapse. There remains time to solve this problem."

I open and close my mouth a few times, wordless. He's actually willing to risk the people of Snowcrest for some fucking dick-measuring contest King Kieran might not even know he's involved in. My whole life, our people have always come first. If he's willing to trade that, there's nothing more I can say to him.

Normally, I'd storm out right now. But Candace wouldn't. Mother appears in my memory, answering some childish question I asked about what being queen was like. *It's like being a parent,* she said, *except you have to raise and care for a whole kingdom.*

"What would Mother think if she could see you right now?" I ask.

Father turns red, then purple. "This is a gift, you ungrateful boy. Responsibility, power, all these things I've given you. You asked for them and were allowed to prove you might handle them. I will happily take them back."

"I have proven myself." I hold my ground against the storm of his rage. "That's how I know you're making a mistake."

"Get out." Father storms to the door and yanks it open. "Until you've learned to hold your tongue again, do not return."

I march out the door with my head held high. He slams it behind me.

Maybe I didn't get everything I wanted, but I've never spoken to him like that before. Never even considered it. He may have kicked me out, but I'm still the prince. The only responsibility he took from me is our meetings.

Each step I take down the hall feels like another down a path to that new future Candace makes me want.

ONE STEP FORWARD

Candace

"THERE'S GOT TO BE SOMETHING WE'RE MISSING." HEAVY BAGS HANG under Kieran's eyes as our stay in Kar Castle stretches into the second week.

"I don't have a clue what," Taner replies, equally tired. "He hasn't even replied to any of our attempts conclusively enough to figure out what's pissing him off."

"I know what's pissing him off." Ingrid scribbles aggressively on the scrap paper she's started bringing to these planning meetings. I asked her once, and she said she's sketching, but she won't show me what it is. "It's the fact that he's awful and trapped us here to torture us permanently."

Finn snorts. Ever since he pulled me aside, I've been looking at his boredom differently. It seems patently obvious that his eyes are trained on the middle distance because he's listening now. I honestly don't know how I could've missed it—I've never had to catch him up on the conversation because he stopped paying attention or repeat myself when I wanted his attention.

"No matter how right I may privately think you are"—Kieran sighs—"that's not really helpful right now, Ingrid."

She rolls her eyes and slumps in her seat.

"So, do we have any other ideas?" he asks.

The room goes silent. Taner furrows his brow in thought. Kieran stares at the table like the dark wood might contain an answer we've been ignoring. Ingrid shakes her head. And Finn? Finn glances at me.

Ice shivers over my skin. I know what he's thinking. But after this much failure, no one wants to hear my idea. I'm the one who got us into this mess.

My mark throbs. In my mind's eye, under a newly rejuvenated oak tree, I ask Hollis if he believes me, and he says, *of course*. I put a hand on his mother's necklace, pinned inside my bodice, and take a deep breath.

"I might."

Kieran and Taner both look at me. Neither of them immediately start offering an idea of their own instead.

"I know what everyone thinks, but let's be honest with each other —I'm the problem here."

Ingrid starts to object, and I put up a hand to silence her. She closes her mouth sulkily.

"I know I didn't do it on purpose, and I'm not saying it's fair, but there's no point in pretending the problem we're trying to solve doesn't exist." My pulse roars in my ears. "I think you need to make a concession on that front—and no others because King Andri will see that as weakness. There's a town below this castle. Offer to pay for lodging for Kash and I there for the length of your negotiations. Then, at the very least, he's not being reminded of the woman who tore his kingdom apart every time he reviews his housekeeping ledgers."

I snap my mouth shut, crushing the urge to keep explaining until I'm sure everyone understands.

Silence follows.

My heart pounds. Ingrid still stares at her drawing. Finn nods slowly, but I don't know whether he's actually thinking about my idea or is just pleased I spoke up at all. Kieran and Taner exchange a look I know means they're talking through the mind-link. I press down on my bodice until I can feel the faint outline of the wobbly symbol. If they don't like it, the world won't end. Hollis will still want to see me at the end of the meeting.

"Direct. Simple. Doesn't harm the kingdom." Kieran eyes me thoughtfully. "I've been trying not to remind him of the issue by not acknowledging you, but that may have looked like I was trying to smuggle you in under his nose to a man as blunt as King Andri."

"I agree." Taner starts to smile. "We should probably ask if he has suggestions about accommodations, show that we're not turning our noses up at his hospitality, but I like it."

My stomach swoops like I'm sledding down a massive drop. "You like it?"

Kieran nods. "I'd like anything we haven't tried at this point, but it's a good thought. You know King Andri better than I do."

It worked! They like it! I release the necklace, thinking how I may know King Andri better than anyone but his closest family. Ingrid grins at me.

"I can write this up and get it in his hands this afternoon," Taner says.

"So fast?" My eyebrows shoot up.

"Why wait?" Kieran takes a few notes. "We've been sitting on our asses long enough."

He and Taner leave, talking to each other through the mind-link. I see half of Finn's nod before Ingrid basically tackles me in a hug.

"You're a genius!" she squeals. "I'm so proud of you."

I laugh and hug her back. "Proud? Why?"

"Because Mother is the reason everyone else didn't already know you were a genius, and you're not letting her keep stopping you." Ingrid squeezes me harder. "Maybe you could take up diplomacy as a hobby."

"Not a very un-princessy hobby," I say, noticing Finn slip out the door without a word.

"Oh, hush. We're celebrating." Ingrid releases me. "Want to go scout the town and see if there's anywhere you'd like to stay?"

"I actually have plans." I glance at the table. The dream is still keeping me up, so I've been napping during the day more often, and I promised to meet Hollis in that room off the portrait gallery when I wake up.

Ingrid's grin immediately falls. "With *him?*"

She won't say Hollis's name unless forced anymore.

"You know, he's a big part of the reason I was able to do that." I take a step back. "Him and, actually, Finn."

"I honestly don't know which of those I disbelieve more." She shakes her head incredulously. "Finn barely notices where he is, and Hollis—"

"Has been doing better." I fidget with my dress. I want to defend him, but disagreeing with Ingrid is strangely unpleasant. "He really seems to be putting in some effort."

She snorts. "I will believe it when I see it."

"Will you admit that's difficult right now?" We haven't been hiding since that day, but throwing our relationship in King Andri's face didn't seem clever either. We're just...out of his way.

"I suppose." She shakes her head. "I don't know, I've just seen you with so many men like Hollis. You forget yourself and become whatever they want."

A thousand of Mother's lessons flood through my mind in a single blast, every one teaching me to do exactly that. The best way to have a mate, according to her, is to manipulate from the shadows. Do whatever you have to do to gain his trust, then whisper in his ear. And laying the groundwork with as many eligible men as would step foot in Dun's Crossing was only smart.

And Hollis believed me the first time I told him the truth. He asked for no proof, never wavered. Even in Escuro, when he didn't want to be together, there was only one moment when I believed he didn't want all of me, when he nearly said I was just a body to him, and he apologized. He was just lashing out with what he knew would hurt me.

"I'm falling in love with him," I confess in a rush.

Ingrid freezes, her mouth a perfect O of surprise. I count heartbeats until she moves and start to worry when I reach ten.

"I didn't love him before," I murmur. "I needed him, but love… love is a choice. And he makes me happy."

She melts like an ice sculpture and wraps her arms slowly around me. "I love you. Goddess above, there's nothing I want more than to be happy you're happy. So… I'm going to."

"Just like that?" I hug her gently, waiting for the outburst I anticipated.

"For you? Yes." She sighs. "Finding a way to be happy for Hollis is going to take a little more work."

I giggle. "We can live with that."

"I'd like to see you together sometime," she says. "If he's going to be my brother-in-law, I should probably get used to not rolling my eyes every time he speaks."

"Maybe you should move out of the castle with me." I pull back and hold her shoulders at arm's length. "Tell me you haven't actually been doing that."

Ingrid smirks. "Not where anyone can really see."

The "really" in her sentence is terrifying, but the smirk means the worst of it is over. If there's one thing that's easy to believe about Ingrid, it's that she wants to be happy for me. And I know she'll put in the work to make the rest come together.

"Go, see him, tell him my demands." She waves me off with a smile.

"Nap first," I say through a yawn.

familiar patch of dirt. Grit and debris score my skin. The painful screams and howls of the fighting damned scorch my ears. No matter how many times I have the dream, it never feels less real, just less new.

More certain.

I open my eyes. Charred dirt, looming mountains. The sand-colored wolf lands at my feet and meets my gaze as the darker one tears it to ribbons. I still can't flinch, can't be sick like my stomach begs to. There is no reprieve for me here. Just more carnage to witness.

And I start lifting up above the fighting. The screams blur together. The blood becomes a stink rather than a reek. The violence feels no less overwhelming. There is no peace here, no compromise. I stare out over the end of the world and wait for the dream to end.

It doesn't.

Months of having this dream now, and it has never changed. But where I usually gasp myself awake, hot tears snake down my cheeks, and I keep watching. Someone trumpets. My neck jerks like someone pulled a puppet string too roughly, and I look toward it. The banner of what I know to be the attacking army flies high over the fighting, bringing hope to its soldiers.

The gray and green banner bearing the crest of Snowcrest Canyon flaps louder than the screams of the wolves dying underneath it.

ET TU?

Hollis

"Almost." Standing in the training room in the castle, I adjust the shoulders of a teenage boy, training to become part of the military someday. "But you want them in line with your hips for the maximum draw distance. Try it now."

He relaxes his hold on the bowstring then pulls it back again. At least another inch. I nod. He's got real promise, but he's up against a tough crop of potential recruits this—

'Army approaching the gates,' one of my scouts yells through the mind-link. *'Armed, flags flying. Maybe two hundred strong.'*

Oh, fuck.

Candace was right.

"Zain, take Alek and Val. Get outside before they shut the gates. We're going to need eyes," I bark.

'Do you know who it is?' he asks.

'No. But protocol doesn't give a shit, and neither do I. Move. Father's been jumpy.'

He hurries off to find my other two favorite scouts.

My mark pulses, and Candace's face fills my mind. She doesn't know. I can't warn her through the mind-link. I wouldn't be surprised if Father pettily decided the Dun's Crossing contingent didn't need any warning. My plans shift, and I turn to Kota, the fastest soldier helping to train these potentials.

"Find the Dun's Crossing contingent. Any of them you can. Tell them what's happening and where to find me."

Kota snaps off a salute and sprints away.

"Cadets," I say, even though they're still training to potentially earn that title. "Follow Captain Arjun. Secure the northern crags."

Arjun turns without a flicker of hesitation, but I see his frown the heartbeat before he does. He's thinking what I am—the northern crags are a back way, only taken by those who know the palace well. But I'm not leaving gaps in our defenses just because their use is improbable.

They leave out the back door of the training room, and I take off through the front, firing off more orders through the mind-link as I go. *Corral all nobility who can't fight in their rooms. Locate and protect any civilians.*

No one announces they've found the Dun's Crossing contingent. I keep running even as my instincts scream for me to turn around. I'll protect her better by raining the full hell of Snowcrest's army down on whoever was stupid enough to approach our front fucking gate.

I shoulder open the door out onto the wall over the gate and skid out. Icy air caresses my skin, promising magic will be as easy as breathing if I reach for it. I suck in an invigorating breath and feel the cold burn to the bottoms of my lungs.

The gate crashes shut like a thunderclap, and the portcullis rattles into place a second after.

"Two hundred and fifty strong. Not two hundred." Father's voice is rough and fast.

He stands behind the high stone of one crenellation, protected from attack and holding a brass telescope to one eye. Like me, he has no cloak or coat. He dropped everything to run here. Our soldiers eddy this way and that, preparing countermeasures.

"Apologies for my slow arrival." I step up next to him, as the protocol we've been practicing since my eleventh birthday dictates. The crenellation shields a little more of my body than his. "Preliminary cadet training."

I still haven't apologized for bringing up Mother like I did. He still hasn't apologized for all his bullshit, but I sent out an order for the extra squadron to escort the grain north, and he didn't publicly veto it. All of that disappears as we stand united on the front wall of our castle against a faceless enemy.

"Do you know anything more?" I ask.

He gestures over the wall. I turn, and my stomach drops to the ground a hundred feet below.

An army crawls up to the mouth of the gate like a squirming insect, twisting and weaving through the mountain pass. Two hundred strong seems right, if not a little low. But they walk like they know this land, a mixture of men and wolves confident over the lingering snow, and the reason why quickly becomes obvious. A standard-bearer marches at the front carrying a heavy flag of gray and green. Snowcrest's flag, though the crest in the middle looks a little strange. We're attacking ourselves?

"What the fuck?" I ask dumbly.

With a grim expression, Father hands me the telescope. I press it to my eye, adjust the lens, and peer through. The banner swims into more detail, and I was right. The crest is slightly off. Instead of centering the white-tailed eagle over the peaks, the normally smaller gray owl looms large and dangerous. It's an antiquated version of the crest, one I've seen before but hasn't been used since—

"Find the standard-bearer," Father says. "Look up, then right."

Striding in human form surrounded by a circle of wolves is Soren Skadi. Father's Beta. Eva's father. Riding under a crest that hasn't been used since his family and ours split control of the throne. Ice crusts over my fingers as rage crackles through me.

Another person bobs into the circle of my telescopes, and the ice whispers away like it was never there. Eva. Her hair hangs loose around her thin cheeks, and her chapped lips sag under a heavy frown. She looks tired, sick, worse than when we both got the spotted fever. I should've fought harder to find her.

Someone takes her hand. Goddess above, is that Nessa fucking Winters? I thought she died in a Dun's Crossing prison—but even as I think that, I half remember Candace mentioning she escaped.

I lower the telescope and look at Father. He stares out over the approaching army, his face lined and bleak. There's no anger crackling behind his gaze, no violence in the grasp of his hands on the top of the crenellation. If I didn't know any better, I'd say he looks... resigned.

The vanguard of the army comes to a stop in front of the gate. Another two hundred keep trudging onward. They'll fill the courtyard far before everyone is here, but there's no order to stop.

Soren marches forward with Eva at his side. I clench my hands into fists and wait for the mind-link demanding we open up. Behind me, a trio of soldiers starts boiling pitch in a cauldron. My stomach churns—I can't let them drop that on Eva, no matter what's happening.

"Snowcrest Canyon's throne is a rare one." Soren's voice whisks up the wall to us on a frozen breeze.

Has he declared himself independent and severed the mind-link, or is he showing off his power?

"Shared between two families too powerful to let their opposites hold it in its entirety." His words shake with barely contained rage, angrier than I've ever heard him before. "Until the Goddess offered us a compromise. For three hundred years, the Skadi family has kept its end of that bargain."

The army behind him roars, deafening. I realize this can't just be the guards he keeps around Skadi Peak. As close as he and Father are, no lords are allowed such large standing forces—which means he has spent the intervening weeks gathering allies. A few soldiers have failed to report to duty, not enough that it caught my attention, but enough that they might've been sneaking off to recruit others.

One of the trio of soldiers steps up to Father, a searing fire pot of pitch in one leather-gloved hand. Kar Castle is impenetrable to many things, but not to ladders, so all defense plans dictate that attacks start as soon as possible to give attackers the least chance to prepare. Father waves him back. Not on his Beta. Not yet.

"As have we," he bellows. No magic, no mind-link, just pure power and volume. Soren may have numbers—especially since I sent the third squadron away—but I wouldn't want to fight Father.

"Ha!" His mirthless laughter makes his wind shimmer. "You've spat in our faces. Betrayed us in front of the assembled world. Stabbed us from behind like common cowards."

Without the telescope, I can't see any details, but it looks like Eva turns her head away as he says that. My ribcage crumples. It takes all my willpower not to vault over the wall just to talk to her, whatever the consequences of the fall might be.

"Duplicitous Kar, I charge you to cede your throne in apology," Soren demands.

Father's jaw works, but his posture never falters. "I offer no apology for the Goddess's will. It is Her compromise to break. Perhaps She saw this cravenness in you already."

"Andri Kar, I knew you before your first steps," Soren declares. "You speak of Snowcrest superiority, but you marry a woman from another kingdom. You speak of tradition, but you break our most sacred. You speak of trust, but you hide me away just when my family needed me most. You have not been an Alpha our kingdom can rely on since Queen Lara's death, if not before that. If the Goddess broke our compromise, it was only so I could savor striking down a false king."

I stare down at the vague shape of a man I grew up alongside. In almost all my memories of Father, Soren stands nearby. The loss of his wife made him more effusive where it made Father less. Eva and I both went to him with exciting news to be congratulated, celebrated before enduring Father's gruff nod. His shaven head shines in the sun, uncovered, proof he truly believes everything he's saying about Father. There should already be an arrow through his eye, a fire pot cracking on his skull. Father's hesitation would look like weakness to Soren—to Father himself, if anyone else showed it. But I can't wish he'll do anything differently because a fire pot would catch Eva, and so might an arrow.

"Return your renegade army to Skadi Peak, and let us talk like men," Father hollers.

This time, Soren isn't the only one who laughs. The bitter, searing chuckle echoes up from the whole army, mocking Father with his unwillingness to act. It ricochets up his spine and winds his posture even tighter.

"For my daughter's honor," Soren says. "For my ancestors' honor, I will retake our kingdom. I suggest you open your gates before I have to. You have twenty-four hours."

ENEMY OF MY ENEMY

Candace

Freezing wind whips my hair into a cyclone around my head and stings my cheeks. Kieran desperately clings to his hat. Ingrid's teeth chatter, and her face turns pink.

"You have to love springtime," Finn mutters under his breath.

I stick my tongue out at him. Maybe it's colder than any spring I've ever experienced, but I haven't yet walked into a building up here and not been offered something hot to drink. The quiet, relaxing break between activities is something I could get used to.

And I might have to. If everything goes well.

Kash shudders audibly. "Hardly a fucking place. I can't believe folks actually scraped out a living up here."

"I like it," Ingrid says through chattering teeth.

I squeeze her mittened hand. Ever since our talk, she really has been trying to be happy for me.

"If you're all so cold, we can do our goodbyes here." I squint at the vague shape of the eastern gate Hollis led me through a few days ago, apparently the easiest way into town, where an inn called the Skyship awaits Kash and me.

King Andri actually replied to my idea—brusquely—and said he would discuss setting a meeting after we were gone. An ember of victory burns in my chest, keeping me more than warm enough. It was the first progress since arriving at Kar Castle, and it was my idea!

Kash puts down our bags with a grunt. "Can't say I'm pleased about any of this, but rest assured, you'll still be seeing me."

Kieran nods at him. Impressive diplomacy. Then, everyone turns to me.

"Are you sure about this?" Ingrid asks. "You'll be so far—"

A trumpet sounds, high and loud. Just like in the dream. I whip toward it.

Across the snow, a dark shape moves toward us. Quickly. Kash shifts without a heartbeat of hesitation and shoves in front of me. Kieran, Finn, and Ingrid fall into preparatory stances but wait. Chills ripple over my skin, colder than the breeze.

It's happening.

The dark shape turns into a reddish wolf who skids to a stop a few feet away and drops something in the snow. Kash prowls slowly forward, sniffs, and snatches it up in his maw. He gallops back to drop a drool-soaked piece of paper at my feet, and I read it aloud.

"An army approaches. Prince Hollis is on the gate wall. Move quickly. Barricades going up."

My stomach knots. My heart hammers. And a very small part of me warms. Hollis didn't want me to leave, or at least, to leave without knowing.

As one, we take off. Kash grabs both bags in his mouth and sprints ahead. Ingrid and I both yank up our skirts and drape them over our arms, despite the cold. Kieran's gaze goes vague for a moment— warning Taner, I assume—and then he's running with the rest of us, crashing through the icy top layer of snow to the powder below. Only Kash seems to have half a rhythm, a strange bounding hop I don't know how to recreate on two legs. Shifting tempts me, but I won't have time to get a new dress, and I don't particularly want to stand outside—or face King Andri—in the nude. Instead, I just watch Kash pull ahead and pray the snippets of what seem like the real him I've seen are enough to convince him to help us.

My breath scrapes in and out of my throat. My legs go numb. More trumpets sound, and as we draw closer to the castle, I start to hear *clangs* and *thuds* that sound an awful lot like closing doors.

We careen into view of the door we exited through—already half closed! But there's something in the half-closed door. The curve of a thin, pale gray-yellow wolf butt. I don't know anyone with that pelt.

But I don't know exactly what Kash's coat looks like from behind.

A whining bark leaks through the gap as the door opens slightly, then closes harder. Another inch disappears.

We're so close, I yell through the mind-link to him.

Pick it up, kiddo. This bastard's got a real grudge against your old man's rib cage.

It's Kash, I tell everyone else, grinning wildly. *He jammed his body in the door to buy us a few more seconds.*

Wow, Ingrid says softly.

I pour on what little speed I was keeping in reserve, and my family does as well. Snow puffs and swirls in powdery clouds around us. Someone yells at Kash, demanding he get inside.

Finn hits the door first, shoulder forward, and whatever soldier was trying to squeeze it closed can't take the impact. It swings wide open, and the four of us barrel inside.

Thank you, I tell Kash. *From everyone.*

Ah, I did it for you and the sauna. He saunters off, bags still clamped in his mouth.

Ingrid and I will lock down the rooms. Finn bolts down a hallway.

My sister, who was slowing down and panting, shoots me a brief, irritated look before following him at a jog.

Kieran and I wheel the opposite way. There's no discussion needed—we're both going to the wall. My legs scream for relief as we pound up and down the million staircases that make up Kar Castle, but finally, we explode out a door and back into the cold.

Hollis and King Andri stand at the wall, islands of stillness in a sea of moving soldiers preparing to repel a siege. When Kieran slams the door shut behind us, they both turn. Hollis, with a breathless smile, touches the spot on his chest that mirrors where his mother's necklace hangs on mine. A silent gesture of… love? And perhaps all we can do, this close to his father.

King Andri looms, as dark and sullen as the mountains surrounding the castle. "Have you come to mock us?"

"No," Kieran says. "We—"

"How did you know to come here?" King Andri turns back to the wall.

"I told them." Hollis raises his chin, still looking at me. "I wanted my mate safe."

King Andri scoffs. "Childish. Were she at Skyship, we might have had something to trade."

Fear prickles over my skin. The army wants me?

Would King Andri really make that trade?

"If you don't like it, you can leave," Hollis says.

King Andri tenses. "Not while there is light. Soren must see me here, as strong as our walls."

"Soren?" Kieran's eyebrows shoot up. "Lord Soren Skadi, your Beta?"

"Now, my betrayer." King Andri sounds surprisingly worn down.

Finally, I turn and look out over the wall, my heart in my throat. Even knowing that it's impossible—I smell no blood, and the courtyard at the front of the castle isn't large enough—I expect to see the carnage from my dream.

I come face to face with an army. Not yet drenched in blood, slavering for the death of those they once called friends, but they march under the banner of Snowcrest I saw. I clap a hand to my mouth as my stomach roils. This is it. The beginning of the end.

"What's happening? Do you know anything?" Kieran steps over to the wall like he'll be able to see any more.

"You missed the big speech." Hollis sighs and runs a hand through his frost-covered curls, barely seeming to notice the chill. "He's attempting to retake the throne."

"This is a coup." Kieran's voice grows heavy and worried. "Do you know why?"

King Andri laughs humorlessly. "Guess, bastard-lover."

His words hit like rocks. It is about me. I meet Hollis's gaze, begging him for anything else he knows.

"He's doing it for Eva," Hollis whispers. "And… she's here."

My knees turn to sand, and I sway. Hollis catches my arm before I collapse. His hand is an anchor, a point for all my thoughts to swirl around. Eva is here. This is my fault. Every time I went back to Hollis, I guaranteed even more that we would end up here. All because I couldn't tell my friend a painful truth.

"His allies?" Kieran asks.

"Many southern lords," King Andri says. "Your envoy's daughter."

Kieran blinks. "Ty Sulick has a daughter? He was unmarried when we sent him off to you."

King Andri growls. "Floyd Winters. Your envoy, whom you killed."

I jerk my head up. "Nessa? Nessa's here?"

Hollis nods. "Surprised me, too. I really thought she was dead."

I lean heavily into Hollis for support. Nessa is very much alive—and fairly recently escaped from the cell right next to Mother's. She's not a fighter, though. If she's with this army, she must be doing something else for them.

Like feeding them information? Twisting their opinions of what happened in Escuro? Nessa is one of the most devious, manipulative people I've ever met. Leaving her alive was too kind on Estrella's part, though I agreed at the time. The only person who beats her for deviousness is Mother.

And me, before I started trying to change.

"The troops in Dun's Crossing are able to mobilize with an hour's notice," Kieran says. "We have some much closer to the border, could get here in a day or less."

"Pah. We need no help." King Andri shakes his head. "Snowcrest handles Snowcrest's problems."

Kieran points over the wall. "That's a siege tower. Kar Castle might be difficult to breach, but to trap? You've done half the damned work yourself with these mountains. Which means, if you can get outside reinforcements, Soren will be pinned with nowhere to go, and I'd bet my whole kingdom's coffers his army has fewer supplies than Kar Castle."

King Andri clenches his jaw. He pounds his fist against the high wall of the castle, once. "Starvation is a coward's gambit."

"He's using it." Kieran stares the older Alpha down steadily.

King Andri looks out over the army silently. Hollis squeezes my arm, though I can barely feel him through the numbing cold. The numbing terror.

"You will come to my office tomorrow at nine. We will talk," King Andri says.

Kieran barely hides a triumphant grin. "I'll be there."

There it is—the meeting we've been fighting for two weeks to earn.

The smell of armor polish reminds me we have very little to feel successful about right now.

THE PRICE OF INDEPENDENCE

Hollis

Father's private sitting room as he finishes pouring two steaming mugs of mulled wine. The smells of clove and nutmeg make my mouth water.

He joins me, offers me one mug, and takes the other armchair in front of the leaping fire. I fold my hands around the clay gratefully. It's a little too hot to hold, but after almost six fucking hours on the wall, even I'm cold. Father refuses to show any weakness, but I see the slight chatter in his teeth as he lifts his mug to his mouth.

Six hours down, twenty-four to go. There's only one reason Soren would give us this much time—he's preparing the perfect siege outside. To go against the terms he set would violate the rules of honorable warfare, and I know Father would rather die than do that, so we can only plan until the time runs out. Or so nearly runs out that anyone arguing we acted first wouldn't have a shred of proof, a tried-and-true strategy.

I lift my drink to my lips and sip. Warm spices, rich wine, and the burn of a harder alcohol hidden somewhere inside. Mother used to call this muddled wine. She also used to call it her favorite drink. I haven't had it in years. Over the rim of my mug, I glance at Father, but he's too busy staring into the fire. The peace between us will last as long as I focus on the larger threat. Maybe I'll ask why he chose it later.

"Have you thought about King Kieran's offer?" I ask.

Father huffs a sigh. "Nothing but, since he spoke it."

That's a good sign. If he wasn't even considering it, he'd say he hadn't thought about it at all.

"Do you know what you're going to say?" The next sip of my muddled wine actually starts to pierce the lingering ice inside me.

He stares quietly at the fire for a long moment then looks at me, the flames flickering in his dark eyes. "Have you heard how we became allies with Dun's Crossing and King Gavin?"

"No." Not for lack of asking, either. Once I figured out what a monster King Gavin was, I demanded my tutors tell me why we had anything to do with him for months. None of them had answers. The one time I asked Father, he told me to run and fetch him a drink first then disappeared before I got back. It never made sense how Snowcrest could be so powerfully good and work alongside such a piece of shit.

"Before you were born, I lived in a much simpler world. King Gavin's father, Kellen, was a weak and unambitious man, ruled by his people rather than ruling them," Father says.

I nod. This part, I've heard.

"Upon his death, Gavin came to power, and my peaceful world ended." He rubs his thumb over the outside of his mug thoughtfully. "I remember sitting here with my Lara much like this, reading the evening's mail and watching kingdoms fall."

My heart skips a beat. He never brings up Mother, especially not unprompted. I swig my drink so I don't smile or stare or do anything that might stop this story before it reaches its conclusion.

"Before, dozens of powerful kingdoms vied for spits and scraps of land. After, through our early days of marriage, they began to crumble. Kingdoms with centuries of history. Kingdoms we considered allies, even friends." He sighs heavily. "Yewbrush Stream fell to a steady, ravenous military campaign. Pebble Forest ate itself alive, and only after did anyone discover King Gavin had planted an advisor in their court. Starfall Mountain simply disappeared, their royal family missing and their people aimless." Father glances at me out of the corner of his eye. "That last happened when my Lara couldn't sit down without complaining how much her little heir loved to dance on her bladder. I told her amidst a tirade, and she fell silent. A terrible, sickbed silence. Our world fell to a disease named Alpha King Gavin."

"And you just let it happen?" Maybe I shouldn't say anything, but if it was as bad as he's saying, I can't imagine staying locked up in Kar Castle. I certainly can't imagine Mother choosing that.

"What can you do when your neighbors are plagued?" That resignation creeps back into his voice again. "Send food, supplies. But your own people will only carry plague home in their knapsacks."

"I can't believe you just let them die." I shake my head.

"You will believe when you must make similar choices." There's no room for argument in his tone. "And you will, or you are not my son."

I look at the cranberry surface of my drink instead of him.

"Even when you do not tempt plague, though, it comes knocking. As Gavin did, very much like his son these weeks ago. From rumor, I expected a bear of a man, but I dwarfed him." He smiles grimly. "Gavin smiled, he laughed, he begged a way inside our doors. I should have shut them in his face, hospitality be damned." Quickly, Father dips two fingers into his wine and flicks the droplets over his shoulder to ward off bad luck. "After dinner, he looked at me and said he liked Snowcrest Canyon quite a lot. He would do anything to get a piece of it. Would I like to be allies?"

Through Father's mouth and a handful of decades, I can still hear the threat in Gavin's words. I shiver even though I'm not cold anymore.

"How many of my friends, I wondered, stood before this killer king and heard his offer? How many had eyed his lands, soldiers, and decided he was no equal?" He meets my gaze, hard. "This is being king—looking at others' mistakes and refusing to make them again. I am proud of our land, our people, our name, but I will not drive us to death for pride alone. I shook plague's hand and spoke what words would make him unshadow our door. I had no other choice."

Father's eyes burn into mine, the fire only intensifying his already heavy expression. I realize this is a confession. He believes every word he's saying; he thinks he didn't have a choice, but he regrets it. He's humiliated.

"Gavin left," Father says. "And he sent his envoy, not two weeks later. When his foot hit our threshold, my Lara's eyes changed. They never changed back. Not when looking at me."

I blow out a long, slow breath. Mother hated the alliance with Gavin, hated what it did to Snowcrest. A thousand little memories of her pursed lips when his name came up, her polite excuses when conversation surrounded him, make sense. She would never have made the deal Father did.

How much else don't I know about her, or only know in pieces? I open my mouth to ask about the drink, or maybe just about Mother.

"We do not need King Kieran's aid," Father says. "He is no plague. He is not even a knife in darkness. King Kieran is a wolf at a supper table—strong, but obvious. To a man like him, I will cede nothing."

"Cede?" I repeat. "You don't have to cede shit. He didn't ask for land, for alliance, nothing. He just offered his help."

"That is where supper-table wolves start." Father nods. "He lacks his father's subtlety. If his men march in, they will never march out."

The soft, easy moment between us shatters. "That's completely paranoid."

"Perhaps." Father sips his wine and smiles softly. "But I want to leave my kingdom independent. Snowcrest deserves to stand on its own feet, does it not? And Soren is an old blowhard. Tomorrow, we will talk, and I will soothe his ego. This is why I did not strike today. He does not mean war."

I stare at him, dumbfounded. "You just said you wouldn't kill our people for pride."

"We will not die." He pats my knee with one large hand. "My Lara looks over us still."

"I love Mother, but I'm not willing to stake a siege on her power in the sky," I say. "You have to take Kieran's offer."

He sighs. "I do not wish to fight now. Sit, drink."

"No. I have to get ready to fucking fight. Someone has to." I start to stand.

"Hollis Kamari Efrain, sit and drink with me," he orders.

I sit back down automatically. "Fine. This conversation isn't over."

"If Soren will not hear reason…." Father purses his lips. "Honorable combat cannot be had with traitors. We will strike before his preparations are complete. And now, it is over."

I grit my teeth, but I'm not going to get anything else out of him tonight, and the fire is warm. If he tries to kill Snowcrest, I'll talk to Kieran.

After all, there is no honorable combat with traitors, and I won't let Father become one.

NEEDING HELP

Candace

I sit in my bedroom in Kar Castle, staring at the metal-reinforced sheet of wood over my window. The bag I packed to move into town lays on its side at the foot of my bed, saliva drying on the handle, but I can't imagine being frustrated with Kash right now. Holding the door like that… it proves there's still some hope for him. For us, I guess. I believe him when he says he wouldn't have done that for the others, but even if it was only for me, the pain in his whine feels important. He risked something.

The scrap of fabric in my lap I'm supposed to be embroidering tears. I look down at it with a wince. Worrying the unfinished edges maybe wasn't the best idea, but the tear hasn't technically reached the lopsided, ugly skycatching warbler I've been trying to replicate. With a groan, I throw the fabric onto the table beside me and squeeze my eyes shut.

Thinking about Kash is easy. Thinking about the warm, smoky smells of cooking fires from the army camped outside the gates, the blood that's going to follow, and the betrayal at the heart of all of this is much, much harder.

Halfway through the vigil on the gate wall, Hollis offered me the telescope and said I could see Eva if I wanted to. I accepted, and part of me wishes I hadn't. She looked like she hadn't slept or smiled since that moment in Escuro, and Nessa's hand was tucked tightly in hers. The shining, smiling woman I met in the chaos of the assassination attempts around Estrella is gone, stomped out by a combination of my selfishness and the influence of the people around her. Eva, as I knew her, would never want all this.

I sit up. Maybe that's the answer. She's got Nessa and her father in her ear—maybe hearing from someone else will shake her out of their grasp. I just need to talk to Raven and—

She's back in Dun's Crossing. Obviously. So I can't have any friendly birds or mice deliver a message for me. Not that, I now realize, a bird wouldn't be shot down the second Soren's archers spotted it.

My magic is useless—all I can do is foretell tragedy with enough vagueness that I can't stop myself from being the cause of it. And what else do I have to offer, really? A few half-decent diplomatic ideas, most of which need to be refined still and all of which apply to people inside the castle walls. A trunk full of pretty dresses, chosen to highlight me a little more or a little less within a strict set of rules. A few dance routines. I'm useless.

Before I can even finish the thought, my brain offers up the arguments I know Ingrid and Hollis would make. I'm not useless, I'm specific, or I'm learning, or I might not have the skills to do this exactly, but I have many others. None of them stop hot tears from streaking down my cheeks. All I want to do is talk to my friend, honestly, like I should've done from the very beginning, and I am built to look pretty and manipulate people into liking me. I can't even finish embroidering a bird without ruining it.

Eva's voice floats through my mind, repeating a line from one of the many letters we exchanged between Anwen's wedding and the rejuvenation ceremony. *Sometimes, I feel like a stone dove, building impossible nests in unlivable coves and corners. But so many of those doves raise strong, happy families that it's hard not to wonder if maybe the attempt is what matters.*

I stare around the small room I've been given. I packed up my clothes to take with me, but it's been over two weeks, so other errata dots the floor, errata Ingrid was supposed to move to her room because it wouldn't fit into the inn with me. The embroidery hoops, with their spare fabric and thread. The canvas, easel, and paints. Delicate, silken dance shoes with ribbons that lace up the calves. A few chunks of softwood and a sharp knife to whittle them. A set of calligraphy pens and inks. The scattered remains of almost a dozen tried and discarded hobbies.

The fluting birdcall from the days I spent refusing to leave my tent after Mother revealed my true parentage to me echoes through my memory. They had as little as this, maybe less, to construct it with. The attempt was what mattered.

I slide off my bed and get to work.

HOURS LATER, I DROP INTO THE CHAIR IN FRONT OF MY DESK AND LIFT A quill carefully with two bandaged fingers. Finn agreed to lure the soldiers watching the roof of Kar Castle's highest tower away with a game of cards, and he left a few minutes ago, so I don't have long to actually write my message before Ingrid arrives to smuggle it and the contraption up to the chosen point. My hand hurts, but I haven't stopped smiling since I came up with the final plan for the beast behind me. A particularly elastic length of yarn from my failed attempt at knitting cranks back like a crossbow string with a makeshift handle salvaged from a parasol I really shouldn't have brought on a wooden base, constructed from my brief foray into bookbinding. My paint brushes created enough of a lever to peek out the window and see the largest campfire outside, clearly the one belonging to Soren and Eva. All I need to do is write my letter, fold it into the shape I know lets seabirds soar for long journeys without flapping their wings, and send Ingrid off with what was supposed to be a hat but turned into far more of a windsock to measure the breeze before launch.

Eva, I write at the top of the page. Then, my quill stops. What can I say? The words to explain this have eluded me since I woke up next to Hollis that first morning.

The attempt is what matters. I re-ink my quill and begin writing.

I am sorry. If there were bigger, more powerful ways to say that, I would use them. There are no words for the hurt I've caused you. And as much as he is at the heart of this, I don't mean by mating with Hollis. As painful as this is, both of us know there was no decision in that. If there was, I wouldn't have made it. No, what I owe you an apology for, first and foremost, was deciding not to tell you it had happened. I had a myriad of chances, and I chose over and over again the safety of not speaking up. It was selfish, and cowardly, and I understand if you can never forgive me. I'm not writing this letter in the hopes you'll forgive me. I'm writing it because I love you as much as I love him, and it hurts me to see you like this.

Nessa Winters cannot be trusted. She is as manipulative as I was at my worst, clever enough to find even your weak spots and prod you into the worst decisions. I don't know who chose the army or marching on Kar Castle, but if she at any point suggested it, know that means it is a hurtful choice. Maybe not to you, or at least not now, but she doesn't care about loss of life, and that is guaranteed in this fight. I don't want you to have to live with that for the rest of your days.

You once told me you thought attempting something alone is what matters. I never attempted to speak to you until it was too late, and I can't take that back. I also won't lie to you—I don't see a world where Hollis and I can leave each other now. But I am sorry, with every fiber of my being, and I will be until I join the Goddess in the stars that I didn't try to talk to you sooner. I love you, and I hope you can find your way to a place that hurts less. If there is any way I can help with that, please let me know.

I dot the final period onto the letter, scrawl my name at the bottom, and take a deep breath. Speeches have never really been my strong suit either, and this feels more like that than the letters we exchanged before, but this is the best I can do.

No. I'm proud of the letter. I've poured my heart out, and every word is true. If it really is the best I can do, that's impressive on its own. I start folding the thick paper along soft charcoal lines I pre-marked on the back.

Ingrid knocks on my door, then steps in quietly. "Ready?"

I hold up the letter, wings stiff and proud, with Eva's name on all sides. "As I can be."

"Thank you for letting me help." She grabs the contraption, the windsock, and the letter.

"King Andri is watching me." I smile bittersweetly at the covered window. "And… I'm still learning, so of course I needed help. Thank you."

'Got them,' Finn says through the mind-link. *'But apparently there's a patrol coming by before long, so we've only got one hand's worth of time.'*

Ingrid nods, kisses me on the cheek, and darts out. I look around the scattered remains of my construction. Dawn can't be far off now, and I'm exhausted, but it was worth it. Even if it changes nothing. Eva needs to know I tried. I step over to my bag and start extracting my pajamas. I might still be able to steal a few hours of sleep before morning.

'News from Solberg castle!' One of our couriers, Rege, pants through the mind-link like he's been running for a long time.

I sit up.

'Rowena Solberg has escaped the dungeon!'

DESPERATION

Hollis

Warm wine humming in my veins, I knock on Candace's door. Father managed to schedule a parley with Soren tomorrow morning, before his meeting with Kieran, through the mind-link, and I need to warn her.

And, fuck, I want to see her. We haven't been able to talk alone yet. She was supposed to be leaving the fucking castle today, even though we made plans for how to still see each other, and I can't fall asleep knowing she's still here.

The door explodes open. Candace stares at me, hazel eyes wild. My heart jumps into high gear.

"What's wrong?" I step inside and close the door behind me then scan the room for danger. A smaller area will be easier to defend unless the problem is already in here with us.

"My mother," she says.

My heart skips a beat. Of all the things I expected, Rowena is not one of them. "Isn't she locked back up in Dun's Crossing?"

Candace shakes her head and tugs on one ink-stained sleeve. "She's supposed to be. She was, until a bit ago."

"She broke out." My guess sounds dull and heavy in the quiet room.

Candace's breathing picks up. Her eyes go hazy with a mind-link. "She's not from Dun's Crossing originally. She's from Lightning Cape, so she has wind powers."

All those weird gusts in Escuro snap into place. "I didn't know that."

"They used to be weak!" Candace snatches an embroidery hoop off her bed and begins nervously picking out stitches. "Father—King Gavin–liked keeping them secret because they weren't impressive to show, but discovering she had secret powers made people nervous all the same."

I grab her hands and hold them still. "Okay. What does all this have to do with you–here?"

"She used her powers to break out. She's stronger than anyone thought." Candace shakes her head like she's refusing the words coming out of her mouth. "And... and she came here. Or she's coming here. We don't know exactly where she is, but she escaped and turned this way, and people at home are hurt."

I barely swallow a snarl. Let her come here. If she has fucking anything to do with this, I'll tear her head off myself. My mark pulses as I look at Candace's panicked face. Maybe I'll tear her head off anyway just for making the woman I love react like this. She shouldn't have to be scared of her own mother. Even when Father's at his worst, I'm never actually scared of him.

"You have healers in the castle to take care of those people," I say in my best soothing voice.

It seems my best isn't particularly good. Candace's eyes get even wider, and she starts shaking in my grasp.

"If she's coming here, who is she coming for? Did she cause all of this somehow? Is she in league with Lord Soren, or Nessa—they were cellmates, you know." She shakes even harder. "My dream... Hollis, there's going to be a battle. Probably a war. And if Mother's here, someone is going to have to fight her. If it's me… I don't know if I can do that."

Tears streak down her reddening cheeks. I release her hands to swipe one away with my thumb. I've always been awful at cheering people up, even Eva. There's a trick to it I don't understand. I glance at the door out of the corner of my eye and wonder if she'd be better off alone.

I can't do that. If I was this upset, she'd stay with me. I just need to figure out the impossible fast enough not to make this a lot worse.

"Look at me," I say softly.

Candace jerks her gaze up to mine. My heart pounds. I've watched her do this the whole time I've known her, with me, Eva, and even Kash. I just need to channel her.

"This is terrifying," I say.

She nods. Her tears flow faster. Mistake or success? I have no way to know.

"But right here, right now, your mother escaping doesn't change anything."

She opens her mouth to object, and I cup her cheek.

"If she fights, and you don't want to fight her, I will." I leave off how happily I'll do it. "And if she is behind everything that happened in Escuro… shit, that means you don't have anything to feel guilty about."

Candace blinks. "I… don't?"

"Rowena didn't lead us to each other in the Haze." I stroke my thumb gently over her skin. "But she made all those announcements. She could've convinced Nessa to come—hell, she could've had Nessa do anything, even send Eva to come find us that last night."

Candace shakes her head. "We still should've told Eva. Mother didn't make me lie."

"I did." My chest aches at the memory of Eva's face. "And I'd take it back if I could."

"I went along with you." Her voice is soft now, fragile.

This is actually working. "What did you say the other day? Your mother trained you to listen when people speak."

"To be seen and not heard." Candace smiles ruefully. "That's what a perfect wife is supposed to do."

Fuck, I hope Rowena's on her way here. Her blood on my claws will taste so sweet.

"Not my perfect wife." I gather Candace to my chest. "You made choices, but she guided them. Maybe you still have apologies to make, but she's at least as much to blame."

Slowly, she stops shaking. A moment later, she puts her arms around my waist.

"Then your father's at least as much to blame for you," she murmurs against my shirt.

I endure the immediate gut-punch of refusal. I'm not scared of him. He doesn't control me like her mother controlled her. But that's not what she needs to hear right now.

I think. Copying her seems to be working, but I'm not completely sure how. "Don't worry about her for tonight." I slide my hand through her silken hair. "Tomorrow, Father has a parley with Soren. We can—"

She jerks back from me. "He what?"

"That's what I was coming here to tell you. We can figure out how involved Rowena is then. Tonight, just…." The right answer feels like rest, but I ache with the loss of her warmth. Sending her to bed, alone, seems impossible.

"Just?" She steps back up to me and braces her hands on my chest.

There should be answers in my brain, on my tongue. But I'm all out of words. I bend down and kiss her.

Candace responds immediately, pushing up onto her toes to get closer to me. The taste of sunshine warms the cold castle. I lap at the seam of her lips, chasing more. She opens for me, and I flick my tongue inside.

I nestle one hand in her hair, holding her close, and skim the other down her side. She's half-dressed, gown loose without a corset but still thick and limiting. I groan and grab what I can. Under all the layers of fabric and fur waits a warmth I've never found in anyone else. This parley tomorrow… I have no idea what's going to come of it. Or the meeting with Kieran, or the war Candace has been dreaming about since the day we met. We've spent all our time together saying goodbye, and this could be another.

If that's true, I can't think of a better way to say it.

I drop to my knees in front of Candace. She stares down at me, lips kiss-swollen and eyes wide.

"Hold on." I nod at the nearest post, then duck my head under her skirts.

Down here, her smell is even more powerful. Summery and sweet, like the few best months we scrape out here in the mountains. I run my hands up her legs, savoring the warmth, and thumb over the wetness gathered between.

She keens, and her knees shake. I dive forward and press my mouth to the heart of her heat. She's so foreign up here, in this land of ice, and I want to melt away just from touching her. My tongue dances over her skin, lapping, flicking, drawing wails and moans from her lips. I can't believe I didn't realize, the moment I woke up next to her, what I had. I can't believe it took months to reach this point, the one where I worship her like she deserves. Fuck tradition—this is where I belong. The Goddess knew it, and now, so do I.

So does she, judging by her quivering thighs. I soak a finger in her wetness, then slide it inside. My name falls from her lips, broken and desperate. My tongue and fingers move faster, in perfect rhythm. My cock aches.

Candace comes apart around me, a symphony of pleasure. Want shatters my resolve, breaks every thought in half. Almost before she's done, I shove out from underneath her skirt and leap to my feet. The sight that greets me stops me dead. One of her hands is snarled in her own hair, turning it into a spun-sugar cloud. The other clutches one of her breasts hungrily, exposing a sliver of rosy nipple over the neckline of her dress.

"Fucking gorgeous," I growl.

I slide one arm under her legs, the other behind her shoulders, and lift her. She writhes in my grasp, still wracked with euphoria. Cock throbbing, I toss her on the bed. She yanks her own skirt up to her waist, and I don't need any more permission than that. I unfasten my trousers, free my cock, and thrust into her.

It's like putting in the last piece of a puzzle. Her hot, hungry body swallows me down. Her muscles flutter around me in tantalizing patterns, the final echoes of her explosion. I bend down and crush my mouth to hers. She throws her arms around my neck, dragging me even closer. There's no rhythm in this position, no grace. Just her breath in my mouth, her hands in my hair. Mine on her exposed breast or hitching her legs higher for the angle that raises her moans an octave.

If Soren attacked right now, I wouldn't even fucking move. I love her too much.

My orgasm hits me like an avalanche, all at once and overwhelming. As I freeze over her, Candace's screams reach a new pitch. We shake together.

When the last throes of pleasure start to fade, my brain comes back to life. At the end there... did I really...?

Candace's sleepy smile is too familiar, sated rather than shocked. I didn't say anything. But as she cards her fingers gently through my curls, the words dance on the tip of my tongue. She deserves to know. I open my mouth—

And close it again. Tomorrow, after the parley, when we know what's coming next, I'll tell her.

The tower is falling, and fuck, it feels incredible.

KASHADIEN

Candace

THE FIRST RAYS OF SUNRISE FIND ME ALREADY AWAKE. I WANTED TO sleep—I really meant to—but after the last round, Hollis showed no signs of leaving. His dark curls stuck to his face with sweat, and the softest smile curved his lips. He cuddled down under my blankets, draped an arm around my waist, and fell right to sleep.

I meant to rest, but I spent the whole night watching his face. It was my first real night with my mate. I didn't want to waste a single second.

But now, with the parley and King Andri's meeting with Kieran threatening, I have other seconds I can't waste. I brush a kiss over Hollis's forehead, trying not to wake him. There's no point in pretending King Andri will let me anywhere near that parley, so I need Hollis sharp. I need to know if my message reached Eva, if it made any difference at all.

As quietly as I can, I dress and creep out of my room. I have one last card in my hand to attempt to play. Not for Hollis and me, not even for Eva, but to try to stop the war haunting my dreams.

The hallway outside is dark and quiet but studded with more soldiers than I've seen before. I can't turn a corner without Snowcrest green and gray winking from the shadows. They move in tight patrols of two, one human and one wolf, both arrayed in the colors with what I've been told is the crest of the Kar family displayed proudly.

Every pair I pass looks quickly away, eyes hazy with the mind-link. My presence is being tracked through the castle. Is that specifically another symptom of King Andri's distrust? Or just the procedures of this small, heavily militarized kingdom? In times of trouble, King Gavin barely increased security in Solberg Castle because he said no enemy would ever reach us.

I need to focus. I draw in a deep breath, hunting for the charcoal smell not completely unlike my own.

As always, it stands out amongst the crisp Snowcrest scents and the more familiar ones of my family. I turn in that direction and hurry. Hollis only said the parley was before the meeting with Kieran, not when.

I find Kash in a small, glass-walled orangery jutting off the side of one of the towers. Despite the protections on every other shred of the castle, half of the windows here remain uncovered, letting in shafts of golden light that illuminate him below the branches of some fruit tree, eating a rich breakfast.

"Only damn place you can get a breath of fresh air," he says. "Coffee?"

I sit on the floor across from him and accept the mug he pours me from a carafe. "How did you sleep?"

"Better than I would've in that inn." He snorts.

I sip the burning brew and take a deep breath. I've learned so much over the past few months, gained skills I could never have imagined, but that doesn't mean my old skills are useless. If I want Kash to stand with us, maybe even fight with us, I need to use what I know.

My heart.

"I am sorry about that. It probably felt like being thrown under the cart for political gains you don't care about."

He raises his mug to me. "Hear, hear. Your brother doesn't have much in the way of manners."

I glance briefly at the spray of crumbs caught in his facial hair and covering his chest. But I know what he means. Rogues like him operate by a different code, one I've slowly been figuring out.

"It was my idea," I say honestly.

Kash eyes me. "Huh. Turning on your old man already?"

I shake my head. "Acting like the princess I was raised to be. But I don't want to lie like one."

"Well, I can respect that." He takes a massive bite of an unfamiliar pastry. "Just here to tell me that?"

"No." I sip my coffee to steady myself. "I came to say thank you for holding the door. You wouldn't have done that when we first met."

"For you?" He grins. "Course I would've."

"I don't think so. I've been learning a lot about freedom lately. The idea that I don't have the destiny I assumed, that I can make my own path in this world alone, is pretty exhilarating."

"Maybe after all this, you and I hit the trails," he says. "I'll show you the real world."

I glance up at him. "But that freedom has also taught me a lot about loneliness. Being the only one responsible for myself, having to make every decision on my own… it's overwhelming."

"You'll get used to it." Kash flips his hand dismissively. "Always takes a bit of adjustment, but it's in your blood."

"Just like sacrificing you to get that meeting with King Andri is," I say. "I don't think it's a good idea to be fully one or the other. Princesses are too restricted, and rogues are too lonely." I take Kash's leathery hand in mine. "Now that we've found each other, you don't have to be lonely anymore either."

Kash snatches his hand back, a snarl painting his face. "What the fuck do you know about loneliness? You've still got your whole family around you, and you always Goddess-damned did."

I recoil. Kash has never spoken to me like that before. I want to shrink, to apologize, to give up the plan and let Kash do whatever he wants. But I remember Finn's words and steel myself.

Hurt boils in Kash's dark eyes, hot and fresh as the day he first felt it. This is the thing making him so angry, the thing I've sensed just below the surface more than once. And it just might be the only way anyone can reach him.

"King Gavin took a lot from you," I say quietly. "Is that what he took? Your family?"

Kash stares at me for a long moment, tense like he's about to spring. I meet his gaze steadily and wait. There are so many things I don't know about him, but if he'll put his body in the door to make sure I can get inside, he's not going to attack me. I know that in the same place I knew he was my father before that woman from Cirrus Summit confirmed it.

He exhales, and his whole body deflates like a broken toy. "Just had to get your mother's smarts, huh?"

"If I can use anything from her for good, I want to," I reply. "Were they caught in one of his campaigns?"

"You could say that." Kash shakes his head.

I hold my coffee and wait.

"Kash is my name, and the only one I've answered to for twenty-five odd years now. But it isn't the one I was born with." He smiles tiredly. "You're sitting in front of Crown Prince Kashadien Jair LeClair."

My jaw drops. A prince? The crumb-coated, brusque rogue who's been pestering Kieran about compensation for his lack of a relationship with me?

"I shed a few of the habits." Kash runs a hand through his hair. "Course, I did that after I abdicated the throne. Never figured myself much for rulership, and being first in line sounded more like a death sentence than an opportunity. Soon as I came of age, I snuck out of LeClair Castle and never looked back."

LeClair. The name rings a faint bell in my head but not enough to put my finger on why.

Not when the rest of my mind won't stop screaming that I might be a bastard, but I'm a royal bastard. I'm still a princess.

"King Gavin?" I ask numbly.

Kash's bitter chuckle slices through me. "You haven't figured out where I'm from yet, have you?"

I close my eyes and try to sort through half-remembered geography lessons. LeClair belongs to…

"Starfall Mountain."

He nods. "My sister Luci, my parents, all my younger brothers, burned alive in the temple on her wedding day because Gavin's invasion wasn't working. If I hadn't run off, I'd have been right there next to them."

I rock back with the weight of information. The man I believed to be my father slaughtered my true father's family in cold blood. Mother had to have known about it—according to her, all of Father's best plans were hers first.

"Went ahead and slept with Rowena just as soon as news reached me," he offers casually. "I wasn't planning for a kid, but I can't say I regret it. Gavin paid handsomely to hold onto you."

My stomach churns. "I don't believe that. Not that you didn't want me, but that I'm just a payoff to you."

"No?" His smile is sharp as a knife. "Then why'd I only come back when a pretty little thing named Nessa told me Rowena was willing to offer a spit of Dun's Crossing land to do it? A perfectly private patch, all to myself, where no one'd ever bother me again. All for the low, low price of making myself a nuisance."

"Because…." My mind fights to wrap around all the information he's just handed me, hints slotting into place one after the next.

I'm thinking too much. I have a mind, one worth using, but I can't outsmart a former prince who's been surviving alone longer than I've been alive. In truth, I don't want to—or need to. Because it's as plain as the nose on his face that he's spent that time building up armor around his heart as thick as the coating of grime he arrived with. Cutting through that is my only way.

"Because that was what you thought you wanted," I say.

"Thought?" He laughs. "And what do I want now?"

I hear his pained whine when he was caught in the door. "I think you want a chance at a family again. With me."

He looks away sharply. "Land still sounds pretty good."

"If that's what you really want," I say, "it's yours. No tricks, which I'm sure Mother can't promise."

"What's the catch?"

"She sent Nessa to you." The words burn—she orchestrated my public destruction, seemingly just for fun. She couldn't have known I'd mate with Hollis, where all of this would lead. "You've been working with her. Just stop. Whatever information you've been feeding her, whatever favors you've been doing, don't."

He picks at his breakfast. "Why bother? Why not report me in and have me hung from the rafters?"

"No matter what you think, I have lost my family. That they still love me doesn't mean it's not different now. And if you work with us, make this deal, I'd like to try to have a relationship." I meet his gaze. "I don't see any good reason for both of us to be lonely."

He studies me for a long moment. My resolve starts to waver—I've overestimated myself, flying high off a few fluke successes.

"You remind me of Luci," he says. "Got the same hopefulness even when the world keeps kicking you down. It's how I knew she was gonna be better for Starfall than I ever could." He sighs. "I'm all yours, baby girl."

Hot relief floods through me. I throw my arms around his neck, babbling thanks. He hugs me back, more awkward this time, like it's actually real for him now.

As I bounce out of the orangery, I realize I didn't ask him to fight with us, and he didn't say he would.

Maybe he'll surprise me.

PARLEY

Hollis

FATHER AND I MARCH IN LOCKSTEP UP TO THE SMALL DOOR BESIDE THE front gates. Early morning sunlight promises spring might actually arrive in the mountains someday soon, as soft and sweet as waking up to Candace slipping back into the room with a sheepish smile on her face. Low conversation and clattering from the far side of the wall make it impossible to forget what we're walking into, though. Why we're using a side door instead of the main one. Why Father's heavy, furred coronation robe flaps from his shoulders and why I'm wearing the circlet of silver that represents my station.

On the other side of this wall is war.

A soldier lifts the miniature portcullis over the side door with a rattling wheel.

"Drop this behind us," Father declares.

"Your Majesty?" the soldier asks.

I square my shoulders and meet his gaze. "We cannot leave punctures in our defenses. King Andri and I can hold our own long enough to reopen it, if this is an ambush."

The soldier nods. Tension falls over the surrounding crowd like a thick quilt. This isn't a meeting with Soren; this is a parley. Thinking of it as anything else is reckless.

Another soldier unlocks and opens the wooden door, and we step through.

Immediately, the sheer number of Soren's forces confronts me. From the ground, I can't see an end to them. Just a string of smoke trails from cooking fires stretching to the horizon, a thousand tents and weapons and siege towers in the making. But Father doesn't miss a step, so neither do I.

A low, wooden table was lowered down from the gate wall last night, after this talk was set, along with two benches. Father and I take the one that puts our backs to the castle and wait.

'Do not give ground,' he warns me through the mind-link.

'Even if that's the only way to avoid fighting?'

'Then, we retreat and act quickly,' he replies.

That's better than a promise that this is going to work, at least. In the cold light of day, Father seems less sure of his Beta.

Soren steps out of the crowd to a trumpet blast, his armor shining silver and emblazoned with his family crest. Behind him, Eva follows, surrounded by the whole pack of her sisters—and Nessa.

Instinct surges. Before I can stop myself, I reach out to Eva through the mind-link. *'Are you all right? I'm so fucking sorry.'*

Nothing in return. She doesn't even look at me as Soren takes the seat across from Father. Eva and her sisters stand at his right, like a council. Soren and Father exchange the traditional prayers and promises to initiate a parley, both swearing not to attack while the laws of parley apply, but I barely hear them.

Eva looks a little better rested than she did yesterday. Barely. She stands a bit taller, at the front of the pack just as often as surrounded by it. Maybe she got more confident overnight, surrounded by this army.

"You challenge my claim to the throne," Father starts abruptly.

"I challenge the Kar claim." Soren whips a glance at me. "Your bloodline has forsaken the ancient pact, so the Skadi bloodline merely does the same."

"The Goddess assigns our mates. You know this as well as I do, Soren."

"Lord Skadi," he corrects crisply. "I hereby remove myself from the position of your Beta as well. I will not serve under a traitor."

Father scoffs, and my stomach sinks. Soren just hit his pride, killed just about all chances of a helpful parley.

'Can you convince your father to back down on the traitor talk?' I ask Eva. *'Mine won't listen unless he does.'*

More nothingness.

"Rich words from a man attempting a coup," Father says. "Tell me how others' actions make me a traitor."

"You honor the false mate in your home." Soren gestures at the castle behind us. "We have seen her."

"The bastard was leaving when your attack fell, trapping her inside." Father crosses his arms. "Would you have me violate hospitality laws as well? Or is that for clan Skadi alone?"

"One time," Soren snarls. "My mother failed to offer you a meal one time, and you throw it in my face for two decades."

"She refused her newly crowned king and queen!" Father slams his hand on the table. "I should have known then you could not be trusted."

"She did not yet recognize your queen, your marriage was so hasty."

Something hot bubbles in my throat. Soren isn't allowed to talk about Mother that way. I find myself leaning forward, opening my mouth.

"Snowcrest loved my queen," Father says first. "Can the same be said for your wife?"

It's like looking in a mirror—well, like looking in a shitty mirror that emphasizes all the worst parts of one's self. These two grown men, one of whom shares my square jaw and heavy features, scream at each other across a table in the snow. They turn red in the face as they unearth old, petty hurts like hundreds of lives don't hang in the balance. They're too Goddess-damned proud, the both of them, to take a single step back and think.

Before Candace, I would've been yelling right alongside them. Fuck, I almost still did. And I have no idea how to talk them down.

My gaze drifts to Eva. She watches the two of them dully, almost disinterested, but she has her arms wrapped around herself the way she always does when she's upset. Holding herself together.

She and I weren't supposed to see all the same tutors, I remember suddenly. While I studied government, she was supposed to learn how to manage a household. We refused to be separated—and Father was actually the one who changed the schedule, against Soren's wishes. What Candace said last night about being seen but not heard flickers through my mind.

Maybe I don't need to talk them down. Maybe, aside from giving the orders, Soren and Father aren't actually the ones who matter here at all.

"What do you want to do, Lady Eva?" I ask.

Soren chokes on the end of the sentence I interrupted. Father freezes. It almost feels like the breeze hesitates to blow through. Eva lifts her head and meets my gaze for the first time. Pain and rage simmer through the dullness.

"This is what she wants," Soren says. "As I was saying—"

"No." I stare at the man who was such a large part of my child-hood. "I want to hear it from her."

"Rein in your son," Soren snarls.

Father clenches his jaw but doesn't look at me. "Prince Hollis is a man. We come to this table together."

I grin. His united front is working in my favor for once. "Eva." I meet her gaze, hold it even though it hurts. "Tell me what you want, and I'll make it happen."

Soren lunges up like he's actually going to fucking hit me. "She is not at this table—"

"I want you to hurt," Eva says roughly. "You and Candace, I want you to feel what I feel."

Acid burns through my veins. Hard certainty stiffens her shoulders. Maybe she didn't ask Soren to gather an army or march on Kar Castle, but she's not upset that he has.

And here I was, making fun of Father for believing he could get through to Soren. I had no idea how badly I hurt my best friend.

Soren grins hungrily. "The best way to make them hurt stands behind us, darling."

She nods sharply and looks away from me.

"What if Candace and I—"

Father interrupts me. "You will not compromise."

"Not for my family." Soren leans back, pleased as a cat. "You heard her wishes."

"We have wasted time and breath." Father stands. "I will meet you in battle at your chosen time."

He turns with a flourish of his cape and starts marching back toward the side door. I scramble to my feet and follow after him. Arguing with him out here is a real waste of breath—anything I say in Soren's earshot means less than nothing—but he threw away the only chance Soren offered us to end this, and I'm not letting him just walk off.

With a flurry of rattling, the door opens, and we step back inside.

"He would've accepted Candace and I," I say.

"Eva would have." Father continues marching away like he's trying to escape the cluster of men by the door. "Soren has grown greedy in his pride. He will not concede for anything but our throne."

"*His* pride?" I scoff. "You brought up his mother. What kind of parley was that?"

"What it needed to be." He wheels on me. "Say what you mean or allow me to refuse Alpha Kieran."

Fuck, I forgot about that meeting. Half my brain is still sitting at that table, staring into Eva's eyes, but I've got one fucking chance.

"A few days before we lost Mother, she talked to me alone. I think... I think she wanted me to cry with her." I swallow. I've never told Father this before—usually, any mention of her ends conversations. "I couldn't because *you* told me Snowcrest needed me to be strong, to maintain the pride of the kingdom through this loss. After that, she never looked at me the same."

He clenches his hands into fists. "Snowcrest did need you. They still do."

"And so did Mother." I shake my head. "I didn't choose not to. I couldn't. She asked me for something, and I couldn't fucking do it because I was so busy trying to be a paragon of emotionlessness, closed off to anything but my duty."

"Should I have wept for Soren?" Father sneers.

"No." I cross my arms. "It's too fucking late for that, and I think you know it. But you also know there's a world of difference between bending the knee and opening the door to welcome a potential friend. Think about that while you go to this meeting."

Father stares past me. A large clock ticks the passing time loudly. His meeting approaches.

"I spent years terrified you were my Lara's son." He sighs. "Were she here, she'd have reminded me that was nothing to fear."

He claps me on the shoulder once and strides away. I wait until he's out of sight, then punch the air. He actually fucking listened to me!

COOPERATION

Candace

'*He's in,*' Kieran says through the mind-link. '*Everyone convene in the main dining room in fifteen minutes.*'

I look up at Ingrid, painting on the other side of her sitting room. She grins at me. I don't know what comes next from here, and I doubt she does either, but we won't be trapped in Kar Castle while a doomed fight rages outside.

To think, a few months ago I was worried about a dream of a slightly bloody mate.

As we ready ourselves, I reach out to Kash and give him the information. I haven't heard from him since this morning, haven't even seen him, but I'm holding out hope.

By the time we reach the main dining room, one of the biggest spaces I've seen in Kar Castle yet, it's already halfway transformed into a massive war room. King Andri, in a simple shirt and trousers, no sign of the imperious cloaks he usually wears, orders staff this way and that with simple nods of his head. Hollis confers with a small knot of soldiers behind him. Taner and Kieran lean over a massive map.

My heart speeds. I take Ingrid's hand and squeeze it. We only have a few hours before Lord Soren's twenty-four-hour deadline—it's time to find out if I can stop a dream in its tracks.

Hollis looks up as I enter then smiles. My chest warms.

"Should we get started?" he asks King Andri, loud enough for everyone to hear.

His father glances at him then surveys all of us slowly. His gaze catches on me, hard and distrustful. I hold my breath. "Yes." He marches to the head of the table and sits.

Everyone else filters in around him. Hollis takes the spot on his right, Kieran on his left. I sit next to Hollis. Finn ambles in and shuts the door behind him while we're settling—no sign of Kash.

Him showing up was a long shot. I swallow my disappointment.

King Andri spreads a map of the castle and grounds out on the table. Hollis places a handful of tiny tent markers outside the gate.

"Do we have solid numbers?" Kieran asks.

"Scouts report as low as 175, as high as 215." Hollis keeps placing tents. "We don't know if he has any reinforcements."

"He does not," King Andri rumbles. "Soren shows his strength and lacks patience. This is his force. Within our walls, we have one hundred soldiers, thirty potential recruits, and those in this room."

Hollis plunks singular men inside the castle walls.

"We've already sent a messenger back to Dun's Crossing for a battalion of reinforcements, which should be here within a few hours." Kieran studies the map. "I'm sure you've been made aware of my mother's escape."

King Andri grimaces. "Do you believe she will fight?"

"Can't count it out."

"She's been training her powers," I say. "That's how she got out, but she's been working on them since she was deposed. She... told me."

Ingrid squeezes my hand on my left. Hollis, on my right, rubs my shoulder. King Andri watches the movement like a hawk but doesn't say a word.

"Wind powers," Kieran says with disgust.

Hollis glances at the small pile of bow-wielding miniatures he was pulling out. "So then there's no point in arming the walls."

"She is one woman," King Andri says. "Archers will avoid her."

"We could also try to counteract her," Taner says. "What about reinforcements from Escuro?"

King Andri's frown deepens, the message clear—he's allowed one ally, but a second is pushing it.

Then, he looks at Hollis. Hollis looks at him. Something has obviously happened between them because King Andri sighs and says, "How would we reach them?"

"I'm mind-linked to the pack," Kieran offers.

"Not at this distance, unless Luna Delaney and Alpha Cole are on their way here now," Ingrid says. "And if we've got a hundred and nine people, we can't lose the only one who's killed an Alpha."

"Did you kill him in combat?" King Andri asks.

Kieran swallows. A heartbeat of quiet passes. There's no sign of the haughty king I remember from Anwen's wedding or the bristling, brusque host I've grown used to over our days here, but it feels like he could reappear at any moment. This question threatens to blow what little cooperation we've managed to pieces.

"Paw-to-paw," Kieran says.

King Andri nods. "When this ends, I will tell others that. It will earn you much-needed respect."

"Thank you."

Breathless tension deflates. King Andri actually wants to work with us, now and in the future. I shoot Hollis a tiny grin. He must've said something—and if King Andri can do this, maybe he can accept us.

"Are there any other kingdoms worth reaching out to?" Hollis asks. "What about Sundrop Gem?"

I shake my head. "They'd help if they could, but they have no standing army, and we have even less of a way to talk to them."

"Somebody has to ask," Ingrid says abruptly. "We're not sticking to Soren's timeline, right?"

"There is no honorable combat with traitors," King Andri replies severely. "We will strike once prepared."

From there, the planning moves easily. I contribute whenever I have ideas—mostly about Mother, since I'm the only one who's really talked to her since Kieran took the throne. Miniature archers are placed on walls, removed. Castle defenses are interrogated. Military terms are argued over. Slowly, a plan starts to come together as minutes tick away. The longer we wait, the longer Soren has to complete his siege preparations.

The doors swing open. We leap to our feet at varying speeds, like Soren could've gotten this deep into the castle without us hearing a peep.

Kash strides in, an easy grin on his face. "Sorry I'm late."

"I do not believe you were invited," King Andri says coldly.

So his change of heart has its limits. I start to shrink. Hollis catches my eye.

"I did," he says. "I thought—"

"No," I interrupt, "I told him about this meeting. I hoped he might be able to help—he's already agreed to stop assisting my mother."

'Assisting?' Kieran demands through the mind-link. *'Why didn't you tell me?'*

'I figured it out this morning, and you've been a little busy,' I reply. *'And... I didn't know if it would make a difference.'*

"Nice to meet you all," Kash says. "I'm Kashadien LeClair, former prince of Starfall Mountain."

Ingrid shoots me a wide-eyed look. Hollis grabs my arm. Finn nods like he already knew, but he might just want to look smug.

King Andri stands. "By the Goddess, you are."

"Long time, no recognize." Kash smirks. "My girl convinced me I was on the wrong team, and I was getting tired of sulking by myself. Hollis, want to give me a couple of those little toys?"

Hollis frowns as he obeys then whispers to me, "Do you believe him?"

I don't hesitate. "Yes."

Kash sets a dozen of them at different points behind Soren's army. "Ain't many rogues in the area this time of year, but I managed to reach a handful that owed me a favor or two. I figure harrying the bastard from the back'll bridge the gap between us marching out and King Kieran's army showing up."

King Andri studies Kash for a long moment. "Smart."

Kash winks at me before taking a seat. "Glad you think so. They're already in position. What else?"

My chest warms. He's here. For me—for us.

I've got a father.

A few more plans fly. Ways to start the fighting without opening the main gate, traps to set inside the castle in the event of a breach, optimal timing. But it quickly becomes clear that there's not much left to do. We're outmanned, potentially out armed, but there is a reason Soren didn't lead with a full-frontal assault. Fighting from a reinforced position like this gives us a lot of advantages, and between the minds at the table, we're taking advantage of all of them.

Finally, King Andri bangs his fist on the table. "Go, dress. We strike in thirty minutes. May the Goddess guide your steps."

"May the Goddess guide your steps," I echo with the rest of the table.

Hollis takes my hand as I stand. Wordlessly, the two of us leave, and he leads me to his room. It's massive, a bed larger than any but the Alpha's at home in the middle of the room and weapons and armor lining almost every wall.

"Aren't you worried about someone killing you in your sleep?" I offer him a small smile.

"With my reflexes and you at my side?" He strides to one wall and starts pulling down leather armor for wolves and humans. "Never again."

Step by step, he shows me how to put on the armor, how to adjust each buckle so it fits correctly. His hands glide over my skin temptingly.

"Why are you teaching me this?" I ask. "It's not like I'm going to be able to put it on in the middle of battle, and I only barely know how to fight as a wolf."

"Self-defense training. That's what we should've been spending our time on." He groans playfully, but I can hear the real worry underneath it.

"I'll take care of myself," I say.

"If you can put the armor on, I need to know you're able to." He caresses my cheek. "Okay?"

"I need to know you won't try some heroic sacrifice." I stare up into his eyes.

"On one condition." He touches the spot on my bodice his mother's necklace hides behind. "Wear it for me?"

That warmth in my chest redoubles, almost painfully pleasant. I unhook the necklace from its hiding spot, offer it to him, then spin around and lift my hair. He clasps it around my neck with gentle fingers.

"I will put on the armor if I can." I twist to face him and touch the symbol on my breastbone.

"I will come home to you if I can," he replies.

Our mouths meet, and I have no idea which of us moved first. The hunger of last night is missing—banked, not gone—and in its place, a soft wishfulness shines. I trace my desire for better timing, better choices, an easier path onto his lips. He kisses back an aching hope that what comes next will be easier, a want not to be saying goodbye again.

I pull back, meet his emerald gaze, and know exactly what to say.

"I love you."

The warmth in my chest suffuses my limbs, my whole body. I love him. No tricks, no hiding, just the truth, naked between us.

Hollis opens his mouth.

'Rowena's here,' Taner says through the mind-link. *'And she's headed for Skadi. I don't think we have any more time to lose.'*

I look at Hollis to see if he's heard the same thing from his own scouts.

He grabs my hand. "Let's go."

FOREGONE CONCLUSION

Hollis

I STAND WITH MY SQUAD AT ONE OF THE SIDE DOORS, WAITING FOR THE final signal from Father. Pinning Soren's forces in, making it so their numbers are useless because they can't get enough of them out to change anything, is the highest priority, so everyone is attacking from different angles. Candace is already somewhere on the west side, where fighting is expected to be thinnest, because she barely has any training.

My stomach churns. I touch the smooth bow on my back, the one-handed sword on my hip. The familiar weapons don't steady me. My mate is dozens of feet away, about to risk her life, and there's no more I can do to help.

And I didn't even tell her I loved her.

'*Ready?*' Father barks.

'*Ready!*' I roar in return with a hundred other Snowcrest voices.

'*Now.*'

One of my squad mates slams the door open, I whip my bow off my back, and we pour out. Nock an arrow, breathe, release. A soldier falls. A maid shuts the door behind us, and the lock clanks into position. I prowl across the stretch of snowy ground surrounded by men I've known all my life, men I trained with and trained, like death in a cloud of arrows.

Shouts go up. Trumpets sound, nearby and farther away. Soren's men leap to attention, grabbing weapons, shifting, screaming war cries. The element of surprise didn't last for fucking long.

A group of three wolves barrels toward us, too fast for me to take aim. I shove my bow and sword into the bag over my shoulder, drop it, and shift. Fur explodes from my skin. I hit the ground a heartbeat before they arrive and slash out with a paw. My claws rake over flesh. Someone howls.

Instinct takes over. Mind-links fly between my squad and me, tracking enemies from every direction as we fight deeper into the fray. My claws grow sticky, and my mouth tastes like iron. For all my training, I've never fought in a real battle before. I never expected it to be so second nature, so like a hunt.

I throw myself to the side when snow crunches in an unexpected place. The enemy wolf plows headfirst into the nothingness where I once stood, earning himself nothing but a mouthful of snow. With a flick of my snout, I solidify the snow in place.

The answering whine catches my ear. It's… familiar?

Like I'm not in the middle of pitched battle, I look closer at the wolf on the ground, and realization hits. The mottled brown-and-black coat, the amber eyes. This is Karsen, a soldier I trained with when I was younger. He was particularly good with a crossbow.

Claws sear into my back. I wheel, a small part of me grateful I don't have to keep looking at Karsen's panicked face. A gray wolf bares his teeth at me. I feint like I'm going to leap at him then dodge to the side and try to snag his back leg between my teeth.

He dodges instinctively. Not just dodges but whips around and sweeps my feet out from underneath me.

Which is what I teach people to do if anyone tries to use that move against them.

I suck in a breath as I crash into a snowdrift. I see ink and some winter tree I half-recognize through the blood. That's Johan, a recruit I trained a few years back.

Fuck, he can't be more than seventeen now.

My stomach riots, and the rhythm breaks. With a little magic, I tunnel through the drift and come out on the other side. Another wolf lunges into my path—who's that going to be? One of the trainees who just washed out, no more than twelve or thirteen? Someone who trained me, who I respect?

The first thing I learned about war was the sweetness of victory. The glory, the pride, the glow of success. I feel that on hunts.

Here, I'm nothing but a butcher.

'Captain?' one of my men asks.

'I'm strategizing,' I snap as I back into the drift again.

Wolves howl. The air reeks of blood. I can't think about who I might be fighting, but I can't forget either.

It already feels like the fate foretold in Candace's dream is coming true. This whole fucking battle is a foregone conclusion, a step on the path to the nightmare world she saw. We're going to lose, and Soren is going to march over the world. As bad as Gavin or worse. There was no damn point to any of this because she already dreamt the future, and those dreams always come true.

'I love you,' Candace says in my memory.

That only makes me sicker. I love her—at least, I'm pretty damn sure I do. And obviously, she doesn't think we should wait until the dust settles. But I looked at her, and all I could think about was finding her body among the dead.

If I don't admit I love her, maybe the Goddess won't think to take her from me like She's taken damn near everyone else.

All together like that, it sounds fucking stupid. Like a kid trying to keep the monsters under the bed from becoming real by saying they're not there. Like screaming into the wind against fate.

Which I've done a fucking lot lately, if I think about it. Every time Candace and I walked away from each other, that's what we were doing. We're back together now, but that feels like a choice.

Maybe her dreams aren't set in stone either.

I explode out of the drift, a plan taking shape as I run. *'Follow me. We're looking for a grayish-yellow wolf. Only attack as you must to get through.'*

My squad follows orders without a breath of complaint, even though I've just taken a hammer to the plan. Together, we tear through the scrum of wolves locked in battle.

Distracting Candace right now sounds like a fucking death sentence, but she gets her powers from Kash. He'll know the answer, and I'd bet the rangy old rogue knows his way through a fight. He strikes me as the sort of bastard that can't be killed, no matter how impossible it seems or how much you might wish he could sometimes.

I somersault into a snarling tan wolf, roll to my feet, and keep running even as someone else slices across my ribcage. My eyes water with the sharp burst of pain, and the spatter of blood on snow chases my footfalls. It's not lethal, so it's not worth my fucking time. I have to know if we're wasting lives out here.

Banners sway over the crowd, and I avoid them. Soren is a fighter, so I doubt he'd stick by the side of some kid with a flag, but I can't risk the chance. Wherever he is, Eva will be, and I know I won't be able to stop myself from going to her if I see her. I'm not even sure what I'd do. Protect her? Try to get her out? The hurt in her eyes burns worse than the cuts on my ribs, and I still know I couldn't fight her.

Time crawls by with no sign of Kash. Someone gets their teeth around my shoulder. One of my squad mates takes a deep claw to the haunch and has to fall back. I sniff like my fucking life depends on it, but everything just smells like blood.

I keep running. He'll be near the back, with his rogues, and nothing is more important than answering this question right now. If I was thinking fucking clearly, I'd have asked before we even got out here. I'll fight until my dying fucking breath for Snowcrest and for Candace, but I don't want to die for a battle already decided.

Not without telling Candace I love her. If we're both going to die, she has to know.

Slaloming side to side, I slip through a brawl so chaotic I don't even know which wolf was on which side and emerge into a slightly clearer patch of battlefield.

Kash stands on the far side, surrounded by two darker wolves. One swipes at his back legs. The other rears back for a leap.

Finally, instinct clicks back into place. I throw myself over the snow and catch the leaping wolf broadside. We tumble away in a pile, and I scratch my way to the higher position. With the other wolf in the snow beneath me, I exhale a gust of icy air. He freezes into place.

Someone yelps. I turn to find my squad already dragging the other wolf away from Kash by the haunches and tail. Between the remaining three of them, he doesn't stand a chance.

I take a deep breath and shift into human form. The freezing air is bracing, restoring some of my strength but stinging my still-bleeding wounds.

"Your dreams—Candace's dreams—do you ever have ones you know are prophetic but don't come true?" I dodge a spear hurtling through the air with a wince. "Can we change the outcome, or are we just going to die here?"

Kash cocks his head to the side, then shifts. "Sometimes they fail."

"How?" My voice breaks with desperation.

"It's tough to explain." He sighs. "I guess the easiest way is… well, they come true if those involved act the same way they would've before knowing about them."

I fall back into a shift and bolt off in a new direction.

FACE TO FACE

Candace

A WOLF DIVES AT ME OUT OF THE SCREAMING, CLASHING MAYHEM, ITS maw drenched in blood. One half of my brain orders a paw to swing. The other shouts, *RUN!* I manage a hopping scramble that seems more likely to get me killed than anything else.

And one of the men Hollis picked to stay at my side through the battle catches the attacker's back foot between his teeth and yanks him back. Two of the others swarm out from behind me like a cloud of death, and the reek of blood in the air intensifies.

I heave. It's so much like my dream, so little like anything else I've ever experienced. I'm just grateful Ingrid didn't fight me when I told her she should stay in the castle. I only got a few self-defense lessons, but she barely had any at all.

More claws swing toward me. The final member of the team Hollis assigned to me attempts to interrupt them, but some instinct a trainer actually managed to inculcate into me fires, and I dodge out of the way before he has to. Adrenaline courses through my muscles.

'You're small, decently quick,' I remember the trainer saying. *'Fighting's a waste of your energy. Just try not to get hit.'*

That, I might be able to do without losing my breakfast in the snow. And since I'm here at least partially to draw attacks from our other fighters, it's all I really need to do.

Look pretty, do nothing.

An arrow zings through the air, aimed for my head, before I can get upset. Trying to survive is distracting, at least.

The longer I spend in the chaos, the duller my nose becomes to the scent of blood. I begin to pick out other smells, just enough to identify my guards, then enough to track basic movements. I dodge left, right, down. An enemy wolf rolls away from one of my guards, and I manage to replicate the move the next time someone swings on me.

My heartbeat throbs in my ears. I am seconds away from death at every moment, which the corpses already littering the ground make impossible to forget. If I didn't know my dreams were actually prophetic, I would now. The only thing missing is the ground destroyed by battle after battle on the same land.

And the creeping dread of failure. I have never been more scared, but I felt the change when we were planning inside. We're working together. Reinforcements are coming. I don't know what's going to happen to me, to Hollis, but I don't think the world ends here.

I'm holding onto the hope that it isn't because I want to know if Hollis loves me, too.

A gust of wind pulls snow off the ground into a miniature blizzard. I squint against the sudden obscurity, waiting for enemies to jump out.

Then, I smell it. Black tea and violets.

That's not the wind. That's Mother.

I turn and try to scramble back, but it's already too late.

'Candace,' she calls through the mind-link. *'I've come so far to see you.'*

A retort burns on the tip of my tongue, but I can't bring myself to say it. Goosebumps raise under my fur. I can't do anything—not only is she here, she's right in front of me. Hollis's men look at me in confusion.

The fighting ahead parts as she advances, surrounded by a miniature tornado of her own making. I can just barely make out the four-legged shape of her within the swirl of air and snow. My heartbeat pounds louder than her storm.

It's one thing to leave Mother in the dungeon. To resent everything she did to me in Escuro. To maybe even, in the private corners of my heart, dislike her.

But to *attack* her? To risk tasting her blood, knowing I ended her life? That's completely different.

The storm breaks for a breath then reignites behind me. Cutting me off from Hollis's men and the entire rest of the battle. Her pale fur shines dully, almost lilac in the strange reflection of the wind and snow. Her eyes narrow, and she pads toward me.

I scurry to the side. *Dodge, don't fight.* It's only the wind keeping me here—I should just be able to leap through it and escape.

A sword swirls past, caught in the cyclone. Like the tornadoes that plague Lilywind and Lightning Cape, she's picked up whatever she's passed over. Any jump could send me into a cloud of blades, a caught wolf—a corpse.

'*You truly were my favorite,*' Mother snarls through the mind-link.

'*I'm sorry,*' I blurt. '*I never meant—*'

She barks a laugh. '*You never meant anything I didn't intend for you, darling, until that Escuro bitch started whispering in your ear.*'

'*Raven?*'

Mother prowls closer, and I skitter back.

'*Who else?*' she replies. '*Or do you have another reason why the children I dedicated my life, my soul, my* everything *to would abandon me like a week-old carcass?*'

I trot in place, looking for a way out. Mother's long strides whip her around the tornado almost as fast as the wind itself, and every time I try to avoid her, she pushes me farther toward the middle of the circle she's created.

'*Ah,*' she says like she's finally cracked one of the secrets of the universe. '*It wasn't Blanca, was it?*'

'*Help!*' I yell to Kieran, Taner, and Finn. The rest of our reinforcements aren't here yet, so they're my only hopes.

'*It was you.*'

A finger of wind lashes out and flogs my back, like I remember her doing to Raven so often with the fireplace poker or a horsewhip. Agony shakes my bones, and I whine. Mother has never hit me before.

'*I suspected it, you know.*' A smile parts her black lips, and more tendrils of wind sprout from her cyclone. '*You always had too much of your father in you. Willful. Unmannered. Nasty. Goddess above, Gavin would've loved you if you only had a cock. Instead, I had to endure.*'

Memories of myself before Raven and Kieran's Haze ricochet through my brain. The lies, the preening, the endless times I convinced everyone to torture Raven or some other whipping girl of the week with a gesture. Just because I was bored.

'*Of course, he also would've killed you,*' she snarls. '*And we would've all been better off. Killing you now is just fixing an old mistake, darling.*'

At the center of Mother's tornado, surrounded by her in every way, I shrink. Another tendril crashes into my side, knocking me off my feet.

'*I'm sorry,*' I mumble through the pain. '*I'm sorry, I just wanted to be happy.*'

'*Happy?*' she shrieks. '*I was raising you to be happy. Strong men, proud men like Gavin, they don't want a partner. They want a pretty little bird who sings on command. If I wasn't enough, you never would have been on your own. You aren't! Your own mate loathes you.*'

I lift my head. That's not true. I don't know if Hollis loves me—by his eyes when we're together, by that soft little smile I've been seeing more often, by the way he speaks to his father about me, I think he does—but I know he doesn't hate me. Not anymore.

Mother's eyes blaze with something hot and wild. '*If you can be anything near happy with a woman who would've given her life for you in a cell below your feet, you're colder than me.*'

She's at least as much to blame, Hollis said last night. He meant for everything that happened in Escuro, but… for every memory of my own viciousness I dredge up, there's a matching one of bragging about it to Mother. Her cool smiles, her faint praise. I made every choice, but she wanted me to.

A tendril cracks through the air, and I roll to the side.

'You are my one regret!' Mother's voice cracks at the top of her register. *'If I had a mother as good as I was to you, I would've known to destroy you before Gavin ever found out. I'll make certain every single one of your siblings is ruined by the time I'm done, but you, I'll take out of the world myself.'*

Her cruelty batters against the flimsy armor of Hollis's words, but it doesn't break through. I dodge another cudgel of wind. I've heard her scream like this before, the worst possible things she can think to say, with weapons of all kinds in her hands. Always at Raven, always with the silent promise that she'd never turn on the other five of us.

Or did I just imagine that promise? Because her voice lives in my head, picking at every mistake I make. Telling me to keep silent, to make myself smaller, to never forget that I come last. Mother never hit me or spoke to me like this before Kieran claimed the throne, but cruelty, she dealt in spades. All while wearing that polite little smile of hers and reassuring me that I needed every word she said to survive.

'No,' I say quietly.

'You don't say no to me.' Three bursts of air explode out of her storm. *'Not here. Not ever!'*

I dart to the side, trying to find an ebb in her rhythm. Knocking my head against a sword can't be worse than standing here and letting her talk to me like this. If I lure her out, maybe Hollis's men can—

'You stupid bitch! Just sit still like a good dog!"

The wind whips faster. I slide up to it, then my head passes through.

Chunks of ice and snow lacerate my skin like tiny knives, even through my fur, and I can't see the other side. She's thickened the barrier, cut us off further, and my body screams for relief.

I yank back. She cackles through the mind-link. One thing becomes painfully obvious: I will never be happy with my mother in the world. She won't rest, and she'll only get angrier.

But even knowing she's a monster who needs to die, can I kill her?

BEHAVE DIFFERENTLY

Hollis

ALL I HAVE TO DO IS BEHAVE LIKE I WOULDN'T HAVE BEFORE I HEARD about the prophecy. Before that night under the oak tree with Candace, before I knew her shy smile, before all the ups and downs of these weeks.

A deep, bassy howl splits the air. Wolves around me twist toward it. Footfalls echo off the mountains. Does Soren have reinforcements, or—

Dun's Crossing's flag flies over the horizon. The reinforcements are here! I throw my head back and join my howl with the others. Focus splits, and fighting breaks out anew. This is all we need to win.

But not all we need to keep Soren from escaping, licking his wound, and trying again, from someone else on this battlefield deciding that winning the fight is their first step. This battle doesn't change anything unless I behave differently.

It should be fucking easy. Ever since I woke up next to Candace, I've been behaving in ways I barely recognize. But the truth is, I didn't change; she changed me. I fought her tooth and nail the whole

Goddess-damned way, but she did it. So I need to find a way to act like her. Look at this fucking nightmare and see what she would see.

Another wolf launches himself at me. We tussle, claws and teeth everywhere. Blood paints both of our coats, and I don't even know where all of it on me comes from anymore. The other wolf snarls, a show of dominance belied by the wild fear in his eyes. Fear I've seen in a thousand trainees—in soldiers I'm training alongside.

And I know exactly what Candace would see. She's so much a part of me now that I was already feeling it on the run to find Kash.

'*Fight to subdue,*' I shout through mind-link to every damn person I can reach. To Father, to anyone on Soren's side who hasn't fully detached themselves from the pack. '*Not to kill. Snowcrest is Snowcrest, and we don't kill our own.*'

Father's voice rumbles through my mind, a private message. '*You would limit our abilities?*'

'*I wouldn't spill our pack's blood,*' I reply. '*If we want it to be, this could be one fight, not the first battle of a war.*'

My thoughts are my own for long seconds. I throw myself between the jaws of a silver Dun's Crossing soldier and a wolf with a Snowcrest-red pelt. No matter what Father says, no matter what the rest of them do, I have to behave differently.

'*Obey your prince,*' Father says.

I meet the Dun's Crossing wolf's gaze, then freeze the paws of the wolf behind me to the snow. Soren's man whines, but he doesn't take the chunk out of my shoulder I know he could at this angle. One breathless heartbeat passes, pinned between two unreachable strangers with every reason to tear me to shreds.

The Dun's Crossing wolf steps back, allowing me the freedom to get up. Soren's warrior doesn't swing on me as I move away. When I glance at him, he's fighting with the ice shackling him to the ground and nothing else.

I howl, high and bright. My squadron hurries to my flanks, and we charge deeper into the battle. The silver Dun's Crossing wolf joins us, falling into formation like he's been training with us all along. We find another cluster of fighting and plunge into it. I knock a clawed paw away from someone's throat without glancing at who it was headed toward. Flags and insignias blur to nothing in my vision. I may have only told my men to stop trying to kill Soren's soldiers, but the silver wolf moving with the same military precision through the scrum as my own squadron reminds me that I'm not fighting to end this fight, to protect my people, but to end that world-burning war Candace saw touching every kingdom.

That, more than anything else, is what Candace has changed in me. Candace worries so much about being selfish, being cruel, but she's got the biggest heart of any person I've ever met. She accepted Kash when no one else would because she wanted to give him the chance to prove us all wrong. Hell, she kept giving me chances to repair my past mistakes.

It seems so fucking obvious now. If we all stand together, joined for celebrations like the revitalization of Escuro or royal weddings, there's no threat we can't face. There can be no next King Gavin, no tyrant that runs through the world like a plague. Not if we don't allow him to. Alliances aren't chips to trade like a global game of cards. They're proof of our bonds with each other, the only things that keep us from descending into the true anarchy of rogues.

A dull brown wolf—a rogue—clobbers one of Soren's to the ground and uses his paws like fists until the other wolf lies still beneath him.

Not even rogues. The animal chaos of unshifting wolves, fighting only for themselves and their pack. I'm not going to be one of them, and I'll drag all of Snowcrest with me. By force, if I have to.

The tide of battle shifts around me, slowly but surely. Instead of the furious frenzy of blood I saw mere moments ago, things start to ease. They don't stop. They don't even really slow. But I watch fewer throats get torn from the fur surrounding them. Fewer wolves, whimpering in pain from wounds that will take hours to kill them, litter the ground at my feet. Wolves of all colors are actually fighting to subdue. Magic courses through the air, not as spears of ice or clubs of snow, but as traps, restraints, blocks. When I throw myself between killing blows and their recipients, the delivering wolf hesitates a little less before turning away. A handful of people shift out of wolf form, seemingly just to be able to manage the force of their blows more closely. Bladed weapons disappear in favor of blunted ones.

Soren himself was one of my most common trainers when I was learning to fight. He taught me the basics of honorable combat, the rules of violence within Snowcrest. Those rules were simple and clear: if you start a fight, you end it. An enemy left alive is an enemy with another chance to kill you. Don't let enemies suffer—a lethal blow from the start means you don't have to waste time on mercy killing. A thousand little ways to say, anyone you face in combat dies or kills you. There is no other way. This is how it's always been.

Just like the tradition entwining the Skadi and Kar lines. Maybe the change was a sign from the Goddess, just not the one Soren thinks.

Since losing Mother, I've put everything I have, everything I am, into being the prince Snowcrest has always had. Under Father's instruction, under Soren's, under my fucking own more often than I'd like to admit. But as one wolf helps a fallen enemy stand back up instead of hitting him while he's down, I realize what a waste of Goddess-damned time that was. Tradition isn't good for its own sake. And, hell, I don't want to live in the world Father did. I want to live in a new one—one I build with Candace at my side, guiding me with her heart. I'm not the prince or the son he wanted. I'm going to be the man I want to be.

And that means I don't want to watch people I'm responsible for get hurt over my fucking mistake, even if they're not dying. This whole fucking battle is about a personal conflict Soren is blowing up into something dynastic. It comes down to how Candace and I— really I—treated Eva. None of us can control the Haze, but we can control our actions after it. The look in Eva's eyes when she said she wanted us to hurt sears through me like a coal through snow, but she's not a stranger to me. She never could be, and pretending other-wise is the same bullshit that made me avoid telling her the truth in the first place. I wanted to maintain the way things had always been between us like any change would destroy what used to be and erase our chance at a better relationship moving forward. Snowcrest has to change, and so do I.

I shift into human form, grab the armor in the bag around my neck, and start putting it on while running at the silver wolf still fighting alongside my squadron. He looks up as I hop toward him, one foot in a boot.

"Tell Candace," I say breathlessly, "to meet me at the center of the courtyard."

The wolf inclines his massive head, and I take off running before he attempts any other reply. There's no time to wait. I have to reach the center of the fighting.

Because I still know Eva, so I know where she's going to be.

FIGHTING FOR MYSELF

Candace

MOTHER'S WALL OF WIND REACHES OUT TO ENSNARE ME, AND I REALIZE it doesn't matter if I can kill her. I need to fight, or there's no way out. Heart pounding, I dodge away from reaching fingers of wind, so close they ruffle my fur, and turn. She lurks across the circle from me, obviously waiting for my response.

'That is your strong suit,' I bark through the mind-link. *'Waiting for others to act.'*

She snarls, and in her split-second of distraction, I charge her. I've never spoken to her like that before. The words burn through me, hot and electric. If I can do that—

A club of wind slams into my side, sending me skidding through the snow. Pain radiates through my ribs.

'Do not mistake patience for passivity,' Mother replies.

The club rears back, ready to strike again. I kick my back legs and roll away. A cloud of snow puffs into the air where it lands beside me. I only have a split second to breathe before I have to roll again. Avoiding the heavy thuds pushes me back toward the wall once more.

We're playing keep-away, I realize. Mother may be stronger than she was, but her weakness was always concentration, which her power requires a lot of to use. She was always pulled in too many directions, managing too many things, to control anything more than the smallest breeze. The dungeon obviously gave her time to focus, but the battlefield is overwhelming. There's less of it, locked away in here, but if I can break her concentration, I can get her to drop the wall or even just stop attacking for a moment.

'*Kieran removed your royal portrait from the gallery!*' I yell.

The club hesitates in midair. It's all I need. I scramble to my feet and bolt toward her.

'*Liar!*' she shrieks. '*Petty, childish little brat.*'

I glance to either side, watching for another club, but none appear. When I look back to the front, I realize my mistake. Needle-thin whips of wind explode out of the wall behind her and lash at me in a single, furious wave. Pain runs through me like a river originating from a thousand different points. My vision goes white, and I stumble.

She cackles. '*I taught you everything you know. Do you really think such a small lie will stop me?*'

I hoped. But as my senses start to return, I realize how stupid that was. Mother struggled with focus because she was such a talented multitasker. Nothing happened in Solberg Castle without her knowing about it. I never got away with a single rule-break, never kept a secret for more than even a few hours. Some of her information I know came from me, but the rest remains a mystery. Sometimes, I thought she was lying about her powers, and she actually could see everywhere within the walls. Single, small distractions like that won't affect her.

As I struggle back to my feet, I say, '*I just thought you should know.*'

If I insist it's true, maybe some small part of her mind will keep worrying about it.

She throws spikes of air at me. I dance side to side, trying to replicate footwork I've learned in a wolf body. The steps aren't quite right, but holding onto them keeps me focused, in rhythm.

'*You always insist on drawing things out,*' Mother says. '*At least I know destroying Finn will be quick. I doubt he cares enough to resist.*'

'*Then you don't know your son.*' I roll out of the way of a club that appears on my left. '*Finn will see you coming from a mile away.*'

She laughs. '*So, you've become delusional. I suppose that explains your betrayal. Perhaps I'll just break the news to Blanca—that ought to be enough to ruin a fragile little thing like her.*'

'Raven *is one of the strongest women I know.*' I edge a little closer to her. A spear of wind shoots out of the ground like I triggered a trap, and I leap out of the way. '*If you don't know that after beating her for two decades, you might not be as smart as you think you are.*'

'*She always collapsed into a ball after the first hit,*' Mother sneers. '*Kieran, though—he would have been trouble, if not for that beautiful baby boy. I think I'll keep little Altair alive, raise myself a better heir.*'

Iron rage floods me. Ignoring any other threat, any whisper of wind, I spring at Mother. '*You don't touch Altair.*'

My claws graze her snout. A few beads of blood bubble on her nose and mouth before a shield of wind slams me back. My breath gasps out of my lungs as she crushes me down into the powder, but I burn with victory. She didn't anticipate that.

'*This, from the daughter who once told me she'd hire an army of governesses so she'd never have to touch a baby,*' Mother says acidly.

'*I started liking them when I realized I liked anyone.*' The reminder of my old self makes me sick, but I can't think about it when the shield is still crushing down on me. I claw at its featureless surface, scrabbling for any kind of break, but it's perfect.

'*Does your precious Hollis truly believe that?*' She scoffs. '*I know the little bitch I raised. He should've stuck with his refusal.*'

'*But then how would you have lured us all here?*' I wheeze. '*What is your plan? To make Soren your new king?*'

'*Darling, I could lead every one of my children around by the nose without them noticing. Soren is an afterthought, just like you. Stepping stones on the path to my army, my kingdom, as it always should have been.*'

There. The break I need. '*Gavin wouldn't let you lead, would he?*'

The shield flickers for a moment, and I crash through it. Sweet air courses into my lungs. I can't waste the moment, so I charge at her blindly.

'*I kept him as my figurehead*,' she howls. '*I did not need his permission to act. I needed him as a shield.*'

Dodging strikes, I manage to weave in even closer and sink my teeth into her foreleg. Hot blood fills my mouth. I choke.

Something wraps around my tail and throws me back. As I fly through the air, I can only think about the slight taste of violets in her blood. My mother's blood. Half of what flows through my own veins. I land with a sickening *snap*, and pain radiates up my front leg.

'*Anwen has destroyed himself*,' she shouts before I get my thoughts together. '*Shackled to that pompous Sundrop bitch and the lands across the sea.*'

'*Shackled?*' I drag myself up on three legs. The fourth makes stars dance through my vision when I try to rest weight on it. '*Is that what you think a mate bond is? Because I have never seen Anwen happier than he is with Estrella.*'

She barks a jagged laugh. '*He's forgotten everything that made him useful, everything Gavin gave him. He's a shell.*'

'Good.' I grit my teeth as I limp forward. '*You, Gavin, you only ever hurt us.*'

'*Selfish, ungrateful—*'

The wind grows louder behind me. I glance over my shoulder, hoping Mother is too lost in her rant to strike while I'm not looking. The back of the wind wall gusts feet closer to me than it was a moment ago. She's closing us in together.

She's preparing for one massive attack. First, she chipped away at me—like she did by speaking to me in the prison wagon or introducing Kash. But that's all a smokescreen for her endgame. Plan, prepare, then finish it. I peer through the whipping snow and the pain, looking for any hint of her plan.

Her gaze darts left for a split second before a gust of wind sends thicker snow dancing between us. Warmth fills me. She may have taught me most of what I know, but she taught me nearly everything she knows as well. I recognize the trick—if you want someone to think you're paying attention to them while focusing on someone else, use a fan to disrupt their line of sight. In a pinch, a snowstorm will do just as well. Whatever her final move is, it's coming from the left.

I don't look to see what it might be. Knowing what Mother is planning has never helped me before. It didn't make finding her on the battlefield, or watching her beat Raven, or standing beside her while she humiliated the staff any easier, and it won't now. I just limp to the right, putting her between whatever she's working on and myself.

'Would you like to know what I'll do to little Ingrid?' she asks as traps and attacks try to force me left.

'I already know.' I hobble side-to-side, hoping to use unpredictability where I can't use speed. Blows glance off me, but none truly land. *'You'll leave her the hell alone because I'm going to stop you before you try anything.'*

'Ladies don't swear, darling.' Mother bares her teeth at me. *'But I shouldn't be surprised you're not one of those anymore.'*

She looks left just before shielding her eyes again. Her timing is off. Maybe she's fading.

'I don't care.' The words ripple through me, almost more powerful than the pain. I really, truly don't.

'Ingrid will be locked in a cell,' Mother bites out.

'You don't scare her.' I take a deep breath, brace on all four legs. *'Or me.'*

I jump. Instead of hitting wind, I impact fur. Mother and I land in a pile, her underneath me. The wind immediately starts to die down. Her muscles are weak, trembling under my paws. I could knock her out—or kill her.

'I'll keep her away from her hobbies, trot her out only to attend parties until I find some awful king to marry her,' Mother hisses. *'A lifetime of torture because you've tainted her. You've tainted all of them. Their agony is on your head.'*

'No, it's not.'

For Ingrid, for Finn, for all my siblings, I clamp down on Mother's throat and tear. It's a quick death. Maybe better than she deserves. I spit the flesh onto the snow beside her and turn away.

Relief makes my knees shaky, and I realize that wasn't just for them, to save them from the tortures she described. It was for me. I wouldn't have been responsible for them even if she'd lived and carried out every plan. But now, I can build a future. One where I'm happy, and battles like this don't haunt my nightmares.

'Prince Hollis wants you in the center of the courtyard,' a soldier informs me through the mind-link.

I don't wonder what he wants or why. I need to put Mother's body behind me, despite the future it represents. I turn and start limping away.

Hollis's men surround me, now that the wind is gone, pressing their sides into mine so traveling with my broken foreleg is a little bit easier.

THE HEART

Hollis

At the same moment as I reach the wide ring of defenders and ranged fighters encircling the heart of the battle, Candace limps to a stop at my side. Blood stains her gray coat in a dozen places, and my heart leaps into my throat. I meet her huge, dark eyes. She melts into a human before me. Her left arm dangles, boneless. Mottled black-and-purple bruises cover her bare torso. A myriad of small cuts spit tiny tributaries of blood, and a few massive gashes split her back.

My blood boils. I whip to the men I assigned to her. "You were supposed to—"

Candace puts her good hand on my arm. "They couldn't. My mother…." She squeezes her eyes shut. "Rowena Solberg is dead."

The blood on her mouth. Candace killed her, maybe even by herself. My chest aches. I send a futile prayer to the Goddess for time, but the battle doesn't stop.

I brush a soft kiss over her forehead, then start fastening the buckles of her armor. "You'll tell me everything later."

She nods against my face. Her exhaustion is palpable, almost painful, but when I'm done, she turns to the fight ahead.

"There's not a woman alive I'd rather have at my side," I murmur.

She quirks a smile. "Which dead woman should I be?"

I snort, take her hand, and we step forward without having to talk about what comes next. A few mind-links, and the wall of fighters directly ahead of us parts.

Eva, her hair streaming behind her as she pulls back a bowstring to fire, is the first to turn. Her eyes narrow as she takes in Candace and me, our linked hands. Her gaze clouds, and then everyone else turns. Her sisters and Nessa, in a motley mix of human and wolf forms. Soren, heaving, his pelt soaked in so much blood that it drips off him in a ruby trail. A small handful of other soldiers, but nothing compared to the piles of bodies draped around this clearing at the heart of the battle. There's no point wondering how it got cleared.

Soren howls and braces to charge, the rest of the Skadi sisters with him. Candace is seriously hurt, and we have no back-up, but I just keep staring at Eva. Despite everything that happened, despite the corpses on the ground, I know her.

"You want us to suffer?" I say. "Here's your chance to do it yourself."

Eva looks me up and down one last time, then lays a hand on her father's shoulder. Her oldest sister, Eyana, objects, but Eva ignores her. She shoulders her bow, unsheathes a long, wicked knife, and steps out of the protective circle of her family—and Nessa.

"All the better to enjoy it," she says.

The only thing Eva likes more than watching something she enjoys is doing it herself. She crosses the snow between us in a few bounds and slashes out at me with her knife. I throw my forearm up, but even my armor doesn't stop the blow from rattling my bones. One of the many reasons I was so shocked Candace had such little combat training—Eva and I trained side-by-side for most of our childhood, so I know how lethal she is.

"Candace is hurt," I tell her over the cross of arm and blade.

She smiles joylessly at me. "So you're taking that fun from me, too."

Eva rips away from me and spins toward my mate. Candace is much more mobile on two legs, and she clutches a dagger in one hand, but the pain of her broken arm paints her face. She's too slow. I grab Eva around the waist and drag her back a step, shortening her swing just enough that Candace can duck away.

"Nessa found your ridiculous letter," Eva snarls. "And she told me how all you Solbergs use pretty words like bandages."

Candace clutches her ribs and backs up. "I wrote that letter to warn you about Nessa! I had to apologize—I owed you that much—but I know she's a snake. She did this to Estrella as well."

"Lucky she's here to prove it—oh wait." Eva twists in my hold and stabs.

Hot pain lances into my side. The armor softened the blow, but at least an inch of serrated metal lodges perilously close to my gut.

"I can," I say through gritted teeth. "Father had me in all those meetings. Either Nessa did what Candace is saying, or he and King Kieran colluded to make me think so."

"Who cares?" Eva yanks her knife back. The resultant shock of agony loosens my hold enough that she can break it easily and chase after Candace. "I've always known that Nessa's a bitch, but this time, she's right. You were lying to me. You were sleeping together behind my back. Maybe I can't trust her, but I can still trust my Goddess-given eyes."

She slices at Candace, who drops to the snow with a whimper.

"I'm sorry," Candace says. "I should've told you, but I was being selfish. I love y—"

"Don't," Eva barks.

Candace barely dodges another slash. Her face goes green, like she's going to vomit or pass out soon.

"*I* love you." I freeze a shield of ice around my arm, then grab Eva with the other and yank her back again. We need to face her, need to talk, but I won't let her target Candace alone just because she's injured. "Just the same as I did before all this. And I'm fucking sorry. I was trying to find a way to tell you."

Eva scoffs and smashes the hilt of her knife into my fingers around her arm. "When have we ever had trouble talking to each other?"

"Exactly." My fingers throb as I wrap them around my sword. "That's why it was so hard."

"Bullshit!" Her voice cracks. "Just tell me. Four little words. I found my mate."

I blink, lost in the storm of her hurt. For the first time, I imagine what it would've been like if I woke up alone, then found Eva in the arms of another man later. Betrayal tears through me. Not jealousy, just hurt at the lie. We've never lied to each other before.

"I wanted to find a way that didn't hurt you," Candace says.

"Lying to me probably wasn't the best start." She hammers against my shield. "And sleeping with him on the night I *told* you I wanted to was a shitty end."

"Blame me." I reinforce the ice as she chips away at it. "She warned me about that. And I kept telling her nothing could happen. That I was going to go home and marry you."

Tears fill Eva's furious eyes. "Why didn't you?"

"Because Candace changed me." I hold her gaze, knowing deep down that she doesn't want to take advantage of her friend's weakness. As long as I'm here, the biggest target, Eva will stay focused on me. A choice I wouldn't have made before. "The Hollis who would've done that ran into the Haze, but he didn't walk back out."

"And because I never actually shut that door," Candace says.

Eva whips around. I almost scream. She's been understanding me perfectly for days—why can't she now see I'm trying to keep Eva's attention?

"I wanted him to change his mind." Candace balances on her toes, ready to dodge, but she still looks green. "I wanted to get the thing I wanted for once."

I circle around, shield and sword aloft.

"I would have wanted that for you." Eva feints left, then stabs right.

The tip of her blade grazes Candace's armor before I can throw myself in the middle, and Candace's face goes from green to gray. "If you'd bothered to tell me the truth instead of treating me like a child."

I slide in front of her as she pulls back, my whole body shielding Candace's. "And we're sorry. We were wrong. We shouldn't have done that."

"But you still want me to let you ride off into the sunset?" She shoves my shoulders, and her knife scrapes my cheek. "Live happily ever after? No consequences? Why should you get to do that?"

"No innocent lives lost, yes." I stand, strong and still. "You can hate us, want us to feel whatever the hell you want, but you're lying to yourself if you actually believe this war was your idea."

Doubt flickers in her burning gaze. Over her shoulder, I watch Soren claw a Dun's Crossing wolf open and wonder where Father is.

"That's why I was trying to warn you," Candace says. "Because I love you, and I don't want to see you surrounded by people I know are going to chew you up and spit you out in pursuit of their own goals."

Eva kicks the side of my knee, and it buckles. As I crash to the snow, she taps the blade of Candace's dagger with her own knife mockingly.

"Which is why you'd much rather I spend time with you two, people who would never hurt me." She raises her blade to Candace's throat. "At least with them, I know."

Seen, not heard. We haven't been listening to Eva either. Even when I asked, it was in public, where anyone could twist her words to their own ends. Where she had to perform.

Which means I've got one card left to play.

My mark sears as I climb to my feet beside Candace, rather than in front of her. I know Eva—and the fact that I could be wrong about that means doing this has any point at all.

"You're my best fucking friend, and I do still love you. Probably always will. And"—I meet Candace's wide, worried hazel eyes—"I love her, too. She's the love of my life, and I've been lying to myself about that since the Haze."

Candace sucks in a sharp breath and offers me a tremulous smile. I smile back at her, then turn to a seething Eva.

"So if the only way to keep the two people I love most in the world from killing each other is my suffering, then so be it." I throw my sword down and let my shield melt away. "Take whatever you need from me. Just end this."

Eva stares at me, a muscle in her jaw working. Candace looks from my sword in the snow to my face, but I can't break Eva's gaze. Not even when Candace drops her dagger next to my weapon.

"We both did this to you. Just stop your father," she says.

She finds my hand with her good one. My mark howls to protect her, but deeper than instinct, this feels right.

We face Eva's decision together.

HELL TO PAY

Candace

My heart hammers in my throat. Our weapons shine dully in the snow, Hollis's sword dwarfing my dagger. Eva drags her gaze from them up to our clasped hands. My other arm throbs, a reminder that I don't think I could fight her off if I wanted to.

She adjusts her grasp on her knife to a stabbing angle. All my various physical aches melt away, replaced by the painful knowledge that Hollis loves me and that still might not matter. That we may have been too selfish, too reckless, to have earned our happy ending. My body screams for it. It's so close I can almost taste it in the copper of Mother's blood still burning on my tongue, but this is how I don't turn into her. I have to face the consequences of my actions head-on. I acted cruelly, even if I did so in trying not to be.

Eva meets my gaze. She raises her knife. I smile at her, even though it wobbles at the edges. Goddess above, I don't want to die, but I understand. And at least I have Hollis, my mate, my love, beside me.

She lunges the short distance between us, throws her knife down next to ours, and wraps her arms around our necks. Hollis hugs her back. I bury my head in her neck, unable to move my shrieking arm, as her shoulders heave with sobs.

"I thought you didn't care about me anymore," she gasps. "Would you really have—"

"Yes," I say at the same moment Hollis says, "Without a doubt."

"Then I can't." Her tears come faster, harder.

Pain, exhaustion, and the bone-deep sadness of missing Eva these past few weeks roll over me like a wave. Tears stream down my cheeks.

"I'm so sorry," I murmur.

"So am I." She laughs wetly. "I listened to Nessa."

"We didn't leave you a lot of options," Hollis says.

"No, you didn't." Eva squeezes us both tighter. "Never again."

"Never again," Hollis repeats.

"No more lies," I say through my own increasing sobs. "I promise."

"And we'll all talk to each other," Eva adds.

Hollis nods. "About everything."

"Maybe not what happens behind closed doors." I blush.

Eva giggles. "I don't know… you've got a lot to make up for."

My tears and burning face blend into a blur of heat, but I don't mind one bit. This sounds a lot better than settling down with some stranger in the town below the castle.

"We're all going to have to hold each other to this," Hollis says seriously. "After all, we're about to share Kar Castle for the rest of our days."

The easy way he discusses our future almost knocks me off my feet. He loves me. He wants to marry me, move me here as his Luna, spend forever with me. And I get to believe him. The tower has fallen, and this is the moment where we're finally united.

"Oh, I'll show you all the best places to birdwatch," Eva gushes. "He doesn't know any of them."

"He has been useless." I smile to myself. "I don't suppose Lunas get Betas in Snowcrest?"

Eva sucks in a sharp breath.

Hollis glances at me out of the corner of his eye. "Certainly not traditionally… but nothing about this is traditional."

Somewhere outside the breathless circle of our hug, a wolf screams in pain. The rest of the world, its stink of blood and cacophony of violence, explodes back into my attention. Eva tears away from the hug, and I sway without the additional support for my weight. Only Hollis's arm, threading around my waist, keeps me from toppling face-first into the snow under the sheer weight of all the injuries I've taken.

Eva bolts toward where Soren, her sisters, and Nessa still fighting. Hollis helps me after her as I slowly regain my focus.

"Father!" She waves her arms wildly.

Soren glances at her, then past her at us. His top lip raises in a snarl. One of her sisters, who all look like copies of her at slightly different heights, draws a bead on us with her bow.

"Don't shoot!" Eva yells.

Soren shifts into human form. One of his daughters hands him a loincloth and broadsword. My pale face reflects in the massive blade.

"And why shouldn't she?" he bellows. "You've failed."

"I haven't failed. I've realized how ridiculous this all is."

"Ridiculous? The Skadi name has been dragged through the mud."

Hollis pauses a few feet away from the brewing conflict between father and daughter. Belatedly, I realize we're probably just outside the reach of Soren's massive sword.

"Has it?" Eva shakes her head. "My pride was hurt."

"They broke an ancient treaty." Soren takes a menacing step forward. Hollis blocks his path to me. My chest warms—I don't need more proof of Hollis's love, but him choosing to risk himself to protect me time and again provides it anyway.

"The Goddess broke it," Eva says. "But you took the fight to King Andri instead of Her."

"You said—"

She holds up her empty hands. "I know what I said, Father. But I was wrong. I don't need them to suffer, and I certainly don't need this war."

"No!" Nessa shrieks. "I warned you about this, about her. She's twisting your mind."

Eva laughs in her face. "*She's* twisting things?"

Nessa darts to Soren's side and grabs his arm. "We can't stop. Rowena said there would be hell to pay if—"

Hollis gestures sharply with the arm I'm not holding onto. A melon-sized chunk of ice rises from the ground and smacks into the back of Nessa's head. She collapses like a marionette released by her puppeteer, and I gasp.

"She's all right," he murmurs. "Just unconscious."

Soren gestures at Hollis. "You see his violence? I am saving our kingdom from it. Our line is owed the throne after this insult."

Eva bites her lip. "He—"

"Rowena was going to dispose of you." I free myself from Hollis's hold and take one shaky step forward. Fainting in the middle of battle won't help anyone, but Soren needs to take me seriously on my own merits, not as an accessory to Hollis's betrayal. "Once you stopped being useful. She called you a stepping stone to her own conquest."

He eyes me, his broad chest and massive sword promising he could strike me down without a second's thought in any form. "Why should I believe you?"

"Because Nessa just tried to convince you to keep fighting on her behest." I meet his gaze. "And because she admitted it to me just before I killed her."

Eva covers her mouth. Her sisters exchange looks. I sway slightly as nausea rocks me.

"The Solbergs are parent-killers," Soren says with markedly less heat.

"And you are a traitor to your king, from a certain point of view." I hold my ground. "I was born to a mother who needed to die. Is there any crime in being the one who did it?"

"No," Hollis says. "I think it's bravery."

"Kindness." Eva nods sharply. "Choosing to put the world's safety first."

Soren clenches his jaw. "One poorly chosen ally does not negate my rights. Rowena was a stepping stone to me. Snowcrest's throne is owed to my line."

I look at Eva. Her brow knits in worry. She may have set this war into motion, but it's taken on a life of its own, and she can't stop it anymore.

My whole life, everyone has laughed at my dreams. Treated them like a funny fixation of mine to be ignored or teased at will. Now, they're all I have.

"My father is former Prince Kashadien LeClair of Starfall Mountain," I declare.

Every Skadi eyebrow raises in unison, like they rehearsed it.

"I have his power of prophecy. Since the Haze, I've been having the same dream over and over again. Every night—every time I fall asleep."

Hollis rubs my shoulder, carefully avoiding the gashes from Mother's whip he only saw for a moment.

"In it, I stand on a battlefield not completely unlike this one, surrounded by violence. If that was all, I'd assume I was dreaming this moment." I take a deep breath. "But then, I rise, and the scope of the violence is revealed. Ruined land, charred blood, abandoned corpses —the wreckage an army leaves in its wake when it crawls across the whole world, stretching as far as the eye can see. I know, as I sometimes do in these dreams, that I'm witnessing some late point in the campaign of a tyrant to control every kingdom, with no concern for the damage he leaves behind."

"By the Goddess," Eva murmurs.

"That's no proof." Soren plunges his sword into the ground and crosses his arms, keeping my words further away from him.

I stare up at him and pour as much certainty as I can into my voice. "Last night, for the first time, I saw the flag they ride under. That flag." I point at the banner flying overhead, emblazoned with his family crest. "If we don't end this here, today, you won't be able to stop until you've turned the world to ash underfoot."

Soren opens his mouth, then closes it again.

Eva turns to Soren, looking nauseous. "Then this ends."

"Andri—"

"Will discuss terms," Hollis says. "Candace has made the very interesting suggestion that she takes Eva as her Beta, when she becomes my queen."

"A secondary placement is an insult." Soren glances around at the fighting. "You said you saw this battlefield destroyed?"

"Or one a lot like this." I take another step closer. "I know how intoxicating power is. My mother got me addicted when I was too young to know better. No matter who you think you are, it makes you someone new."

"I won't let you do that," Eva says in a tone that brooks no argument. "I suggested we march on Castle Kar. Now, I'm telling you I'll stand in the way of every sword or arrow you throw against it."

"Do you really trust this bastard?" Soren asks her.

"Yes." There's not even a breath of hesitation—far more than I deserve.

Soren's eyes go hazy with a mind-link. The fighting slows, then grinds to a stop.

"It's done," he says.

TOMORROW

Hollis

'G*OT SOME MORE OVER HERE*,' Z*AIN CALLS THROUGH THE MIND-LINK*.

I drag the heavy cart across the red-mottled snow toward my Beta. My muscles burn with exertion, but I'm not stopping until this whole battlefield is clear. I won't let a wolf suffer longer than they have to.

Zain nudges ice off a half-covered wolf. Blood paints his coat, but he's still wheezing in shallow breaths.

'Can you hear me?' I attempt to ask him.

No answer. It's impossible to tell what side he belongs to with all the gore on his side, but being able to talk to him would only make this a little easier. I shake my head at Zain, and we both shift to either end of the injured wolf.

'Three...two....'

We lift in unison. The wolf between us whines in helpless pain—a good sign, I've learned, because it means he's still conscious—and we lay him as gently as we can on the back of the cart of wounded.

Another team manages the cart carrying the dead. Thankfully, Zain and I have been returning to the gates to unload ours much more often.

"Fuck." He wipes sweat off his brow. "Didn't expect this to be so hard."

"It's harder for them," I reply.

He shakes his head. "Prince of the people now, I see."

"Prince led by his princess of the people." My thoughts drift to Candace, among the first rushed inside for treatment. I haven't heard anything about her condition—which probably means she's fine. But the grayness on her skin is hard to forget.

"But you're still going to manage the army?"

"Of course." I shoot Zain a smile. "I love her, but she has as much combat training as your littlest brother."

He snorts. The youngest in his family turned five last month.

We make another pass, hunting for anyone we might've missed. Even though every corpse I spot buried in the snow stings like a fresh cut, I hold onto how much they're outnumbered by the wounded. I did that, maybe even more than I got the wolves left behind killed. And I've learned. Tomorrow, the new training for the army starts. We fight to subdue unless ordered otherwise, not the other way around. A new Snowcrest is going to emerge out of this fight, and I intend to build it the way I want.

'Soren will not cede his demand for every third generation,' Father snaps through the mind-link. *'Soon, I am going to slit his throat just to silence him.'*

I shake my head. Inside, King Kieran, Father, and Soren are deep in peace negotiations. I wasn't invited because Soren wouldn't agree to allowing one of us without allowing all three, and I knew Candace would insist on being there rather than getting some fucking medical care. Eva said she needed to make sure Nessa was actually locked up securely anyway. So instead, Father has been keeping me up to date. I think he's doing it less to be inclusive and more so I can check his pride for him, but hey, it's better than reigniting the Goddess-damned war.

'What would Mother say?' I reply.

He sighs heavily in my mind. *'I preferred when we didn't speak of her.'*

I roll my eyes. He's not angry, just irritated that I'm right. And as long as he's willing to admit that, these peace talks stand a real shot.

Zain and I trundle up to the gate and release the last cart of the wounded to a team of healers, apothecaries, barbers, and midwives—anyone we could gather on short notice with some knowledge of the body—who are managing their care. The smell of blood mixes with stinging alcohol and sweet, pain-dampening plants. My stomach lurches. Still too much like Mother's sickroom. I hurry inside while Zain turns toward the outdoor sauna entrance.

The warmth stings my cheeks. I scoop one mug off a table laden with them and sip the drink inside—muddled wine, more proof Father doesn't mean any of his complaints about Mother. I should go to my room, bathe, see if I'm more injured than I think. Instead, I grab another mug and head for Candace's room. Everything else can wait.

I rap on her door. No answer, but I can smell the sunshine and berries of her inside. With a slight push, the door opens, and I step through.

Candace lays on top of her blankets, hair splayed wildly, mouth slack with sleep. She still wears the leather pants of her armor and her boots, but her torso is bare except for a column of bandages, and her broken arm lays at her side in a heavy splint. I expect her to look weak or vulnerable, but all I can see is her strength. She barely knows how to wield a dagger, has no combat magic, and without her, hundreds more would be dead. I set the mugs down, creep across the room, and brush a kiss across her forehead.

Her eyes flutter open. A slow smile spreads across her face. "No dream."

"No...dream?" The meaning sinks in, and I grin. "No war. We ended it."

She nods. Her dark eyes glow with excitement. The necklace I gave her lays proudly on her breastbone, framed by nothing but skin and gauze. And it finally sinks in—the thousand battles we've been fighting since I woke up next to her are over. There are no more goodbyes to say—just a world to set to rights and a future to build.

I press my mouth to hers, mapping the curve of her smile with my tongue. She laughs up into me, breathless with relief. I trace the fullness of her cheek, the slope of her neck. She nips my lower lip. I climb into the bed with her, careful of her many injuries. Someday, we'll talk about her mother, what happened between them. For now, I need to greet this new future the way I intend to greet every day from here on out—just her and me, nothing between us but air.

"I'm not made of glass," she grumbles as I graze my hand down her side.

I pull back and raise an eyebrow at her chest of bandages.

She pouts in response. Fuck, she's too cute. I dive immediately back in, kissing her as hard as I can without bouncing her on the bed. Her mouth survived unharmed—for now.

With a gasp, she starts to arch into me, then stops. I smile to myself. She doesn't need me to say I told her so. I'll just take good enough care of her that we both forget the injuries exist.

Blindly, I untie her grubby leather leggings. Blood flakes off on my fingers. I can't even imagine what my armor must be shedding, but I free her warm skin. She hisses when I run my cold fingers over it. I huff a laugh then drag my fingers up and pull back from the kiss to press them against her lips.

She parts like a blooming flower. I fuck two fingers into the warm wetness of her mouth. She laps at them, rolls her tongue around them, sucks like she's got my cock instead of my hand. All the blood leaves my head, and my armor pants become uncomfortably tight when she opens her eyes to meet my gaze. An interminable moment stretches out between us, vibrating with connection and want.

I have to touch her. I pull my fingers back with a wet *pop* and slide them beneath her loosened pants. Her warm, hazel eyes roll back as I find her core and circle. Her mouth remains open, the perfect plushness of her lips so pink and alive. She grabs my arm with her good hand, clamping down with all her strength. If I wasn't wearing armor, her claws would break my skin.

Maybe next time. We've got a whole fucking lifetime of next times to look forward to, after all.

She moans and scratches from my arm all the way to my waist, tugging at my pants. Anything she managed to learn during my impromptu armoring lesson earlier seems to have disappeared. I grin down at her, watching her desire quickly turn into something animal. She wants me as much as I want her.

Loves me as much as I love her.

"I love you," I say for the sheer pleasure of hearing it, of saying it without the words needing to save the world.

She locks her gaze on mine. "If you love me, you'll help me."

I chuckle and obey, though she whines when I have to pull my hand out of her pants. With her eyes dark on me, I strip out of my armor. She bites her lip, then threads her hand into the place I just abandoned. My skin burns with her attention. I'm far from at my best —mud and blood still streak my skin in places, and my few small injuries boast crusty scabs that break as I twist through the motions. But Candace looks at me like I'm the most beautiful thing she's ever seen, and fuck, I don't want to disagree.

That is, until I tug her pants down to see her fingers dancing over her own wetness. My mouth waters—but she asked for help, and I don't need to clarify what that means. I position myself over her. She lines my cock up with her entrance, and I sheathe myself inside.

We moan in harmony. It's like finding a patch of wild berries I didn't know about on a summer afternoon. A perfect surprise, exactly what I didn't know I wanted. Her fingers swirl between us, and I crush my mouth back to hers.

I match the rhythm of my hips to that of her fingers, her wordless guide rippling through my limbs like she's woven into my very muscles. Like we're actually rejoining into one, as the old legend claims. I can't imagine a better fate.

Her fingers speed, and so do I. Our breath, in harsh pants, echoes through the room. My hips struggle to keep rhythm as pleasure overwhelms me.

We climax heartbeats apart, shaking and holding onto each other like there's nothing else in the world.

Tomorrow, we'll build the future we deserve. Today, I love her, and that's all I need.

ONE MONTH LATER

Candace

I DRAG A COMB THROUGH MY THIN HAIR AND STARE AT MYSELF IN THE mirror on my vanity. More accurately, the new mirror on my new vanity. Hollis and I had to exchange one more goodbye because I had to return to Dun's Crossing long enough to pack up my life. Some things weren't worth the trouble of escorting through the mountain passes—mostly furniture—so I'm still getting used to the foreign, Snowcrest fixtures. And the rest of the castle's little quirks. Eva's guidance has been massively helpful, but I keep finding myself in strange towers, looking through windows at the rooms I want with no idea how to get there. Without Kieran's diplomatic party around, the castle is emptier than I'm used to. Their late spring helps some. Maybe I can convince Hollis to take an annual trip when spring arrives somewhere warmer. Raven was saying something about turning the festival in Escuro into an annual event.

I adjust the angle of the mirror then meet my own gaze.

My hair falls around my shoulders like a pale waterfall. After so much time, I'm finally able to admit the hazel eyes suit my face better

—they warm my complexion and make me look more alive than a Solberg ice blue ever did. Hollis's mother's necklace remains proudly around my neck, the symbol of her kingdom joined by an equally poorly made combination of Dun's Crossing's and Starfall Mountain's. His work, of course. I smile at myself.

The door bursts open, and people flood into the room.

"By the Goddess, Snowcrest knows how to talk," Ingrid complains.

Eva laughs. "We have to be blessed before we can help her!"

"Why doesn't she have to be blessed?" Ingrid grumbles.

Estrella rubs my shoulders with a soft smile. "Because she already was last night. You just said we could only demand one party out of you in a week."

Ingrid meets my gaze in the mirror, obviously looking for me to defend her, and I laugh.

"It's my wedding! I'm not going to make excuses for you."

She scowls then laughs at herself and joins Eva at the towering wardrobe in the corner.

Raven hurries in, Altair balanced on her hip. "Sorry, sorry, I had to run and get him."

"How did he survive the ceremony without you?" I ask as Estrella starts styling my hair.

"Kieran says he cried the whole time, but I think he was teasing me." She frowns down at her little son. "At least, I hope so, or the wedding will be very difficult."

"The Goddess might make an exception for him because he's so cute." Eva dangles a ribbon in his face on her way over to me. "Come on, stand."

"I'm not done!" Estrella braids sections of my hair close to my scalp, slowly twisting them into the halo we discussed.

"She has to get dressed!" Eva tugs on my wrist, and I have no choice but to obey.

Estrella stumbles after us, still tangled in my hair. Ingrid holds my gown high, positioned for her to be able to rain it down over my head. Eva strips me out of the robe I was getting ready in. Raven steps closer, the ribbon Eva had now in her hand. Estrella releases her braid with a grumble and steps back.

My wedding gown settles over me in a rain of heavy silk. The day after the battle with Soren ended, Hollis asked me to marry him over breakfast—no fanfare, no preparation. I almost choked on a bite of toast and seriously thought about refusing him. After everything we'd been through, didn't we deserve for this to be special?

I'll never forget the look in his emerald eyes when he explained— we'd waited long enough. He'd marry me the very next day, if I'd let him. He just wanted to tell the world that we were mated, together, forever.

It made him very hard to refuse.

My head emerges from the neckline, and I look into the tearful eyes of my family. Even Ingrid gets a little misty, though she ducks her head.

"Does it look good?" I twist, trying to see the fine, pale-green dress I had made so quickly.

"Perfect," Eva whispers.

Raven brings over the veil, the same one from her wedding, and places it on my head. Estrella makes a small, frustrated sound.

"I can wear my hair down." I pat her hand comfortingly. "It's what my hair does best."

She fixes a few strands. "You do look beautiful."

Ingrid throws her arms around me. "Tell him I'll still kick his ass."

"Tell him yourself," I reply. "At dinner."

She groans. "I really think that might count as two parties."

With a laugh, I let them lead me out of my new bedroom in my new home and down to the temple to start the rest of my life. Ingrid, Estrella, and Raven leave to join the crowd, but Eva stays with me. According to Snowcrest tradition, she walks me down the aisle because she's my best friend now, too.

Kash meets us outside with a low whistle. "Damn good thing you got your mother's looks."

I smile at him. The more time we spend together, the more I

realize how he falls back on his roguish habits most when he's uncomfortable. "I'd like to show you something."

"It's your day, baby girl." He shoves his hands in his pockets.

There's talk of rebuilding Starfall Mountain, like we did Escuro, but Kash doesn't want to lead, so the plans are kind of stalled. For now, he's been hanging around Kar Castle, soaking up the amenities like they're going to get taken away. But I was still part of an exploratory mission to see how much of Starfall remained, and I found something I knew I had to take with me, no matter what else happened.

I lift my veil and show him a bit of lace sewn onto the bottom. Just barely, if you look close, the threads read *Luciana LeClair*. His sister, whom King Gavin murdered on her wedding day.

"I hope you'll tell me more about her someday, but I wanted as much of my family here with me as I could have."

"Well, shit." Kash's voice is choked with rare emotion. "I think she would've liked that."

I hug him briefly, tightly.

"It's time," Eva says.

Kash waves me off and hurries into the temple. Music reaches a crescendo, and Eva and I stride in.

The crowd almost overwhelms the aisle. Every noble from Snowcrest and Dun's Crossing is here, as well as smaller groups from Sundrop Gem and other kingdoms. Half a world, in full support of us. My eyes sting with tears.

"I'm so happy for you two," Eva whispers.

"I'm just happy you're staying," I reply. "I'd be lost without you."

"Literally." She grins. "But there's nowhere else I'd go. Even if Hollis isn't my mate, he means too much to me—and so do you."

I squeeze her hand. "I love you."

"I love you too." She squeezes back. "And I'll expect you to do all of this, whenever the next Haze finally rolls in, and I find my mate."

"Deal."

I look up and find Hollis right in front of me. A small scar still slices through his cheek from Eva's blade, but it makes him look dashing. And it matches the thick scars on my back, the creak in my arm when I try to bend it still. He takes my hand from Eva, winks at her, and pulls me close.

Somewhere in my mind, I know there's a holy woman performing the ceremony. I think it's even the one from Dun's Crossing. But I don't hear a word she says because all I can do is stare into Hollis's eyes and think about how happy I am. How impossible this felt at every moment before it happened. How he was right; we could've marched down to the temple and done it right then, and it would've been nearly just as good. But we're royalty, and that means always thinking of our people, our world, a little more. How knowing he'll do that with me doesn't feel like a compromise—it feels like a miracle.

Ribbons wind around our hands, binding us together for all time. I clasp his fingers between mine as magic hums. Whatever words someone asks me to repeat, I say. I've already made all the promises I need to him.

Hollis sweeps me into a huge, hungry kiss. Teeth on lips, searching tongues. Tonight will be a long night after all our guests go home.

'I love you,' I tell him through the mind-link.

'Fuck, I love you too,' he replies.

"Are you shitting me?" Kieran demands.

We break apart, shocked. Kieran scowls out the window while Raven tugs on his shoulder, obviously trying to get him to shut up. I follow his gaze and see exactly what made him respond like that.

Another Haze, rolling over the horizon to start this whirlwind all over again. Hollis laughs helplessly. I look at Eva, and she winks at me.

I'm glad the Haze is here. Everyone deserves a chance at happiness like this.

Thank you for reading! Book 4 will be out soon!

The Alpha King's Breeder series:

Bought by the Alpha: The Alpha King's Breeder Book 1

Loved by the Alpha: The Alpha King's Breeder Book 2

Lost by the Alpha: The Alpha King's Breeder Book 3

Luna of the Alpha: The Alpha King's Breeder Book 4

Legacy of the Alpha: The Alpha Kings's Breeder Book 5

Daughter of the Alpha: The Alpha King's Breeder Book 6

Descendants of the Alpha: The Alpha King's Breeder Book 7

Shadow of the Alpha: The Alpha King's Breeder Book 8

Son of the Alpha: The Alpha King's Breeder Book 9

Spare of the Alpha: The Alpha King's Breeder Book 10

Claimed by the Alpha: The Alpha King's Breeder Book 11

Atonement for the Alpha King: The Alpha King's Breeder Book 12

Rejected by the Alpha: The Alpha King's Breeder Book 13

Abducted by the Alpha: The Alpha King's Breeder Book 14

Wolf Shifter Fairy Tale Retellings series

Beauty and the Alpha Beast

Sleeping Beasty

Tangling With the Alpha

The Luna's Vampire Prince series:

The Culling

The Kingdom

The Conquered

Pregnant With Four Alphas' Babies

Chosen As the Breeder

Mated to Four Alphas

Threats Against the Breeder

At War for the Breeder

The Stolen Breeder

Four Alphas, Four Babies

Becoming the Luna Queen

Descendants of the Breeder

Desired by the Devil series

Whispers of the Devil

Banter of the Devil

Murmurs of the Devil

The Mafia Kings series

Indebted to the Mafia King

<u>Loved by the Mafia King</u>

Claimed by the Mafia King

Secrets of the Mafia King

Burned by the Mafia King

Kidnapped by the Mafia King (coming soon!)

Dark Stalker Romance series

Tempted by Sin

Fated to Sin

Secret Billionaires series

Finding the Secret Billionaire by Olivia Bhelle Kildare

Falling for My Secret Billionaire by Bella Moondragon

Driven by the Secret Billionaire by ID Johnson

Wolf Shifter Alpha Kings series

Ravens and Ruins

Sundrops and Shadows

Snowflakes and Sabotage

The Vampire King's Feeder series

Claiming the Alpha's Daughter

Loving the Alpha's Daughter

Finding the Alpha's Daughter

Writing as B. Moon

The Boy Who Died

Sign up for Bella's newsletter here.

Or get a free novella from The Alpha King's Breeder series when you sign up here:
The Beta and the Maid

Follow Bella on Facebook here.

Follow Bella on Bookbub here.